MĀTŪTŪ

Ann, with lots of

love,

Sally.

MĀTŪTŪ

SALLY ASH

Goodfellow Press

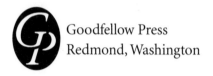

Goodfellow Press
Redmond, Washington

Matutu

Copyright © 1997 by Sally Ash

ISBN 0-9639882-9-8
Library of Congress Catalog Card No.: 97-74221

Edited by Pamela R. Goodfellow
Cover illustration and chapter art by Barbara Levine
Cover photography by Susan Talbott
Cover and book design by Scott Pinzon

Printed on recycled paper in Canada

Acknowledgements

My thanks go to the following people:

To Bruce, for his unstinting generosity,

To Robin, John, and Jocelyn for
their help in research and authentication; and

To Marjorie, for her many hours correcting
and verifying the Maori vocabulary of this book.

Whangapouri does not exist outside my imagination, although it will be easily identified as an amalgam of many similar small places along the East Coast of the North Island. I have borrowed the tale of Hinemoa and Tutanekai from the rich fabric of Maori lore and legend, but the story of Te Manawanui and Waikura is exclusively my own.   —S.A.

PROLOGUE

ill Thackeray let his eyes follow the swift changing patterns created by the clouds on the surface of the southern Pacific, while he tried to formulate the correct words. He was thinking about his mother. With every intention of writing to her today, he'd gone as far as putting a fresh sheet of paper into his typewriter. He saw this as a sign of progress. Not so many weeks ago the challenge inherent in that sterile, blank expanse would have been enough to trigger a wave of panic. But today, he felt, he could face it.

The address was easy, so was the date, and they had the advantage of defacing the paper. Once mutilated, it lost the inherent threat of unsullied whiteness. So far, so good. There was a long pause, as he watched a tern sweep across the washed-denim sky. The jet black head appeared briefly to be surrounded by an aura of light as it bisected a late sunbeam.

"Dear Mom," read the stark letters. What was important for her to hear? What might she want to know? Obviously, that her only son really was recovering from the blackness that had knocked him so badly off track. It was easier to call it his blackness than to say that he'd had a breakdown. But his mother knew that. She might not be able to reach inside his mind to identify with the desolation against which he'd fought because hers was a very different makeup, but she could, and did, sympathize. Come to that, she'd probably had some experience from living with his father.

He could say, "I'm getting along fine, although slowly. I'm eating okay, gaining a little weight." Trite. Ungainly English, too. She'd notice that immediately, and know he'd not put any thought into the words. He tried to imagine her, looking at a very similar seascape, because she lived on Cape Cod. Still winter over there, of course. The black oaks not yet in bud, the cranberry bogs dormant. He could see her in his mind, standing at her easel, putting together one of those god-awful pictures that she created for taste-deprived tourists in the summer months. She knew they were tacky, but they sold. And thus put butter on her bread, clothes on her back. Even thinking of the atrocious character of her painting made him smile, but it was a smile rooted in love for her. In his mind's eye he could envisage her so clearly. Hair graying at the temples, but still tall and well-built. Aging well.

The evening was fast setting in. Twilight in this part of the world was fleeting, even in high summer. If he wanted to keep the deadline he'd set for himself, he'd better get typing.

As the light faded the small, blue penguins would re-appear. It was a spot of enchantment in his daily life, walking along the beach to watch the birds come ashore after their day's fishing out at sea. Perhaps that would interest her, that was what he could tell her. And, best of all, it was totally impersonal.

Dear Mom,

They're very diminutive, the little blues. One of the smallest variety of penguin. They nest all along the less inhabited stretches of coastline, preferably in the dunes, occasionally in the safety of sand beneath the wooden cottages which New

Zealanders call baches. Of course, the stink of fish under your living room isn't so welcome and they're inclined to hold noisy soirees, but I guess the locals accept that for the pleasure of having such entertaining house guests. When they emerge from the waves, they look for all the world like middle-aged husbands who've managed to wangle a night out with the guys, and must now come up with an explanation for their wives. They're very reluctant to take the first step, so they bob about in the fringe surf, occasionally venturing a few, brave paces homewards, then scooting back into the water as if gaining courage from another nip of bourbon with their pals. But once the first plucky bird makes up his mind, the rest follow like so many lemmings. A veritable cavalcade of solemn little men returning to face the music.

It felt good, having written so much. A full paragraph. More than he'd written for months; for more than a year. He, who used to consider himself a twenty page-a-day guy. But it was still progress.

Would she find his description of the birds bizarre? No, she would understand, appreciate the effort.

He was about to close the letter when it occurred to him to add, "I think I'll find peace in this place. It suits me. Bill."

Then he thought of another P.S. "I hope you're well. Love, B."

ONE

t the crossroads, the driver slowed the bus to a wheezy stop. He pointed. "You oughta knock on that door, there." Not that she had a great deal of choice. He was indicating the solitary building that appeared to serve in the double capacity of service station and general store. "Jack Muller has a taxi. He'll run you down to the beach, if he's not busy with milking."

Jack Muller's taxi had seen better days at some time in the distant past. It bounced and rattled its way down the rutted, gravel road which appeared to go on forever. Never had thirteen kilometres seemed so long. Emily sat in the front, beside the silent driver. Her two cases slithered and bounced across the rear seats. She clutched her violin case to her chest and hoped that the seatbelt would do its stuff should an emergency materialize. But it was probably only her frame of mind that gave the area through which they were traveling a feeling of utter desolation. That, and the rain. Now and then the lights of farmhouses pierced the grayness, there were wire fences, substantial clumps of thick, dark trees, and dense valleys of native forest. Finally the road dropped down, turned a corner and leveled out along the bay. At least, peering through the fast-gathering winter's night, Emily thought it was a bay.

"Where didja say you were staying?"

Jack was built like a wrestler gone to seed, and clearly he did not believe in idle chit-chat. Talk for the sake of talking, Emily surmised from his speechlessness, was seen as a gratuitous waste of energy and vital resources.

"Bateman's bach. Do you know the place?"

Jack grunted and turned the taxi northwards, along the track that skirted the trees. You could not grace such a shabby trail with the title 'road.' They passed one or two wooden cottages with glowing windows, then the reassuringly cheerful lights of a general store. Probably the well-stocked one to which Marge, the real estate agent, had alluded when Emily signed the lease. At last, a mile or so along the track, they pulled into the sandy drive of a small, wooden dwelling.

"This is it. Okay?"

"Okay," Emily echoed. "Yes, of course. Quite okay. How much do I owe you?"

The place, seen in the gloom and general dampness, looked terribly uninviting. She peeled some notes from her billfold. "Keep the change."

Jack lifted her suitcases from the back seat. He deposited them on the wooden porch. Then, eyeing the violin, he said unexpectedly, "You play, then?"

Emily swallowed, despite herself. After all, she'd had enough practice recently responding to this very question. "I did. I was with the City of London Symphony. But I had an accident." She held out her hand, the scars from her most recent surgery still in vivid evidence.

Jack cleared his throat as though he found his foray into the world of words, and her response, extremely embarrassing. "That's tough."

"Nobody said that life was meant to be easy."

"Right." He smiled, the action transforming his plain, weather-beaten face. "I'll wait until you're inside, ay."

"Oh. That's good of you."

She knew where to locate the key; at the real estate office, Marge had been nothing if not thorough with her instructions. She'd find it under the step of the front verandah. She would see a piece of driftwood, but shouldn't just feel for the key in case she came across a *katipo* spider. She was to turn the driftwood chunk over, the key would be there.

Emily located the gnarled, water-smoothed knot of wood and tipped it gingerly. But any *katipo* previously lurking there had already sought another refuge. She slotted the key into the lock. The hinges creaked as she swung the door open. The light switch was one of the old-fashioned type, with a little knob on the end. A single, bare bulb was suspended from the middle of the ceiling. Although the room was small, the light's unshaded beams didn't quite penetrate the corners.

"I'll be off, then," said Jack.

"Yes, right. Thank you, Mr. Muller."

She heard the taxi door slam, the sound of reversing, the engine coughed crossly, and gradually the sound of the decrepit vehicle receded. Emily, feeling that with Jack Muller's departure she'd severed her last connection with civilization, looked bleakly around her new home. This was to be her catharsis, then. Her fresh start. She felt like weeping.

The room was neat, clean, and sparsely furnished. There was a chrome-legged table with an elderly Formica top and three sort-of-matching chairs, an extremely ugly sofa with a hideous crocheted afghan folded across its back, and two armchairs, one on either side of the fireplace. A single bookcase leaned crazily against the wall, its purpose to house the dozen books which lay haphazardly on a shelf. One door, half ajar, led into the kitchen. Four others were closed.

Emily pushed aside her suitcases and placed the violin case carefully on the table. Then she tried the first of the doors. It opened into a bedroom that was scarcely furnished with interior decorator's chic, although elderly, feather quilts like the one that covered the iron bedstead did have a certain intrinsic appeal, should they be to your taste. As well as the bed, there was a solitary, sad chair with one leg too short to touch the floorboards, and the sort of dressing table you saw in tacky, junk-filled stores, purporting to be a valuable antique. The veneer was peeling away in some places, and the mirror was flecked with half a hundred gray spots.

When she turned the large key in the lock of the back door she could step outside onto the verandah, facing the obscurity of the trees. Rain was thudding on the corrugated iron of the roof. From somewhere in the darkness the dismal hoot of a bird pierced the monotonous drumming. She stepped quickly back inside and shut and locked the door.

Marge had told her what to expect. Tea and biscuits in the kitchen, plus a few staples. Cans and that.

She filled the electric kettle and found a jar of instant coffee. The powder had set into an ebony mass, so it needed some rigorous scraping to obtain enough for one cup. And that tasted foul. In the crock she discovered a loaf of bread, left by a previous tenant. It had developed an interesting pattern of mold along the crusts. Emily cut the worst bits off and shoved two doorsteps into the toaster. Those, and a can of spaghetti hoops, were her supper. Clearly, if she elected to stay, the first thing to do in the morning would be to make a list. On top of the list would be proper coffee, even if that meant infusing it in the chipped enamel jug.

Her hunger at least partly assuaged, she lay in bed under the frayed patchwork of the quilt and listened to the night noises: the incessant tattoo of rain against the roof, punctuated by a sporadic squeal from the bed as she changed position, waves softly slapping against the shore. Occasionally a bird on the wing cried something like *mo-poke!*

And she wondered whether she had, at last, fallen off the twig. Here she was, stretched out on the meager mattress of an iron-framed bed, somewhere at the very end of the Empire, or where the very end would be, should the Empire still exist. Here, when she could just as easily be back in her childhood bedroom in Gloucestershire, under the oak beams, with her mother's cat curled in the bend of her knees in the perverse manner in which it elected to sleep.

Or she could be in the cozy bedroom of Jay's and Chelsea's house in Melbourne, knowing that her little niece was sleeping peacefully in the next room, and that along the hall her brother and his wife were whispering the things that married couples whispered, and doing the very private things that married couples did.

And instead she had committed herself to three months in this god-forsaken place. She must, indeed, be a certifiable lunatic. A candidate for Bedlam.

"Whangapouri." She said it out loud, and the very name sounded forlorn to her ears. "Whangapouri, Whangapouri." When repeated it began to take on a rhythm, musical and soft. "Whangapouri ..."

She wondered what the word meant in Maori.

Her first conscious thought in the morning was that the drumming of the rain had ceased. She could still hear the shush-shush of waves, but even they sounded less insistent than last night. She glanced at her watch. Nearly seven. When she climbed out of bed the wooden floorboards felt cool on her soles, but last night she'd unpacked only basic essentials. She padded on bare feet into the living room and drew back the apology for a curtain which hung across the ocean-facing window. Then she stood still in wonder.

Never before had she seen the sun rise over a watery horizon. The beauty of the panorama before her was as unexpected as it was breathtaking. While she watched in silent awe the line between ocean and sky was divided by an arc of brilliant, burnished metal. The pale-washed sky glowed like buffed copper, and wisps of thread-like cloud reflected peach and mauve.

It didn't last long, probably only a few seconds, before the arc became a fiery semicircle and the spell was broken. But those few seconds were enough to transform Emily's thinking. Her final, waking thought last night had been that today she'd be heading back to Auckland, and to civilization. Perhaps even back to Australia, to make her peace with Jay. That was why she'd not even bothered to unpack. Now she decided that she might manage to stay a few more days. Enough time, anyway, to watch another dawn over the Pacific.

Two

One thing could be said in favor of the cottage, or bach, although the strange New Zealand word still did not come easily to her lips. Someone had done a great job of cleaning it. The decor might not be everybody's idea of luxurious, but, apart from the inevitable sand associated with beach-side living, there wasn't a scrap of dirt to be found. And with early morning sunlight streaming through the two windows and opened door, it seemed considerably more cheerful.

In her mind's eye she refurnished the living room. It could be rather nice, if somebody cared enough to take the place in hand. A comfortable sofa in place of the existing grotty object, with cushions, possibly a seashore theme? Gulls and shells, maybe patchwork. Perhaps a decent rug. Certainly, she'd get shot of that atrocious table with its dated Formica pattern of zigzags and blotches. She substituted a simple, wooden piece in its stead, with sensible, solid chairs.

She might think of doing something about the bathroom, too, were this place hers. Right now it could have been featured in some film about the early settlers. The elderly tub that abutted the far wall had, over the years, acquired a long trail of rust that united taps and plughole like an umbilical chord. She'd used the shower earlier in the day, and knew it to be a similarly hoary example of plumbing, and the linoleum which covered the floor had been cleaned so frequently that the original pattern was almost a memory.

The mold on the bread appeared far more vivid in the morning's light. She wondered whether she might have contracted anything from eating it last night. Like Lord Carnarvon, after the opening of Tutankhamen's tomb. Fungus growing in her lungs. Tiny wisps of it invading her respiratory channel, emerging eventually from her nose. She could almost read the obituary. Emily Merivale, struck down in her prime by a medical phenomenon, baffling all the top brains of the country. Perhaps she should leave a note in her diary:

> *I ate the mold on a loaf of ancient bread in Whangapouri, New Zealand. P.S. I love you all.*

But at least a premature death would remove the arid wasteland before her that was her future.

Breakfast was the final, tired cornflakes that she found in the cupboard. No milk, of course. As she ate them she made a list of the barest essentials necessary to remain here a week. She thought she could manage a week.

Because of last night's rain-sodden darkness she had very little idea of how the bay might look. So when, a decent interval later, she set out on her walk, it was with her senses alert like a terrier on the trail. Thank heavens she'd thought to toss a pair of rubber boots into her luggage. The previous day's rain had made the track into a rutted series of potholes and puddles. But it had also bequeathed a legacy of freshness. The air felt sweet and clean against her cheeks.

The bay was a wide sweep of grayish sand, light and silvery over the low dunes to the south, gleaming metallic where the retreating tide had left it smooth and wet. She tried to estimate the length of the strand; two miles or three, possibly. To the south it ended abruptly, where the foot of the cliff was firmly rooted in the sea, but the headland to the north was less stark, softened by a sprinkling of foliage. Between where she stood and that end of the bay a lower projection of rocks thrust itself into the ocean like a row of blackened teeth, dividing the stretch into two parts.

Marge had called the forest something. Bush, that was the New Zealand word. And bush there was aplenty. It was almost as if the track along which she was walking created a demarcation line between the shoreline and the tree-covered hillside. The bush came closest immediately behind Bateman's bach, maybe only a hundred yards to the rear. Somehow it looked benign and protective, as if it were sheltering the little wooden structure.

A small, plump bird fluttered out from the greenery. It had a buff-colored breast and a wren-like tail which opened and closed like a fan. Enthralled, Emily watched its darting flight for some minutes, until it swooped again into the undergrowth.

She passed a sheer rock face, down which water trickled in a hundred rivulets. The rock was sleek with algae, and a host of tiny ferns and mosses clung to the surface, verdant and delicate. The water formed a miniature lake at the base, before spilling out across her path.

The time, according to her watch, was ten-thirty. In her pre-accident life, she'd have been rehearsing right now. She'd have been following the pre-ordained agenda of other people's schedules. This hour for practice, that hour for warm-up, prior to a performance. Recording sessions meant being at the studio for nine, or ten, never later. Wasted minutes spelled loss of money.

Where the bush line receded there was a cluster of cottages. Baches. She should try to use the local word. They weren't exactly Cannes. They weren't exactly Newport, either. More like replicas of her present address. And their appearance reminded her of Marge's description of Whangapouri. A popular place for summer holidays. These small dwellings had obviously been closed down for the winter. They showed no signs of habitation at all. But one house was freshly painted, and had a garden which must have looked lovely before last night's deluge. There were sorry yellow lupines in their final flower, and the glossy leaves of sand-plants. Several large clumps of pampas grass hung their rain-laden heads.

There was no way she could miss the store. To begin with, it was the only building so far to offer any indication of life. And if that were not enough, the words were painted on a large, cheerful sign. **HORI'S STORE.**

To her English eye it did not look like a shop at all, but a larger version of all the baches, with its deep-roofed verandah across the width of the front. There were several tables on the verandah, with chairs upended upon them, a miniature thicket of slender, wrought-iron legs. Six broad steps led up to an open door. As Emily mounted the wooden treads she could hear music from somewhere in the back. She recognized it with a jolt. Cani, from *I Pagliacci*. Of all places, of all arias.

Entering the store was like entering Aladdin's cave; an overwhelming experience of smells and sights screaming for attention. She paused in the doorway to allow her senses time to adjust.

"Hello. Can I help you?"

The voice had the texture of rich treacle. Emily turned toward its source. The woman behind the counter was either a giantess, or she was standing on something. She was built along statuesque lines, with a full bosom and what her mother would charitably call a firm foundation. Her hips, clad in rather faded cotton, spread generously like the base of a Mayan pyramid. But her face was the most interesting part. Emily could not recall such a remarkable example of serenity. Like a Maori Madonna, perhaps.

As Emily remained bereft of words the woman repeated her question. She appeared to be descending from something, because at least in height she assumed more human proportions.

Emily found her tongue. "I need practically everything, please. So much that I don't know where to start."

"You got a list?"

Emily nodded.

"Let me see it. I'll tell you what we have in stock."

She handed her scrap of paper across the counter. The woman slipped on horn-rimmed glasses and surveyed it.

"Hmm. Coffee. That's easy." She walked with the deliberate step of someone who has all the time in the world. "You staying here?"

"Yes." Emily was casting an exploratory look round the store. "In Bateman's bach."

"We don't get too many visitors this time of year. Only the local fishermen." The woman picked up a packet of coffee. "You want the beans, to grind yourself?"

"Oh, no thank you. There's nothing as sophisticated as a grinder in the bach."

"Ready-ground, then." She peered again at the list. "Sugar. That white, or brown?"

It was the sort of store you associated with a frontier town in a Western. There were all the supplies you could imagine, and then some. Fishing gear, axe handles and heads, pails and bowls and bottles and groceries, fresh and canned. One stand held clothing, sweaters and sturdy, weather-resistant garments, but there was also a freezer in one corner and a rack of videos to rent. The accouterments of the twentieth century.

"Are you Hori?" Emily asked.

"No. Hori's my husband." The woman did not look up from the list. "You'd better choose your own cereal. Over there."

Emily picked up a packet of cornflakes and put it beside the growing pile on the bench. She was beginning to wonder how she would transport all of her purchases.

Clearly Hori's wife was trained in mind reading. "How you going to get all this home?"

"I don't know. Perhaps I'll make two trips. Half at a time."

She propped herself on the high bentwood chair by the wooden counter. Chairs such as this were probably valuable antiques. Mrs. Hori regarded her with her head a little to one side. Her eyes were deep, brown pools in the flawless skin of her face. But she was older than Emily had first thought, because her thick, straight hair was heavily streaked with gray. She wore it in a huge bun at the nape of her neck.

"Hori will be home by lunchtime. He's gone in the truck to get fresh vegetables. I'll have him run your stuff down to Bateman's this afternoon."

"Oh, could he? That would be wonderful."

Perhaps she should stock up on more things, to avail herself of the offer. But then she paused. How much was needed for a few days, and anyway, what was she going to do tomorrow, to keep herself occupied? At some point she was bound to want a walk. And where else was there to walk, but to the store?

She peeled some money from the wad in her wallet. The notes were in dollars, but more like the Australian paper money than American greenbacks. Colorful, with native patterns and birds. She'd have liked Mrs. Hori to ask her to stay a little longer. "Cup of coffee?" she might ask. "Keep me company for a little while. If you're not busy."

No, Emily was not busy. But Mrs. Hori remained silent. She simply gave her back the change, smiled at her pleasantly, and started to remount whatever it was behind the counter that she'd been standing on before.

"Good-bye, then." Emily felt that she'd been dismissed, like a school child, or a guest who has overstayed her welcome. A small seed of loneliness took root and sprouted in her heart.

She wandered back along the beach, scuffing with her toes the driftwood and the brown, pungent strands of seaweed. She picked up a long stick and trailed it behind her. Apart from the seagulls that were gathered in a squabbling crowd around some piece of cast-up carrion, and a flock of tiny, busy waders that flew before her, she was totally alone with the sea and the sand.

Bill took his time climbing the hill. Not for physical reasons, but because he found something enjoyable about every part of the climb. The track began along the gully, through which the fork of a stream tumbled toward the Pacific. The bush was thick and verdant, rich with tree ferns the New Zealanders called *pungas,* and stands of *rimu* and *totara.* In the five and a half months since his arrival at Whangapouri he'd learned to recognize most of the local flora. And Hori had introduced him to the native fauna as well, so that these days he could identify the less obvious song of the *tui,* as well as the easily recognizable night cry of the *morepork.*

Once the track left the gully it zigzagged up a ridge that eventually led to the headland, but that was not Bill's destination. Where the path branched he took the inland fork. It led to the remains of the old *pa.* There was not a great deal of the hill fort left because, according to Hori and reinforced by local reckoning, it had been abandoned about a hundred and fifty years ago. Perhaps longer. Anyway, Bill mused, not many structures built of timber survived so long. Nevertheless, on previous forays he had established without much doubt the outer perimeter of the fortifications, and there was some satisfaction in even so small a discovery. And he found the association of the *pa* and the legend of the lost lovers interesting.

When he reached the crest, he turned to appreciate the view. There was the wide sweep of sand, the pewter-gray ocean stretching to the horizon. Apart from several dinghies beached on the low tide it must have looked like this when the *pa* was occupied. Most signs of habitation were screened by the forest: only the barn-red roof of Hori's Store was semi-visible. A lonely figure was walking across the beach, trailing a stick. The mark left behind in the sand resembled a snail's track.

He decided, by the way she walked, that the figure belonged to a woman, but it was difficult to be sure of much more. Boots, blue jeans, an olive-green jacket, short brown hair.

The image of JoBeth formed itself, unwanted, in his mind. And the bile rose in his throat as panic hovered, far too close for comfort, on the edge of his consciousness.

He sat down heavily on a log and gave himself a mental shake. Idiot! Not every woman with short brown hair was JoBeth. And, anyway, she was part of yesterday, and a long way behind him. Still, for a moment he resented that figure down in the bay, that unknown woman who inspired in him even ten seconds of pain. He resented her being there, invading his territory, his safe haven, giving rise to unwelcome thoughts.

The person below on the beach had seen him. She waved in enthusiastic greeting. Bill hesitated. He had no intention of responding to some stranger who had just conjured up alarm in him. But to ignore her would be rude. He lifted his arm in a half salute. Then he purposefully turned his back on the bay and began to climb again. He hoped that she was not staying in Whangapouri. He'd thought, with three more letters to his mother safely in the mail, that he was well on the road to recovery. He hadn't realized, until this moment, how fragile that recovery was, and the realization was bitter.

〜〜

Hori sounded the horn of the battered pick-up truck to announce his arrival, as if the rattling and splashing that accompanied his journey were insufficient warning. To Emily's amazement, he quite dwarfed his wife. Not exactly in height, although he was no shrimp, but in girth. He closely resembled a sumo wrestler about the middle, and as he carried her boxes of groceries into the kitchen his bulk temporarily blocked out the light. Surveying the fruits of her morning's shopping spree, Emily wondered what could have persuaded her to buy so much. She looked as if she were laying in food for a siege.

"Planning a long stay, are you?" Obviously the same thought had occurred to Hori.

"Oh, no." She was about to say that she'd almost certainly leave on the first available bus back to Auckland, probably not last the week, but politeness held her back. It would be awful if he thought she didn't appreciate the place where he lived. "Actually, I've not yet made up my mind."

They looked at each other over the piled up boxes. Hori's hair was just sprinkled with silver and his nose was a splendid, aquiline affair, very aristocrat. He must have been a handsome man in his youth, and even now he was out of the ordinary good looking. Avuncular perhaps, like an elderly St. Bernard.

"It can be quiet here, in the winter. Especially without a telly. You brought plenty of books?"

The extent of her reading material was three paperbacks designed for airplane consumption. She realized as he spoke that it was a serious omission on her part.

"Probably not enough. Do you sell them at the store?"

"A few paperbacks. But there's a library in the town which isn't too bad, and they'll get anything extra you want."

Goodness only knew how far away the town might be. "Well, thank you, Mr. Hori."

He turned to leave. "Just Hori. That's my name. Translates to George, in English. No formality."

This seemed a golden opportunity. "Could you tell me a bit about the bay, Mr... Hori? I have the distinct impression that there are about four of us living here, at present."

He grunted. "More like thirty, but most of the year-round residents are fishermen. They're out in their boats a lot of the time, if the weather's halfway decent."

"And they live in those cottages . . . baches, near your store?"

"No. They're holiday places. Most of the fishermen live south of the store. The bay's more sheltered, that end. From the southerly storms."

Which explained why everything seemed so abandoned. She wondered if she could offer him some refreshment. A choice of tea, or some of her freshly delivered coffee.

But Hori solved her dilemma. "I'll be on my way. I've a load of stuff to tidy up at the store. If you're in need of a bit of company you can always come along." He turned back to her. "What did you say your name was?"

"I didn't. But it's Emily Merivale."

The hand he held out by way of greeting shared its dimensions with a bear's paw. But his smile, above the paw, was open and friendly.

"Well, Emily, it's nice to meet you. You walk along to see us, if you feel like a spot of conversation."

"Thank you, Hori." She felt a bit inadequate, in the face of such genuine friendliness. But that was what Marge had said and repeated. New Zealanders, she had explained, were warm, welcoming people. Not judgmental. "I'd enjoy doing that."

A pattern began to emerge in her way of life. Wake up in time to watch the sun rise, if the day was propitious. Somehow she felt better, on those mornings which blessed her with the privilege of watching the sun bisect the horizon. On cloudy or rainy days she considered herself cheated.

Then breakfast. There was a radio in the kitchen, an elderly battered object, but she found that it was tuned to the national station, and she could listen to the news as she ate her cereal.

Housekeeping was minimal. There was, after all, nobody about to stir up dust. She did tackle the iron stain down the tub but discovered very quickly that far more than elbow grease would be needed to remove that orange slick. If the place were hers, she decided, she'd have the tub re-enameled. Or buy another, also with claw feet. And put up fresh, cheerful curtains, paint the walls.

Mid-morning, she walked along to the store. No point in arriving before they opened. There was a pattern about the walk, too. She began to recognize landmarks, like the glossy rock face down which the slender waterfalls tumbled. After three dry days in a row the flow decreased by about half, and the tiny ferns lost some of their fresh greenness. Farther along there was a huge, moss-covered tree trunk. It must have fallen across the track and been pushed back to lie parallel with the rut marks, because the other half lay at an angle up the hillside.

She bought things from the store that she did not need, for an excuse to be there, even though Hori had invited her to come along to chat. And when Hori was in the store it was all right. He seemed to enjoy passing the time of day. Mrs. Hori was another matter. Emily would sit on the bentwood chair by the counter and try to conjure up questions that required answers of more than one syllable. Not that Mrs. Hori was rude, or unfriendly. It was just that she did not appear to have the same needs. Swapping confidences was not for her. Behind the serenity of that lovely Polynesian face lay a personality that was totally private.

Generally she walked home along the beach, searching for shells and gathering pieces of driftwood with which to augment her fireside supply. And despite herself, despite the loneliness that was starting to pervade her soul, she began to recognize the therapeutic nature of this existence. She started, very slowly, to feel at one with the sand and the sea. Perhaps, she rationalized, people were right. Maybe you could find comfort in different ways of living.

She wondered about the man she had seen, that one time. He'd waved to her, but since then seemed to have vanished.

The evenings were bleak. That was when she felt most isolated, and the series of events that had brought her to Whangapouri invaded her mind, and bobbed, uninvited, into the forefront of her thinking. There was the radio of course, which provided a little companionship. One evening she fiddled with the knobs and hit upon the classical station. Someone was playing Mendelssohn's *Violin Concerto*, beautifully. She had played it, once, at a concert to raise funds for her father's hospital. Far less well, of course, because she'd been young, still at the Meinhardt, in fact. Sitting in the sparsely furnished little room, listening to it, was horrible, soul wrenching. Despite her best resolutions tears welled up in her eyes, and she found herself shaking.

The fierceness of her reaction frightened her, and it took all her willpower to switch off the machine. She stumbled into bed to cry herself to sleep. But even that was denied her, as memories of the accident vied desperately with fiery recollections of her spat with Jay. It was the awful realization that her hitherto omnipotent brother could not, would not, understand the helplessness that had triggered her flight to New Zealand. Quite soon the fragmented jumble of half-memories culminated in a racing brain, followed by a blinding headache that scattered any hope of sleep.

THREE

The noise had the suddenness of rifle-fire. It wrenched Emily from sleep into wakefulness. She sat up like a jack-in-a-box released from its prison. There was something on the roof. No ... there were at least two somethings, possibly more, and, if the noise overhead were an indication, they might well join her inside. Shock was her first reaction, but common sense came quickly upon its heels. Several thuds were followed by the sound of claws scrabbling against corrugated iron in long, metallic screeches. There was a chattering of excited animal voices, scurrying the length of the roof, then back. The fauna of New Zealand had chosen her roof to hold a midnight party. She wondered whether they could be cats, but the vocalization wasn't feline. However, she knew of no other animals given to leaping onto roofs in the small hours of the morning. Come to that, did these creatures harbor any hostility towards *Homo Sapiens*? Especially isolated, female members of that breed. She wasn't too sure that her bravery quotient, as of this minute, was sufficient to mount a foray.

She lay back in bed, pretending that the feathered quilt could protect her from nocturnal predators and decided that discretion was, as the saying went, the better part of valor. And, overhead, another thump and agitated babble indicated that the party had been gate-crashed by an interloper, and to the screamed announcement of this fact was added a series of grunts and growls.

The night seemed very long.

Five days in Whangapouri, each day the length of a week. Emily had almost decided that there was a limit to this solitary existence, and she had nearly reached it. As things stood, loneliness was superseding every other thought. All very well to discuss with Chelsea, her much loved sister-in-law, the therapeutic nature of solitude, to agree with Marge the advantages of seeking a retreat. Somehow in that scenario she'd included a sprinkling of friendly faces which added up to more than one and a half. Because you could scarcely call Mrs. Hori more than a half, when she was so sparing with words.

Totally wrapped up in herself and her isolation, she began to question whether anybody could find a purpose to life when feelings of disconnection overrode all else. It was probably time, she reflected, to accept defeat and call it a day.

Whe afternoon was fine, but cool. She shrugged herself into a jacket for protection from the chilly off-the-sea breeze and wandered along the beach, scuffing with her toes through the debris thrown up by last night's southerly wind. Above the high tide mark there was a mess of seaweed and driftwood, scallop and mussel shells and the occasional dead crab. Below, the sand ran sleek and smooth to meet the water. She walked above the driftwood, not wanting to spoil the immaculate condition of the wet expanse with her footprints.

Halfway to the headland the outcrop of rocks she'd noticed jutted into the sea, like the buttresses of a cathedral. She had almost reached them when she saw the man, and she recognized him at once as the figure she'd seen in the distance the other day. If nothing else, the growth of beard that covered the lower half of his face was identification enough. He was seated on a flat face of rock, and appeared to be sketching. Beside him lay a small open paint box, and he was concentrating on an object that she couldn't see. He had his back towards her.

"Hello." She was quite close when she spoke, and the man jumped. "Sorry. I didn't mean to catch you on the hop."

The man got hastily to his feet, closing his sketchbook quickly. When he stood she saw that he was very tall. With scarcely a glance in her direction he leapt from the rock and set off in the opposite direction.

"Hey," Emily called after him, "You've forgotten your paint box." She waved it in the air. She need not have wasted her breath. Apart from a quick look over his shoulder he gave no indication of having heard her.

"Well!" she exclaimed to the cliff face and the water. Then, "Well." She sat down heavily on the slab that he had vacated. "I suppose it's sensible to know who your friends are."

But she felt her loneliness like another garment, and there was also a sense of hurt. It was as if he had seen her scars, and found them repulsive. He had waved to her the other day. When he couldn't see her too clearly. She regarded the small tray of water colors bleakly, then tucked it into her coat pocket.

Immediately in front of her was a rock pool, filled with a microcosm of ocean life. It reminded her of the shadow boxes she and Jay and Sarah used to make as children; occupation for a wet afternoon. As she watched, a small fish darted out from among the crimson anemones and daringly traversed the length of his miniature world.

The chap must have been sketching the inhabitants of the pool. She had thought him very attractive, without being able to put her finger on exactly what it was she found appealing. Clearly, though, he had not reciprocated this sentiment. Nor could she identify what she had said or done that inspired such hasty flight. Common sense told her that it couldn't really be her scars, unless he possessed x-ray vision.

She wondered where he lived. She'd not yet explored this next part of the beach, and the afternoon seemed promising. If she located the artist, she could at least return his property.

Traversing the northern half of the bay did not prove too testing. Twenty minute's steady walking brought her to the high bluff which marked the end of Whangapouri. The base of the headland was protected from the sea by steeply angled rocks, over which trailed dark ribbons of rubbery kelp. Unlike the earlier outcrop, which invited exploration, these sentinels appeared hostile and forbidding. In this part of the bay she passed three signs of human habitation; two small baches and one rather fancy place, all timber and glass, with a balcony the length of the front. They'd have views of the sunrise, at that house. It was interesting to speculate whether the peculiar man lived in this handsome house.

She'd noticed quite a bit about him in that brief flash. His eyes, to begin with. They were an unusual, light gray. His beard was a bit untidy, in need of trimming, and his hair was receding a little at the temples. It gave him a slightly scholarly air.

Should she confront him by walking up tand ringing the bell? "Here are your paints," she might say, "You left them ." And risk having the door slammed in her face. She thought her fragile self-esteem might not survive two rebuffs in one afternoon.

"Not today, thank you." She spoke aloud again. The words bounced across the sand left shining from a retreating wave, and a black-backed gull rose, screaming, perhaps affronted by someone talking to herself. Perhaps another day. She was curious to know more about this man.

She turned at the bluff and retraced her steps along the track. As if to confirm her conjecture, a lamp inside the house was switched on at that moment, and she could see inside, like viewing a television screen. There was a fire glowing. The man had shed his thick sweater, and held a mug in his hand. He put down the mug, and was crossing to the window. Then he closed the curtains, briskly, as if he knew she were out there, watching him. It made her feel like an intruder, like a Peeping Tom.

☙

They met again the next day. Or, more accurately, they collided. Emily was leaving Hori's Store with provisions as the tall man entered. She was backing out, pushing the door behind her, and when he pulled it open she all but toppled against his chest. In such circumstances it was hard for him to run away.

"Sorry." Emily scrambled without too much success to stop all her groceries from precipitous descent. Then she glanced around, saw who was supporting her, and said, "Oh!" From her laden arms a packet of soap powder dropped to the ground. She stooped to retrieve it and half a kilo of apples shed their paper bag and scattered themselves across the floor. The man looked as if he might turn tail and flee. "Wait a minute. Please," Emily called. "Don't go. I've got your paints. Here, in my pocket."

He hesitated, turned back, and stooped to help Hori gather the scattered fruit. But she had a feeling that it was a near thing. His escape mechanism was hair triggered.

"Here. Take this." Mrs. Hori appeared from behind the counter with a cardboard box. "You know you can't walk home like that. You need to buy yourself a shopping bag some time."

"Thank you. Yes. A shopping bag."

The man picked up the last of the apples and Emily, not to be put off by yesterday's rebuff, smiled her thanks at him.

"Please don't go." She balanced the box against the counter so that she could dig into her pocket. "Here are your paints."

He smiled back, and she was arrested by the sweetness of his expression. It crinkled the corners of his eyes. She'd been right in her recollection. They were light and gray and very attractive. In a woman you might say, beautiful. There was a pattern of little mosaic flecks in them.

"Thank you."

He slotted the small tray into the back pocket of his jeans, then held the door open for her politely as she stepped onto the verandah of the store. He followed her out.

Emily smiled again, in the hope that he would reciprocate. "Do you live here permanently? All year round?"

Her hope was rewarded. "Yes, ma'am. No, ma'am."

Ma'am. So he simply had to be from America. No New Zealander spoke in that way.

"What?"

"Yes, I live here, right now. No, not all year around."

"Ah."

She looked about for a sign of any sort of vehicle, truck, jeep or bike, and discovered none. She wondered how to continue this conversation, prevent him from escaping for a little bit longer, because she really did need further human contact. Very badly. But, if she were being honest with herself, there was more to it than that. Her first impression had been confirmed today. In that brief moment when their eyes first met across the rocks she'd recognized a kindred spirit. Another lost soul.

Somewhere like an espresso bar would be perfect, so she might suggest buying him a coffee, to thank him for his help. But Hori's Store had no such token of civilization. She rested the box of groceries on the rail of the verandah.

"I saw you the other day, up on the hill. And you live in that lovely house round the point?"

"That's right."

"But not your main home? I mean, you say you don't live there all year?"

"No, I'm house sitting."

"I see." She wanted to say, "What did I do that frightened you?" but the feeling persisted that he might, very easily, take to his heels again. "Do you have to buy groceries? I could wait, if you'd like to come back to my bach for a cup of coffee. You have to pass it, to get to your place."

From his considerable height the man looked down at her, as if assessing things. His gaze implied that she might have grown a pair of pointed ears. It didn't do a great deal for her confidence. She wasn't used to being the one who initiated conversations. It took more courage than she knew she possessed to try again.

"I don't bite, you know."

There was another, agonizing pause, before he said, "I didn't mean to be rude. Coffee would be fine. I'll just get my mail."

He carried the box of groceries as they retraced their steps towards the cottage, and although each of his strides was as long as two of hers, and he moved with the easy athleticism of a long distance runner, Emily had the sensation of a large, wary dog loping beside her. They passed the fallen tree, they passed the rock face and the ferns.

"By the way, my name's Emily . . . Merivale. I was about to say Williams, because I've called myself that for some years, and Merivale still doesn't leap to my lips."

"You're divorced." That was the very first comment he'd proffered without prompting. They were making progress, even if the steps were excruciatingly small.

"No." She shook her head. "Williams was my professional name. I play . . ." She swallowed and corrected herself. "I played the violin." They walked in silence for a short distance. He should at least have volunteered his name. Conversation was a two sided affair. When nothing materialized Emily said, "What's your name?"

"Bill Thackeray."

"And you're American. Isn't that clever of me?" He smiled in agreement. His smile really was charming. "So what are you doing in New Zealand?"

"Recovering."

The tilt of her head suggested that he might elucidate, but he didn't appear to notice. "Nothing life threatening, I hope?"

"I hope not, too, ma'am."

And he lapsed into silence.

The sky was threatening further rain as they approached the bach. Emily led the way, clicked the switch and the solitary light bulb came to life. The place really would benefit from a couple of lamps. She crossed to the hearth and added several more pieces of driftwood to the smoldering logs.

"Sit down. I'll get the coffee started."

When she returned a few minutes later, with a tray on which were enamel mugs, sugar and a plate of shortbread fingers, he wasn't actually sitting, but was leaning against the wing of the armchair, as if he'd thought better of her invitation and was poised once more for retreat.

"There isn't a milk jug, so I hope you don't mind the bottle. My mother would have a fit."

However, as neither of them took milk in their coffee, there was no fear of offending anybody's sensibilities. Emily sat in the armchair on one side of the fire, the one with the crocheted square over the back. Bill Thackeray continued to lean against the other. Not intending to seem rude apparently didn't extend to small talk.

Emily cast about for something to say which didn't sound too nosy. Occupations were generally safe. "What do you do?"

"Do?"

It didn't seem like such a difficult question, but his tone suggested that she'd asked him to solve the riddle of the sands.

"Yes. To keep the wolf from the door."

There was another small pause before he spoke. "I write. Or rather, I used to write."

She looked at him. "Should I know you? What do you, did you, write?"

"Books. Fiction."

That was scarcely adequate. She scanned through her mind to recall a modern Thackeray.

"You'll have to tell me more. I'm sorry, but I'm not much of a reader." Which was one hell of a lie. Perhaps she should she be crossing her fingers. "I can't place any Thackeray, apart from the famous William Makepeace. Was he an ancestor? And what sort of fiction do you write?"

He returned his empty mug to the tray. Hers was still far too hot to do more than sip with care. He must have a gullet lined with galvanized iron. "The *Vanity Fair* fellow might well be a connection, although I've never investigated."

"I'm sorry. I still can't recall a modern Thackeray."

"I wrote under a pen name, because my agent thought it could lead to confusion."

This was as bad as drawing teeth, but she persisted. "What's your pen name?"

"W. L. Martin."

That did strike a chord. There was a book by W. L. Martin a few years ago, which received wide critical acclaim. She hadn't read it, but . . . "I know!" Memory sprang to her aid. "You wrote *One Witch Too Many*, and it was made into a movie. Right?"

"Yes."

"Wow!" She was about to add that Jay had composed the score for that movie, but there were more pressing things to discover. "But you said you're not writing at present? Because you've been ill?"

"Yes."

"What happened, or do you prefer not to talk about it?"

"I talk about it." Bill straightened, preparatory to leaving. "If people keep on prying. I had a breakdown. Last year. "

The silence that followed seemed to echo upon itself. Emily was caught up in the web of her own, searing embarrassment. Then she cleared her throat. She spoke very quietly.

"I'm sorry. I didn't intend to pry. I just thought we might have something in common, because I'm recovering, too."

Bill Thackeray didn't sit down, but he didn't head for the door, either. "From what?"

"An accident. Look." She thrust out her arm so that he could see the pattern of red scars across the fingers.

"And you mentioned that you were a violinist?"

"Yes." She tucked her hand into her jeans pocket.

"I see. I'm sorry, too."

She regarded him curiously, her cheeks losing their fieriness as her embarrassment ebbed. "Why? There's no need for you to apologize, just because I came across as a nosy parker."

"I could have chosen my words better."

Emily stood up abruptly. "Would you like to stay for supper? It's nothing much, but I bought a ham hock and made a huge pot of split pea soup. They seemed to swell up into enough soup to feed an army. I'll never manage to eat it all on my own. And there's toast and fruit."

Bill accepted the olive branch. "That would be very nice, ma'am."

To hide her lingering feelings of awkwardness Emily spoke more sharply than she'd intended. "I wish you'd stop calling me ma'am. You make me feel like an elderly schoolteacher, with *pince-nez* and her hair in one of those tight, squashed-up buns."

Bill remained silent but he smiled at her, and she was again aware of the sweetness of his expression. She decided that, when he allowed himself to be so, or when not backed into a corner by her unwitting intrusiveness, he was a very attractive man.

"I'll heat the soup, then. Would you supervise the toast? I recovered an ancient toasting fork from the dark recesses of the kitchen cupboard. And the loaf is in the earthenware crock."

There is something about the sharing of food, even when it is as humble a meal as split pea soup and unevenly browned toast. Emily noticed as Bill relaxed the muscles across his shoulders, and consequently felt more comfortable herself. Conversation became easier as they progressed, as though both were out of the habit of verbal communication.

"I thought at first that I could manage with just my own company." She used a crust of toast to sop up the final traces from her bowl. "But within a week I'm going round the twist. I find myself walking down to the store, even when I don't need anything, just for the opportunity to say hello to Mrs. Hori. That was my second visit today, when I rammed into you."

"Heneti."

"What?"

"Heneti. Her name is Heneti Webber."

"Oh. Well, she's not the world's greatest conversationalist."

Bill helped himself to another piece of over-charred bread. "She respects your privacy."

"That's very nice of her. But what if I'm longing not to have my privacy respected?"

"Then you must initiate the conversation."

That seemed choice, coming from someone whose communication skills had appeared to be so deficient. Emily forgave him, for the niceness of his smile if nothing else. She watched as he spread the slice liberally with apricot jam.

"Until then she'll assume you wish to be alone. You would enjoy talking to her. She's a remarkable woman."

Emily, although impressed by the fine looks of the store keeper's wife, did wonder privately what they might have in common, but she kept such thoughts to herself. She steered the conversation along another path. "The other day. Why did you sprint off so fast?"

"You caught me unawares. It was a gut reaction."

"You mean, you always leap to your feet and bolt when somebody says hello?"

"Only certain somebodies. Young women."

Emily looked at him assessingly. "I see. You have an aversion to young women. And I thought, for a moment, that you'd seen my scars and taken fright."

Bill reached across the table and gently took her hand. He scrutinized it carefully, as if it were a foreign object rather than a part of her. "Somebody did a great job on this."

She felt a bit awkward, having her fingers inspected in that way. "My godfather, Reggie Moore. He's one of the best micro-surgeons in England."

"And it works okay?"

Emily withdrew her hand. "It's a bit feeble, still. But getting stronger daily."

"But not strong enough to play professionally again?"

She shrugged. "No. And not much feeling in the fingertips."

"Does that make it hard, on a day-to-day basis?"

"Not really. Not now. I had problems with make-up and fiddly things like threading needles, but neither's relevant in Whangapouri. And Reggie says that I'll regain at least some sensation, given time."

"And what else? What other injuries?"

She drew back the fringe of hair which covered her brow to reveal the vivid zigzag. "Some ribs. One lung was punctured, and I was a mass of purple bruises, but all that is well and truly healed. It's really the scars to my psyche, now, that I'm coming to grips with."

"So that's why you're here, in New Zealand?"

"Yes. There wasn't anywhere further I could run, I suppose."

He leaned back in his chair. "Then you're right. We have a lot in common. I came here to heal, too."

Emily started with surprise. And yet, she'd half expected something similar. One survivor recognizing another. She hoped that he might continue, because she knew that this was a topic she could never, never initiate. Not with that word, "pry," hovering there between them, even if he had apologized. But Bill remained silent.

She stood up. "Would you like coffee?"

"Yes, please."

She realized that their shared confession time was over, at least for the present. "Tell me about your book. I'm sorry I haven't read it but, as they say, it's a small world. We do have a tenuous connection there."

Bill stirred two spoonfuls of sugar into his coffee. Emily watched him surreptitiously. If she ladled sugar in like that she'd probably have hips like panniers.

"What's the connection?"

"I have a brother, Jay Merivale. He's the resident conductor of the Royal Victorian Symphony. He composed the music for the film."

"Ah. Yes."

"You don't sound too enthusiastic. Didn't you like the music?"

"I believe it was very good." But he didn't appear exactly thrilled, and he didn't elucidate.

She tried again. "Jay said the movie was really funny."

"It wasn't meant to be funny."

"It wasn't?"

Bill tilted his chair back in a manner that would shock generations of school teachers. He stretched out his legs. "The whole experience of Hollywood and *One Witch* brings back bad memories. It was not a laugh a minute."

Not wanting to spoil the easy atmosphere, but hoping to hear more, Emily selected her words with uncharacteristic care. "Can you tell me about it?"

He shrugged slightly. "I wrote what I thought was a pretty biting satire. Don't forget, memories of Vietnam were still fresh. I saw connections with the attitudes of certain people and the original witch trials at Salem. That's what I wrote about. I set it in the seventeenth century, but the allegory was pretty obvious."

"Then what went wrong? I mean, I know absolutely nothing about the literary world, but don't you have any say, as the author, when it's adapted for the screen?"

Bill shook his head. "Not in general. In this case my agent was so eager to close the deal that he skipped over minor details like author's approval. In my stupidity I signed my rights away. Had no say in the screenplay whatsoever. So instead of biting satire we have instead a dose of whimsy that makes *The Sound of Music* look like an R-rated show."

"Oh dear. No wonder you weren't too delighted."

He smiled somewhat ruefully. "No. Not too delighted."

"Then what? What next?"

"I found another agent. One who wore good strong bifocals and could read the fine print. Not to mention being extremely capable in other ways."

"That was sensible."

"It's vital. You're totally dependent upon your agent, as an author. Unless you have a hot line to your publisher. My present agent happens to be the tops."

"And is that the only book you've written?"

"No. It's the only one to reach Hollywood."

"But you've not written anything recently? Since your . . . breakdown?" Pray, God, that he didn't think she was prying, that she hadn't overstepped the line. But they'd come a long way towards friendship over supper.

"That's why I'm here. To rekindle the spark."

"And has it been successful?" Wanting something to do, she stood to feed the fire and spoke over her shoulder. "How long have you been in Whangapouri?"

"Nearly six months. The owners of the house have spent the summer in Europe. They'll be back in two weeks."

The sense of desolation she felt was out of all proportion to so new an acquaintanceship. Friendship. "Does that mean you'll be leaving in a fortnight?"

"Probably."

"Oh dear." Would he read in her response a desperate, knee-jerk reaction, or someone who had enjoyed his company? She badly hoped the latter, but she had no way of knowing.

Bill stood and began to stack the tray. "I'll help you with these. Then I must get back. I've got a crack of dawn start tomorrow. Hori and I are hoping to catch the early tide."

She raised an inquiring eyebrow.

"Trawling for *terakihi*. Fantastic eating." He carried the tray into the little kitchen. "Would you like to share some of our catch? Tomorrow evening? I'm quite a dab hand with a skillet."

An invitation. More than she could possibly have hoped for, when she climbed out of bed this morning. Two shared meals.

"Don't bother with the dishes. I can get them out of the way in no time." She followed him into the kitchen, and hoped that he could hear her pleasure at being asked in the warmth of her voice. "But thank you for the invitation. I'd love to try some *tera* . . . whatever with you."

FOUR

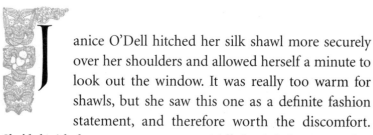 anice O'Dell hitched her silk shawl more securely over her shoulders and allowed herself a minute to look out the window. It was really too warm for shawls, but she saw this one as a definite fashion statement, and therefore worth the discomfort. She'd decided some years ago, practically back in her teens, that she'd employ her height and size as an asset, not something to be camouflaged under all-enveloping kaftans. So shawls and chunky costume jewelry were vital accessories. They spoke of poise and confidence. Lesser women might hide in black and navy. Janice O'Dell wore vivid greens and startling scarlets, and didn't apologize to anybody.

She regularly gloated over the view from her window of the East River. A view to die for, because it cost a fortune, and represented success. And she deserved the occasional moment of self-congratulation, had earned it fair and square. She had, after all, succeeded in the cutthroat world of literary New York. She, that provincial dame from Sydney, Australia-so-help-me, had shown the publishers in the Big Apple that she knew her stuff. W.L. Martin was probably her biggest name, but there was a bunch of talented young hopefuls within her fold and this smart apartment was her reward. Life became sweeter by the hour.

She turned away from the view to pick up the rest of her day, and her eyes strayed to a framed photograph of her most fêted author. It had been commissioned for the dust jacket of his latest book. The photographer had done a brilliant job. The keenness of Bill's mind was hinted at, without his looking remotely nerdy; his sensitivity had similarly been captured, but he didn't come across as sugarcoated. His humorous side was suggested by the lurking smile, the sparkle in his eyes. Heavenly. A truly divine man. She looked with fondness at the scrawled dedication and untidy signature. 'For Jan, a five star agent. Bill.'

She could remember when he'd signed the photograph, at her insistence. He'd objected that only film stars and those with exaggerated ideas of their own importance made such tacky gestures. Jan would have liked to add ". . .or those in love," but had the good sense to refrain. JoBeth was still recent history, Bill was battered and bruised from that union. To cast herself upon him would be an act of madness. Then, while she was sensibly allowing him distance from that set of grisly events, his breakdown had catapulted him, and by association her, into limbo.

She let her finger stray around the ornate silver of the frame and across the cool smoothness of the glass, as though by doing so she was caressing the face behind it. Darling Bill.

Of course, any agent worth her salt could tell you that smoothing the path for your authors was a vital part of the job. Gentling Bill through his breakdown came under that category. As someone who had never in her life experienced more than the occasional pang of PMS, it was almost impossible for her to imagine what had gone on in his mind. She thought it spoke volumes for her ability to empathize that she'd managed so well.

But New York wasn't the same without him, life seemed to have lost a little of its appeal. No good reminding yourself that sensible agents maintained a totally professional relationship with their authors. That was like telling Charles to dump Camilla for the Greater Good. Some things, she conceded, were out of your control, however efficient you were.

God, she mused, looking with deep affection at the finely chiseled features in the frame, how she missed the bastard.

There was something very special about the predawn, Bill thought. That brief period between the darkness of night and the appearance of the sun. If he were writing he'd describe it in shades of silver and pewter, softly gleaming polished metal and fifty striations of gray. Hori reckoned that you caught the best fish at this hour, that the reluctant crawl out of a warm bed was worth it. Hori's friendship had become so important to Bill in the past six months that he'd have dragged himself out anyway, even if they never caught a fish.

Bill's boat was only an aluminum dinghy, so he confined himself to laying set lines; Hori's heavier, larger craft sported a robust inboard motor and was good for trawling. But it was pretty noisy when opened up full throttle, so the men could talk only when they were chugging back to the jetty. Ten sleek, torpedo-shaped fish lay dead at their feet.

"You want to come and eat with Heni and me tonight?"

"Sorry. I'd have liked to, but I have a guest coming." He was aware of Hori's glance and the implied question. "Emily Merivale. The woman who's leased Bateman's."

There was no need to say that. Nothing happening in the bay escaped Hori.

"So you became all chummy-chummy, just walking along the track yesterday."

"Something like that."

Hori's grin was broad. "You're a deep one, Bill Thackeray. I'd never have thought it of you. First unattached female to put in an appearance since the summer visitors left, and you're in there like a shot."

Bill allowed the teasing to wash by him and refused to rise to the bait. "Not quite. She asked me to have a bowl of soup with her. It would have been unkind to say no. And rude."

Hori slowed the motor as they approached the small wharf. "She's a skinny little thing. Not enough flesh on her to last five minutes."

"She was in an accident. Hurt quite badly."

"You don't say?"

Bill repeated what Emily had told him about her injuries and the end of her professional life. Hori listened in silence.

"Poor kid. That's rough."

"Tell me about it."

The smile they shared was born of mutual understanding. Then Hori said, "And you like her, ay?"

"Yes, I like her."

But not, he might have added, in the way you imagine. JoBeth, and the horrors of their marriage, were still too raw for him to think about Emily, or any young woman come to that, in a sexual sense. Possibly it was the medication. In addition to meaning the difference between blackness and life, it seemed to have switched off that aspect of his being. Or maybe it had nothing to do with the anti-depressant drugs and was simply an exercise in self-preservation. Whatever. But he did like Emily for other things, in other ways. He liked her gutsy approach to what had happened, which he sensed hid a despair as deep as anything he'd experienced. Maybe it was that small gesture when she put up her chin and faced him, even when he'd been grossly rude. As, he acknowledged, he had. And the way she'd not been deterred by his feeble, half-hearted attempts to escape. No, he might not be in the business of seeking a lifelong mate, but friendship with Emily seemed a perfectly reasonable alternative.

Hori appeared satisfied with his answer, however brief. He concentrated instead on nudging the boat against the pillars.

Bill leaped out and dropped a clove hitch over the post, then secured the stern. Hori silenced the motor and handed up their gear and the catch. In companionable silence they gutted the catch, their lack of speech amply compensated for by the screams of ravenous gulls. Eyesight to rival eagles, Bill thought. One drop of entrail and they appeared from nowhere in a squabbling, screeching throng.

His mind flipped, unasked, to the moment when he'd made the decision to leave New York. He was over the worst and had decided, almost by chance, to drop in on Jan O'Dell at her office. Her secretary knew him well and smilingly gestured that he go right on into that holy-of-holies, her inner sanctum. Sure, Jan had not been expecting him. The secretary was at fault as well, in not announcing his presence. But maybe his guardian angel had arranged it, so that he could witness Janice off-guard. What had appalled him, what he had never imagined, was that he'd catch her clutching a photograph and gazing at it like some besotted adolescent viewing a portrait of the current crush. Unaware of his presence, she even stroked the picture, pressing her fingertip to the glass and slightly pursing her lips.

"Hi, Jan." He'd cleared his throat awkwardly, disconcerted that he'd stumbled on the soft underbelly of so self-possessed a person. The way Jan dumped the picture, photograph down, and busied herself with rearranging her hair, made him feel even more uneasy. She'd launched into a disjointed speech of welcome, asking about his health, his mother, anything that popped into her mind, and very nearly initiating a full-scale panic attack in him. Then she'd bustled him out of the door, and he'd found himself eating an early and unwelcome lunch, even before his breakfast was digested.

It was only afterward, when rational thought again had a chance to surface, that he understood whose photograph it was in that silver frame.

And so he departed on the first available plane for Cape Cod and, subsequently, to New Zealand. For some reason, it was terribly important to put as much distance as possible between himself and Janice O'Dell. Half the world seemed about right. He knew that he hadn't the strength to enter the combat zone.

But that was six months ago, and in six months he thought he'd again gotten things into proportion. Jan reassumed the guise of a first-rate agent, and her alter-ego faded accordingly. And his inner strength returned daily.

The first rays of the sun were tentatively reaching delicate clouds on the horizon as the men trudged along the track to the store, and Heneti's breakfast.

In the way that a miniature encapsulates a scene and records it for eternity, so the fishing trip seemed to Bill to epitomize the essence of his present life. He found it deeply satisfying.

Emily walked daily, because walking induced tiredness, which helped to combat the invasion of unwanted memories. At first, however, it seemed an exercise in futility. Another reason to escape the bach was the fear that otherwise she would simply curl up before the fire and wither away. That she discovered pleasure in the routine came as something of a surprise. Each day, regardless of the weather, she climbed into stout boots and thick socks, a jacket of some description, and set out to stretch reluctant muscles.

By very small degrees she found a sense of discovery in these exertions and in turn she hoped, perhaps, to open new avenues of knowledge. So she took mental notes of birds she spotted, and the unfamiliar plants and trees of the bush. Then, once home, she'd make herself a cup of coffee and search in the somewhat inadequate volumes to be found on the bookshelves. She would flick through pages to identify this bright-eyed little specimen, that particular fern. The only fly in the ointment was that very few birds were about. They appeared to have abandoned Whangapouri for the winter. And there was limited flora to be researched, because her one edition of native plants was clearly intended for school children. Once she could identify the white-backed leaves of *rangiora* and *manuka* shrubs, it proved to be of no help at all. So much for self improvement.

And so, despite her very best intentions, her thoughts were inclined to stray away from new, fulfilling knowledge, and along much less satisfying trails. Those very paths she had promised herself not to pursue.

This particular afternoon was marked by an absence of rain and the counterpresence of a high, watery sun. She found her contemplations were more tied up with Bill Thackeray than with the less-than-perfect state of her body. She was still trying to assess him, to pigeonhole him in her mind. Attractive, yes. Extremely dishy, truth to tell, in that slim, long-boned way. She liked a great deal about him. The way he sort of unfolded as he stood up, the way he tilted back his chair and balanced it there. But she couldn't slot him into any convenient category. Clearly he was not somebody who accorded you his life history at the drop of a hat. She still blushed when she thought of that word "pry." Possibly that was the reason behind his breakdown, being unable to confide, to spill out his soul. Or the consequence of it? Cause or consequence? The words took on a rhythm as she walked. She found herself humming them to the tune of *Marche Militaire*. Then she realized that her fingers, deep within the pockets of her jacket, were imitating the fingering as she sang inside her head. It had always been so; music was too integral to her life to allow itself a permanent slot on the back-burner. Accepting its reemergence was a natural progression towards recovery. It added an extra spring to her step.

Tonight already took on a special significance, merely because she would be walking along the track to that house with the terrific balcony, to share with him some strangely named fish. As long as they were successful in their trawling, of course, but his words hadn't hinted at the possibility of failure. Dinner with Bill Thackeray. She hoped that Bill was short for William. William Thackeray. His agent was wrong, he should have stayed with his own name. It was far more musical than Martin. Much more individual, like him.

She turned her steps inland. This afternoon she intended to follow the creek, the mouth of which spilled out into the bay from a wide, corrugated iron pipe, before forming a shallow delta across the gray sand. A path of sorts began hopefully along the bank, but it petered out within a couple of hundred yards and Emily had to push her way through undergrowth which clung to the legs of her pants, and vines that attempted to snare her hair. Then, some time later, she rounded a clump of dense bush and almost fell upon a child. A girl, quite small, perhaps nine or ten, with matted black hair and large, wary brown eyes.

"Hello," Emily said. "Sorry if I startled you." She felt that she was beginning to make a habit of doing just that.

"Are you the Welfare lady?" The child's voice was husky, as if she needed to clear her throat.

"No."

"Not nothin'?"

"Nothing to do with them at all."

Emily returned her gaze quietly. The girl remained silent and still, observing the intruder with considerable caution. She made a comic sight as she squatted beside the stream, dressed as she was in an outsized man's sweater which almost engulfed her. From the condition of the ragged cuffs it had certainly seen some wear. The sleeves were pushed back in great bunches above each elbow, displaying skinny, brown arms.

Emily squatted down to be on her level. "What are you doing?" Although it was obvious.

"Washin' clothes."

The packet of soap powder had at one time, probably long past, encountered moisture. Now it was a block of congealed globules with the consistency of slippery, creamish cement. The small washerwoman had ripped down the cardboard side to gain access to the block. Items of clothing were scattered about over the surrounding *manuka* bushes; several tattered T-shirts, an elderly skirt or two, two pairs of faded pink panties. There were also three or four threadbare nappies.

Emily surveyed them all, then returned her attention to the diminutive laundress. "What's your name?"

"Kaffi."

"Kathy?"

"Nah," the owner of the name corrected, "Kaffi."

"And do you always wash your clothes like this?"

"Yeah. Nowdays."

She returned to her labor, scrabbling her fingers against the congealed powder, rubbing the dislodged lump into another tattered garment, then swilling it about in the chilly waters.

"Doesn't your mother wash for you?"

Kaffi shook her head by way of reply. She wrung out the garment with tough little fingers and laid it beside her on the grass. Then she cocked her head sideways and looked at Emily. "You not from the Welfare? Promise?"

"I told you before. No, I'm not from the Welfare."

"What's your name?"

"Emily Merivale. I'm staying here for a few weeks."

Kaffi continued to look at her. Her eyes were wonderful, like polished mahogany. "You talk funny."

"That's because I'm English. I come from England." The words sounded horribly patronizing, although that had been far from her intention. There was a curious dignity about this small figure, squatting beside an icy pool and working so purposefully. To cover her lapse Emily continued, "Who are the nappies for?"

"Me brother. The baby."

"Ah. And what's his name?"

"Gary Cooper."

"Gary Cooper. That's unusual."

"He's me mum's second favorite film star."

"Ah," Emily repeated.

Kaffi stood and wiped her hands on the gigantic sweater. When she was upright it covered her to mid-calf. She rolled down the sleeves and wiped her nose along one cuff. Then she took the latest batch of garments and spread them carefully out over the shrubs. "I've gotta wait till they're dry, ay." She made the comment in a matter-of-fact tone.

"Of course." But in this tentative sunshine it might take hours. "You don't have a line at home? At my place there's a cord along the verandah where things can dry, even if it's raining."

Kaffi shook her head again. "It come down. Me mum hasn't mended it."

Silence followed. Emily could think of half a dozen things she would have liked to ask, but they all sounded inquisitive, and there was no mistaking the caution which greeted even the mention of the Social Welfare people. Clearly in Kaffi's book, Welfare, and anybody associated with it, was not good news.

Anyway, her legs were going to sleep. She stood. "It was nice meeting you, Kaffi. I hope your washing dries in time."

"Yeah."

"Bye, then." Emily rubbed her knotted muscle. "Do you live near here? Perhaps we'll run into each other again."

Kaffi vouched no answer. She stood motionless, watching as Emily started to push her way back through the tangle of undergrowth.

Emily turned and raised her hand in a farewell wave. "Be seeing you, then."

Again no reply. Just the brown-eyed, silent stare.

Emily retraced her steps along the creekside, her mind full of small girls with filthy black hair, skinny limbs and no shoes on this cold day; who wore men's sweaters and carefully soaped and rinsed nappies in a stream. She wondered about a mother who allowed her daughter to wash her garments in snow-fed water, not to mention those of a baby brother. A mother who hadn't knotted together the clothes line, who called her son Gary Cooper, and appeared to have no acquaintance at all with simple, everyday items like shampoo and hair brushes.

It certainly knocked any vestige of self pity into second place. For a while it even crowded out the happy thought that someone else would be doing the cooking this evening.

～

Emily, back at the bach and contemplating her scant wardrobe, wondered just what might be appropriate for this invitation. Her garments fell into two categories, city clothes, from her professional life, and jeans and the like, generally restricted to visiting her parents. Included in the city attire was her penguin gear, the black and white skirts and blouses that are compulsory wear for those who play in orchestras. None of the latter had found room in her bag to New Zealand. So, it had to be jeans, and a sensible, Marks and Sparks pullover.

She found that her pace slowed as her destination came into view. Until this minute she had walked purposefully along the track, using her pocket torch to ensure that she didn't plough into some unseen pothole. What there was of the sun had set fitfully behind a bank of clouds some time ago and the pale moon proved itself an inadequate beacon. To her left the bush was a series of dark and darker shapes, but somehow not threatening. In a place where the thirty-odd residents all knew each other so well that to lock one's door might be considered an insult, the issue of personal safely did not loom large. And the other evening's social gathering on her roof aside, she knew that New Zealand lacked prowling animal predators. No wolves, no cougars.

She'd asked Hori what creatures might have disturbed her.

"'Possums."

The only 'possums she knew of were the American variety, furry gray and white, more often seen squashed on the roads than alive in the trees.

But Hori's next words clarified things. "These are the Australian sort. Bloody nuisances. Kill the native birds, too. And they seem to like playing cops and robbers along the rooftops."

"They frightened the life out of me."

He'd looked at her as if trying to assess whether she had been terrified or whether this was justified exaggeration. "Yes," he'd said at last. "Can sound frightening, if you're on your own."

As she neared the place where Bill was house-sitting, she slowed down to savor the twofold anticipation. Firstly there was her pleasure at being invited and, witness yesterday, there was something about sharing a meal that touched the most basic human need. But the second reason was more vital. It had to do with that transient flash when she had recognized in Bill a fellow traveler. Someone else who was damaged and clawing his way back to the surface. She could not have explained, had her life depended on it, but for all that it was very real. And the knowledge gave her an inner warmth.

The curtains were closed and glowed a bright crimson. Through one chink, a beam spotlit the glossy leaves of a shrub. Two ruby eyes watched her progress as Emily approached the door, then their owner turned and scuttled on noisy, confident paws into the underbrush. It looked no larger than a sturdy cat.

She wondered whether this was an opossum, kin to those which had shattered her peace.

Bill opened the door. He was wearing jeans, a cotton-knit sweater, and nothing more than socks on his feet. It indicated that this house was better insulated than Bateman's bach.

"Let me take your jacket. Come on up." He led the way. "This is one of those houses where the bedrooms are downstairs and you do all your living upstairs."

They emerged into a large room which was both sitting and dining areas rolled into one. The kitchen was separated by a breakfast bar.

"What's your poison?"

Emily considered. "What I'd really love is a G and T. But mostly tonic, please go easy on the alcohol."

"With ice and lemon?"

"That sounds like total luxury."

While Bill was slicing the lemon she looked about the room. From the outside it was really attractive. Inside, it left a lot to be desired. Of course, he was only house sitting, so it wasn't Bill's taste reflected here. Which was just as well because the furniture and the pictures, in her opinion, were decidedly naff.

Bill returned with her drink, professionally garnished with a sprig of mint. "Sit down. I'll be with you in a minute. I just want to check on the potatoes."

She sank into one of the chairs.

"Can I be of help? I'm assuming that you and Hori did catch some fish this morning?"

He smiled. "No problem. Ten. There was quite a shoal, but Hori had to get back to open the store. Heneti drove into town for the day."

The drink was delicious, he had followed her request to the letter, and the smells emanating from the kitchen made her mouth start to water.

"Aren't you joining me?"

Bill looked up from chopping a fistful of herbs. "I don't drink. It doesn't agree with my medication."

"Oh." Not wanting to repeat yesterday's mistake, she lapsed into silence.

He had set the table nicely. The fish was delicious. So was the salad and baked potatoes which accompanied it. So she'd learnt something about Bill. He knew his way around a kitchen.

Emily had to cast about like a beached turtle to initiate a conversation, hating that she found it hard. After all, talking was never a problem in the past. She'd always had confidence. But that was before the accident. Before she became a rudderless ship. The silence stretched.

It was up to Bill, finally, to set the ball rolling. "What do you think you'll do, when you leave Whangapouri?"

"I don't know. I just don't know."

He concentrated on removing a bone which lurked amid the succulent flakes of fish. "Is that why you came here?"

"Yes. I needed to distance myself from everything. And everybody. I went to Melbourne for a while, to stay with Jay. My brother. We always get on tremendously, and I love his wife and baby daughter, but . . ."

"But?" Bill prompted.

She shrugged. "It was all too immediate. Too close to what used to be. You see Jay's a conductor, with the Victorian Symphony. And I used to play with them, in the past, before . . . before the accident."

"Painful associations."

She lifted her eyes fleetingly to his. "Yes. Bloody painful."

Somehow she couldn't share the real reason for her sudden departure, Jay's lapse, and her outburst of rage.

"Wine?" He leaned across and filled her glass. She could smell the lanolin in his sweater.

"You'll think I'm a soak. And I still have to find my way home along the track."

"Don't worry about that. I'll walk with you."

It came to her mind that he was a very kind person.

"Why did you invite me tonight? I mean, you told me that you find young women frightening. Then, hard on the heels of that you ask me to have dinner here. I suppose I am a bit surprised."

He pushed back his chair and the legs scratched against the wooden floor. "You told me you were lonely. I decided you could do with some cheering up."

"Oh." So he saw her as charity case then. Someone to be pitied. While she was busy assessing his charismatic qualities. So much for mutual attraction.

"Would you like fruit? Or coffee?"

"Coffee would be heaven. Especially if it's made in a proper machine. That sieve I have lets through too many of the grounds which, as you'll have noticed, gives it the chewy consistency of pulverized acorns. Mouthfuls of grit."

She stood to clear the table, stacking the plates and glasses on the breakfast bar. Even though she had been staying in her bach only seven days, its primitive nature already seemed more familiar than the trappings of this kitchen. She looked with interest at the array of high-tech gadgets. A month ago she would have been lost without a microwave. She had known no other way to create edible little somethings out of leftovers. Two weeks ago a dishwasher would have taken priority. Of course, the bach could do with a bit of upgrading, were it hers, but there was nothing in this fancy set up that she couldn't manage without. In fact, it all appeared a bit incongruous.

As the percolator began to gurgle noisily she surveyed the living room for signs of Bill's occupation. Was it possible to live five and a half months in a place without imprinting some of your own signature? There was an open book on one chair. She glanced at the title, careful not to lose his place. *The Europeans*, by Henry James. She had read one or two books by James, when still at school, but not *The Europeans.* Anyway, two minutes discourse would reveal the superficial nature of her understanding. No subject for discussion there.

On a table in front of the east-facing window an elderly typewriter sat with its cover pushed back. She wandered across to look at it. It bore all the scars of long usage, so perhaps it was on these keys that he had tapped out *One Witch Too Many.* The open cover made the typewriter look expectant, in some way, as though this were only a small hiatus, prior to future action. But Bill had talked about his writing in the past tense.

Lying beside the keyboard was a tattered photograph. She picked it up. There were two men in the picture, and one of them she recognized as Bill, despite the cleanly-shaven chin. Clearly it had been taken some years ago, because he had quite a bit more hair, in the fashion of the time, and he was looking very cheerful. Was he ever as cock-a-hoop these days? The snapshot must have been taken at a party, because he and the other man held wine glasses, and there were several other figures, slightly out of focus. And she could tell at a glance that the pair knew each other. Bill's arm rested across the shoulders of the shorter man in a way which suggested longtime camaraderie.

"Here's your coffee." He joined her at the window table. She hoped he didn't consider she was being nosy again, snooping into his concerns. He followed the direction of her eyes and glanced down at the snapshot.

"Taken at the launch of *One Witch.* My first major success."

That explained it. The glasses which could well have held champagne, his obvious elation. "Who is the other man?"

"Garth Jordan. A fellow writer. We knew each other for years."

"Knew? In the past tense?"

Bill took the photo from her and considered the images of the two young men. "Yes. Past tense. Garth died last year. Of complications arising from AIDS."

※※

He walked her home along the track, lighting her path with a gigantic torch. They didn't talk much because Emily had dried up since the discovery of that photograph and Bill was not a great one for keeping the conversation flowing. Then the other matter of the day suddenly surfaced.

"I walked up the hill this afternoon, following the brook. And I met a little Maori girl."

Bill took her elbow to prevent her stepping into a puddle. "I don't think there are any children here in Whangapouri. Apart from summertime. There isn't a local school."

"Well, I can tell you she wasn't an apparition. This child was solid flesh and blood. Her name is Kaffi, and she was washing her clothes in the stream."

"I can't bring to mind any family that lives in Whangapouri. The Webbers have two grandsons, but they're away at college."

"She wasn't anywhere near that age. Perhaps eight or nine. She told me that she has a brother. Gary Cooper. Honestly. And I had not been hitting the gin bottle."

They turned into the drive by Bateman's bach. "Mention it to Heneti. She knows everybody. She'll be able to tell you."

"Kaffi was terrified of the Social Welfare people. Asked me several times whether I had anything to do with them."

She couldn't read his expression in the dark, but the remote quality of his voice suggested that a child washing garments in a wintry stream held no interest.

"They're probably transients. On their way from one branch of the tribe to another. I doubt you'll ever see her again."

FIVE

he senior officer of the Social Services Department leaned back in her chair and contemplated with gloom the pile of papers overlapping each other in front of her. She was a tidy person by nature, so the state of the desk gave her no pleasure, but that was the price one paid for ten days of holiday. It was her obsessive neatness that her husband, one Liam Kelly, had cited as the last straw before he moved out. Having fallen for a slip of a girl half his age however, she comforted herself with the thought that he was desperately seeking justification. However flimsy that pretext might be.

Too much paperwork, too little time to pursue the vocation for which she was trained. But no doubt, she thought ruefully, you could find the same sentiment voiced a thousand times across the country, reflected in as many minds.

She'd entered the social services embued with youthful zeal to reform and to save. Up to a point the enthusiasm was still there, but tempered these days with a cynicism that came with maturity, and diluted by countless doors slammed in her face. She'd assumed, at first, that people were crying out to be helped. Rather like heathens falling with stunned amazement onto their knees, as early missionaries introduced them to Christianity. That was the notion conjured up by convent school scripture classes. The same cynicism that had rendered her fervor a bit dog-eared, made her wonder now whether those heathen types weren't actually kneeling to assess the estimable preacher's pot-worthiness. Long pig, they called human flesh. Good eating.

She picked up the first of the papers and scanned it. The normal stuff. A tale of repeated truancy, the father known to be alcoholic, more than a hint that there might be sexual abuse of the daughters. She used her own shorthand to indicate that this report needed immediate follow-up.

The second paper dealt with the return of a family who had been taken into custody while the mother came off hard drugs. According to the case history, she'd gone through hell and emerged clean, determined to reclaim her kids and make up for lost time. Rare. The optimist in the senior officer felt warmed by the effort of the young mother; the cynic wondered how long before she found her old chums, and the cycle repeated itself.

She wrote a note to authorize action, with all the supportive bells and whistles available. That made her smile wryly. There'd been a time when the department could offer a heavy brigade of supportive services. Now the budget was so tight that you expected the toilet paper in the bathroom to be rationed out.

The third item in the pile was only a single sheet. Across the corner a colleague had written in red, "Know anything about this pair? Nothing under Missing Kids."

It was actually a note from a teacher. She let her eyes flick up the sheet . . . from a school in Taranaki. The other side of the Island from here, and the good woman was making enquiries about a brother and sister. John and . . . was that Kaffi? Crikey, the names people called their kids . . . Morrison. Particularly Kaffi, for whom the teacher appeared to have a special fondness. No mistake about the spelling of that bizarre name, this time. Evidently the family had just up-sticks and left about eight months ago, and dropped from sight.

She put the letter down, feeling annoyed. There was no reason to fear for this pair, unless the teacher was holding back. Losing from your class a girl you liked didn't constitute a crisis. Families were quite often known to leg it, if debts had been incurred, or there'd been a bust-up with the in-laws. Was the woman living in Cloud Cuckoo Land? With so heavy a work-load, and so few resources, no one could burst a blood vessel following up a couple of kids who'd moved home. She scrawled WHO KNOWS? in large, red capitals, and refrained from adding something rude. Then she shoved the teacher's letter into a rarely opened file, and dismissed it from her thoughts.

Marge had suggested that Emily have her mail sent to the store. As she explained it, there was bound to be a rural delivery, but no reason for Emily to use it. It was probable that she'd be picking up daily supplies, anyway. How did Marge know that? Probably from first hand experience. Anyway, Emily had given her nearest and dearest the address of Hori's Store, and sat back to await long and cheering epistles.

She waited nine days, more than a week, before Hori said casually, "There's a letter arrived this morning, for you." He handed her the air mail envelope along with her change.

Australia. Jay. She'd have recognized his characteristic scrawl, even if the stamp were not a clue. She propped herself against the rail of the verandah as she tore the top open and extracted the folded sheets. She wondered whether he'd start by apologizing, but decided not to hold her breath. She couldn't remember a time when Jay had admitted a fault; in fact, it was more probable that he was anticipating an abject expression of regret from her. Tough. He'd have to learn to live without it. But Jay appeared to have forgotten the reason for her hasty flight. Other, far more important news was pressing.

Dearest Emms,

I hope the weather where you are is a touch more benign that the foul stuff we're experiencing. Non-stop rain for four days, and Charlie, in her frustration at being cooped up indoors, is driving her mother mad.

Emily stared with glazed, unseeing eyes across to the tufts of pampas grass that dotted the southern dunes and imagined Jay and Chelsea and Charlie in the Hawthorn house, a perfect trio. Complete. Lucky them, lucky Jay. Smug, patronizing Jay.

She set off along the track, walking slowly as she read her brother's untidy handwriting.

However, I'm really writing to keep you abreast of the big news. The ultra-sound indicates that the new member of the family will be a boy ...

A boy. Marvelous. Once more everything fell into place for Jay, like a well-crafted jigsaw puzzle. She knew they wanted a son, to complete the family. So it was infuriating that as she read her eyes filled with tears and her stomach felt as if she'd been dealt a body blow. She was happy for them, wasn't she? Delighted. But her knees apparently didn't share the pleasure that she was forcing by sheer willpower through her veins. They were buckling like straws beneath her.

She sat down on the moss-covered trunk of the fallen tree and gave up the pretence. She cried as if hope had died, for the pain of the moment and for the pain of the past, and for the apparent uselessness of all her tomorrows. She did not even attempt to stem the sobs.

～☙～

Bill, on his way to Hori's Store, found her there. As ever, his first instinct was to depart on winged feet. Weeping was the primary weapon in JoBeth's arsenal. He'd begun to wonder quite early whether she was capable of turning her tears off and on, like a faucet. And the route between that opening, moist salvo and a gut-wrenching battle of wills was merciless and swift.

But he quelled the impulse to escape and forced his legs to stop. In his mind, at least, he'd accepted the responsibilities that accompany friendship. Not to mount a rescue mission at this moment would be to deny that friendship, and was the ultimate action of a jerk. And these were not pretty tears. Emily, wracked with sobs and swollen about the eyes, was scarcely employing feminine wiles. Come to that, he rationalized, up close she was not at all like JoBeth. Emily was soft about the edges, where JoBeth was sharp and sophisticated.

"What's up?" He sat down on the fallen trunk and put a comforting arm around her. Emily rested her head against his shoulder as if it felt too heavy for her neck.

"Nothing. Everything," she gulped, through shudders.

"Something wrong with the day?"

"Yes. No!"

"Immediate problem or long-term?"

"I don't know," Emily wept. "I don't know."

Bill delved into a jacket pocket and found her a tissue. "Here. Wipe your eyes." He waited for her to do as instructed, still providing support with one arm. "Are you on your way to the store?"

"N . . . no. I've been."

He noticed that she was clutching a crumpled letter in one hand. "Have you gotten bad news?"

She shook her head and sniffed. At least the weeping appeared to be coming under control.

"Then can you share what it is?"

"Chelsea's having a boy."

"Aha." Who the devil was Chelsea? "And that's bad news?"

Another sniff, more emphatic this time. "No, it's very good news. They've already got a daughter."

"So what I'm seeing are tears of happiness?" In a pig's eye.

"No." Emily mopped fiercely at her eyes and then blew her nose. "Not happiness, although I'm really pleased for them."

"Then who is the other half of this happy announcement?"

"Jay."

"Ah, Jay." Bill waited for her to go on. He didn't have to wait long.

"I thought I was doing so well. That I really was on the way to recovery. Of the soul, not physical. My body's okay. Well, bearable. But of my psyche. Then I read his letter, and it's so glowing with ... happiness. Togetherness. I don't begrudge them that, or anything. It's just that it brought me, my situation, into such sharp relief."

Bill said, "Aha," again, by way of encouragement.

"There's nothing there." Emily dabbed at the tears which showed signs of a resurgence. "I look into the future and it's gray. Nothing, stretching away to the horizon. And further."

"That's because you're aiming too far." His fingers smoothed down the fabric of her jacket, tracing the seam that secured the sleeve. "Even ordinary people, who haven't been through the ordeal you've experienced, don't attempt that. The body doesn't heal all in one great leap. Nor does the inner person."

He squeezed her shoulder to give his advice emphasis, wondering, as he did so, how it was that he'd been so unable to follow very similar advice. But it was always easier to offer wisdom to others than to comply yourself.

"You need to set your goals less ambitiously. See where you're going. Then the steps are small, and you can manage them one at a time." He stood up. The dampness from the bark of the tree was permeating his jeans. "Let's walk. Physical action is curative, especially walking. I should know; I'm a case in question."

Emily stood too, still clutching his soggy tissue. "Aren't you going to the store?"

"I was, but it's unimportant. Let's climb the hill. Have you ever been to the *pa?*"

"What's a *pa?*"

"I take that to mean no. A *pa* is a fortified village. This one was abandoned nearly two hundred years ago, as far as I can ascertain, but you can still make out where it was."

He led the way, taking the apology for a path which left the track and followed the gully for about a mile. The climb took most of their energy, because the ascent was steep and the ground rocky. Emily followed a bit snuffily, but she appeared to have emerged from the worst of her misery.

When they reached the open ground above the bay Bill turned as usual, to survey the panorama spread below. Emily used the break to catch up with him.

"You were here the other day." The climb had rendered her somewhat breathless, and her voice reflected this. "The first time I saw you. You waved to me."

"Yes. We can wait here while you get your wind back."

Emily sank down with every appearance of gratitude. She filled her lungs several times, long and slowly.

"Tell me about your accident." Bill seated himself alongside her, on the same felled tree as the other day, but maintained a decent space between them. Friendship didn't equate with unwarranted intimacy.

"There's not much to tell. I was on my way to the French Alps for a week's skiing. I was with the City of London Symphony, and we'd just completed several recording sessions. There's this tiny village, sort of tucked on the edge of the hill. I stopped because a little old man was crossing the road, and this gigantic truck came pounding round the corner. The truck hit my rental car and catapulted it down the hillside. That's all."

"The stuff of which nightmares are made?"

"I suppose so, although I can't remember much of it. Evidently the car somersaulted several times."

"You were lucky it didn't catch fire." Bill refrained from pointing out that to emerge alive from something so drastic was a miracle in itself. He knew far too well that reminders of what one was to be thankful for seldom improved a foul mood.

"In retrospect." Emily shifted her seat restlessly.

"And that was the end of your career as a musician?"

"Yes. You can't do much, violin-wise, with fingertips that lack any sensation at all."

Her voice was so bleak that he glanced down at her. She wasn't exactly pretty, but there was a great deal of appeal in her vivid coloring and neat features. Her eyes were remarkable, when not red-rimmed with crying. They were the color of toffee. English toffee.

He put a carefully friendly hand over hers on the smooth, weathered surface of the felled trunk. "There must be other things you can do, with your talent. Teach, for example."

Emily averted her gaze. "I thought of that, but I can't. I'd be totally hopeless. I haven't the patience, or the aptitude."

"Have you ever tried it?"

"Yes. For two summer sessions, after I left the Meinhardt. That's the school where I went; and Moshe Meinhardt invited me back as a student teacher. So I did give it a go."

"But you can't have been too bad," Bill pointed out gently. "If they asked you twice; if you went back."

Emily looked a bit uncomfortable.

"There were other inducements." He put his head to one side to indicate interest and she laughed. He thought that was a more encouraging sign. "Oh, very well, if you have to know. I was in love with one of the visiting teachers. He, Marco, was the reason I returned the second summer. There. Are you satisfied?"

He smiled to himself at her unintentional double entendre. "More than satisfied. Very happy for you." He stood and pulled her to her feet. The color was returning to her face. "Now, shall we continue our climb?"

≈≈

The further they ascended, the more Emily became aware of how unfit she was. Bill was very gentlemanly. He didn't stride away on his long legs and abandon her, but in a way she wished he were a bit less gallant. Then he wouldn't hear the noises she was making as her lungs protested such exertion. It was with considerable relief on her part that they reached the hilltop and were able to survey all that lay below them.

"This is the easterly entrance to the *pa*." The sweep of his arm indicated the approximate limits.

"How can you tell?" To her there was nothing to distinguish this point from anywhere else in the vicinity.

"You see that shallow ditch? That was the demarcation line, although it would have been much deeper then. A stockade of sharply pointed stakes would have been here, so the enemy couldn't enter the outer fortifications unseen."

"Did they fight a lot?"

Bill led her through the entrance to the long-ago *pa*. "They were a very warlike people. Rivalry was intense, especially when it came to matters of honor, and victory meant slaves and booty. But they were also very chivalrous. There were complicated rules which each side had to obey."

The area was sparsely covered with low scrub and coarse, waving grass. She could recognize the stunted *manuka* bushes, and the almost-palm shape of cabbage trees, but not much else. There was no more than a handful of trees, and they grew grotesquely low to counter the fierce winter winds.

"How do you know all this?" she asked.

"I did post-grad work on Polynesian culture, in Hawaii."

It made sense. The common link between America and New Zealand. "Is that why you came here?"

"One reason. The other was serendipity. The house where I'm staying belongs to friends of my mother. It became vacant when I was in need of a refuge."

"I see."

She paused as her gaze swept the inland panorama. Hill upon rolling hill led toward the jagged skyline, grassland spotted in an irregular polka dot of wooly-white sheep. She could see the dark clumps of trees that sheltered farm homesteads, and deep, bush-clad gullies similar to the one they had climbed.

Bill followed her gaze. "When the *pa* was occupied this entire area would have been forested. Totally covered."

"And all evergreen?" She'd noticed the marked lack of autumnal color, even this far into the season.

"The only deciduous trees you'll see are those brought in by the pioneer farmers, planted when they cleared the land. Like that line of poplars."

Emily looked about for something upon which to sit, and found a slab of low rock. She eased herself down, resting aching calves. She knew that tomorrow she was going to be very stiff indeed. "But the settlers haven't been here all that long? You said the *pa* was deserted about two hundred years ago."

"Move over." He sat beside her, stretching his legs out. "That's right. The tribe had left long before anyone started to farm the land. Actually it's quite an interesting story, if rather sad. Would you like to hear it?"

Emily slid across so that she could use his back as support. She leant against him and closed her eyes. "Yes. Please."

"There's a clue in the name of the bay. Whangapouri means Bay of Sorrows. And the headland, with the twin rocks, is called Nga Ipongaro. That translates to mean the lost lovers."

"Don't tell me you can count a knowledge of Maori among all your other accomplishments."

"No. Hori told me."

Emily recalled the large pillars of rock that seemed to guard the point. The name gave them new meaning. "Go on, then. About the lost lovers. What happened? Did they fall over the cliff at their moment of passion?"

"Probably not off the cliff, but they certainly disappeared. That's part of the mystery. This tribe, the one which built the *pa* originally, was the most powerful hereabouts. Their chief, or *ariki*, was a very fine warrior, and evidently they had subjected all the surrounding tribes, so they were very well established and rich. They weren't nomadic you know, like the Plains Indians."

"You mean they lived all the time in the *pa?*"

"No. That was for use only in wartime. It was carefully selected so that any enemy would have to climb the hill to attack, and it needed to have a supply of fresh water, in case of siege."

"Like the European hill forts," Emily murmured. The sun was warm on her face.

"Similar. I found their water supply. A spring, over there."

He must have been indicating with a sweep of his arm, because she could feel the movement behind her shoulders, although there seemed no reason to open her eyes.

"Anyway, most of the time the tribe lived down in the bay, leaving sentries posted to ensure that they weren't taken unawares. The bay must have seemed perfect, because at that time they called it Place of Many Fish. The chief had a son who was the original hero, ripe for Hollywood treatment. He was handsome, brave, all the things a chief's son, a *rangatira,* is supposed to be. Only problem was, he fell in love with the wrong girl. He fell for a slave girl, and then the fat was in the fire."

Emily kept her eyes closed while she listened to the story. "A singularly appropriate metaphor." She could feel Bill's shrug through her jacket, and sensed his accompanying smile.

"Whatever. Anyway, to cut a long story short, they eloped and disappeared. No sight nor sound of the pair, ever again. The *ariki* was heartbroken, to the extent that he gave up caring. Just ceased to rule. Squabbles broke out, and finally there was a slave uprising. The *ariki* was killed, and the tribe began a decline, until they were defeated by the Ngati Tarapunga tribe. The irony of it was that they were the very people from whom Waikura came. Waikura was the slave girl."

As Bill fell silent, Emily sat up, allowing his shoulders to slump suddenly backwards. "Is that all? What about the middle bit? About the disappearance."

"You'll have to ask Hori to tell you. It's his legend. His people."

Emily wanted to shake him. "That's not fair. You're cheating. You get me all involved in the story and then you hold back on the interesting part."

He swiveled round on the rock and grinned at her. Most of his smile was in his eyes, she noticed. It was the first time she had seen him so animated, and she found his mood infectious.

"I wouldn't do it justice. It's a Maori legend, so it needs a Maori storyteller. But it helped you forget about the new baby."

"The new baby?" And then she remembered. Jay's letter. And how upset she had been, because it had brought her own future so bleakly into contrast. Bill was right. She'd completely forgotten, during their climb. She eyed him consideringly. He was looking like the Cheshire cat, as if he had discovered a pot of Devonshire cream. Funny, that such an expression should look so good on him, when only recently she'd rounded with considerable fury upon her brother for similar complacency.

"And you can wipe that smug look off your face, too. There's a word for people like you, Bill Thackeray . . ." and she returned his grin, "but I wouldn't lower myself to say it out loud."

SIX

"H ello."

Emily started. One minute the track was empty as ever, the next there was Kaffi in her disreputable pullover, appearing like an elfin jumping-jack.

"I saw you before, on your way to the store, ay." She was carrying a battered plastic bag which held something lumpy. The day was scarcely warm, but she had no footwear.

"Then why didn't you come along?"

She fiddled with the handles of the bag and shook her head. "We don't go near the store. Me dad said."

"I see." Emily started off again, and Kaffi matched her pace to the adult steps.

"I saw you the other day, too."

"Really?"

"Yeah. You and that man."

Emily wondered if she had become the subject of a minor exercise in sleuthing. "I didn't notice you."

"No. You was crying. Ever so loud."

"Oh," she replied stiffly. "That day."

"Yeah." Kaffi paused to scratch herself vigorously through the sweater. "Can I come 'n visit you?"

"What, now?"

"Yeah. Now."

She glanced down at the girl. Her lips were chapped. There wasn't a part of her which didn't appear filthy, from the caked mud on her feet to the tips of her brown fingers. But the eyes were luminous, and held a silent appeal. Emily, in her present frame of mind, found it impossible to resist that look.

"Of course, Kaffi. I'd love to have a visitor."

Now, as they walked, there was a new spring in the girl's step. She began to skip, swinging the plastic bag so that it clanked against her legs. They turned into the sandy drive beside Bateman's bach. Kaffi ran ahead to open the back door, to let Emily enter with the groceries. Then she followed with a series of enthusiastic bounces reminiscent of Tigger arriving in Winnie-the-Pooh's forest.

Emily put her purchases on the countertop. "I was going to make a pot of tea. Would you like that, or a glass of milk?"

"You got some sugar?"

"Yes."

Then there was no room for doubt. "Tea with sugar. Please."

While she was speaking she was looking about, practically sniffing the air in her curiosity. When Emily went into the living room to replenish the fire Kaffi trailed after her, touching this, toying with that. Emily was tempted to say sharply, "Keep your fingers to yourself," but bit the words back.

"It's nice, here."

Emily could recall thinking very recently that the decor within this little place was positively Spartan. "Yes. It's nice."

Kaffi stopped before the case which lay, propped against the wall, on the bottom shelf of the bookcase. "That a violin?"

"Yes."

"You play it?"

Emily was loath to embark on a litany of explanation. She made her voice as discouraging as possible. "Occasionally."

Kaffi was not so easily deterred. "You play it for me?"

"No."

Kaffi moved on to inspect the books on the upper shelves. "Maybe another time, ay."

"Maybe."

She took her time setting the tray with mugs, sugar and chocolate fingers. Then she added several slices of brown bread, liberally covered with jam.

Kaffi, half seated on one of the chairs, watched her every move. Then she jumped to her feet. "Just a minute. Wait for me." She disappeared outside and returned a few minutes later with an assortment of dried grasses. "You got a vase?"

"I don't believe I've seen one."

"Don't matter," said Kaffi. "You got a jam-jar?"

That was easier. Emily found a small glass jar in the pantry cupboard. "Here you are."

The child arranged her collection with care. "That one, it's tinker-tailor. This one's bunny tail. I don't know the name of this one, but it's pretty, ay."

"Very pretty."

She stood back to admire them. "They're for the tea-table."

A lump formed in Emily's throat. "Oh Kaffi. That's lovely. You can set the jar right in the middle. Then shall we wash?"

This idea met with approval. Kaffi skipped into the bathroom. She watched while Emily ran the water, then made quite a show of pushing her pullover sleeves well up her arms. She took the tablet of soap and sniffed it appreciatively. "Nice, ay."

"Yes. It does smell good."

Side by side they washed their hands, Kaffi creating a fine old lather and working it with vigor the length of her exposed arms. She rinsed with equal care, then took the towel which Emily proffered and dried every square inch of skin. The kettle began to sing. Together they returned to the kitchen and Emily poured boiling water into the pot.

"Are you hungry?"

"Yeah." There was a world of meaning in that single syllable.

Emily gave her a cup which was half milk, half tea. Into this Kaffi measured six teaspoonsful of sugar, concentrating as she did so and stirring energetically. She eyed the food; Emily pushed the plate across towards her.

"Help yourself."

Kaffi did so. In total silence she ate four slices of bread and jam and nearly cleaned up the plate of biscuits. She ate tidily, closing her mouth as she chewed. Then she remembered her manners and pushed the remaining chocolate fingers toward her hostess. "You like some?"

"No, dear, but thank you. I'm not hungry at present." Emily sipped her cup of tea and watched her visitor complete the demolition. "Tell me about your family, Kaffi. I know you have a brother called Gary Cooper. Are there just the two of you?"

"Nah." She talked around a chocolate finger. "There's John Wayne, he's me big brother, and the babies. Ani and Tama and Gary Cooper."

"Five in all?"

"Yeah. And me mum."

"But no dad?"

Kaffi's eyes concurred. When she put the tea down there was a milk mustache along her upper lip. "He went away."

"Just like that? Just disappeared?"

"Yeah."

"But when?"

The child shrugged. Clearly the time was immaterial. "I dunno. I know he'll come back, sometime, because he loves us. It's awful now. I miss him. Me mum's no good without him."

"But Kaffi, dear, what happened?"

Again she shrugged, as if trying to make sense out of the nonsensical. "He went to town. He promised to bring us back a treat. And he never come." She paused and passed the cuff of her sweater fiercely over her eyes. Kaffi picked up the last chocolate finger and carefully sucked the coating off one end. "And now nothing works. The water doesn't work and the lights don't come on when you switch 'em."

Emily hoped the horror she was feeling was not reflected in her face. This sounded terrible. An errant father, five kids and a mother clearly living without electricity, probably in squalor, were Kaffi anything to go by. Perhaps starving.

"Can't your mother do something about it?"

Kaffi shook her head.

"But . . .?"

"She can't. I told her we should go back to Kui. That's me dad's nan. And the tribe. She said she didn't know the way. She's like that, me mum." Then she gathered together her inner resources in a manner which was almost palpable, and spoke defiantly. "But we get on okay." She stood up. "I gotta go now. I gotta get some *pipis* for tea. Before the tide comes in, ay."

"What are *pipis*?"

"Shellfish. Taste yummie. I'm good at digging them. Better'n John Wayne. He's too slow."

"I see."

A little awkwardly Kaffi transferred her weight from one foot to the other. "Ta for the tea. It was nice."

Emily stood too. "That's all right, Kaffi. I enjoyed having a visitor." And it had given her a great deal of food for thought.

"Can I come back and visit again?"

"Of course. I'll look forward to seeing you."

She shifted her weight again, as if aware that she might be overstretching her welcome. "Tomorrow okay?"

"Tomorrow would be fine."

The girl made for the back door, gathering up the plastic bag as she did so. Its contents, Emily now realized, smelled decidedly fishy. So she had probably been digging for pipis while waiting. She wondered what they tasted like.

Kaffi turned to raise her hand in a gesture of farewell.

Emily returned the salute. "Bye, Kaffi."

Clearly Kaffi did not believe in letting grass grow under her feet. She appeared the next morning from the general direction of the bush as Emily headed for the store. She was carrying the same bag as yesterday, but this morning it looked lighter.

"Hello. I got a present for you. While the tide was out."

"You did? Thank you. That's very thoughtful." What on earth could it be?

The child held out the bag. At the bottom lay two objects, completely unlike anything Emily had ever encountered. They were about the size of large scallops, but appeared to have one shell apiece, and the shell was neither scallop-shaped nor fluted.

"What are they, dear? *Pipis?*"

Kaffi giggled at such ignorance. "Course not. They're *pauas.*"

"*Pauas.* I see." What on earth did one do with *pauas?* The parts that she could see were a dark, slimy-looking green, almost black. Totally revolting.

"They taste good. Me nan used to make them into fritters."

"Fritters. Is that so?"

They headed towards the store, Kaffi skipping and taking every opportunity the track afforded to demonstrate her skill at jumping and balancing. But when they reached the fallen log she stopped.

"I'll just wait here for you, ay."

"All right. I won't be more than a few minutes."

Inside the store Emily found Hori semi-squatting and stacking cans of baked beans. As the small bell above the door jangled, he looked up and waved a casual welcome. Over the days they had developed an easy camaraderie.

She came right to the point. "Hori, I've been given a couple of *pauas*. I'm told that they make delicious fritters, but I've absolutely no idea how to set about it."

"*Pauas*, eh?" He stood slowly, allowing his bulk to adjust. "Yes. They're good eating. But a bit fiddly to deal with. You scoop them out of the shell and put them through a mincer."

She made a mental inspection of the bach. She wasn't too sure there was a mincer. And, if there was, she wasn't sure she could bear to touch those evil-looking objects.

"They make a grand chowder, too," Hori continued. "Perhaps you'd like that better."

And he proceeded to explain the intricacies of the recipe.

When Emily returned to the log Kaffi was practicing her gymnastic skills, walking the trunk with her brown toes splayed across the mossy bark and her arms outspread for balance. It was taking all her concentration. Today she was wearing a skirt that might once have been gray or brown. Above this she had on a matted, pink cardigan and a T-shirt so old that its original pattern was now only a guess. But she had taken trouble with her face, which was shiny clean, and she swung the bag containing the two *pauas* with her usual chirpiness. Her high spirits were catching.

They chatted as they walked. Kaffi identified the small, buff-colored birds which intermittently fluttered before them as *piwakawaka*, or fantails, and the tiny green birds with white-rimmed eyes as *tauhou*, or silver-eyes.

"And what do you call that plant, Kaffi?"

The specimen to which Emily pointed was one of hundreds which dotted the gentle slope of the hillside. Huge, spear-like leaves pointed towards the sky, topped by dark brown growths several feet in height which gave the appearance of dried flowers.

Kaffi's tone suggested that Emily was probably the most ignorant person in the whole world. First she confused *pauas* with *pipis*, now she asked about this. "You don't know flax?"

Flax, to Emily, was a small, delicate plant with crimson or blue flowers. "Not this sort."

"Me nan uses the leaves to make *piu-piu*. And *pois*."

"She does?" Although heaven only knew what *piu-piu* and *pois* were. Or whether you ate them, wore them or drank them. No wonder Kaffi's voice was scornful. "You'll have to explain for me, Kaffi. We don't have those things in England."

Kaffi stopped her skipping while she elucidated. "A *piu-piu* is the skirt they wore in the olden days. Nowdays they wear them for dances and that. They kind of rattle, when the flax is dried. Me nan showed me how to scrape the leaves. *Pois* are the little balls that you use for dancing. You sort of flick 'em."

"You do?"

Kaffi took the response literally. "Well, me nan showed me, but I gotta practice to be good enough." She paused and dragged her toe along the soft mud, forming a miniature valley into which a trickle of brown water seeped. "I'll practice again when me dad's home."

Tread carefully, Emily thought. This was delicate territory. "You think he'll come home?"

"Yeah." Kaffi spoke with all the confidence in the world. "Course he'll come home."

"I usually make myself coffee at this time," Emily said as they went into the kitchen. "Do you like coffee?"

Kaffi shook her head. "Nah, tastes awful." Then she added, "Thank you," politely.

"Milk, then? Or hot chocolate?" That suggestion received vigorous approval. "And some toast?"

"Please." She cast a sweeping look about her. "Can I wash me hands again? In the bathroom?"

"If you want to." Emily opened the appropriate door and switched on the light. "Don't you have a bathroom in your home?"

"Yeah. But the water comes out cold. And dirty."

Cold and dirty. "How horrible for you." And how ghastly, to have a baby and be without hot water.

Once more Kaffi looked appreciatively round the room. She laid her fingers reverently on the elderly taps on the tub, and let them wander gently down the smoothness of the white enamel side. Emily regarded her with dawning wonder. What she was witnessing was very nearly an act of adoration. She was thoroughly obtuse yesterday, not to have noticed. But then she realized that yesterday things were on a different footing. Yesterday they weren't equal in their friendship. If she'd made the suggestion then, the girl might have been offended.

"Would you like to take a bath, Kaffi?"

The voice was very nearly a whisper. "Can I?"

"Will your mother mind?"

That question was greeted with a vigorous shake of the head. "Nah. She don't care."

"I've even got a bit of bubble bath left, if you like."

Heaven, she knew well, meant different things to different people. It was apparent Kaffi had just discovered her particular heaven. She spoke with the awe others might use describing nature at its most marvelous. "Bubble bath."

"Shall I run the water for you?"

Her eyes were shining now. "Yeah. Please."

Emily squirted a generous allowance of liquid soap into the flow. "I'll get you a fresh towel. Do you need any other help?"

Kaffi was watching the foam. "No. Thank you."

Emily turned off the taps. "Okay, dear. Enjoy yourself. I'll have everything ready when you've finished."

✕✕✕

She made coffee for herself and prepared the hot chocolate. She wondered how Kaffi was doing. Not flooding the place, she hoped. She thought with renewed wonder about her visitor's desperation to take a bath, and linked it with the memory of her washing clothes in the stream. This time, poor kid, she'd be putting her squeaky-clean little body back into those grubby garments. Not to mention walking home bare-footed.

There wasn't a lot she could do about shoes, but she was pretty sure she could improve on the filthy attire. Kaffi was a lot smaller than herself, of course, but some things were meant to be worn large.

"Kaffi?" She knocked, out of courtesy. Silence. She knocked again, louder, then put her head round the door. To all intents and purposes the bathroom was empty. On the floor lay her guest's outer clothing and some apologies for underwear, but of Kaffi there was no sign. Then the frothy surface was disturbed as a sleek head emerged, eyes tightly closed, mouth gasping for air. Black hair clung wetly to the nape of her neck.

She shook her head like a dog emerging from the sea and opened her eyes wide. "Washing me hair," she announced, and disappeared again beneath the foam.

"KAFFI."

Again the head emerged. "Yeah?"

"Look. Put on these clothes, when you're dry. I know they'll be a bit on the large side, but I'll wash your other things for you, next time I put through a load of laundry. Okay?"

Kaffi looked at Emily and then at the pile of garments. She thought about this for a moment. "Yeah," she said at last. "Ta."

✕✕✕

It was more than half an hour later that a new child emerged from the bathroom. Her hair now hung down her back, smooth and darkly shiny. It occurred to Emily, suddenly disconcerted, that she had probably made use of Emily's hairbrush. Who knew for how long small, hoppy insects could hold their breath under water. A good soaking in disinfectant would be sensible.

But the change was remarkable. Kaffi was clad in Emily's shortest skirt, which hung loosely on her and nearly to the ground, and above that a sweatshirt embellished with "Victoria, BC." She shone with cleanliness and her small face glowed with the pleasure of it all.

"You enjoyed that?" A rhetorical question.

"Yeah."

"And I'll bet you're hungry, now."

"Yeah!"

Emily poured hot milk into the mug and stirred it. "Don't burn yourself. And what do you like on your toast?"

"You got Vegemite?"

Once more her ignorance was manifest. "I'm sorry, Kaffi. But I do have a choice of honey and several jams."

Kaffi settled for honey, but clearly it was second best. She sat neatly on her chair and spread the toast carefully, concentrating on what she was doing.

Emily tried to keep her voice nonchalant when she spoke. "What's your mum's name, dear?"

The girl looked at her a trifle warily. "Winnie."

"Doesn't she have another name?"

"Yeah."

Emily held her breath.

"Morrison."

Again she tried not to sound too nosy or too concerned. "Has she reported about your father leaving you all?"

At once she knew that she'd made a mistake. The look which crossed the child's face was the one she'd seen before, when first they had met.

Even Kaffi's voice altered, becoming closed and guarded. "Not the Welfare lady. Dad made everybody promise."

"I see." But why? If ever there was a situation which cried out for help, this was it. She paused to consider, replenishing their mugs to fill the time.

But Kaffi was still anxious. "You promise you won't tell the Welfare lady? You promise?"

"Tell them what, dear?"

"About us. Me dad says they'll take us away. Put the babies in a home. He made us promise."

She wasn't too sure she could she make an undertaking like that. It was as plain as the nose on her face that, in encountering Kaffi the other day, she had stumbled upon a family in need of help. A family barely surviving, in impossible circumstances. It made absolute sense to report such things. Then they'd be handed on to the correct authorities. She looked at the worried little face.

"You know, it's not a punishment, sugar. People don't just come along and cart you all away, without reason. I do think they're the ones to help you."

Kaffi slipped off the chair and stood up. She was four foot and some inches of pride and fury. "You said you wouldn't. You said when I asked. Now I can't come and visit again. It's spoiled."

Emily hastened to repair the damage. "Kaffi, don't be cross. I promise I won't tell about you." And anyway, tell them what? All she knew was conjecture and the evidence of her eyes.

The girl looked at her warily. Emily patted the vacated seat. "Finish your chocolate."

But Kaffi was still defensive. With studied disregard Emily changed the subject. "I told Hori about your present. The *pauas*. He suggested that I make a chowder. He even gave me a recipe."

Kaffi sat down again, but left her hot chocolate untouched. "I thought you was my friend."

"I am. And you're my friend."

She looked across the table suspiciously. "Did you tell him that I give you the *pauas?*"

Emily shook her head. "I just said, someone."

"And you won't tell, cross your heart and hope to die?"

Emily smiled and nodded mutely. They'd used those very words on occasion, she and her siblings.

"And can I come back, for me clothes?"

"Of course. I'll look forward to seeing you."

The small figure in the over-long skirt stood again and made for the back door. "I'd better get back home. Help me mum."

"Kaffi?"

She paused, her fingers on the door handle.

"You gave me a present, which was lovely; and I've got one for you, although it's nothing like as special as your *pauas.*"

"You have?"

Emily went into the kitchen. "It was really silly of me, but I bought too much at the store, yesterday. This stuff will spoil, if it's not eaten in time. It seems a pity to waste it. Do you think your mother could help me out?"

"What you got?"

"Oh, just a few vegetables, and some sausages. Could she do me a favor by taking them?"

"Yeah. Ta." She gathered up the bag. "Thank you for the bath," she said a little awkwardly. "And for the chocolate. It was nice."

"It was good to see you. And thank you for your gift."

The small figure turned and waved in farewell.

"Bye," Emily called at her retreating back. "Take care."

"Bill, you're not listening." She leaned across to take his plate and ladle a second helping onto it. She'd made a sort of goulash, using the ingredients which the store could supply. She knew that no Hungarian worth his salt would claim the finished product as his national dish, but Bill appeared to find it tasty enough. "Something has to be done. All I am asking is, what?"

"I did hear you. I've no other answer." He shrugged slightly. "You dial directory inquiries for the number. You tell the correct authority that there's a family you suspect to be in trouble. They take over from there."

"And break my promise to Kaffi."

"For what it's worth."

Emily pushed her chair back abruptly. "A promise is a promise, regardless of the age of the person."

"But what's more important? If they are starving as you think surely, for everybody's benefit, you should ignore that."

Emily had related the tale of Kaffi and the bath, even telling him about the way she had employed two twigs to gather up the discarded articles of clothing. Nor did they look much better after lengthy soaking and a vigorous session in the machine that came with the bach. Finally, cleaning the tub itself had taken quite a bit of elbow grease. She didn't begrudge the effort. She could still pause, and conjure up that look on Kaffi's face as she said the words, 'bubble bath.' Like a child entering Santa's Workshop. She wasn't sure that she could ever break her promise to the girl.

And yet the Morrisons needed help. The problem was that she had no idea precisely what to do, which was why she had turned to Bill. And a fat lot of use he was being.

Now, as if aware that he was not proving himself her knight in shining armor, he said, "You could ask Hori. He'd tell you."

She'd considered that. There was something comfortingly avuncular about the storekeeper. And, as he was Maori, he should be able to offer guidance for a fellow Maori family. All she really wanted to do was help, in the most sympathetic manner possible; to offer support to one small girl, for whom she felt a great deal of respect. But Kaffi had said that they weren't to go near the store. Her dad had forbidden it. Why? It was hard to imagine anything threatening about the Webbers. But perhaps they represented authority, too.

Bill finished the last of the stew. "That was good, thank you."

"Coffee?"

"Please."

These days she could carry quite heavy things without fear of her arm resenting the strain. She began to stack the dishes while her mind circled the problem of the Morrisons. But, actually, it was Bill who stood and carried the laden tray into the kitchen.

Clearly his thoughts were following a parallel path. "What did you say the father's name was?"

"I don't know. I didn't ask. She was edgy enough, as it was."

"Then perhaps you could find that out, and then try a few calls to trace him."

That made sense. The bach was not connected to the phone, but there was a public call box outside the store.

"Mmm. I could do that. And I might visit them. Then I can decide whether I should notify somebody, and . . ." She was about to say 'shop them,' because that was what she would be doing. Breaking a promise. It was funny how deep these things went, although Bill was probably right. She should be considering the greater good.

When the kettle began to sing she poured boiling water onto the coffee in the enamel pot and stirred it a couple of times. She had bought a new sieve from the store, but it was a case of beggars can't be choosers. The only one on offer was too large to sit neatly inside a mug. It took a bit of skillful juggling to produce two cups of beverage without creating a brown lake on the table. But at least it was potable, and no longer resembled Turkish coffee in texture. She added the sugar bowl to the tray.

They drank in comfortable silence, Bill, as ever, tilting back the chair at a rakish angle. She tried to see the problem from his point of view. He didn't appear exactly sympathetic towards the Morrisons, but then, he'd not as much as met Kaffi. He hadn't experienced her quick mind and sparrow-like chirpiness. Nor had he first hand experience of her pride. When she thought of the way that Kaffi had said, "Course he'll come back," it made goose pimples tingle down her spine. Such trust, so much devotion. But she couldn't really blame Bill. It was scarcely his fault that he knew none of that.

"Are you doing anything on Saturday evening?"

Her thoughts were still with Kaffi and her family. "What?"

"Saturday night," he repeated, as if she were a couple of clowns short of a circus. "Are you busy?"

She tried to recall what day it was. Such matters seemed to have lost their importance. She smiled.

"Well, actually I was going to wash my hair on Saturday. Before writing a treatise on the adolescent behavior of the greater spotted newt. Why?"

He grinned. "Okay, stupid question. But I was wondering if you'd like to join me at the store. They have a get-together there, most Saturdays in the winter. Heneti cooks something, and the local families gather. That's all."

"Sounds wonderful."

"You said it."

"I'm not sure whether, between the spotted newt and my round of frenzied partying, I can squeeze in another function." She put her head to one side. "But I'm certainly prepared to do a bit of rescheduling. I'd love to go with you."

"Great. Then be my guest." He paused while he considered her quizzically. "Oh, and don't bother to unpack that cocktail dress. Correct attire is strictly jeans and sweaters."

"Phew!" Emily retorted. "That was a near thing. And thanks for the warning. How silly I'd have felt, turning up in my tiara."

SEVEN

ou could learn a lot about people by discovering their time-keeping habits. Bill was knocking on the door of Bateman's bach at just two minutes after the allotted hour. It was Saturday evening and damp because a sea mist had encroached, taking advantage of the stillness to spill onto the land. Bill had tiny drops of moisture scattered over his hair like seed pearls.

"I know you said not to put on my glad rags, but I wasn't too sure how literally to take you."

She was wearing jeans, but the sweater was her best Guernsey. He held the door open while she shrugged herself into a jacket.

"You look very nice."

"I was going to put on a bit of lipstick."

"Not many of the men wear lipstick. It does not seem appropriate for Whangapouri."

Emily held back her grin. "The women, you dope! Or am I to be the only representative of my sex?"

"No. There's always a sprinkling of women."

They set out toward the store, Bill lighting the way with his huge torch. Emily walked with her customary two steps to his one stride. She supposed that she'd get used to it, given time, but at present she had the distinct feeling of scuttling alongside him. She wondered whether Kaffi shared the same sensation, when they walked together. But Kaffi, of course, skipped and hopped and paddled through the puddles as though her feet could not feel the cold.

"Tell me what to expect tonight, Bill. So that I don't make a complete idiot of myself."

"I think you'll find it interesting. Generally it's a mixed bunch. Half a dozen fishermen and their wives, Heneti's extremely elderly grandmother, who's as sharp as a tack but very frail, the artist couple who live in a cottage on one of the sheep stations. A couple of bachelor farmers. Heneti cooks a good meal, and after that the entertainment varies from evening to evening and week to week."

"Entertainment?"

"Oh yes. Always entertainment." But he didn't expound.

As they walked along Emily tried to conjure up all manner of jollification, and failed. Possibly charades. She was bad about leaping to conclusions. It was a besetting sin. She lectured herself sternly, hearing her mother's voice like a recurring echo, hearing Moshe Meinhardt take up the theme. Totally void of any form of inspiration, she abandoned the pointless attempt and concentrated on matching her pace to her companion's.

The front of the store appeared to be deserted, but through the damp grayness the rear windows glowed invitingly. Half a dozen serviceable vehicles were parked in the adjoining space. Bill opened the front door of the shop and the small bell above it plinked. The interior, as they entered, was shadowy, a hundred dimly recognizable forms and shapes which in the daylight assumed mundane familiarity.

"Down the back. Just follow your nose."

Emily did so. A murmur of voices came from that direction, anyway. When she pushed open the door which was half ajar it was to step into another world. The back portion of the building was given over to one large living room which stretched the width of the structure. It was warmed by a great, free-standing wood stove, the chimney of which disappeared through the ceiling. A large table was set on trestles at one end, covered with cheerful gingham cloth and candles placed in red glass jars. About a dozen people sat about or stood.

"Hello Bill, Emily." Heneti, a slightly incongruous hostess apron spread across her front, emerged from what, judging by the mouth-watering aroma, was the kitchen. "Get yourselves a drink. Hori will be with you in a minute."

Emily thought that it would be impossible to assemble a more diverse gathering of people. She was used to mixing with disparate groups, but there had been few occasions which included such an ill-assorted bunch. Several of the men sported three days of stubble, one had a strange, knitted hat atop hair which closely resembled dreadlocks. Perhaps half were Maori, including two of the women. They were talking together with the ease of long association. The somewhat ascetic-looking man she adjudged to be the artist, the woman with the profile straight from ancient Egypt, his wife. She looked like a relic from hippiedom. Sandals, shawl, coarse-textured, graying hair braided down her back.

Emily had noticed Bill handing some paper money over to Hori. So this evening was not entirely philanthropic. That stood to reason; feeding those assembled would cost more than a few pennies. Now he returned to her side with a glass of wine.

He took her elbow. "These are all long-time residents. I'll introduce you."

There were far too many names to absorb at one time. She did catch that the artist was called Vernon, and his wife was Ruth. She established that they'd grown up in England, lived in New Zealand for eons, put down roots in Whangapouri. And the fishing community sounded like a *Who's Who of the Old Testament*, Abraham and Talitha and Moses interspersed with the soft-voweled Maori words which she would never remember. And if her life had depended upon it she could never have matched names with faces.

"This is Heneti's grandmother. Kui." She had not noticed the tiny figure seated in a vast wicker chair which practically engulfed her. A rug covered her spindly knees, and her face had the texture and indentation of a shelled walnut.

Kui. Kaffi had used that name for someone in their tribe.

Emily bent down to shake the hand which was offered her. It was so fragile that she felt one squeeze would pulverize the bones. It was like grasping the delicate claw of a bird.

"How do you do?"

The eyes had faded to a milky white around the irises, but they held her gaze steadily, and the old voice had scarcely a waver. "Not so bad. Not so bad."

"Does Kui mean grandmother, in Maori?"

"No. It translates as wise woman. A title of respect."

"Oh. I see." Now what? Perhaps she could mention her own grandmother, ninety-one this year and no longer wise.

But at that moment Hori came to her rescue. "Will you all find a seat."

By the time they were sitting the number around the table had swollen to sixteen. Kui, escorted with care and propped up with several cushions, sat at the head. It was an overly cozy arrangement. Clearly anybody who ate with undisciplined elbows was in for a tough time. Emily found herself scrunched between Bill on one side and the Maori fisherman with the interesting hairstyle on the other. He wore a hefty flannel shirt of red and black checks which, by the feel of his arm, hid more than your average share of muscles.

Then came the first of what was developing to be an evening full of surprises. Hori sang. He simply said, "Let's bow our heads," and then launched into something lovely that she assumed to be a grace. It was a form of chant, and obviously the words were in Maori; not that it mattered, because the meaning was clear enough. Unaccompanied, his voice had the richness of chocolate decadence, and he sang as if singing were as natural as breathing.

The next surprise was the meal. Heneti had roasted a haunch of venison, which Hori carved with the aplomb of Michelangelo tackling a lump of granite. But the flesh was tender and absolutely scrumptious. There was Cumberland sauce, and Brussels sprouts, petits pois and several types of potatoes. And *kumera*. She recognized the word, because Kaffi had mentioned it on more than one occasion. Now she discovered that *kumera* was a sweet potato, cousin to a yam. And, roasted about the haunch, it tasted delicious. It all tasted delicious.

Maybe it was the combination of the wine and the heat put out by the stove, added to the close proximity of so many people after eleven days of semi-isolation, but a profound feeling of bonhomie began to course through her very being. It was a form of drunkenness which owed nothing to alcohol. She felt that she might have known Bill all her life, instead of less than a week; he was as familiar and as dear as the Jay of her childhood, as her father. Moses, on her right, she discovered to be remarkably poetic, filled with original insights. And it didn't matter that he hadn't shaved for a week, and wore the articles of clothing which a few days ago she would have found alien.

The marvelous venison was followed by a variety of pies. Heneti, it transpired, was famous throughout the Known World for the lightness of her flaky pastry. The known world of Whangapouri, anyway. She had made rhubarb pie, and gooseberry, and apple tart. Too much choice, all vying for sampling. And Hori broached a sweet Sauternes to accompany the pies, which even Emily recognized to be excellent. It slid down her throat like nectar. Then, at the moment when to eat another mouthful was to tempt social disaster, Heneti produced dark, bitter coffee.

As she sipped, Emily listened to the conversation round the table. The artist had tried to photograph a flock of pied stilts along the estuary, involving a lengthy period of chilly waiting, his wife was swapping recipes with the sweet-faced bride of one of the Maori fisher-folk. Bill, with the ease that comes from established friendship, was discussing something which had captured the imagination of the television-watching public. That number did not, of course, include Emily. She let her gaze linger on the diners. Swap suits and ties for the motley assortment of garments, exchange the vehicles outside for Cadillacs and Jaguars, transpose this table to the American Midwest, or the English Shires. Then it might have been any dinner party, anywhere in the world. Although, she reasoned, this evening's food would take some beating.

But the surprises didn't end there, because once they had finished the meal there was a general exodus to the kitchen, where everybody became involved in the matter of stacking the dishwasher, and clearing away the remains of their meal. Emily, remembering countless gatherings at her parents' home, did not need Bill to remind her quietly that here was a difference in culture. Finally they returned to the other half of the living room. There weren't enough easy chairs for everybody, so some of the younger people sprawled out on the floor. Then Heneti asked for requests. One young man piped up from the mat in front of the stove. Emily had given up second-guessing, by now. Even when he asked for the recording of *Don Giovanni*, in particular the duet when the Don encounters the statue, she did no more than blink rather quickly a couple of times.

Heneti crossed to the wall cabinet and folded back doors to display an array of CDs and a complicated arrangement of sophisticated players and amplifiers. She selected the disc and a hush fell over the replete audience.

Emily knew it all by heart. She adored Mozart, had studied this opera during her years at the Meinhardt. She had never, in her wildest imagination, envisioned herself sitting here, in this far reach of the civilized world, listening to it. The music filled the room, abundant and satisfying. She leaned back against Bill's shoulder because it was convenient, and closed her eyes. The voices swirled about her. When, at last, they died down and everybody clapped, she opened her eyes and looked about.

"Bloody marvelous," somebody said.

"Lucky bugger," came another voice, quite clearly.

"Such a gift." That was Ruth, the artist's wife.

"Bill?" She half pulled him down to her level.

He leaned over so that his ear was close to her mouth. "Huh?"

"Who was that? Who was singing?" Although she knew, before he said a word. She had only to link the Cani being played when first she'd visited the store, with this evening's grace.

His breath tickled against her ear. "Hori. With the New Zealand Opera. Recorded a decade ago, before he retired."

Her senses were numb, anyway. Past shock. She looked across to the storekeeper who was sitting next to Kui, the wise woman. Hori's girth spread about him, reminiscent of Jabba the Hut. His eyes were closed, too, and he leaned against the chair's padded back, giving the impression that the recording artist had absolutely no connection at all with him. Then, as if among the praise and chatter he could sense Emily's eyes upon him, he opened his own . . . and winked at her.

For a moment she was aghast, for it was as if he had read her disbelief, and found it amusing. He, Hori Webber, had put down that prissy, English person with her preconceived notions of what could and could not be. But then the wink was followed by a smile which was far more important. It bound them together across the room. We're the professionals here, said that smile. The musicians. We have something in common. And she could smile back, and be thankful for his understanding.

"You could have told me. Given me a bit of warning."

Bill's torch beam caught the glowing eyes of an opossum as it scuttled across the track and lumbered into the undergrowth.

"Why?"

"Out of fairness. So that I wasn't caught on the hop."

She knew him well enough by now to know that he was grinning in the darkness. "You wanted to put me down, didn't you? Teach me a lesson."

"Never!"

"Oh, yes you did." She hoped that she didn't sound peevish. "You thought, here's this pompous person who thinks she's come to the end of the world. Beyond the reaches of culture. That's why you shut up."

Bill said, "Never," again, but she knew that she was right. And that he had enjoyed seeing her flounder a little. Not in a cruel way. He'd probably have leaped to her rescue, had she really shot herself in the foot, but he'd decided to let her discover, as he had discovered, that here, in a remote East Coast bay, an eclectic community could meet to share wonderful food and breathtaking music.

The evening had not ended with *Don Giovanni*. When the last notes faded away one of the fishermen produced a guitar and started to sing a gentle lullaby in his native tongue, and, quite spontaneously, all the other Maori joined in. The way they harmonized suggested that they had practiced long and hard, but that turned out to be incorrect, too. When the lullaby ended somebody asked for one of the more recent songs from the pop charts. A bit of improvised strumming, a few trial chords, and the voices mingled together again in a way that could not have been rehearsed.

"It's part of their heritage. Their culture," Bill explained, when Emily remarked upon the singing. "All they need is three people and one musical instrument to create something pretty fantastic. Even the kids have that ability to harmonize."

"Wow." Emily thought how inadequate that sounded. It was another lesson in not prejudging people. She wondered if Kaffi shared this particular talent. And John Wayne, the big brother.

Bill's hand on her arm brought her to a halt mid-stride. "Shh."

"What?" she whispered.

"Look."

She peered in the general direction of his gesture. Sea mist surrounded them in fine swirls. Somewhere to the right and very high the hunter's moon was a softly opaque disc. Apart from that she could make out only blackness upon blackness.

"Shh," Bill said again, and trod silently toward the over-hanging rock face. Equally stealthily Emily followed him, but it wasn't until she was close to the glossy wall that she could see what had caught his attention. The vertical surface was aglow with a hundred tiny lights. No, more like a thousand, or several thousands.

"What are they?" she breathed.

"Glow-worms."

"Oh."

They were so delicate, so ethereal, it was like entering fairy-land, or a grotto from *Arabian Nights*. They stood in total silence for some minutes, sharing the beauty of the pinpricks of light, the tendrils of mist, the distant sound of lapping waves. A nocturnal predator broke the spell. It passed within feet of them on insistent wings, then screamed *mo-poke!* and swooped angrily up towards the bush.

"Would you like some coffee? Or cocoa?"

"May I have a rain-check on that?"

Emily opened the back door and put her hand around the corner to grope for the switch. "Of course. With food to go with it if you want, although almost certainly not up to tonight's standard." The light behind her clicked and lit the kitchen. "Well, thank you so much for taking me as your guest."

Bill's face was illuminated by the glow, sharply emphasizing the planes and valleys of his features. She thought that the fine bone structure so revealed gave an impression of aristocracy. Handsome, actually. Again, tiny droplets of moisture beaded his hair. They probably did the same to hers. She shook her head and pearls showered about her.

"I'm glad you enjoyed yourself. I was a bit worried that you might find the musical half of the evening a little tough to take."

"And that's why you didn't warn me?"

"In part."

She leaned against the door jamb with her arms crossed while she thought back through the evening. There had been one brief, difficult moment, shortly after she'd learnt about Hori's earlier career. Until then she'd been fully in charge of herself, able to enjoy it all, and feel one of the assembly. Then somebody had requested Mendelssohn's *Violin Concerto*. "No. No," her inner voice had screamed. "Not that, please. Anything but that.' For the second time this particular work managed successfully to undermine the bulwark of her determination. Unlike the Mozart and the subsequent choices, it was far too personal. She knew, she just knew that she was going to make a fool of herself, that, despite her resolution, tears were already forming. And worse than that, for a short poignant moment she felt, once more, an outsider. Totally alien. The sensation lasted only a fraction of a second, but that was sufficient. Through eyes swimming with tears she'd noticed one of the friendly Maori lasses glance at her with concern, and that recognition of sympathy had exacerbated her moment of panic.

But Bill, bless him, had come to her rescue, very quietly, and with the minimum of fuss. He'd merely turned her slightly, so that she no longer faced the other guests, and had pressed an outsized tissue into her hand.

"Can't stand Mendelssohn myself," he'd whispered in her ear. "Sentimental garbage."

And that was exactly the right thing to do, because he had quoted almost word for word what Philip, her father, had said one evening, knowing her love for the work and intent upon pulling her leg. And so that Bill Thackeray, himself an outsider, had proven himself to be her champion. There had been nothing she need do but acknowledge his remark with a watery smile, dab at her eyes, and regain control. She would have liked to thank him right now, couched in the warmest of terms, but found it quite hard to voice. Especially when she reminded herself that she had known him less than a week. Somewhat awkwardly she ran a hand through her damp hair. Ending an evening such as tonight was new to her. A goodnight kiss would be inappropriate in the circumstances, but something more than a handshake was required.

"Well, thank you for coming to my rescue, Bill, when they played the Mendelssohn. And for taking me tonight. I really did enjoy it. Mostly."

And then she did the only, obvious thing. She hugged him. Fortunately he was two steps below her, because otherwise she would have been embracing his stomach region. As it was she could reach around his shoulders and pull him towards her. For a moment she felt him stiffen, and she knew she was going to die of embarrassment if this went wrong. Then his muscles relaxed and he returned her hug, drawing her head into the hollow between chin and shoulder.

"It was great for me, to have your company," he replied, and she thought that he planted a brief, feather-light kiss on the top of her head. Of course, she might well have imagined it.

EIGHT

t was a rare day when Kaffi didn't appear, and to suggest that Emily did anything but welcome her arrival would be to lie. The friendship they forged was lopsided, but no less valuable for that. And, almost as often, they played out the small charade of Emily's habitual over-shopping, so that at the end of each visit the girl would depart with the fruits of the woman's stupidity filling her battered plastic bag.

Emily wondered what the child made of her. Clearly she was far too sharp not to see through the small ruse immediately. Equally clearly, it was important that she did not let on. Emily's foreign-ness provided the necessary clue. Because of that things could be excused. English ladies, in Kaffi's book, would forever be classed as habitual over-buyers, a touch eccentric and inclined to casual generosity. But she was punctilious about repaying in kind. Her gifts were eclectic, ranging from a solitary *kumera* on one occasion, to some rather bedraggled pampas grass heads, which Kaffi told her hostess were called *toetoe*. As they dried they shed their fluffy white seeds all over the floor.

It bothered Emily that Kaffi was not attending school. By her reckoning they should be slap in the middle of the winter term. But when she voiced this concern in a throw-away manner, Kaffi had replied that she'd probably return to school when her dad came home. Everything in Kaffi's world appeared to be hinged upon the return of the absent father.

One morning she arrived as Emily was finishing breakfast.

"I'll clear up for you, ay."

"Thank you, Kaffi. Would you like some toast? I bought Vegemite, while I was at the store." Vegemite was the Antipodean equivalent of Marmite, a yeast spread, salty and sharp.

"Yeah, ta."

Washing one mug, plate and knife was a two minute job. Kaffi stretched it to twenty-five, savoring the hot water filling the sink, squirting sufficient liquid soap to cleanse the soiled dinnerware of a small restaurant, creating swirls and patterns within the lather. When the activity finally palled she trailed after Emily, as she went through the motions of house-keeping her small domain. At the bookshelf, complete with its dozen assorted volumes, she paused to finger one rather lurid cover.

"I got a book."

"That's nice. Do you enjoy reading?"

"Yeah." She seemed about to say more, but held it back.

"What's your book about?" Emily prompted gently.

"All sorts. Lots of stories. The teacher gave it to me when we left and come here."

Extracting anything about her family life from the girl was like drawing teeth, which was why Emily had made very little progress in that direction. It was a constant worry, small but nagging like a splinter under the nail.

"That was kind of her." She kept her voice neutral. "She must have liked you."

"Yeah." Kaffi continued to fiddle with the pages of *Terrible Tom and the Case of the Jumping Bean.* "I keep it hidden from the babies, in case they tear it. And John Wayne. He's jealous, 'cause he can't read."

"He can't?"

Kaffi shook her head. "He's dumb. I gotta do all the thinking, now that Dad's gone."

Another clue, equally tenuous, equally upsetting. In her mind's eye Emily had conjured up a family in which each of the children was very similar to Kaffi. Bright, tough, coping despite the loss of the parent. She even hoped that her contributions to the pot might be tipping the scales. And now here was Kaffi shattering that small, comforting thought.

She prayed that she was not about to put a period to their relationship. "Now that we're such good friends, I'd really like to meet your mother. Do you think I could visit one day? And the babies. I love babies."

Kaffi didn't look directly at her. She drew a pattern with her finger across the shelf while she weighed up the pros and cons of this idea. Then she looked up.

"You won't tell the Welfare lady?"

Emily shook her head.

"Yeah. You can come 'n visit us. You want to come today?"

Emily was a bit appalled to discover just how long was the trek between their two homes. Obviously, the Morrisons did not live in Whangapouri, and just to leave the bay was approximately two miles, by her reckoning. However she had assumed, without giving it much thought, that they would climb the rise over the headland, drop down toward the cove on the other side and be there almost immediately. Instead it took twenty minutes of quite strenuous exercise before the small, decrepit cottage came in sight. During their walk Kaffi alternated between spurts of activity, in which she tried to educate this uninformed foreign woman, and periods of thoughtful silence.

"Wouldn't it be quicker to go along the beach?" Emily asked during one such silent time.

"Round the rocks, you mean?"

"Yes."

Kaffi shook her head. "That's dangerous. If you get caught by the tide you can't get away."

Emily had not walked along the northern reach since the day she'd seen Bill there. Then the sea had been calm and the tide out. Even so, there was water lapping against the base of the cliff. Quite deep water. It didn't take a whole lot of imagination to picture the point with an incoming tide, or a bit of wind to encourage the waves. Kaffi had good sense on her side.

The structure they were approaching made Bateman's bach look like Windsor Castle. Even from this distance the rust on the roof was evident, and the total lack of paint. In size it was too small, even, to be called a bach. More of a fisherman's shack, although it nestled in a sheltering hollow of hillside several hundred feet above the cove. Emily wondered if it had once been used as a shepherd's cottage. She could see a scattering of animals on the far hills.

Kaffi's steps slowed as they approached, as if she were having second thoughts about this visit.

When she broke the silence, her apprehension became manifest.

"Me mum was fine, when me dad was here."

"I'm sure she was."

"She doesn't listen the same to me."

"Probably not," Emily agreed. "My mother doesn't always listen to me, either."

"And we got no electric. Just the fire."

Emily hastened to reassure her. "I know that you do your very best, sugar."

Large, anxious eyes returned her gaze. "It'll be different when me dad gets home."

"Of course it will."

A glade of native bush grew to the south of the shack. When the walkers emerged from this they were hard upon the space which served as a yard for the Morrison's home. Two small, brown children were squatting on the sparse turf, on either side of a muddy puddle. It was impossible to tell their gender, because their garments were unisex and covered them from head to toe. Their hair suggested a complete lack of grooming and their lips were chapped from the seasonal chill. There was abundant evidence that the smaller of the two was suffering from a cold. Kaffi bent down and wiped its nose with one of the tissues that came from Emily's bathroom.

"This is Tama. That's Ani."

"Maori names? Why not film stars as well?"

" 'Cos me dad chose 'em. He said now and then we needed some proper names in the family. Then he laughed. He's like that, our dad. Always laughing."

The pair of toddlers looked up incuriously, Tama not even responding to his big sister's ministrations as she wiped away the evidence of his cold. Their eyes were like great, dark marbles.

"Hello, Tama. Hello Ani."

Her greeting met with no response. Instead the children returned to their previous activity, which seemed to be a form of mud-pie making. Both held short, encrusted sticks with which they stirred the mud rather aimlessly, as if creating a thick broth.

"They always do that," Kaffi remarked. "It's their favorite game. Me mum will be on the verandah. She likes it there."

She led the way to the other side of the shack and Emily, still somewhat dazed, followed her. But if the sight of those dull gazes was daunting, it was as nothing compared with the shock of encountering Kaffi's mother. They rounded the front of the verandah and there was a figure sitting in a creaky old chair, baby to the breast. One glance said she was probably younger than Emily, and she had the same, lackluster look in her eyes as the infants playing in the mud. And she was a white woman.

Of course, there was no reason why she should not be white. It was simply another of Emily's pre-conceived notions. Behind Kaffi she had pictured a Maori family, parents and siblings.

Kaffi made the introductions. "Mum, this is Em'ly. Me mum's name is Winnie."

Winnie was a small woman, but she got to her feet with none of the usual, small woman's grace, and her nipple left the baby's mouth with a plop. The youngest member of the family, who could have been a clone of the pair already encountered, screwed up his face and prepared to voice his protest.

" 'ello. Nice to meet you." She spoke as though somebody had pressed the correct button, like an automaton.

"Oh, please . . ." Emily began awkwardly, "Don't stop feeding the baby, just for me."

Winnie held her bellowing son up against her shoulder and jiggled him a few times.

" 'e's had enough. 'e's always guzzling."

"And this is Gary Cooper?"

His mother turned him around for inspection. The child paused in mid-roar to gaze at Emily. In other circumstances he would have been rated a very attractive infant, with his abundant black hair and large, dark eyes, and the look he gave Emily was alert and curious. But his face was caked with matter, and even at this distance he smelled indescribably awful.

"Mum!" There was a world of frustration in that one word. "Mum, you gotta change him. He needs changing."

Winnie's slow gaze turned from the visitor to her daughter. "Yeah," she agreed.

"Oh, give him to me."

The way Kaffi gathered up the child suggested that she knew all about the care of babies. She disappeared into the house, cooing at her brother like a small, capable nurse. Emily was left looking at Winnie. Winnie slid her breast back inside her dress and looked back at Emily.

"You the Welfare lady?"

"No, I'm just a friend of Kaffi's."

Clearly Winnie thought that something else was needed in her capacity as hostess. "We got no tea."

"That's all right. I'm not thirsty, but thank you, anyway."

And that reminded Emily that she was the bearer of gifts. "I brought you some food. I ..."

She was about to launch into her 'there I go, busy buying more than I need,' routine, when she realized with a shock that it would be wasted on this girl-woman. Winnie wouldn't care about the motivation behind the food, as long as it was there. Kaffi had not inherited her fragile pride from her mother.

The younger woman took the canvas bag and looked into it. Emily had bought saveloys, red-skinned, spicy sausages. "That's nice. The kiddies like saveloys."

"And vegetables," Emily added. "I put in some onions and a piece of pumpkin."

"Yeah. They like punkin."

They stood awkwardly together on the verandah while Emily, at a total loss, searched about for something to say. Finally, as the silence lengthened, she said, "Kaffi's a wonderful girl. I'll bet you're very proud of her."

"Yeah. Very proud."

Again silence descended. From inside the cottage Emily could hear the sounds of soft singing.

"Maybe I could help Kaffi? With the baby?"

"Yeah."

Apparently, to Winnie, this was a normal suggestion. She sat herself down on the ancient wooden chair and stared vacantly out towards the sea. It was obvious that the visitor had slipped from her thoughts. Emily pushed open the door, almost dreading what she would find on the other side.

"Kaffi?"

"I'm here. Washing the baby. Watch where you tread. We got no candles."

The inside of the shack was dim. Emily had to wait several minutes until her eyes became accustomed to the gloom. Then she could make out the baby lying on a rug before the fire, his elder sister kneeling at his side. She had divest him of his soiled lower garments and his plump little legs and tiny penis were silhouetted against the dull glow.

"I'm heating the water," Kaffi explained. "It's taking forever because John Wayne's put damp wood on the fire. He's always doing that."

Emily knelt on the other side of the rug. The baby still smelled ghastly, but she was impressed by the competence Kaffi was displaying. At the age of nine she, Emily, would have died of terror, had somebody suggested she as much as hold an infant. Kaffi stood and went to fetch a bowl. The baby followed her with his eyes and sucked at one fist.

Emily looked about the room. Although there was a distinct smell of stale urine, it was not as bad as her fears might have indicated. Clearly all the living was done in this single space, although there was another door leading off it. There was a table, one large bed, an elderly sofa, an armchair with stuffing spilling from one arm, and the dead face of a television.

There was a small hob attached to the grate by a pivot, and from this Kaffi carefully removed a blackened kettle. She poured some water into the bowl, then tested the temperature. The kettle was returned to the hob. But when she began to wipe the baby's lower regions with gentle strokes of a washcloth, he pulled his legs sharply towards his tummy, opened his mouth and roared.

"Shhh." Kaffi spoke soothingly. "Better soon." She cast a brief glance in Emily's direction. "We run out of cream. It was on me dad's list, when he went away. Cream for the baby. And me mum don't remember to change him, so he gets sore. I do tell her."

Emily felt a rush of empathy. What responsibility, to be heaped on such young shoulders.

"I understand, sugar. But you could have mentioned it, and I'd have bought you some from the store."

The way Kaffi put her head to one side, like a small sparrow, always indicated that Emily was demonstrating her stupidity.

"Then Hori would say, 'And why do you need cream for a baby's bum?' What you gonna tell him?"

"Ah," Emily agreed humbly. What, indeed? She changed the subject. "How do you cook your dinners? On this hob?"

Kaffi nodded. "Yeah. It works okay, when the fire's hot. Me dad and John Wayne put in a whole heap of *kumera*, so we got them to eat. Me mum makes *kumera* stew most days, and we fetch mussels and *pipis* and that. Tastes good."

At this moment the door opened and a boy entered, a boy of about ten or eleven, slightly built, with his mother's blond hair and blue eyes. He stared at Emily, still kneeling by the hearth.

"That's John Wayne." Kaffi's introduction was unnecessary.

"Hello, John Wayne."

His grin held the slightly foolish expression of the very slow. " 'ello." He put onto the floor a bag which clunked. "I got mussels."

"Oh, you always get mussels." Exasperation overflowed in Kaffi's voice. "Then I gotta sort 'em and clean 'em" Again she turned in explanation to Emily. "I told you he was too slow to get *pipis*. You gotta be quick to dig *pipis*."

She finished washing Gary Cooper and folded a fresh nappy. It was a dull gray square of fabric, so thin that you could see light through it. New nappies were added to Emily's mental list of things which should be bought. And talcum powder. The baby smiled and gurgled. Kaffi blew against his tummy as she wrapped the cloth about him and pinned it efficiently.

"There you are. All nice again." She stood and picked him up with professional ease. "Back to Mum."

Winnie accepted the baby without comment, but the expression of love on her face brought a quick lump to Emily's throat. Inarticulate Winnie might be, but her feelings about this child were writ plainly there for anybody to see. She fished out the other breast and jammed it into Gary Cooper's groping mouth. The infant, eyes half closed, gave himself up to the important business of feeding, oblivious to anything else in the world. Beneath the elderly shawl in which Kaffi had wrapped him, his small, light brown toes reflected his pleasure, curling and flexing as he sucked.

John Wayne joined them, grinning vacantly. In clean clothes, and with something done about his unkempt hair, he would be a nice looking lad. Emily added barber's scissors to her list.

"Kaffi," she said awkwardly after a few minutes of silence. "I think I should be getting back."

"You want to see my book?"

The precious book. With so much to occupy her thoughts it was the last thing on Emily's mind. "Of course!"

Kaffi dived indoors and returned in a flash. In her hands was a much-thumbed reader, perhaps dating from the fifties if the pictures were any indication, the edges of the pages grubby with frequent handling. Emily accorded it the respect deserved.

"That's marvelous, sugar. And you've read all the stories?"

"Yeah. Often. I used to read 'em to Ani and Tama when the lights worked."

"Well done, you."

Kaffi beamed in the light of such praise. When she smiled like that she stopped being a little, old person with the weight of the world on her shoulders, and became a nine year old again, enjoying the things that nine year olds enjoyed.

"You'll have to read the children's books at the bach."

Kaffi stood on one leg and raised the other behind her with a hand. "Can I?"

"Of course. Come tomorrow, and we'll look them over together. But I really should be getting back, now. Will you say good-bye to your mother for me?"

"She won't notice."

This response voiced exactly what Emily was thinking. "Enjoy the saveloys."

"Yeah," said Kaffi. "Ta for them. Much nicer 'n mussels."

And she made a nine year old's face at her brother, who responded by sticking out his tongue and crossing his eyes.

❧

Kaffi accompanied her guest as far as the headland. Not because there was any chance of getting lost, there was only one track after all, but as a courtesy. When they reached the top Emily turned back to survey the humble dwelling. Now that she knew what to look for, she could make out the two tiny dots that were Tama and Ani, still squatting beside their muddy pool.

"Kaffi . . . ?"

"Yeah?"

"Dear, I've done some thinking." The words tumbled out, as if by blurting it all she could forestall the girl's reaction. "Please don't get cross until you've listened to me. While your dad's away, I think it would be sensible if I bought a few of the things you need. Like cream for the baby's bottom. Then, when he comes back, your dad can repay me. Sort of like a loan."

"You can't." Kaffi spoke flatly, although she had listened without interrupting. "I told you before. If you ask Hori for bum cream he's gonna be s'picious."

"But what if I didn't get it from Hori's?"

The girl looked at her assessingly, head a little to one side. Again Emily's chest became tight with anxiety on her behalf. It seemed far too harsh that a kid of her tender years should be forced to make such decisions.

"You mean, go into town?"

"Probably."

"How? You haven't got a truck."

"I'll ask somebody. A friend."

Another pause, while Kaffi weighed things up. The notion of the loan didn't appear to bother her; probably because, if she were anything like Emily at that age, money, or the lack of it, held very little meaning.

Finally she said, "You gonna tell your friend about us?"

Emily repeated the same vow that Kaffi, herself, had employed. "I'll make him swear to keep it secret. Cross my heart and hope to die."

Kaffi turned a cartwheel, as though everything had now been decided.

"Okay," she said crisply when she was again right-side up. "Can you get us some tea? And chocolate biscuits?"

❧

Winnie, sitting as she liked to on the verandah, tried to think about preparing tea for the kids, and failed. Better wait for Kaffi to come back, and then Kaffi would get things started. Kaffi was a good kid, and Winnie didn't know where they'd be without her. Didn't even like to think about it.

She knew herself to be slow, because everyone had always told her she was stupid. They used to shout it out, the kids in the street and the kids at school, along with other nasty, hurtful names. Dummy and cretin and thicko. Her mum said not to mind, because sticks and stones could break your bones, but names could never hurt you. Winnie knew better. Names hurt just as much, because they cut you off from other people. And after a while you accepted them as the truth. So Winnie and Jeannie Morrison knew from very early that they were stupid.

She couldn't remember ever being happy when she was young, although perhaps she'd forgotten. She could remember being beaten by her dad, when he came home drunk, and she had similar, vivid memories of his lashing out at her mum and Jeannie, who was two years older than her. She could recall creeping under the table, to be out of the way of his fists, and sitting there, knees drawn up to her chest to make herself really small. Then, perhaps, he'd not notice her.

She hated school, because the other kids always jeered at the Morrison sisters, and teased them in the playground, so quite often they hid instead of going to school.

Then her Uncle Wilf had done that thing, and really hurt her. She was thirteen at the time, because it wasn't long after her birthday, and her mother had made a cake. Chocolate, too.

Winnie had no real idea of what was happening, except for the pain, but she knew that afterwards her uncle always acted sort of funny around her.

Into this unhappy semi-existence had come Matu, like a hero from the old Western movies that she watched whenever possible. Winnie was fourteen when they met, and she thought that she must have died and gone to heaven. Matu was strong and handsome. Even her father listened when Matu spoke. Beneath the strength he was kind and gentle like the heroes she so adored. And, best of all, he fancied Winnie and her long, fair hair and her light blue eyes.

They had been together for ages. Ever since before John Wayne was born. Well, together most of that time, because there had been a long period when Matu wasn't about, after Kaffi's birth. Nearly five years he was away, all told. But they managed okay, because they were living with the tribe then, and Kui told Winnie what to do. Kui was Matu's grandma.

Winnie did all right, when she was told what to do. She could follow instructions okay, 'specially if you repeated them several times, so that they stuck. Once in, she had no problem remembering. It was just making decisions where she was so bad. Tell her what to do, show her the right way, and she would obey to the best of her ability. Matu showed her what to do. He was really good at it; patient, too. And he was great with the kids. Really loved them. Taught them things, like little Maori nursery rhymes and that. So when Matu was around they managed all right.

This time Matu had kissed her, ruffled Gary Cooper's black hair, and driven away to get stores in the town. Sometimes he took the kids with him when he made the trip, but not this time because he was transporting twelve fat lambs for Godfrey Bryant in the truck, to deliver to the stockyard. He'd promised the kids to bring them back a treat, to make up for not taking them. And he didn't return.

By late afternoon the older two were becoming restless for their treat, by nightfall they were whiny and frightened. But not half as frightened as their mother. She didn't like being on her own at night, not in this lonely, isolated place. It wasn't like being with the tribe, even if they only sort of accepted her. It wasn't like living in the city, when she was a girl. When it became dark, and still there was no sign of Matu, Winnie boiled up the last of the shop-bought vegetables for everyone's tea, and then took Ani and Tama to bed with her, as well as the baby. At least that way, surrounded by little warm bodies, the bed didn't feel too empty.

Matu didn't return the next day, or the next. After a while the pattern of days merged, so that she could only remember life when Matu was there, and life without him. And now there was nobody to give her instructions, to tell her in clear, simple terms what was required. At first it didn't matter, she could remember; but that was while everything was almost the same. Then, one day, there was no electricity to make the stove-top hot, and no warm water running into the sink, and the elderly washing machine that Kui had given them refused to wash clothes any more.

Winnie was bereft. She had absolutely no idea what to do, and nobody to enlighten her. About once a week John Wayne or Kaffi would trudge the two kilometers or so to the road, to pick up the letters that were left in the post box, but as Winnie could not read above a word or two they simply piled up on a dusty shelf. Most of them seemed to have little, see-through windows in their centers. She thought of returning to Matu's people, but without Matu to drive them there, she could not even guess where to find the tribal lands.

Without help, without hope, she began a slow, inexorable slide into despair.

NINE

Heneti had always dreaded a fall. It was a terrible dream that surfaced regularly and increasingly often, in direct correlation to her expanding girth. On such occasions she'd waken with a jolt from troubled sleep, a fraction of a second before the agony became manifest.

So when she did slip, climbing rather awkwardly down from the set of steps about which Hori warned her repeatedly, she had a sickening sensation of déjà vu. The topple almost knocked the wind out of her body, and the pain in her knee was just as bad as in her worst nightmares. She lay awkwardly behind the shop counter and, through an explosion of stars and jagged anguish, tried to think constructively.

Hori had gone to town an hour-and-a-half ago. She could expect him back in the early afternoon. Perhaps later, if he met up with a friend or two. Kui was dozing in her chair, and, even should her cries carry to the back of the building, there was nothing physical the old lady could do. Maybe, though, she could ring somebody for help? That was an option, although Kui in general equated the telephone with unfathomable, *pakeha* ways. But this was a crisis. Perhaps she could get hold of Abraham's young wife, if she were about. She was a strongly built, sensible girl.

But even her loudest efforts failed to penetrate the closed door and Kui's deafness. And her own attempts to mitigate the discomfort of the knee, bent sharply back under her, were accompanied by involuntary groans, and totally unsuccessful.

There was no knowing how long she lay there, in a state that could only be compared with purgatory, before the bell above the door broke into her semi-consciousness. It was followed by a voice.

"Hori? Heneti? Is there anybody about?"

Emily Merivale. Salvation.

"I'm here." Heneti opened her eyes. The light was blocked by the shape of the young woman, as she rounded the counter.

"Hello. Oh, crumbs! Are you all right?"

Emily was at once by her side, kneeling down, extending a hand. Heneti tried again to shift into a less painful position. She grunted with the effort.

"I fell," she explained unnecessarily. Nobody would be jammed behind the counter in this ungainly fashion from choice.

"Let me help you up."

But it wasn't as easy as that. There wasn't much of Emily, and there was a great deal of Heneti, and the confined space made the whole rescue business extremely awkward. It took several aborted attempts, and a stoic refusal on Heneti's part to succumb to the pain, before she was finally in a seated position on the floor.

Emily stood back. "Now what? Perhaps phase two should be to get you onto a chair."

"How?" The sarcasm was heavy in Heneti's voice. "Block and tackle?"

She watched as Emily contemplated the options. "You'll have to brace yourself on my shoulders. I'm sure we can do it."

Even in her pain, Heneti warmed towards this helpful attitude. "Kui has a chair. Can you go down the back and wheel it up here?"

The tiny grandmother looked up from her usual seat as Emily pushed open the dividing door. Her voice was querulous with indignation.

"Heneti? Where you been? I need the toilet."

Oh dear, Emily thought in dismay. Not just Heneti in dire straits, but now a frail little woman of great antiquity requiring assistance. From her, Emily Merivale, the last person in all the world to consider nursing as a possible career.

"Heneti's fallen," she explained. "Could you possibly wait? I've actually come to borrow your wheelchair."

Kui grunted. "I've been waiting. I can't anymore."

Emily bowed to the inevitable, feeling as helpless in her way as did Heneti.

"All right. I'll take you to the bathroom first. But you'll have to give me instructions."

It couldn't be too hard, escorting a very old woman to the loo. Her mother had cared for her grandmother, years and years ago when the family was small. It never seemed a big deal, then. But Anna was extremely capable, her daughter was not. Emily had managed to avoid even the easier bits of people-care. And now, suddenly, here she was with two virtually helpless women, both in need of her. Just dumped in it.

She had no idea of much Kui could do, or how much she might expect. And there was her personal pride to consider. It must be quite humiliating, being dependent upon someone else for this most basic of necessities, and Emily was a virtual stranger.

Fifteen minutes later she knew all there was to know. Kui seemed to accept the situation. Her lack of embarrassment made it easier for Emily, drawing her bloomer-like garment up pencil-thin limbs. She returned the old woman to her armchair and tucked the rug across her knees. Then, finally, she negotiated the wheelchair through the deserted store, on phase three of her rescue mission.

It felt good, actually being of use, and concentrating on the requirements of others was certainly a novelty. She wondered if there were someone up there taking notes, making a record of all her progress. If so, she must have gained a line of gold stars alongside her name, by now.

⧘⧙

The free-standing wood-stove did a tremendous job of heating the back living room. The warmth it radiated made Emily feel extremely soporific. Outside the afternoon had slipped into premature, wintry night. She wondered how long it would be before Hori returned home from the town.

She looked about her. It was an interesting room, reflecting those years when Heneti and Hori had lived abroad. Without the normal, Saturday evening crowd, she could inspect it and appreciate all that she saw. On one wall hung a portrait of a much younger Hori, an immensely handsome man with his slightly aquiline nose, full, beautifully shaped lips and dark eyes. There was a smaller photograph, too, standing in a brass frame on the dresser. This was clearly taken by an amateur hand. Heneti and Hori, outside Buckingham Palace, Hori in top hat and morning suit, the necessary paraphernalia for an investiture. It must have been snapped after the event, because Hori was proudly displaying his new award. Heneti's hat was worthy of a picture in itself, the sort of creation you might wear once in a lifetime, should the opportunity present itself.

And there were further tokens of that other life. Beer steins, a picture of Bayreuth, bric-a-brac that meant a great deal to the collector and precious little to anybody else. Finally, twenty bone china cup-and-saucer sets stood on the Welsh dresser as reminders of the past, and the cities they had visited.

She glanced at Heneti who sat in the second armchair, her cushioned leg resting on the coffee table. The burning logs were not the only reason for Emily's sense of warmth, good job though they might be doing. She felt another glow, generated by a certain amount of satisfaction. She could feel justly proud of her rescue mission.

There had been that small moment when both women wondered, in tandem, precisely how they should treat the swelling surrounding the abused joint. Emily knew that ice was called for, but ice cubes were lumpy and not easy to apply, and caused Heneti to groan with the discomfort. They'd come up with a far less clumsy solution, a large package of free-flowing frozen peas. Two applications, of fifteen minutes each, had eased the pain in the joint to the extent that Heneti, with only a little help from her trusty handmaiden, managed a trip to the bathroom too. At which moment the store-keeper announced that there might, after all, be life following her fall. Emily had done a competent job with an elastic bandage as well, and that, along with some painkiller, helped to make her more comfortable.

Nonetheless, Emily felt it beholden upon her to stay until Hori appeared. She had unhappy visions of Kui in need, and Heneti unable to supply that need. And she had no reason to hurry home to an empty bach, apart from stoking the fire.

So she had made them all omelets for lunch, and cups of witches' brew tea, so laden with tannin that she wondered whether she might have chanced upon the very preservative that kept the diminutive grandmother alert.

Kui's days, it appeared, consisted of eating and dozing, watching occasional snatches of television, and excursions to the loo. She also adored talking. Her conversations were very lop-sided, and concerned mostly with reminiscences about life before the *pakeha* had darkened the shores of her native land. For much of the time she talked without the benefit of her teeth, complaining that they hurt her, so that understanding more than half took a fair bit of concentration. It was when she appeared to have come full circle, and was about to repeat it all, that Emily remembered the legend, the tale Bill had started to relate before thinking better of it.

"Kui, could you tell me about the slave girl? The one who ran away. Bill Thackeray says that because it's a Maori legend, you'll be able to tell it far better than he could."

"Abou' Waikura?" Clearly this was a matter of some moment. Kui, dwarfed by the size of the chair/throne, pulled herself upright. "Gimme me teef." Once they were safely slotted in, it was a great deal easier to understand her speech.

"Bill's wrong to call it a legend," she began. "Legends are about gods and that. This is history."

Was it Emily's imagination, or did the tiny woman grow? It seemed that she drew herself together, as if the importance of the story she was about to relate gave her extra stature.

"In the times when our country was Aotea-roa, Land of the Long White Cloud, there lived a great tribe," she began. "Their chief was powerful, and he led his people to many victories, so that they prospered. And amongst this people, no man was as handsome or brave as Te Manawanui, son of the *ariki* himself.

"The time came for this high-born *rangatira* to be wed, and in the manner of our people his father and the elders selected for him a young woman from an allied tribe. She was of high status and possessed many comely charms. But Te Manawanui would have none of his father's choice in bride. He had already given his heart to another, to Waikura, a slave girl."

"You might explain that Waikura was one of our people, Mum," Heneti interrupted. She turned to Emily. "There were always battles at that time. Our tribe, the Ngati Tarapunga, had been beaten by the Ngati Kura, which was how Waikura was captured and carried off to be their slave."

"They were betrayed." Kui looked crossly at her daughter. Emily was amazed in the difference in her language. The old-lady speech was discarded as she retold the tale, replaced by something altogether more dramatic, and far more poetic. She spoke in a slightly sing-song way, as though the words had been committed to memory like an oft-repeated litany.

"Unbeknown to the members of the tribe," Kui continued in her narrative mode, "he and Waikura met secretly many times, while he whispered of his love for her. Away from curious eyes he would admire her beauty and the abundance of her black hair, and Waikura would marvel at the strength of his shoulders, the power of his arms. They would speak together the poetry of lovers, and dream of marriage.

"But marriage was not for them. *Rangatira* were expected to marry for the benefit of the tribe. They did not wed slave girls, even though we knew her to have been well connected in her own tribe. And when the chief heard that his son was rejecting his decision, and prepared to defy his father before the people, his rage was terrible to see. He called together the elders and the *tohunga,* the priest. They sat in council to discuss this matter. Then the chief declared that Te Manawanui must never again meet with Waikura, or she would be put to death, and he set Kapiti to watch his son, and to follow his movements."

The pause which followed was so long that Emily wondered if Kui had fallen asleep again. But then she lifted her head and fixed her audience with a fierce gaze.

"Kapiti was a cunning man, anxious to prove his loyalty to the tribe. Moreover, he harbored in his breast great jealousy for Te Manawanui, who was stronger than he, and braver, and handsome of face. He set about his task with diligence. No move made by the young prince remained unknown to Kapiti.

"Te Manawanui despaired. He felt that never again would he and the beautiful Waikura lie in the sweet grass under the *punga* trees, and dream of the future. And without Waikura there could be no future. He applied himself to being more cunning than Kapiti. He thought deeply, and formed his plans. Then he called to a small boy who was playing with the other children, and he spoke loudly, so that the words would carry to the ears of Kapiti, who was hiding behind a *rimu* tree.

"'Boy,' he said, 'go to Waikura the slave girl, and give her this message from me, the son of your *ariki*. Tell her that now I have considered the wishes of my father, and I turn my back on her. No more shall we meet together under the fine crescent of the new moon. No more shall we hear the sound of *tui* birds where the stream changes color. Tell her that I, Te Manawanui, am finished with her. Can you remember that?' "

Again Heneti interrupted the narration to explain. "Young George discovered the place, where the water changes color. Young George is our grandson."

"And you really can see the difference?" It brought vividly to mind Moses and the River Nile, when that flow reputedly turned to blood.

"Yes. I've not been there myself, but he said the contrast is remarkable. Clay deposits, or maybe iron."

"Can I go on?" No doubting Kui's annoyance, this time.

"Sorry, Granma. I just wanted to make it clear for Emily."

The old woman waited a dignified minute before she picked up the thread. "The boy sped on his way. Waikura was working with other slaves, grubbing the soil to prepare it for the planting of *kumera*. The child related the message from the chief's son. Waikura's eyes filled with tears at his harshness.

"And Kapiti, too, watched the boy deliver the message. But he was not entirely deceived. 'Te Manawanui is cunning, but I, Kapiti, am more cunning,' he thought. 'Within these harsh words there must be another meaning.' And he set about his spying with renewed zeal.

"Waikura was in despair. Since her capture after the terrible defeat of the tribe, her life had been one of drudgery and humiliation. Only her love for Te Manawanui meant anything in so miserable an existence. Then she considered again. Her lover was a man of great cleverness, and had often spoken of his faithfulness to her alone. She knew from the other slaves that he was pursued everywhere by his father's spy. How could he get word to one he loved? It became clear to her that he meant quite the opposite of what the boy repeated. He had a plan. She need only to wait for the coming of the new moon."

There was another pause, which might have been for effect, to allow time for her listeners to consider the implications of the tale. Emily, caught up in the events and carried away by the beauty of the narration, would have liked to nudge her on. Only her determination not to break the spell kept her impatience in check. She glanced up at the window. Outside the last of the day had yielded to the early obscurity of a moonless evening.

"Never did days pass more slowly for the separated lovers. Each night they watched for the moon to shrink a little more. It was vital to the success of this scheme that there be as little light as possible, because only Waikura and Te Manawanui knew well their secret tracks, and the consequences if Kapiti was able to follow the young *rangatira* would be disastrous.

"Finally the moon was a fine crescent in the sky. Te Manawanui waited until he could hear the steady breathing of the other men before he crept on warrior-stealthy feet out of the sleeping house. He hitched his cloak about him and skirted the quarters of the women and the great meeting house.

"'Where would you be going, my friend, on this dark night?' Kapiti's voice was soft, but full of menace. Te Manawanui hesitated. He could kill this thorn in his flesh with one blow of his *mere,* but it would certainly summon the sentries who were guarding the village from night attack.

"'I had need,' he replied, and returned sadly to his mat.

The next night he was more successful. The fishermen had made a fine catch of *kahawai*. Kapiti, a greedy man, feasted too well, and slept too deeply. Te Manawanui was able to creep past the sentries and make for the place which only he and Waikura knew, where they had lain together and listened to the sweet sound of *tuis* in the surrounding bush. He knew that she had been there the previous night, because several *rangiora* leaves lay in a pattern on the grass, and they were not yet withered. For many hours he sat beside the stream where red soil made the flow change color, awaiting his love. But in that long night she did not come. She had been taken to the house of an elder, as was the way with slave girls. And while Te Manawanui waited he watched clouds cover the moon, and felt the wind blow cooler, and knew that the weather was about to become his enemy.

"Could they wait until the next new moon? By then he would be husband to one for whom he felt only coldness. Could he risk sending another message to Waikura? That would alert Kapiti, and might well result in her death. With heavy heart he realized that they would have to try again the next night, and to hope that the gods might look upon the lovers with kindness.

"Throughout the day the wind from the west grew, lifting the waters of the bay and driving the waves angrily. By evening it was stormy and dark. The noise masked the soft steps of the young man as he left the sleeping house and slipped into the bush. "Tonight,' he thought. "Please come tonight, my love.'

"But the sound of the wind also masked the footsteps of Kapiti, too far away to issue a challenge, but stealthily following. This evening they were more fortunate. Nobody had called for the services of the slave girl.

"'My dearest.' Te Manawanui folded her to his heart. "We must be brave. I have a canoe concealed in the cove, where it is more sheltered from the wind. But speed is vital. The tide is on the wane and driven further offshore by the storm. Its strength is such that we may well be pulled far out to sea.'

"Waikura did not hesitate. 'I would rather be far out to sea with you, my only love, than safely asleep among the other slaves.'

"Their path through the bush was treacherous and difficult. Rain slashed at their faces, clinging vines caught at their bodies. Te Manawanui removed his fine cloak and wrapped it around his love, to protect her from the worst. A hundred yards behind them Kapiti struggled to keep up against the fury of the storm. The chief would want to know all that transpired. Then, when the lovers were recaptured, Waikura killed and the young *rangatira* disgraced, honor and glory would be heaped upon Kapiti's head. At a fork in the narrow path he paused. Had they gone down the track towards the bay, or over the headland? He paused to consider. If he took the headland trail he would be able to see the Bay of Many Fishes as well as the neighboring cove. His footsteps sped him along.

"As he climbed to the point, high above the shore, the rain abated but the gale reached a peak of frenzy. He drew his cloak closer to his body. Now, with eyes sharpened by practice, he was able to see quite clearly the tiny figures of the lovers on the sand below. They were making their way towards the next cove, bodies bowed, heads bent low against the stinging wind. That must mean Te Manawanui intended to take a canoe out to sea. The tide must now be on the turn, but the sea was still far away from the coast. Kapiti shook his head smugly at such folly.

"The pair had reached the long spur of rocks which jutted out from the point. From on high he followed their progress, as they picked their way with care. Now he had only to cross the headland to await their reappearance in the cove. He waited for some time. No figures came into sight. He crossed back to the bay. The sand was bare. In desperation he retraced his steps. The worst of the storm was over as he scrambled across the rocks, but as the wind dropped the tide raced in quickly, obliterating any footsteps. There was no sight of the lovers.

"For the rest of the night Kapiti searched among the boulders. He found nothing. By the time he returned with heavy feet to report his failure and face certain dishonor, waves were dashing against the cliff and salty water filled every hiding place.

"Great was the distress of the chief at the news. 'For my obstinacy I have lost my son, who was very dear to me,' he cried. 'Now he and the woman have perished, and we are bereft.'

"Then he ordered that the tribe enter into two full moons of mourning, and in memory of that night he renamed the bay where they disappeared. Until then it had been called Place of Many Fish. Now the chief called it Whangapouri, Bay of Sorrow, and the point where they disappeared he named, Nga Ipongaro, the Lost Lovers."

Silence fell within the room as Kui ended her tale. Emily was profoundly impressed, not only by the simple, haunting tale but also by the oratory this ancient woman had displayed. Her use of words, her wonderful rhythm, suggested that this was a story told and told again, handed down from one generation to the next. Just to hear it was something of an honor.

Finally she cleared her throat. "Thank you for telling me." She paused, anxious to know more, feeling her way. "And is that really the end? Their bodies weren't ever washed up, or anything? No rumors circulating years later, that they'd appeared somewhere else, safely married?"

"Nothing." Kui's tone was emphatic. "A complete mystery."

"But there must have been plenty of suggestions," Emily continued. "Conjecture. I mean, here was this really powerful chieftain, and his son has disappeared. Surely there'd be at least a clue, somewhere. Wouldn't he send out messengers, or offer a reward for news of them, or something?"

Kui shook her head. "No. Those are the facts, as I told you. When the tide came in it obliterated anything there might have been. Kapiti knew they had reached the point, but that was all."

"There's something else you ought to mention, Mum," Heneti remarked. "That tide. It's very rare, really freakish. We call it, *he tai rereke a tino whakarerea te akau*, a tide that recedes exceptionally, abandoning the shore. What happens is that there's a particular conjunction of abnormally low tide and a strong, offshore wind, which drives the water back."

Emily was still working her way through the sequence of events. "It sounds like your version of the parting of the Red Sea."

Heneti smiled. "That's right. But when the wind dropped, the returning water must have surged in like a tidal wave. My theory is that they were caught against the cliff, and drowned."

"They never found their bodies." Apparently, to Kui it was heresy to query her version of the events.

Emily frowned slightly as she contemplated. "Could they have been trapped under rocks? Eaten by predators?"

"Humph!" No misinterpreting Kui's opinion. "Seagulls, perhaps?" she said scornfully. "We don't have lions in this country, *e hine*. Only dogs, and can you imagine a whole stream of dogs heading off along the bay, without somebody noticing?"

To suggest anything else might be interpreted as inferring that the tribesmen of yesteryear weren't much good at the sleuthing business. Emily lapsed into silence. If nothing else it was a tremendous tale, interweaving as it did all the necessary elements of a tragic romance. Kui, in the retelling, had brought the lovers vividly to life, and the story was local and immediate. It was part of the rich fabric of Whangapouri.

And that, she thought to herself, was amazing in itself. Who would have thought three weeks ago, when she arrived, that she'd have dreamed of describing this place as rich?

✒✒

Hori was feeling in love with his world. After a day in the town, in which he had replenished supplies, met with friends and enjoyed swapping stories over the pint of local brew that he allowed himself, there was something deeply satisfying about the drive along the unsealed road which wound down the long gully to Whangapouri. Hori would not have called himself a superstitious man, but in a small, less sophisticated corner of his soul he did believe in omens. It was no coincidence, he felt, that there had been porpoises playing close to shore the day that Bill Thackeray arrived.

Hori reckoned that porpoises symbolized friendship, and Bill had proved to be a good friend. He didn't like to belittle the other long-time residents of the bay, but Vernon and his wife, good people that they were, were inclined to keep to themselves, and there was nobody else, apart from Heneti, with whom Hori could comfortably swap anecdotes of life in other corners of the world. And Heneti had heard his reminiscences before, and was inclined to purse her mouth, so, and find something to do about the store. Even though Bill knew mostly America, and Hori's professional life in the early days had been centered on Europe, they could discuss similarities and laugh at mutual frailties.

And Bill had that one, great accomplishment in a friend. He knew when to be quiet.

Hori hated the thought of his leaving. Whangapouri would be the poorer. But now there was this new, interesting element. Young Emily, overly-slender little *pakeha* that she was. And Bill seemed to be sharing more than a few meals with her, and had brought her to two of Heneti's Winter Gatherings. Hori hadn't been too impressed, at first. Emily reminded him a bit of some of the stuffier English types who got under his skin in the past, but he'd concluded, of late, that he'd misjudged her. She was prepared to have her leg pulled, for a start, and at the last dinner she had rather shyly asked for certain recordings, and told them all a few snippets about her professional life. Judging by what Bill had said, this was quite a milestone for her.

But would she be staying in the bay? And might she be the catalyst to keep Bill there?

It was too early to expect that but Hori, ever optimistic, hoped that she, too, might prove to be a happy omen. It would be good to see Bill settled among them. Good for Bill, too.

He was quite surprised to see the shop closed so early. Not that it mattered, because there was nobody living in the bay who wouldn't hammer on the back door if the need was urgent, but the light at the front always served as a welcoming beacon. Then the sight of Heneti with a towel and a bag of frozen peas draped across her knee inspired several swift responses in him. The first among these was alarm, quickly followed by mirth, as soon as he realized that there was no long-term damage to the joint being treated. The third was annoyance, because, so help him, he'd told her too many times not to climb those goddam steps.

But young Emily, in the role of savior, was worth tucking away inside for future enjoyment. Man, he'd have given the truck's worth of supplies to see the waif getting his old Heni up off the ground. Or half the truck, anyway, because he was a rational man.

After everything was related, and most of it repeated and embellished for good measure, and Hori had reinforced his position as traditional head of the family by having his say, Emily stood and put on her jacket.

"Now that you're back, I'll get home."

They all spoke at once, Heneti voicing thanks and regretting that they couldn't offer her a bed for the night, except sharing with Kui who was a restless sleeper and snored, besides; Kui loudly refuting this charge.

Hori used his most commanding voice to make himself heard. "The truck's there. I'll just run you along the track."

He saw Emily hesitate, and could almost read her mind. "No, *tamahine,* it's no trouble, after you've been so good to my Heneti. Now, I've got a little something that I brought back from the town, and I want you to take it, to say thank you."

Again Emily hesitated, color flushing her cheeks. "It was nothing, really. I didn't do anything . . ." Then her eyes fell on the leg of lamb he was selecting from the piles of provisions strewn across the table and awaiting storage.

"This is special. Smoked mutton. The most delicious food you'll taste in many a day. You just simmer it an hour or so, and it's good cut chunky when hot, and sliced thin when cold." He didn't say out loud, but he was thinking that he'd actually bought the leg with Bill in mind, but there was every reason to think that Bill might share it this way, as well. And perhaps that was all part of a greater plan.

Emily accepted very graciously, he noticed. Just the right amount of reluctance, and she delicately balanced her words so that an elderly man could feel pleasantly gallant, and not patronized for one moment.

Hori pointed the truck into the darkness then, determined to pursue his own agenda, made his voice deliberately casual. "You like it here, among us?"

"Yes, I do, now that I'm getting to know a few people. I walked along the bay the other day to have tea with Talitha, and I'm hoping to get up to see Ruth one afternoon, too."

"You reckon you'll stay?"

One wheel found a particularly hostile rut. Emily grabbed at the bag containing the leg of mutton. "Stay?"

"Yes. Remain. Settle. Live."

"Heavens no . . . . I mean . . . no."

Not quite so gracious, perhaps, but then maybe he'd put her on the spot a bit too hastily. "Not such a stupid idea."

Emily almost fell over herself in her haste not to appear rude. "I didn't mean it like that. But I came to Whangapouri as part of my recovery. There was always a limit to the time I'd be here. And honestly, Hori, I'm a city sort of person. I've always preferred city things."

"I was like that, too. Auckland, Sydney, London, Rome. But people change. I changed."

Emily greeted this with silence.

"I'd never go back to the city, now. Nor Heneti, either."

After a pause Emily said, "I can't see myself changing. Not that much, anyway."

Hori put out a hand and patted her shoulder. "Well, *e hine*, you tell us you've rented the bach for two more months. And who knows what might happen in eight weeks?"

But he was pleased, all the same, that Bill had mentioned he was taking out a lease on the Wallaces' place for a few more weeks. As the saying went, it was foolish to pin all your hopes on one person. Put all your eggs in one basket. A pity, though. She was a nice girl. He ought to find a moment to discuss the end of her career. Compare notes, as it were.

TEN

his idea, like so many, was not conceived in a flash of illumination. It developed very quietly in the recesses of Emily's subconscious. But once it had become discernible, it dominated her thoughts because it was so sensible.

Bill had said his lease expired very soon. The owners of his present home would be reclaiming their property within days. She liked Bill a lot. She was lonely. It needed simple addition to come up with the correct sum. Kill two birds with one stone by asking him to move in as her lodger, to share the bach.

She thought about it, tossing about every angle and point of view, and each concurred with her original. It would be bliss to have somebody with whom she could share the long evenings, somebody to talk to. Of course, there were certain imponderables which she could discover only by asking him. He might, for example, be eager to leave Whangapouri, to return to America, although she doubted that. And he might be reluctant to share anything with her, let alone daily living. So she should not allow her hopes to rise unrealistically.

She contemplated what she knew about him. Although she was no longer daunted by his lack of small-talk, he didn't exactly overflow with conversation at the best of times. She knew that he was an efficient housekeeper, a capable cook; certainly not a slob, despite the beard and collar-length hair. He was always clean. He had suffered a breakdown. And he was gay.

She didn't mind that. It fact, apart from a touch of regret that he favored men above women, it made things a great deal easier. She would be far more circumspect about inviting him to share her dwelling, were he heterosexual. Hormones could do peculiar things and lead one along unexpected paths, witness Marco and the grief that caused. It was after Marco's exit that she had almost decided upon a man-free existence. Certainly in a sexual context. But she felt that she and Bill were already friends, and it was a friendship that could develop unencumbered in the absence of sexual spark. All-in-all, the idea had limitless appeal.

The fact that the opportunity presented itself so soon after her brainwave took root suggested the gods were playing a supportive role.

Bill appeared that afternoon on her doorstep, carrying a large, ugly, red fish. "This is gurnard. It's great eating."

Emily counted herself among the cowardly types who prefer to think the food on the table has never breathed air or swum beneath the waves. She looked at the lifeless eye and great, gaping mouth. "For me?"

"Yes. I put out a set line last night."

She swallowed her distaste and the fear that all its innards would still be nestled within. "Fantastic."

There was enough flesh on that set of fishbones for her to be enjoying gurnard well into the next week. Or month. But it, along with a certain leg of smoked mutton, could easily be shared with another. So the gods must indeed be busily smoothing her path.

It wasn't in Emily's character to begin by testing the waters. Having thanked him and watched the large fish be laid almost reverently on the kitchen table, she simply took a deep breath and plunged headlong into the matter foremost in her thoughts.

"You said your lease was due to end, next week."

"Yes."

"How do you feel about leaving Whangapouri?"

He shrugged. "I've come to like it here. It seems like home."

He hadn't exactly answered her question, but she let that pass. She wondered if he had considered renting any of the holiday places lying empty through the winter. But she had no intention of even hinting at such a notion.

"Would you want to stay on, if it were possible?"

She wished it were less hard to gauge Bill's thoughts. In a way it had been easier previously, when he very nearly fled. At least she knew where she stood, then. And even the beard offered a form of barricade, behind which he could retreat.

"You mean ... er ... um ...?"

"As my lodger." She hastened to spell out her idea. "There's a divan in the sunroom, and a table of sorts where you could put your typewriter. And I'm not at all hard to live with. I don't carry references around with me, but I've shared digs with all manner of people. I'm not madly demanding, or anything."

"Why, that's very ...er ..."

Again she was quick to interrupt his floundering. "You don't have to make your mind up at once. I just thought I'd ask you. And I'm only talking about the next two months, because after that I'll have decided what I'm doing." She might have added, that her future would include shopping malls and street lights.

He smiled. "You're talking about a boarder, not a roommate."

Emily looked blank, because she hadn't realized there was a difference. Some American nuance, lost on her?

Then he came to a decision. "I don't need time to consider. Two more months would be fine for me, too."

It seemed almost too easy. She smiled at him. "Then that is settled. Shall we shake on it?"

She had noticed before how well-shaped his hands were. Wasted on a man, her mother would say. His fingers were long and tapered, but not at all wimpy. Quite powerful in their way, actually. Right now they were also covered with fish scales.

"Pooh!" She brought the interview to an end. "I can't have my lodger appear at the table like that. You stink."

"Only nice, clean gurnard."

Emily grimaced and raised her scale-covered hand to her nose. "Nothing that's nice and clean smells as bad as that. When would you like to move in?"

⟨⟩

It was strange how excited she felt about Bill's impending arrival. It was like awaiting slumber-party guests, or returning to the Meinhardt at the start of a new term.

Bill didn't hang about. He arrived the following afternoon, transporting all that was his in the back of a functional, jeep-like vehicle. One suitcase of clothing, the typewriter, two packets of paper, two boxes of books.

"Gracious." Her voice reflected her breathlessness. "Do you carry your library about with you?"

As it had taken their combined efforts to bring the larger of the boxes into the sunroom, she wondered how he, alone, had managed to get that weight into the jeep. And it made her weak arm ache, although she kept this fact to herself.

"I decided that while I was lacking creativity I should re-read old loves. Henry James and Thoreau. Edith Wharton. A back-to-basics period, as part of my therapy."

"Very wise." She eased her back. It was horrible, being so unfit. Perhaps she should begin more vigorous walking, instead of her present routine of easy ambling. "Well, there's not too much to show you about Bateman's bach. You'll find it awfully primitive, after the luxury of your previous place. There's no lock to the bathroom, for example, so we'll have to be sensible. A closed door indicates occupancy and loud singing is reinforcement."

She pointed out where things were kept in the kitchen, where to find fresh linen. "The towels are scarcely luxury items. Whatever pile they started with disappeared years ago. My mother would say you could shoot peas through them, but I was never too sure what she meant. She's so utterly respectable that I know she didn't mean pees, with two ee's."

"Probably using a pea shooter." Bill started to place his collection onto the wonky shelves of the bookcase. "Dried peas and a bamboo pipe. Or willow bark. We did that as kids."

She nodded. "And the laundry is off the back porch. Verandah, as they say here. The second loo is there, too. And for what you're paying you do your own laundry. It's not included."

Bill made a face of mock disappointment. Emily wondered, not for the first time, what he would look like without the whiskers. Some people grew beards to hide weak chins. Was Bill hiding a weak chin behind that growth? Remembering the small snapshot, she didn't think that was the case. And perhaps she could do something about the state of his hair. Just tidy it up a little, get it off his collar.

The gurnard, it turned out upon subsequent inspection, had been gutted. She baked it in the oven and that, with potatoes and a concoction of vegetables, was their evening meal. She went to a bit of trouble setting the table, creating a sense of occasion to welcome her lodger. The only cloth was faded calico, but there were Kaffi's dried grasses in the center, transferred to a small jug she'd found in the cupboard. She'd bought cheerful paper napkins from Hori's and a bottle of wine, with which she drank his health. Bill reciprocated with water, raising his glass and toasting 'his most gracious landlady.' Then they laughed together, because there was something funny about Emily being anybody's landlady.

"The figure that leaps to my mind when you say that has lisle stockings in wrinkles around her ankles, and isn't a day younger than fifty," Emily explained when she could talk again.

They'd had to pry out very long-time ice cubes from the tray for his glass of water, and that had been funny, too.

They cleared away together, Bill rolling up his sleeves and wielding the small, washing-up mop that came with the place, Emily drying and putting away. The companionship was bliss.

"I dreaded the nights on my own." She set the tea towel over the rail to dry. "I'm used to the days now, and I can see that the time here is working, because I'm starting to get things into perspective and realize that the future isn't totally negative. But the evenings have been grim, despite the radio."

"They do have television in New Zealand, you know. And three whole channels." He swilled water around the sink and tidied the dishcloth. "You could rent a set easily enough."

Emily looked at him questioningly. "Will you miss the telly? Do you want me to hire one? I'd decided not to bother, just for three months. But I don't want to appear a stingy landlady."

"No," Bill replied. "I rarely watched, anyway. I prefer to read."

The two chairs in the living room, one on either side of the hearth, could have been custom-ordered for them. Shabby they might be, but they were extremely comfortable; and while the one on the right was clearly designed for a man, particularly a man with long legs, the one on the left was suitable for a female.

Bill carried through the coffee tray, once the kettle had boiled. He didn't make a fuss. He just did things, quietly and efficiently. She savored the companionship as though it were something material. It was a gorgeously warm feeling that made her sing inside.

She had prepared the divan in the sunroom, and given him the better of the pillows to compensate for the hard bedsprings.

"I'm sorry the curtains are so inadequate, but even on sunny days it's dark until about seven, and I doubt voyeurs will be a problem. Of course, if I were to stay here longer I'd do something about them. It didn't seem worth it. Not for so short a time."

"No problem." Bill was ever polite. "These are fine."

She could hear him in the bathroom, running water, brushing his teeth. The wooden walls provided very little insulation. Each sound seemed to emphasize the intimacy of their shared habitation. She decided that she must learn to pee quietly. Then the loo flushed, and the narrow bar of light beneath her bedroom door was extinguished, only the embers of the dying fire throwing out a dull redness. Emily lay under the patchwork quilt and listened as her lodger went about the evening rituals. For the first time in forever she shut her eyes and offered up a prayer of thanks. Thanks for companionship and friendship. For somebody with whom to share things. She couldn't imagine why he'd agreed to move into the bach, but she couldn't be bothered to question his motives, either. It was enough that he was there in her sunroom, undressing, or reading, or sleeping. It was enough.

Opossums skittered across the roof in the small hours of the night. Emily half stirred, hearing them, recognizing the clattering and the scrabbling. But she wasn't alone. Somebody else was residing in Bateman's bach. She turned over, buried her head under the pillow and slipped serenely back into sleep.

When she awoke in the morning her first thought was of her companion. Was he still asleep? Not possessing any form of robe, she wrapped the quilt about her and padded into the central room. The door of the sunroom was ajar, she could see the divan neatly made. In the kitchen she discovered signs of breakfast; one bowl, one spoon, one mug, all neatly washed and stacked on the draining board. No sign of Bill, which was quite disappointing.

He returned just before lunch, sketchbook and paint tray in hand. She could immediately picture him sitting on a flat rock, creating some form of picture record.

"May I see what you've painted?"

Bill opened the sheets. "Just notes, really. I sketch anything that interests me."

Emily, a total novice in the world of art, thought his bits and pieces were good. With only the barest of pencil lines and the small set of watercolors he'd created a series of vivid miniatures, a bunch of leaves, the tightly curled frond of a fern, several small, olive-green silver-eye birds.

"They're lovely."

He smiled down at her. "That's a bit strong. They're adequate."

"And this is also part of the therapy?"

"Yes."

"Then lucky old you. I couldn't sketch anything that you'd recognize to be a bird, let alone one particular breed."

"I'll bet you have other talents."

She made a face. "Yeah, sure. Name one." But she didn't wait for his response. "Can you do something for me? I need transport. I have to get into a town."

He gathered up his pictures. "The store inadequate?"

"No . . . yes, probably not . . . but . . ." Here was an act of faith. It was vital she elicit a promise of silence, and beg assistance. "It's the Morrisons. Kaffi's family. They're without some things which are essential, and Kaffi is anxious that Hori will ask awkward questions. If I get stuff for them in the town nobody will look at me oddly, when I buy baby powder. And new nappies."

Bill paused. She knew exactly what was going through his mind. "You're the wrong person," he was thinking. "Let the Social Welfare people help. Tell the authorities."

"Please, Bill."

He shrugged. "We can take the jeep. And we'll have to go this afternoon, because I'll be leaving tomorrow and away overnight. I've agreed to collect the McDuffs from the airport in Auckland."

ELEVEN

The jeep bounced along the deep ruts of the gravel road that led to the highway. Even with the presence of a seat-belt Emily found it necessary to hold fast to the handle above the door, and the din of the engine reminded her of the boiler room in some monstrously outsized ship. It certainly put paid to conversation which was just as well, because she'd been rather dreading that Bill might ask a few searching questions about the Morrisons. She didn't want to lie to him, and she knew herself to be the most transparent liar; nor did she want to justify the fact that she had not called anybody with a bit of clout. Instead she clung to the handle, braced her feet against the metal plate which separated cab from motor, and watched the rise and fall of the countryside in a series of irregular jolts. On her arrival, three weeks and four days ago, the combination of rain and darkness had obscured the view, so she was seeing everything for the first time.

"That's the Reynards' place." Bill spoke very loudly over the noise and used an inclination of his head to identify the small cottage. It was framed by a thicket of native bush. Emily was glad that he kept both hands firmly attached to the wheel, which had a tendency to buck in response to the sorry condition of the surface.

"Vernon and Ruth?" The artist and his interestingly unusual wife.

"Yes. Ruth takes in all sorts of injured creatures, you know. Nurses them back to health, then releases them."

Ruth had mentioned this aspect of her life, which was why Emily, immediately curious, had hopes of visiting her some time, but it was impossible to explain all this over the roar.

There were several stockyards, wooden farm buildings, and homesteads sheltered by dark banks of macrocarpa trees. The hills of rolling grassland were dotted with sheep and occasional cattle. They passed the high wire fencing that indicated a herd of deer. It was not at all like the English countryside, with its hedged patchwork of fields and regular pattern of hamlets.

The luxury of being able to hear yourself think, when they reached the main road, was wonderful. At the petrol station by the junction, familiar because it was there she'd located Jack Muller and his taxi, Bill turned the jeep to the south and within a few miles they trundled into the township. Bill pulled in to park alongside other, equally utilitarian vehicles, and Emily looked about her with interest. The small township, too, was as un-English as you could imagine, with its wide single street and small wooden shops, each sporting a covered verandah roof to offer protection for shoppers. It was more like a township in the American West, maybe Dodge City in the Age of the Internal Combustion Engine, Emily thought, and was pleased with herself for having produced such a neat analogy.

"Do you want my help?"

She thought quickly. It was nice of him to offer, but perhaps it would be easier if Bill weren't around to scrutinize her purchases.

"Not really, thank you. Can you just point me towards a chemist? I mean drugstore?"

He smiled down at her. "Two nations separated by a single language? But I do recognize the Queen's English."

"Not two languages," she was quick to rebut. "Three. Think of all the new vocabulary I've struggled with in the last few weeks."

Bill pointed along the street. "Drugstore thataway. Would it be sensible if we met in . . . perhaps an hour? Here, at the teashop."

It would be hard to get lost in this tiny place. Emily nodded and watched him depart in the opposite direction, with what might have been tact or, equally possible, a desire to distance himself from her intentions.

The chemist's shop was one of those functional, all-purpose stores, and the sales assistant was one of those women who knew exactly what you wanted before it was spelled out. Between the two of them they assembled a pile which was quite daunting in its size. For the first time Emily wondered exactly how she was going to convey all of her purchases to the Morrison's home. But, she decided, only a coward would allow so small a consideration to get in the way of the greater good.

She dumped everything in the cab of the jeep and looked about for her next objective. "East Coast Electricity," said the sign. Good. It would have been useful if the girl behind the counter there showed half the initiative of the pharmacist.

"Morrison?" the young woman said vaguely, as if asking her to look up an account was to suggest something wantonly bizarre. She wandered away with all the zest of a battery losing its charge and returned some minutes later. "We got no Morrison on our books."

"But . . ." How else would they be listed? "Perhaps if I described where the house is, would that give you an idea?"

The girl picked at her fingernails. "P'haps." But her tone said, "You're wasting your time, lady."

This scenario was leading nowhere and would soon be spoiled irreparably when Emily lost her temper. Help, however, arrived seconds before ignition in the shape of another young woman. Her brisk gait and businesslike manner said more than words.

She dumped a bag of groceries on the floor as she greeted the fingernail-picker and turned to Emily. "Can I help you?"

Gratefully Emily repeated her spiel. "Your friend said that there's no listing under Morrison. I was hoping you could identify the house." She explained the exact location to the best of her ability, while the new arrival listened with slightly knitted brows.

"That's the Bryant estate, I didn't know there was anybody living in that *whare*."

"What's a *whare*?"

"A house. Cottage used by seasonal workers. Shearers and all."

"Can you look into it? The family has no electricity and I was hoping to settle the arrears, so power could be restored."

She also hoped that this capable person was not renowned for an abundance of curiosity. But perhaps she would simply look upon Emily as one of Kaffi's dreaded Social Welfare people.

"I'll see what I can do." And it took about ten minutes. "Cook," she stated. "Nothing has been paid on the account in six months."

Goodness knew who or what Cook was, apart from the explorer who'd mapped the country in the eighteenth century. Or maybe he was the owner of the Bryant estate.

"What do they owe? And you'd better add something up front to cover the next quarter." Thank goodness for plastic money. And for rich deceased grandparents and a generous insurance settlement so she could pay this bill without flinching. "How long before the supply is restored?"

The service assistant glanced at her watch. "I'll ring the maintenance department right away. Should manage it before tonight."

"That's wonderful, and thank you so much."

"Don't mention it," the young woman said politely. "Only doing my job."

The fingernail-picker, leaning against the counter as though her legs couldn't hold her weight, blew a large bubble of gum in farewell.

◈

"Successful?" Bill looked up as she entered the teashop. She was only seven minutes late for their rendezvous.

"I think so. In all the important matters, anyway."

She had stopped at another place which sold camping gear to buy a very large haversack, and paused outside one which stocked women's apparel. It had occurred to her that some form of robe might be sensible, now that she was cohabiting with a chap. But then she thought again. Given his sexual leaning, Bill was scarcely going to read anything lascivious in her pottering about the bach in her nightie. And anyway, it wasn't exactly the last thing in revealing, being sensible, cotton-knit and knee-length. It seemed pointless buying a garment she'd never again wear, once she left Whangapouri.

The teashop was a complete surprise. Tastefully decorated and it smelled of warm bread and spices. There was even a fire in the grate. It sold all manner of teas, along with scones, cakes and an array of biscuits. Bill was already seated at a small wooden table, reading a newspaper. He stood as she approached, and she was reminded of the niceties her mother had taken such pains to drum into a very young Jay.

"Find all you wanted?"

She placed her jacket over the back of the chair and sat down. "Yes, thank you. You can't imagine how much I've bought." She thought this was wise, forestalling his startled look when his eyes happened upon that pile of goodies in the jeep.

Bill folded his paper. "I can." He paused, looking at the upside-down print, avoiding her eyes. "I suppose it wouldn't help if I suggested that, instead of spending your money, you should be calling somebody and explaining the situation of this family?"

Precisely the reaction she had anticipated. "I know that's your standpoint. But you don't know Kaffi."

"Has it occurred to you that these children ought to be in school?"

"Yes." She was grateful the waitress should appear at this minute, giving her time to formulate a response. It was irritating that Bill should always hit upon the very circumstance that was bothering her. She picked up the menu and concentrated on her selection. When the waitress' nattily clad figure disappeared towards the kitchen she decided that enough time had elapsed, and she could decently change the subject.

"I love the way they've done up this place. That frieze with the old books on it, and the stripped-pine furniture . . ."

"Emily."

So that wasn't going to work. She pleated the paper napkin to delay her reply. "Yes, I've thought about school, too. I've gathered from bits and pieces Kaffi's dropped that they used to attend. She has a book the teacher gave her, when they left. At that time they were living with the tribe."

"Why didn't they return, then? After the father disappeared?"

"I don't know. I have met the rest of the family, and it's not as bad as I feared." The image rose in her mind of the toddlers sitting at their mud hole and Winnie, with her vacant, hopeless eyes. But there was also that moment when Kaffi handed back the baby, and his mother's face reflected her love for him. Surely that was worth something, too.

"I mean, their diet has been dreadfully monotonous; *kumera* augmented with shellfish as far as I can gather. But they're warm enough, and at least they've survived until now. And with the things I've bought I think they'll be fine. Really."

Bill pushed back the chair so that he could stretch out his legs. He waited until the waitress set down their tray of tea and buttered scones. There was a small pot of strawberry jam.

"Has it occurred to you that all you're doing is a shoring up process, which will collapse the moment you leave Whangapouri?"

"Perhaps, by then, their father will have returned." She raised her chin a little defiantly.

"What do you have against social workers?"

Emily might have replied, "What do you have against my helping the Morrisons?" Instead she said, "Absolutely nothing. It's possible that Kaffi's terror of the babies being removed is totally misplaced. How would I know? I simply believe that, having promised her not to report on them, I can't break my word. And it's not as though they were abused. Winnie might not be too bright, but she really loves those children, and you should see her with Gary Cooper."

Bill shrugged and leaned across to take a scone. It smelled delicious and its interior, when he broke it apart, was a fluffy white.

Emily didn't need the shrug to know he was not convinced. She reassembled her arguments and started again on a fresh tack.

"Listen, Bill. Earlier today you asked me about my talents, and I said, 'Name one.' I wasn't being mock-modest, or stupid. All my ability was tied up in music and the violin." She squeezed lemon into her cup while she sought the most apt comparison. "Imagine cross-country skiing. My life was like that. As if my feet were set in tracks, from about the time I was seven. Maybe earlier than that, even. You could even say Jay led, and I happily followed. They were very convenient grooves, and I always enjoyed the way they took me, but they were rather narrow. Do you understand?"

He nodded. "Go on."

"Now, very abruptly, the tracks aren't there stretching before me. That's why I've been floundering about, trying to get some direction back into my life."

"And . . . ?"

"And maybe, just for the present at least, Kaffi and her family are giving me something, apart from myself, to think about. Surely that can't be bad?"

He spread the jam across the scone, thickly and deliberately. "For you or for the Morrisons?"

Emily's temper flared, short and hot. She imagined for one vivid minute how he would look with strawberry jam dripping off his beard, and the temptation to toss the small jar at him was almost too much. But, equally as quickly, she quelled the impulse. In the past yielding to those swift infusions of anger always ended in regret. And Bill was her lodger. He'd also driven her into town and she had no desire to walk home alone.

"Perhaps you should examine your motives, too?" She spoke tautly with the effort of holding her irritation in check. "Exactly why are you so determined not to allow these people, less fortunate than yourself, as much as a moment of your consideration."

Perhaps he didn't hear the annoyance in her voice. If he did, he hid it well.

"I've seen too much of the Do-Good Brigade. They barge in without a thought beyond that moment and the self-satisfaction they can extract from every action and then sweep off, leaving a trail of devastation behind. Bungling amateurs."

Emily wondered whether he was talking personally. Sensing a private pain she took tight control of her exasperation. Now would seem the right moment to offer the olive branch.

"I'll tell you what, I'm prepared to put a time limit on this. If the Morrison father hasn't returned within ... oh, the next month, and if their conditions haven't improved, then I'll go to the Welfare office. And, until then, maybe you'll get off my back. Okay?"

She thought, with a trace of justifiable smugness, that their conditions should be improving quite soon, if Miss Efficiency in the Electricity Office were as good as her word. She rather wished she could be there, to see their faces.

There was a pause which lasted a few seconds, but seemed like an eternity. Then Bill looked about the room, as if seeing it for the first time.

"Yes," he said deliberately. "They've done a great job. I like the decorations."

Hori, returning from his weekly excursion to the wholesale markets, knew the road from the town as well as he knew the lines on his palm. So he needed very little concentration to avoid the worst of the potholes. They came each year, with the rains of autumn and with equal reliability a grader would appear in the spring to smooth out the worst before the holiday crowd arrived.

Today, still intent on pursuing his own plans, his mind returned with the regularity of a metronome to young Emily. It was becoming something of a habit. He thought of her when first they had met, as he delivered that heap of groceries. Her pinched, white face and wan expression. She was so totally out of place in Whangapouri. She certainly looked healthier these days, with more color in her face and more bounce in her step. And, if the amount of her daily shopping were any indication, she had the appetite of a horse.

Since Bill had told what he knew about her accident, and Emily had shared with the Saturday bunch a few of her orchestral reminiscences, he felt he understood her a lot better. Hori could relate more than she knew. His own career had been curtailed prematurely when nodules developed on his larynx. Non-cancerous, thanks be to God, but terminating his career. Probably that was why they shared a fellow feeling. And her arrival at the store at the time of Heneti's fall was a godsend. He and Heneti would always owe her a debt of gratitude for that day.

He still wondered what Bill thought about her. He was mighty quick to shut up whenever Hori broached the subject. A decent chap, Bill, always ready to lend a hand, to muck in when things got tight. But so quiet. So private. Hori did know all about his being a writer in his other life. These days he said he'd run out of steam, which seemed a pity. Hori wasn't much of a reader himself, and didn't know a great deal about the publishing world, but it stood to reason that Bill would be good at his job.

And now he'd moved into Bateman's bach. Surprising? Perhaps, upon reflection, cash was a bit tight. If he'd not been writing for some time that figured, and Emily could do with company. Or perhaps he wasn't so far off the mark after all, despite her vehement disavowal when he'd tentatively suggested she might stay on. Perhaps he should keep his eyes open for an omen. Not that he was superstitious, exactly.

His thoughts strayed in another direction. The McDuffs would be back this week, after their worldwide excursion. Bill had mentioned that he'd be driving to Auckland to meet them, and handing over the keys to their house.

Hori liked the McDuffs . . . in very small doses. He liked them even better when they were away, in Auckland, or in New York, or in Singapore. They rarely missed a Saturday evening gathering, and Mrs. McD., Vera, always tried to dominate the scene. She was a born manager, that was her problem, and Heneti resented it. Heneti, quite rightly, thought that the evenings were theirs. It might be sensible to catch Gordon McDuff and suggest into his ear that he put a muzzle on his fair lady.

He swerved to avoid a *pukeko* which was stupid enough to stray into the road. Then he thought what an idiot he was. *Pukekos* made delicious eating, and this one wouldn't have known what hit it. Kui would have been delighted, bless her. Proper eating, she'd have said, a change from pappy, *pakeha* food. It was part of Kui to pretend that she could remember life before the white men came. All rubbish of course, because she'd been born well into this century, by which time Aotea-Roa had been New Zealand for seventy-odd years. What she remembered were the tales her grandmother told her of the tribal days, and the times when the Maori-folk rose in battle against the encroaching *pakehas*. Better forgotten, while they looked towards the future. That was what Heneti would say, and Heneti was a sensible woman.

Still, Kui would have enjoyed that *pukeko*.

TWELVE

E mily was close to resenting the fact that, only two days after moving in, Bill should be disappearing overnight to collect the McDuffs from Auckland. The drive, he said, was really too long to undertake easily in one day, more particularly as the flight from Hong Kong landed at seven fifty-five the following morning.

There was no reason why she should feel so proprietorial towards him. It was just that . . . well, it was just that she did. Despite all the logic which she counter-engaged, the small sense of grievance gave her something to mull over as she walked across to the Morrisons with all her newly acquired goods. And perhaps that was just as well, because the one thing she did not do, after the first mile, was walk. Laden like some beast of burden, the haversack causing her shoulders to wilt, the handle of each bulging carrier bag fast cutting a groove through her palms, she puffed and panted her way up the rise to the headland. With each step her legs became increasingly tottery, the stitch in her side correspondingly evident, and the pauses to muster fresh reserves closer together and longer in duration.

Just as she reached the peak of the climb Kaffi appeared, on her way to Whangapouri.

"Hello." She gave a skip and turned a quick cartwheel. "We got the power back on. Yesterday."

Emily took advantage of this welcome interruption to lower the plastic bags onto the grass. She rubbed her palms to encourage circulation to return. "That's wonderful."

Kaffi appeared to make no connection with this latter-day miracle and Emily's foray to town. She looked with interest at the stuffed-to-the-brim backpack and carrier bags. She was rather like a puppy dog, scenting treats to come.

"You got all that for us?"

"Yes."

"Ka pai!" It was marvelous, the way Kaffi could imbue two words with so much meaning.

"Maybe you could help me carry some of it, the rest of the way?"

For a kid built on slender lines, whose diet over the last few months had been nothing if not scant, Kaffi was surprisingly strong. The easy way she lifted one of the bags onto her back made Emily envious. Allowing a sense of the dramatic to color her thinking, she had seen herself appearing at the shack like some Mother Teresa, a modern saint bearing salvation. Even the effort needed to climb the col had seemed appropriate, in that scenario. Now, the downhill part of the tramp was almost an anti-climax.

She hadn't anticipated an overflowing of gratitude from Winnie; her personal sense of achievement was sufficient reward in itself. But she had hoped for a little more enthusiasm. The younger woman's almost silent acceptance seemed proof of her slowness. And Ani and Tama, uprooted from their mud hole, sat watching the proceedings with silent incomprehension. Only Kaffi and John Wayne came up to expectations.

"Tea," Kaffi exclaimed. "And sugar. I'll put the kettle on, ay."

"Chocolate biscuits. Choice!" John Wayne scrabbled his fingers under the protective cellophane coat and distributed the booty. Not even the richly-coated cookies elicited much response from the smaller Morrisons.

Emily had sensibly packed those requested treats high in the backpack. But there was also cream for Gary Cooper's raw little posterior, and two packets of pristine, snowy nappies. There were three stretch outfits for him, and a warm sweater apiece for the older children. She'd added cleaning materials, and washing detergent, shampoo, toothpaste and toothbrushes. Unpacked, their new acquisitions overflowed the table.

Winnie, completely unresponsive, had watched this Christmas-in-July as if the family belonged to total strangers. Now she picked up the tube of toothpaste.

"That's nice. I like that flavor," she remarked. "Kids like it, too."

"And look, Winnie, I got this for you."

Emily had wanted something that could have special appeal to the young mother. At the suggestion of the helpful woman in the pharmacist's, she'd chosen a pretty barrette decorated with yellow-centered daisies, and a matching necklace. Among all the things that they actually needed, Emily hoped that she would enjoy a gift which was purely for pleasure.

"That's nice," Winnie repeated politely. "Thank you."

"Make some room. Here's the tea."

Kaffi produced a chipped, china pot and several greasy cups. Emily knew it was going to take a supreme effort on her part not to let the girl see how distasteful she would find drinking out of such a vessel.

While Winnie and John Wayne were helping to clear a space, she looked again about the room. The return of the power supply revealed a far more sorry state than she had been aware the other day. Perhaps just as well, really. Had she seen then what she saw right now, she would almost certainly have broken her promise to Kaffi and made the treasonous phone call.

The place was filthy, the floor littered with debris, the linen on the communal bed indescribably soiled. At a guess those sheets had not encountered water since the father disappeared, and the pillows, in the total absence of cases, were dark greasy ticking. When she stopped to consider it, the smell of stale urine was even stronger today.

She had taken upon herself the task of helping this unfortunate woman, and her children; but with that acknowledgment came no automatic indication of where, on earth, to start.

"Here. Drink your tea." Kaffi pushed a cup toward her, and Emily took a hesitant sip. "Good, ay."

Kaffi, while Emily's attention was elsewhere, had laden the cup with half a dozen spoonfuls of sugar and a hefty infusion of milk, which she never took. She swallowed and willed her stomach not to retch.

"It's delicious."

Courage has many faces. Drinking that beverage called for far more than Emily knew she possessed. Each sip was a shuddering, mouth-distorting exercise in self-control. Halfway down the cup she felt that she had done her duty, and gave up.

"Winnie, is the washing machine working?"

Winnie's eyes, over the rim of the cup filled, doubtless, with a similar milky mess to Emily's, signaled incomprehension.

Kaffi answered for her. "We haven't tried."

"Would it be sensible if we tried now?"

She slipped from her chair. "Okay. What you want to wash?"

"Could we change this bed? Do you have other sheets?"

"Yeah, but they're dirty, too. The babies pee in the night." She looked a little defiantly at their benefactor. "I can't take sheets to the creek. They're too big."

"Sugar, I'm not here to be cross. I'm here to help. And if we launder one set today they can dry overnight. Then we can do this lot tomorrow. And we'd better mend the clothes-line."

Kaffi glanced sideways at her. "You coming again, tomorrow?"

"Yes. I can come each day, if you like. At least while I'm in Whangapouri."

The look was once again that of little old woman with the weight of the world on her shoulders. It was remarkable, the way the girl could slip from the carefree child in one swift movement.

"Okay." She inclined her head like a small, wise owl. "While you're here."

※※

And this time around, Emily felt relief that Bill was not at the bach when she returned. It was about eight hours later, and she was totally exhausted. So tired that the effort of heating as much as a can of baked beans for supper was beyond her. She flopped down onto her bed without removing more than her shoes. The fire in the living room was out anyway, because it had not really occurred to her, when she'd set off that morning, that such a day was before her.

Of course, she had overdone it. She knew that at the time. The Morrisons had managed, despite the grime, until now. They could easily survive another day. The problem was that one chore led, inevitably, to another. And Kaffi became so enthusiastic about the whole business that she showed every indication of ransacking the house for potential laundry.

While the much-used machine rattled and sloshed, Emily set her to work attacking the floor, first with brush and then soapy water. John Wayne was co-opted to tackle the mire in the bathtub and kitchen sink.

For the first hour or two Winnie watched all the activity impassively, wrapped in her shroud of indifference or playing pat-a-cake games with the baby while he was awake. Then she seemed to come to life a little. She abandoned a sleeping Gary Cooper in the bed and picked up one of the new cloths. She did quite of good job of cleaning the hand basin, and smiled shyly in response when Emily praised her efforts. To Emily, it was the first token that suggested the other girl she might once have been.

But it all took time, and energy. The long walk home in the semi-dark had been the last straw. So, when you came to think about it, Bill's being in Auckland was heaven-sent. Under other circumstances she might have enjoyed describing the whole day to him, but probably, upon reflection, she'd have held her peace. He'd have been sure to start on his do-gooders speech again. She could almost hear his voice.

〜〜

Bill appreciated the length of the drive to Auckland. It gave him ample time to reflect. He worked backward in his thoughts, so that yesterday's small spat about Emily's rescue mission was early to surface. Without seeing the contents of the load that had filled the cab of the jeep, it was quickly apparent that she'd spent a small fortune. Maybe that wasn't an issue. She probably had a ready supply of cash and, anyway, it had nothing to do with him.

What she did with her time didn't affect him, either. But that didn't explain why he had to fight down feelings of revulsion, whenever this particular topic was mentioned.

And yet, in all honesty, he knew. He needed to go back no farther than JoBeth or, more fairly, JoBeth's mother. Awful woman. Correction: she-vampire. Always there, egging her daughter on, feeding her social ambitions. And the most infuriating thing was that JoBeth, scarcely noted for her retiring disposition, should have embraced her mother's aims so whole-heartedly.

And that, in a nutshell, was what stopped him. Bill wouldn't have cared if the whole apartment were taken over by lame dogs and hard-luck cases, camped out on his sofas. He wouldn't have minded if his wife had asked him to share their last crust with a deserving panhandler. But he did resent, more and more as time went on, that his mother-in-law should use him, and his small claim to fame, as the vehicle to get her daughter onto this and that charity committee. And the pair's determination that they be seen among the glitterati at every benefit evening that New York threw their way. It might seem a puny claim, but to Gloria Sullivan it was better than nothing, as a vehicle to climb the social ladder. And position, darlings, was everything.

He allowed his gaze to leave the road briefly and stray over the countryside through which he was traveling. The road had wound across rolling hills of grass for the first part of the journey; marvelous sheep country. Now he was entering the lush, green hectares that lent themselves to dairying. Cow-cockies, the New Zealanders called dairy farmers. He'd found the name hilarious, and wished that Garth had been there, or his mother, or anyone with whom he could share his amusement.

His thoughts drifted back to the days of his marriage, to the constant bickering that accompanied his admittedly feeble attempts to dissociate himself from the Gloria-and-JoBeth-show. And, were fuel required to feed the flames, he had vivid memories of those occasions when he'd been left to pick up the pieces of their latest, short-lived crusade. Having been seen to advantage, preferably by someone with a camera, Gloria and JoBeth would sweep on. Compassion dictated that he would be the sucker left explaining to some hopeful kid that the charade had a way of running out of steam. Fast.

Of course, to suggest that this was the sole cause of his wrecked marriage was ludicrous. Far more important was his profoundly depressed mental state, and JoBeth's inability to deal with it. Or his inability, come to that. But the professional do-gooder mother-in-law still left a bitter taste in his mouth. Probably always would.

He made a deliberate attempt to readjust his thoughts, before its negativity took ascendance, and concentrated on the scenery. In the wire-fenced fields were herds of black and white Holsteins and the smaller, softly-brown animals from Jersey and Guernsey. In some ways it all reminded him of rural America. The Midwest, he mused, dispossessed of its rust-red barns and their characteristic Dutch roofs.

He knew that he was being unfair to Emily, which was why he'd been prepared to compromise and accept her truce. That was fine, as long as she didn't try to get him involved. And he had a hunch that she would, given time. Emily, he reckoned, was the sort of person who, having espoused a cause, expected those about her to jump eagerly onto the bandwagon. Fine. But she'd have her work cut out hauling him aboard.

He was still wondering why he'd agreed to move into Bateman's bach. Befriending a very lonely young woman was one thing. Becoming her boarder was another, especially when he'd been about to sign a lease on the pretty little place further along the beach. A moment of weakness? Or compassion.

And yet she was an engaging person. He liked her. In another life he might have singled her out, because she had looks that attracted him. The springiness of her rich, brown hair, the way it curled at the nape of her neck was very appealing.

He gave himself a mental shake. This was a ludicrous musing because there was a vast gulf between liking someone, sharing accommodation, and seeing her as a life-long mate. And Emily, come to that, was as damaged in her way as he was in his. Walking wounded, the pair of them. Her scars were external and, given time, she would surmount those small handicaps.

He expected to live with his for the rest of his life.

THIRTEEN

ill, Emily soon recognized, was the most docile and comfortable of all lodgers. He ate what she put on the table with easy acceptance and quiet praise. Twice, in that first week of co-habitation, he cooked the evening meal. Evidently the collection of the McDuffs had gone smoothly, ditto depositing them at their Whangapouri residence. Emily did wonder, in a mild way, what sort of people they might be, but she was pretty involved with the Morrisons and the gigantic clear-up. Anyway, Bill mentioned in passing that they'd almost certainly be attending Heneti's next evening.

It was exactly eight days after his moving into the bach that Emily said, as they sat drinking post-prandial coffee, "You've been here a week now. Is there anything about the arrangements that you don't like? Anything that I could improve?"

"The bed's not exactly luxurious."

"I know that, but it doesn't belong to me." She handed him a plate of shortbread fingers. "And, come to that, neither is the one I'm sleeping in. I wake each morning with a pattern of embedded diamonds that actually penetrates through the mattress from the wire base." This was something of an exaggeration, but created an interesting picture in her mind. "If the place were mine I'd invest in new beds. Immediately after new towels."

"I was going to mention them."

"You probably think I should get us some new ones."

"It had crossed my mind."

She fiddled with the cuff of her sweater. "But buying things like towels is a bit like putting down roots. I've never done that." She looked across at him. "Does that sounds silly to you?"

"Not so much silly as downright dumb. Cutting off your nose to spite your face. Or, in this case, denying yourself a comfort in case it's shaped like a millstone."

"True enough. But if you felt strongly enough you could buy some for yourself."

He smiled. "I'll suffer these. For now."

Strange, to feel so comfortable with a person you'd known hardly any time at all. Especially if you remembered how he'd actually run away at their first meeting. She knew at this minute that he was teasing her, in the gentlest way. Of course the bathroom linen was awful. Almost not worthy of the title, and completely threadbare.

"Taking towels and uncomfortable beds as given, what else?"

"I guess I can handle Bateman's bach."

"That's a relief. I shan't lie awake at night fretting that my lodger's about to fly the fold." She smiled briefly. "Tell me more, though. What in general don't you like?"

Bill tilted his chair back. "In the generic sense?"

"Yes. Meaning all lodgings, all landladies."

He gave this weighty topic the attention it deserved. "Dirty dishes left in the sink, perhaps. Grunge lying about until it starts to sprout whiskers, especially in bathrooms. And, worst of all, wet pantyhose clinging to my face when I shower."

Emily laughed. "Not a problem here. I've not as much as unpacked my pantyhose since I've been in Whangapouri. But you sound as if you're speaking from bitter experience."

"You've said it."

She wondered to whom he might be alluding, in his earlier life. Sisters? Other roommates?

"And what do you like?"

"Generic again, or specific?"

She shrugged. "Whatever."

He took quite a long time to reply. Finally he said, "Driftwood burning in the fireplace."

"Is that all?"

Bill looked across at her. "No. If we're into specifics, I like you."

That startled her. "Me?"

"Why not?"

"No reason. I'm just a bit overwhelmed."

He smiled. "You mean, you thought I didn't like you? That I'd become your boarder even if I detested you?"

"No, not that. I thought you'd say something neutral, perhaps Thai food, or classical jazz."

But, although she quite speedily changed the subject before embarrassment had time to surface, she was nonetheless pleased. It was only later, when she was re-thinking the surprising way the conversation had developed, that she wished she'd had the presence of mind to add, "And I like you, too."

Another snippet of conversation lodged in her memory. It was to do with that black period in his life, his breakdown. She'd inadvertently introduced the subject by asking him about his writing. Almost six months in Whangapouri, and had he put nothing down on paper in all that time?

"I write to my mother," Bill replied. "Give her progress reports."

She was making a caper sauce at the time, to go with grilled snapper fillets. Hori's store came up with a surprising assortment of gourmet items. Fat, juicy capers was one such discovery. She allowed the walnut of butter to melt, holding the pan lightly over the element.

"So do I, to my family. 'Dear parents, I'm okay, not too lonely.' Stuff like that. You can't call it writing."

Bill was standing at the bench, preparing a winter salad to accompany the snapper. "It's better than I was doing."

He began to cut up the white-leafed heart of a cabbage. He took a great deal of care, so the slices were almost wafer-thin. Emily, observing this, refrained from mentioning that her winter salad quite often came out in jaw-exhausting chunks. And that it was nothing to do with her accident, but because her endurance level precluded such exact shredding.

"You're saying that . . . that since your illness you've found even letters to be hard?"

"It has to do with the medication." He glanced across, noticing her perplexity. "A depressive state has peaks and troughs, far more extreme than a storm at sea. When I was on a peak the creativity soared. I could write like Hemingway, like Fitzgerald. With total passion. When I was in a trough I felt that there was no tomorrow. Words refused to surface. That's not disastrous, as long as you can function during the trough. I found that I couldn't. It's very hard to climb out of despair like that."

"How did you?"

"With drugs, eventually. Prescribed medication. On rational days I came to realize that I couldn't do it alone. I needed outside intervention."

In the past Emily would never have describe herself as a patient person, but it was certainly a quality with which she was gaining more than a nodding acquaintance. She stirred in a spoonful of flour, turning it gently so that it would not brown. Then she began to add milk and stock.

"And now?"

"Now I'm in control."

He had always appeared totally in control to her. "Surely that's only a good thing."

"In a way. But it has its flip side. Without those peaks I've lost the creative urge. The passion refuses to ignite. Nothing flows."

"That's why you came here, to Whangapouri? To rediscover whatever it is that drives you?"

"Yes." He was grating a carrot, very carefully, very tidily. "Or at least inspiration."

Emily wanted to say, "And have you?" She did not want to be associated with the loss of his motivation, even if only by inference. Instead she said, "How's the salad coming along? The snapper's about ready, and this sauce."

～

Early in the next week, the two dwellers in Bateman's bach became three. Bill had hiked up the hill leading out of the bay, and was on the way back when he heard a gut-wrenching wail. At first he was unable to locate the source in the gloom, looking in all the wrong places. Then he noticed a pair of yellow eyes.

If ever eyes pleaded for rescue this pair did. They belonged to a cat. It must have been swept downstream with the flooding brought about by several inches of downpour, and had by the skin of its teeth avoided a watery death. There was a conflict of wills about whether or not the cat would release its deathlike grip on the willow bark; Bill was finally forced to lever each claw away separately, while the animal complained vociferously. As he was perched on a bank of dubious stability, at the edge of a swollen creek in which it appeared more than likely he'd end, Bill finally brought the tussle to a close by yanking, and then stuffed the bedraggled beast into the front of his jacket. There was every reason to think that such an ungrateful rescuee might manifest its terror by attacking his chest. Any sensible rational guy would simply have dumped the animal onto terra firma and gone about his business. As it was, it seemed to find the warmth of his sweater and the semi-darkness of the jacket comforting. Bill turned his footsteps homeward.

§

"I've something to show you."

"What?"

Emily viewed with horror the way the front of his jacket subtly changed shape, in a manner that brought vividly to mind some ghastly scene from a sci-fi movie. It looked set to develop into that hideous moment when an alien creature erupts from the stomach of the innocent character in whom it has gestated.

"A refugee."

Remembering the startling experiences when they played cops and robbers on the roof, Emily hoped that it wasn't a 'possum. But from within the jacket Bill drew out nothing more exotic than a cat. Not a kitten, but a full-sized animal whose sodden fur made it look like a piece of flotsam. Straddling the security of his palm the cat made a half-hearted attempt to shake itself, and mewed plaintively. The mew found an immediate response in Emily's breast.

"Oh, the poor thing. What happened? Where did you find it?"

"In the stream. Or, rather, clutching an overhanging branch. The stream's in flood."

Emily fetched a towel and enveloped the creature. It repaid her by yowling louder, and managed to gain purchase on Bill's wrist. He swore softly at such ingratitude and extricated his hand with care. Emily enfolded the cat within the cloth to forestall any escape attempt and sat it on her lap, talking reassuringly as she gently toweled it dry. After a brief, token struggle it submitted to her ministrations, finally going so far as to assist with an occasional swipe of the tongue.

"Do you think it's wild? A feral animal, or somebody's pet?"

"How can you tell? There are wild cats about, that I know, because they do awful damage to the ground-dwelling birds. But my guess is this one's domesticated."

Emily continued to remove as much moisture as possible from the spiky fur. "We're becoming quite a twosome, you and I, in the rescue stakes. Me coming to Heneti's aid, now you saving Felix from drowning."

"Felix?"

"Felix Mendelssohn, of course."

Bill raised one eyebrow. "You reckon we could set up a brass plate? Merivale and Thackeray, Saviors Inc."

"Let's hope we aren't needed too much. But it added a new dimension to Bill, his role as Official Benefactor.

She lowered the newcomer onto the hearthrug, where it sat and completed the cleansing process in the time-honored manner.

"It must belong to somebody. We'll have to put up a sign in the store, or ask the postman."

"Okay."

Personal toilet complete, fur at least adequately rearranged, the cat stood with dignity, walked purposefully into the kitchen, sat itself before the refrigerator and meowed. It was a demand that brooked no refusal.

"That solves one problem. Not feral," Emily remarked. She filled a saucer with milk for their guest, then selected potatoes to scrub, prior to baking them. "I think that's what you might call learned behavior."

A week later the cat was still with them, unclaimed. Hori suggested that it might have been swept downstream from one of the hillside farms, but no homesteader came forward to acknowledge a missing pet. Then the storekeeper ventured that it had, perhaps, been abandoned by some townie, looking to dump a pet that had lost its initial, kittenish appeal. Emily thought that to arrive here the townie had gone some distance out of his way. They would probably never know. Thus Mendelssohn, for so he became, quickly established himself as an intrinsic member of the Bateman's bach family. Nobody would call him halfway handsome but, as Emily remarked, once his fur dried his snowy chest and single white paw gave him a very distinguished air, and it was unfair to penalize one of God's creatures for being short-changed by nature. Added to that, having a cat about was marvelously homey. And a description of his arrival more than filled a letter home.

Since Bill's arrival Emily rarely entered the sunroom. It had become his domain. They had rigged up a pole for use as a make-shift wardrobe, there was an ancient chest of drawers that housed his other garments. Its top served as a sort of dressing table, but was remarkably devoid of anything personal. The bed was always neatly made, on the bedside chair lay his current reading with a folded envelope marking his place. They had unearthed a truly hideous lamp, originally marketed to commemorate the impending marriage of Princess Elizabeth to Prince Philip of Greece, which served for bed-time illumination. On what must originally have been a sewing-machine table sat his elderly typewriter, the top back as if anticipating a flurry of activity.

But Bill had been in Bateman's Bach nearly three weeks, and during that time the keys had remained silent and unused.

Once a week Emily paid her dues to housekeeping and ran the fourth-hand vacuum cleaner over the mats, and a cloth along the ledges and surfaces where fine sand relentlessly settled. It was necessary to sweep the wooden floors more often than that, because the beach had a habit of intruding, but she usually excluded the sunroom. If her lodger disliked grit under his bare feet, well, he knew where the broom was kept.

On this particular day she altered the rules somewhat. Bill saw to his own laundry, as they had agreed when first he moved in. Today several shirts, half a dozen pairs of socks and some underwear billowed on the outside line, and it was coming on to rain. Yet again. Winter in this part of New Zealand seemed to include an amazing amount of precipitation.

Only a very inconsiderate person would leave dry washing out in such circumstances. Nonetheless, there was something surprisingly intimate about folding shirts and briefs. She took the neat pile through into the sunroom and put it on top of the sun-bleached divan cover. There were windows the full length of the small room. On sunny winter days it was deliciously warm, in the summer she could imagine its becoming scorchingly hot. Bill, she noticed, was reading another of his Henry James collection. *The Turn of the Screw.* That was one novel with which she could claim at least slight knowledge. The delight of Britten's opera bearing the same name had been one of her earliest discoveries.

She had turned to go when her eye was caught by the unexpected whiteness of paper protruding from the typewriter. So he was writing again, without her having realized it. She knew she was prying, but some inner compulsion was in charge, urging her to read.

Oddly enough, it was a list, partly obscured by the roller:

- There is elegance in the arch of each eyebrow.
- The hollows of her back are reminiscent of the curves of an ancient, finely crafted, musical instrument.
- Her eyes are the color of liquid caramel. Sometimes warm, sometimes wary.
- Her hair reflects firelight in cadences of copper

Emily stopped reading, torn between being very moved and somewhat embarrassed. She couldn't doubt for a minute that he was writing about her. Even though not given to boasting, she could generally recognize her physical features, when described. She'd not have thought about caramel, herself, but someone at school had once mentioned runny toffee, in reference to her eye color, intending to be funny.

And Bill had sat here, at this typewriter, and thought enough about her to create a list of things that he liked. Expressed extremely beautifully. She was so touched that she felt like crying.

It certainly added another dimension to the day, that list. It made writing home to her family quite awkward, because the words Bill had used intruded between her and the airmail letter. He seemed to have noticed such strange parts of her. Eyebrows, for example. Eyebrows? Not her figure, which she knew to be quite trim, unless that reference to her back being like something ancient could be considered "figure." Nor obvious parts, like her breasts, which were at least moderately attractive too.

But after a while, by which time the letter writing had been abandoned, it began to make sense. You had to remember that she was being seen through the eyes of a chap whose orientation was different. It would be out of kilter for a gay man to note the parts more noticed by the general male populace. Come to that, he'd never seen her legs out of jeans, apart from the ankles and feet visible beneath her cotton nightie. And he had said that he liked her, the other evening. Her *in toto*, rather than disembodied bits.

She doodled the length of the aerogram, creating a border of kelp. Now she was faced with the small matter of whether or not to mention that she'd invaded his private retreat, actually read what he'd written. Perhaps she should say something, casually, in a "by the by . . ." throw-away manner.

But, of course, that was impossible. Not to be considered, not with that word "pry" still lodged within recent memory. What she had happened upon was something to be considered on her own, to be appreciated and cherished.

FOURTEEN

The senior social officer had forgotten all about the kids who'd departed so suddenly from the school in Taranaki. She'd dumped the memo in a rarely opened file and not given it a second thought. So to find a personally written letter in the day's mail was quite a surprise. It also showed a bit of enterprise on the part of the teacher who'd put about the initial request. Knowing just how busy the school boards kept their staff, it did mean that the good woman must care a heck of a lot about this pair.

She scanned the letter quickly. Probability that they were in this area, known to be an earlier address, albeit some years ago. No request from a new school for reports and records of attendance to be forwarded . . . potential neglect . . . possible danger warnings . . . Certainly stronger stuff than the carefully worded memo which had first landed on her desk.

But surely not her concern, or not right now. If there was proof of truancy it came under the auspices of the Special Education service, not her department. She fiddled with her red pen, then wrote, *Ref: Jim McGuire. I'll be happy to follow up if you can trace this family. Thanks. MK.*

Then she dropped it into the Out basket. Jim was a lazy bastard at the best of times. It wouldn't hurt him to get off his behind and initiate a search.

Tending to the immediate needs of the Morrisons was time-consuming, but that aside, Emily's days were open to anything; reading, walking, exploring. Bill suggested that she avail herself of some of his literary favorites, and she began by reading *The Turn of the Screw.* Rediscovering Miles and Flora in the printed word was like picking up the threads of an old friendship.

But it was the evenings which took on a special flavor, and Emily came to anticipate them with pleasure. After they had cleared the meal away they would sit, one on either side of the hearth, and discuss everything and anything. She couldn't say why it was so easy to open up, especially after her discovery of Bill's list. At other times, in these exact circumstances, she might have dried up completely, become tongue-tied in the light of her unacknowledged information. Probably, she decided upon reflection, it was a combination of many small details.

The fire, to begin with. The driftwood which replenished it could be anything, although according to Bill the majority of the logs were black pine and *totara.* They burnt in differing ways, flaring sometimes orange, sometimes blue, creating miniature caverns of brilliant light, then collapsing into heaps of glowing ember. Emily could follow the changing patterns for long hours. She had unearthed two blue-rimmed, enamel candlestick holders, probably squirreled away as insurance against loss of electricity. The store supplied her with candles of the old fashioned, no-nonsense variety. Rather than tolerate the harsh illumination afforded by the single bulb, they would extinguish that, and light the two small wicks.

Maybe it was the dimness that encouraged intimacy, maybe it was the lack of television. Certainly the absence of a sexual spark helped immeasurably. Little things couldn't be misinterpreted. For whatever reason they would talk, and drink coffee, and talk some more, until the candles guttered in their holders, and Bill would remember that he had a dawn start to trawl with Hori, or to tend his set lines. As far as Emily was concerned, they could have conversed the night away and she would not have minded.

At first she was the one who opened up, which stood to reason as there was less reserve in her personality. She told Bill all about her family and her time at the Meinhardt. Bill now knew quite a lot about Philip Merivale, and his wife. He knew that Anna bred Welsh ponies, and showed them, that she named them after characters in operas.

"Mum would have liked to be a professional musician herself, I think," Emily explained. "But her generation rarely had the opportunity. Anyway, she married Daddy when she was quite young, and devoted herself to family."

"Happily?"

Emily took time to consider. It was quite hard to stand back from her parents and look at them with adult eyes.

"I think so. It's not one of those topics bandied about over the Sunday joint. Anyway, she got a tremendous kick out of Jay and how well he's done. And me, to a certain extent."

"What about Sarah?"

Emily tried to appraise her older sister dispassionately, trying to envisage how other people would see Sarah.

"She looks like Dad, where Jay and I take after Mum. But she's got nothing of his personality. She's . . . different."

Early childhood was memorable for the feuds that erupted in the nursery, always Sarah pitted against Jay and Emily. And Sarah was so prickly, so difficult to befriend. She was her own worst enemy, as Granny Williams used to say when she was still rational.

"Luckily she's the only one of us to share Mum's interest in horsey stuff. That gave them something in common, even before Sarah's sons were born."

A log crashed into the grate, sending a shower of sparks up the chimney.

"Tell me about the Meinhardt."

It was easy to talk about Moshe Meinhardt, who wasn't immediate family and didn't threaten to expose less than perfect relationships.

"Moshe came to England as a young man, escaping the Jewish purge. He was immensely talented. He set up his own conservatorium in a disused village school, on the Welsh border. At first it was only for British children, those he thought had sufficient talent. Then, as its fame spread, kids from all over the world started coming. The school expanded. We had a wonderful auditorium, donated by a grateful old boy."

"And what were you? The local genius?"

She shook her head slightly. "No, certainly not that. I was a bit precocious, because Mum had taught us all, but nothing like some of the other students. Music is like maths. It seems to attract infant prodigies. Some of those children were so gifted that they were soloists at the age of five. Never me. I discovered very early that I wasn't of their caliber."

Bill rested one ankle on his knee. She couldn't see his face because the wing of the chair, and its angle, prevented firelight from illuminating his features.

"Was it painful, reaching that conclusion? After all, each of us hopes to be seen as a star."

"At first, I suppose. Finding out that you're not actually a world-beater does tend to deflate the old ego, but Moshe was tremendous at handling that, too. He never suggested that we were less valuable to the world, we second-stringers. I can hear him, now. His English was always pretty awful. 'Think now,' he would say. 'Can you ever imagine an orchestra filled only with soloists?' And he'd wag his finger like this . . . 'That is my idea of purgatory. Sixty soloists, all determined that the world will appreciate their genius.' Then we'd laugh and feel better. Useful, because we weren't the ones to throw prima-donna screaming fits."

"Excellent psychology."

"Yes, in retrospect. But he really meant it. He's just that sort of very special chap."

"And has it all changed, now? If it's true that you're performing career's over."

This was something she'd thought about at length, especially in those early days. "You can't just dismiss such a huge part of your life, simply because you can no longer make an acceptable noise. I've lived and breathed music all my life. When I'm walking, I walk in time to music. I fall asleep to it. I do the dishes, going through a familiar score in my head. It will never leave me."

"Then that, in a way, is also a gift."

"You think so?"

" I know so. Believe me."

"Ah, I'm not sure your judgment's to be trusted. You also think Mendelssohn writes sugary garbage. And I'm not referring to the cat."

"Where did you come up with that idea?"

"You told me so."

"I did?"

"Yes." She could allow a justified frisson of smugness. "The first time you took me to the Webbers' evening party. Don't tell me you've forgotten?"

～

It was embarking on a voyage of discovery, Emily decided, learning about her lodger. Though he appeared reluctant at first to divulge anything remotely personal, and the snippets might be carefully rationed, each conversation revealed new facets of his character. It was salient to remember that the first time they'd made eye contact he'd taken to his heels like Tom the Piper's son.

"You know an awful lot about my childhood," she encouraged him this particular evening. "Tell me about yours."

"What, exactly?"

She gave a sigh. "Start at the beginning. Carry on to the end."

"At conception?"

She could visualize his grin without seeing it. She knew that his eyes would be gleaming in the shadowed darkness.

"We can skip that part, especially as whatever you tell me can scarcely be based on first-hand knowledge."

"True. Well, my father was much older than my mother. A generation apart. They met when Polly, my mother, was hired to nurse his first wife, who was dying of something."

"Most people do. Die of something. Deaths from nothing are extremely rare, I've been told."

"Okay, smart ass. I'll rephrase. She died of some cause about which I am ignorant, having probably been told, but forgetting."

She smiled. "Okay. Go on."

"My father was in his late fifties, newly widowed and with two teenage daughters, who were something of a handful by all accounts. My mother was twenty-six, nearer the age of the daughters than their father. Nevertheless, she married him."

"Were they happy together?"

"Yes, very happy. It was a marriage of total opposites that managed to work. My half sisters, took a bit of bringing around, but my mother has a vast reservoir of optimism. She always assumes that she'll win through."

"And then you were born."

"After several years. My father was sixty-three."

"Sixty-three!" A grandfather, rather than a parent.

"And he died thirteen years later."

Into her mind leaped the image of an elderly man bent over his cane, holding the hand of a very small boy. In this vision he looked more like Old Father Time leading in the infant New Year, the babe clad only in some scrap of cloth for decency's sake.

"What was he like, your father?"

"Patrician. Educated and gentle. He left me, as a legacy, his depressive tendency. He was very fond of me, and proud that his name wouldn't die with him. I know I adored him, and childish worship is totally unconditional. My mother says we're very alike, in looks as well as personality."

The heat of the fire was searing Emily's ankles. She tucked her legs under her. "Then what happened?"

"Two things, pretty close together. Polly was from the South, born and raised in Charleston. While my father was alive we lived in Alexandria. When he died he left a huge legacy, in land and investments, the lion's share to Polly. After all they'd been very happy, and she had produced an heir. By that time my half-sisters were comfortably established, married and with families. However, they weren't too keen on the apportionment."

"You mean he disinherited them?"

"No. They were left a sizable amount, as was each grandchild. And they had their mother's money. But that didn't mean that they were prepared to settle for what they saw as a grossly unfair situation. To them, Polly was a usurper."

"And?"

"I told you my mother was a born optimist. She's also capable of seeing only the best in everybody, so she comes across as pretty naive, at times. She wasn't going to fight her step-daughters in court. She said she'd not be able to sleep with herself afterwards. So she agreed to retain enough for my upbringing and education, and handed the rest over to Allison and Evie."

Emily was appalled. "All of it? Just like that?"

"All of it. Just like that."

"Crumbs."

She looked across at what she could see of him with renewed interest. When leaning against the faded back of the old armchair in that way he didn't exactly resemble a person whose mother had blithely waved farewell to a fortune. If she could conjure up a stereotype of such a person. She thought about Polly Thackeray. Was she very idealistic? Or very stupid. Possibly six of one, half a dozen of the other.

"You said two things happened. I know your father died, but what was the other?"

"We moved to New England. Cape Cod."

The silence which followed this deceptively simple remark suggested that the move was monumental in its nature. To Emily, who had chosen to wander the world in preference to putting down roots, it sounded like small beer.

"So?"

"It probably seems strange, but to me it was like moving to another country, another planet. I was fourteen, a gangly kid with a strong southern accent, dropped, in my perception, in the heart of the Union."

Emily stood to allow the circulation back into her calves. She felt that she needed the small pause caused by this mundane activity to ingest all that Bill had told her.

"I'll put the kettle on, for coffee. Tell me the next part when I get back."

Being the recipient of so much in the way of personal history was like over-binging on chocolate. The system required a period of adjustment. She resettled herself some minutes later.

"Okay. So now you're living on Cape Cod. Why did your mother choose there?"

Bill had also taken advantage of the pause to restoke the fire and to bring in chunks of driftwood from the back verandah.

"She needed money, and something to do. She could have returned to nursing, but she'd been out of circulation fifteen years, and there was her son to consider. So she started to paint."

"Gracious." Emily could certainly identify with someone faced with such a radical, life-altering move; and to admire her method of solving it. "How brave."

"Or ignorant. Cape Cod has quite a few artists' colonies, but she was sufficiently savvy to know that they might look upon her little daubs with a jaundiced eye. Instead she became a fringe-dweller. We moved to Truro."

"Is she a good artist? I mean, has she any training?"

"No, on both counts," Bill replied. "She paints two types of pictures. Little fluffy kittens and puppies with enormous eyes and soulful expressions, and small, urchin-like children with huge eyes and mournful faces. But they sell.."

Emily did her juggling trick with the sieve and the enamel jug, while she thought about the subjects Polly Thackeray had elected to paint. She'd seen their like at tourist resorts the world over, and articulated her scorn at such tastelessness. She handed Bill his mug and the bowl, so he could add his own sugar.

"Tell me about Cape Cod. It always sounds wonderful."

"In some ways it's very like here."

She was pleased that, with characteristic subtlety, he'd not pursued the topic of his mother's artwork. Instead Bill went on to describe the dunes and the black oaks, the pitch pines and glossy, box-berry bushes, the beaches where he had wandered and explored, that first lonely summer. He told her about the flocks of white egrets and the long, solitary bike rides he'd undertaken, and about the gleaming red of the cranberry swamps.

"Then, finally, school started. And I met Garth."

Garth. His friend, his lover, who had died of AIDS last year. The laughing young man in that photograph. She'd not seen the snapshot again, since Bill had become her lodger.

"Can you tell me about him?"

Bill leaned back in the chair and there was so long a period of quiet that Emily began to wonder if she'd strayed into taboo territory. Then, finally he began.

"As I said, I knew nobody in Truro. Not one soul. And, of course, when school started I was the new kid. I was built like a beanpole, just entering adolescence and outgrowing clothes faster than my mother could replace them.

"Garth sat next to me in biology. He was everything that I wasn't. Popular, good at sports. His family was long established in the community. I was still my mother's son, speaking with my southern accent, which the other kids loved to mimic. I said, 'Yes, Ma'am,' and 'No, Ma'am,' and they fell about laughing. Garth spoke right. He did everything right. I had trouble knowing what to do with my feet and hands, they always seemed too big. He was neat and coordinated. The football flying through the air managed to miss me by yards. It found his hands as if they were magnets. And he became my friend. Rescued me, because after that it didn't matter that I was the odd guy out."

Mendelssohn chose this moment to interrupt. Without a cat flap for his special needs, they were always opening and shutting the door at his request. And, in the contrary way of all felines, he was no sooner out on the verandah than he was wailing to be let back inside. Emily rose for the second time in answer to his stridently voiced demand, then settled herself back in the chair. Mendelssohn sampled both laps before selecting Bill's, and began the rhythmic kneading that preceded his hunkering down.

"Go on," Emily prompted gently. "You were telling me about Garth."

"He wanted to write, which was our first, and major, common link. By the time of our senior year we were joint editors of the school publication. Two raw kids, overflowing with ambition, and sharing dreams. We'd be discovered, we agreed, because of our brilliant use of language. Somewhere, sometime, a literary scout would stumble upon a copy of *Seashell*, and be swept away by our purple prose. We didn't bother much with distribution to fellow students, arrogant young snobs that we were. Why cast pearls such as ours before swine? Instead we left copies lying open in the smart offices of Hyannis Port lawyers and dentists. Anywhere that the literati might drop in during a summer vacation. And, in a way, it worked."

He paused in his narrative, and Emily could imagine the pair, poised on the brink of manhood, sharing the vision.

"We separated to go to college. Garth went Ivy League; I didn't. But the bond was still there, as strong as ever. Summer vacations we'd be back together, swapping anecdotes, laughing at the pretensions of others. I could draw a strength from him that I would never have found on my own. Garth had enough confidence for both of us." He paused again, raking his fingertips gently along Mendelssohn's back in a manner known to delight. "After we graduated, Garth's father paid for him to spend the summer in Europe, and I was taken on as a cub reporter with one of the smaller Village papers. Nothing fancy, but it was a start.

"'Clark Kent on the outside,' was how Garth described me. 'Literary Superman inside, lurking about while seeking the right phone box.' He had that quick sort of wit I really admired. After his European jaunt he got a job writing advertising jingles, which he saw as camouflage. We shared a miserable little apartment which we kidded ourselves was chic because the address was nearly Greenwich. Six flights of stairs to be climbed, and central heating which rattled so loudly, when and if it deigned to work, that the din kept us awake at night. Garth got cracking first, on his career. It was all pretty erratic, leaping as he did from doing advertising copy to theatrical reviews, with a handful of television scripts thrown in. My progress was less spectacular. It took a few years, and a lot of small steps, but in the end I managed to achieve a column in the syndicated press."

"But that wasn't enough?" Emily thought that most people might well be content to remain right there.

"It was okay at first. But not long-term. I always wanted to write novels. Then Garth found a sponsor, a blue-rinse divorcee a year or two younger than his mother."

"A woman? But I thought . . ." The exclamation surfaced uninvited. Emily bit her tongue with chagrin. The last thing in the world she desired was for Bill to imagine her homophobic. But if he'd noticed her slip, he didn't show it. His tone scarcely changed.

"She was prepared to establish him, while he tapped out his masterpiece on a state-of-the-art word processor. So he moved out of our apartment. And that's about that."

Bill fell silent, fondling Mendelssohn's ears so the only sound was the cat's appreciative purr. Emily had the distinct feeling that for some long seconds Bill wasn't with her, but was back in New York, with his erstwhile lover. That he was editing his reflections for her ears. Clearly she had been right; such memories were still too painful to share.

"Don't go on unless you want to." Although she was praying that he would, because it seemed so much the key to his character. Garth, and his tragic death.

"It's okay. Where was I? Yes, with Garth and his masterpiece. In the end it wasn't a best seller, but it wasn't a failure, either, and the reviews were all that you'd want to hear. Critics used words like 'brilliant touches,' and 'a completely fresh approach.' I snipped out the cuttings and posted them into a scrapbook for his parents, because I knew that Garth wouldn't remember to do so."

"What was it about, his book?"

"The title was *A Reason for Murder*. The plot revolved around a young writer who is sponsored by a rich, middle-aged woman. When she becomes too demanding and too smothering, he kills her. Ostensibly to preserve his talent. But the underlying theme was more about the influence of parents on their kids. The over-demanding patron is supposed to be symbolic."

"How ghoulish."

It was good to see Bill smile. Maybe Garth's death was sufficiently in the past. Or maybe talking about him was therapeutic.

"So, established and fêted by the literary set, Garth kissed his blue haired matriarch good-bye, and moved out."

"I'm surprised that she didn't take offense. Didn't she think that the woman in his story was based on her?"

"I guess not. Perhaps she didn't read. Or maybe Garth could explain the underlying message to her. He could argue that black was white and you'd believe him."

Emily saw that debating the relative merits of Garth's book would lead them up a cul-de-sac. "Go on, then. Please."

Bill waited for Mendelssohn to rearrange himself comfortably before picking up his narrative.

"He had great generosity of spirit. When *One Witch* hit the bookshelves, he was first in line to congratulate me. And the same when the Hollywood contract followed. Then, of course, I expected *Murder* to be followed by his second, equally clever novel. And it never happened. Somehow he'd gone off track. Lost his momentum. We'd meet for lunches, and he was always full of cracking ideas and wicked plot lines, but the words didn't appear on paper. Maybe it was all that unexpected luxury. Without such a cushion, I knew from the very beginning I had to discipline myself, sit before a typewriter for the prescribed number of hours each day and sweat over every sentence. But in the end it paid off. I landed a contract for three more books." His voice was reflective, as though reassuring himself more than Emily. "Of course, I could have gotten myself a word processor by then, but I'm attached to that old machine, I know the keyboard. It's like a pair of well-worn shoes. Your toes don't need telling where to go."

"And what happened to Garth?"

Bill continued to stare into the flames. "He died. Not quickly and cleanly, but a long, slow decline. Flesh melting off him, pain that was terrible."

There seemed to be quite a large leap in the story, like any mention of his being gay, but Emily accepted that this was the bowdlerized version, and was grateful that he had shared so much. She could use her imagination to fill in the gaps.

"All that talent. How dreadfully sad."

"Yes," he commented. "All that boundless spirit. And so many of his friends seemed to disappear, just when he needed them most. I tried to compensate. I was with him as much as possible ... until ... "

"You became ill, too."

The was a long pause as though Bill was sorting through things for his own satisfaction. At last he spoke very quietly. "Yes."

They sat in silence, but there was no awkwardness in the stillness. It was a mutual appreciation of the companionship which follows the sharing of memories, happy and sad.

Finally Emily said, "Thank you for telling me about him, Bill. He must have been very special to you."

"A friendship like ours doesn't come along too often."

And together they watched the fire create miniature dragons' tongues of brilliant scarlet and hot coral. Emily was mulling over his use of the word friendship. Surely their relationship was considerably more close than that. Perhaps it was difficult for Bill to express such intimacy, even in these more accepting times.

When he spoke it was to turn the thrust of the conversation back to her. "What about you? Did you have a best friend?"

"Gracious, yes." Emily was amazed that he suggested anything to the contrary. "Dozens of them, when I was small. A new best friend each week. But some who lasted. And at the Meinhardt there was a trio of us. The three musketeers. Of course we split up when we graduated, but I'm still in touch with the other two. Susie married and settled down to happy domesticity and a baby a year. Five at the last count, and I'm godmama to number one. Maria Blumstein you might have heard of, if you're into musical matters. She plays the cello, absolutely superbly. This year she was off to Moscow and Beijing, on the concert round."

Bill altered his position in the armchair slightly, and the glow lit his face. "I don't know too much about music, I'm afraid."

"And I know that by your standards I'm almost uneducated, when it comes to literature," Emily responded. "Perhaps we should do a swap. You continue to tell me what to tackle, book-wise, and I'll give you the lowdown on things musical."

"In six weeks? Make a silk purse out of this sow's ear? Heneti's been trying without success for months." But he extended a hand for her to shake, sealing their small pact. "You've got yourself a deal."

Although Emily had the distinct feeling that he was mostly agreeing to please her.

Bill found that sleep evaded him. It was all that talking about Garth which was so disturbing although, goodness knew, he'd thought about him often enough. Now his head was filled with the other half of the tale, the secret part which, out of respect for his friend, he'd chosen not to reveal.

He was back in that gruesome apartment in Greenwich, at about the time when the divorcee had put in so welcome an appearance. It might have been seen as serendipitous, because her arrival coincided with the period when Bill was having doubts about how their relationship was developing, his and Garth's.

Garth had always been able to turn on the camp, doing it so brilliantly that Bill would laugh until it hurt. Like a cabaret act. The limp wrist, the exaggerated, mincing walk, the works. Then, at other times, he was busily dating women, scores of women, and portraying the macho guy who got things done. With so much play-acting it was pretty difficult to separate what was genuine from what was sham. But there was something new in the way he looked at Bill, letting his gaze linger below the waist, combined with how he'd trail a finger slowly across the back of his neck, along his shoulder, that Bill found decidedly unsettling.

He was profoundly grateful when Garth announced he was moving to Long Island to become a kept man, because Bill was struggling with the correct phrases to explain that friendship had its boundaries, and that Garth's overtures were making him thoroughly uncomfortable. Probably Garth would never actually have followed up these initial advances, had Bill voiced his distaste, because he appreciated their camaraderie too, but at the time it muddied the waters.

"Wonderful woman, darling," Garth had said of his new sponsor. "Generous to a fault. I'd marry her tomorrow, if it weren't for the physical side." He'd accompanied this with a droll face. "It's the sex, dear chap. Totally gross. I have to shut my eyes and think of my fans, lining up in their hundreds while I sign copies of my bestseller. You have to consider the long term, you know. Be prepared to make sacrifices for your art."

Bill had found so blatantly materialistic an angle mildly repugnant, but had been too craven to voice his opinion. No, that wasn't being fair to himself. More important was that debt of friendship. He'd thought about Garth's decision from his point of view, and from the widow's, and decided that on balance she would be the winner. Garth was witty and fun. Great company. And maybe he was exaggerating about the sex angle. Maybe.

Bill had heard Emily's implied question and taken the coward's way out in not responding. He was pretty sure that the divorcee with the blue hair had no idea that Garth was gay. Not then, anyway. Perhaps later, when his casual liaisons had brought him in contact with the Black Death of the late twentieth century, but by then it was too late to turn the clock back, and what useful purpose was served by the good woman's knowing, anyway?

Fifteen

ori . . . " Emily rearranged the already tidy pile of candy bars on the counter of the store.

"Hello?"

"Next time you're going to the town . . . may I hitch a ride?"

Hori stopped adding up a column of figures to look at her over his glasses. "No problem. I'll actually be going to the depot in the morning. But I can drop you in the town on the way, and pick you up on the way back. Can you fill in a couple of hours?"

She nodded. Unwittingly, he'd given her the very opportunity she sought. "That would be wonderful. Perhaps you could point out the library to me."

There was no real reason for her to feel like a traitor, nor was there anything remotely hinting at underhandedness in what she was doing. Still she felt uneasy, maybe because she was keeping a secret from Hori, who had become a friend. Or because she knew that Bill still thought she was wrong; or, at best, misguided.

But part of her mission was totally reasonable. She needed to buy the sort of shampoo that killed head lice. Quite a lot of it, actually. She hoped that the same, sensible woman would be on duty at the chemist's, and that she could solicit her advice.

Hori's truck was a great deal quieter than the jeep in which she'd last made this trip or, perhaps, Hori knew to avoid the worst of the potholes. They drove through an early morning in which pockets of heavy mist filled the valleys and clung in threads to the hillside. It added a touch of the ethereal to everything.

Hori smoothly shifted down one gear as they rounded a curve and began the climb out of Whangapouri.

"Bill busy, then?"

She understood what he meant. Hori knew that he had only to say for the McDuffs to offer their vehicle. They thought the sun and moon circled around Bill. She'd met the McDuffs at Heneti's most recent evening. She'd watched them fawn all over him.

Major McDuff was a very small man who walked as though he'd swallowed an iron rod, every step precise. Vera McDuff, too, wore the sort of clothes that made you think of corsets, and which Sarah had rudely described, in days gone by, as tools of the meat packing industry. Once seated, it seemed probable that Vera would have to stay there until hauled perpendicular by a crane. Emily had avoided her, and spent her time talking to Talitha and Abraham's wife, Minnie. They listened to *Aida* that evening, and Minnie had shown them how to dance with *pois,* so Emily knew, now, what Kaffi was talking about. She'd even tried to manipulate the small flax balls herself, and laughed at her awkwardness.

She switched her thoughts back to the present, and answered Hori's question. "Bill's busy writing."

"He is? Another book?"

"I don't know what. But he's very pleased about it. He's been fighting some sort of writer's block, to do with his breakdown." She didn't add that she felt proud, too, as though his mastering this impediment were her personal hurdle as well.

Hori swerved to avoid a hole that could have engulfed the truck, causing Emily to slide across the seat to the limits of her seatbelt. She righted herself, clutching at the overhead handle.

"It's Whangapouri, does that. Helps you to mend." Hori spoke reflectively, and she looked up at him. "Same with me. I came here after my operation. Nodules on the larynx, and there was the end of my career."

"Why Whangapouri? Did you grow up here?"

"Nope."

"But Heneti did, didn't she? Isn't that what Kui said?"

The truck picked up speed as they reached the flatter land of the interior.

"That's Kui talk," Hori explained. "She might have lived here, for a short while, as a girl. But the Ngati Tarapunga people moved away years ago. Heneti grew up in Auckland, same as me."

Emily thought about this. In a way it was as big as the move Bill had described, when he and his mother moved to Cape Cod. Practically enemy territory, in his adolescent opinion. Of course, to compare the shift from city to bay with Bill's shock of perception was rather over the top, but the winter quiet must contrast sharply with all that Auckland had to offer.

"What on earth inspired you to come here, then?"

The big man glanced across at her. "Dear me. I think I'm hearing someone who's hungry for traffic lights and shopping arcades. Done enough rusticating, have you?"

She tried to be fair. "I can understand what you're talking about, because this place has helped me, too. But there's a great deal of difference between being here three months, and thinking about staying for the rest of your life."

"Not once the magic of the area has caught you."

"I like concerts and movies, and visiting other cities, and never quite knowing where I'll rest my head tomorrow night. And your life must have been like that, too. While you were singing."

He grunted. "Sydney, London, Rome. We lived in all those cities. You ask Heneti. It never suited her. She was always missing our daughters, hankering for home."

"Why did she accompany you, then?"

"You'd better ask Heneti that."

"But you could have settled in Auckland once you'd retired, couldn't you? Or Hamilton."

"We could have done a lot. It was the Lord guided us to Whangapouri. Same as he guided you."

Emily turned her head to look fixedly out the window. She certainly didn't want to enter into a discussion about religion, however profound the storekeeper's beliefs might be. Nor did she want to nail her own colors, pallid as they were, to the mast. Not in the light of such fervor. So she decided to switch topics, and at the same time tackle the subject most close to her at this time.

"Hori, how would I go about tracing a person, in this country?"

He replied calmly. "Like any other country. Ring the police." He paused, and there was a tense moment when she imagined herself parrying difficult-to-answer questions. "You seeking a long lost relative? An identical twin abducted at birth? Or an uncle who's made a fortune in the wool industry?"

She laughed. "That I should be so lucky. As they say, chance would be a fine thing."

Bless him. Hori had to be the most sympathetic, most understanding person in the Southern Hemisphere. He must have sensed her anxiety, because he did no more than glance shrewdly across at her, and smile.

The library did have a telephone and a selection of directories. She set out her coins before her in a line, remembering from experience how quickly public phones could gobble up money. She summarized exactly what she knew of Kaffi's father, which wasn't much. His name was Matu. He'd gone to town with a list of things to buy and a truck full of sheep. He hadn't returned. But, despite a number of likely leads, she could find nobody who knew Matu Morrison. Not with the police, nor at any hospital. It was as though he'd vanished off the face of the earth.

She had taken her haversack to accommodate the books that she borrowed, and it was just as well. As Kaffi was wont to repeat, what would Hori have thought, seeing her select readers and spelling lists, and a copy of *Elementary Arithmetic?* She noted the indifference with which the librarian checked out her supply, and tried to see herself through the young man's eyes. Maybe a farmer's wife, mother of a growing brood, gathering additional help for her children. Then so be it. She was, after all, about to undertake that very role which had been the last she sought for herself, about as unlikely as nursing. Emily Merivale, tutor.

Marco, could he but know, would laugh until he wept. It was with him that she'd shared her hopes and passions in those halcyon summers at the Meinhardt. Knowing her revulsion to teaching, he'd have teased her unmercifully.

Anxious to avoid having her reasons to seek city life again placed under Hori's personal microscope, Emily had decided to employ diversionary tactics on the return trip. However, she might have spared herself the bother. Hori had other matters he wanted to discuss.

"Not easy, having to swap careers, is it."

"You're probably right. Except about the word 'swap.' That suggests an option. I have no idea what I'll do."

Hori grunted in reply, or maybe he cleared his throat. It was certainly a characteristic Hori-noise. "Rudderless ship still, ay?"

Emily could only agree. "You know Hori, once, when we were small, we walked along the lane to the farmer's, my brother and I. Mum had sent us to buy eggs. And we arrived just after Mr. Prince had killed a chicken. And it ran round and round the farmyard, headless. After I'd recovered from the physical side of my accident, I felt just like that bird. As though all I could do was run and run, until I dropped down dead. It was awful."

"And you ran to New Zealand? As far as Whangapouri?"

"Not all at once." She allowed herself time to reconsider those steps that had led to this place, at this time. Hori, having been there, was so easy to talk to that confiding in him felt very comfortable. "The accident happened in France, but once they could move me I was transferred back to the hospital where my father's a consultant, in Gloucester, and after that I went home to recuperate."

She could recall it so vividly, the early snatches of pain, sharp and intense at first, woolly and nagging at others, and also the inexplicable sensation that the familiarity of a time-ordered existence was being denied her. For the life of her, she could not have made sense of the confused jumble of images, and sensations, which characterized that bleak period.

"My parents tried so hard not to fuss, and in a way it was worse than their fussing, if you can follow that."

"Didn't offer you a focal point for your anger."

Emily was grateful for his accurate assessment. "Precisely. In retrospect, I was hideous to them. The nicer they were, the more concerned about me, the waspier and snappier I became. And they sort of skirted around what had happened to my hand, and to my fingers."

Another grunt of agreement. "Same with my throat. Talk about this, about that. Never talk about nodules on the larynx."

"Then Jay, my brother, suggested that I should convalesce with him and his wife. In Melbourne. And I jumped at the idea."

"You get on well with them?"

"Oh, yes. Most of the time. And they have an enchanting little girl, called Charlotte."

"So? Tell me about it."

Again Emily allowed herself a short period of reflection. "We'd always been so close, Jay and I. He led, I followed adoringly. All my childhood, even at school. He was the bright star lighting the way, I followed, trailing behind. I thought he could do no wrong." She felt Hori's glance as she paused. "Melbourne's a lovely place. Charlie, my niece, was a delight, and Chelsea was her usual, wonderfully supportive, self."

"But . . .?"

"Jay just didn't understand. I think he imagined it was only in my mind. A mental block that wouldn't allow me to play properly. He kept on sort of suggesting that I ought to give it a go. Just pick up the bow and let it happen. It was ghastly, because he made me feel like a coward when I refused to try. It all came to a head one evening, after I'd been in Melbourne about a week." She paused, her throat tightening even at the memory.

They had been discussing her future, not for the first time, but certainly in greater depth.

"It will happen, Emms," Jay had said with the buoyant confidence that she assumed came from never having faced failure. "Things will come right, gel. You wait and see."

"How can they?" Emily had replied bitterly. "I played the violin. Now I can't. That's it. There is nothing to gel."

Hori, bless him, was infinitely patient, aware that she was remembering what had transpired, and feeling the hurt all over again. "I've got a *Vuillaume*. It's a lovely instrument, early French and modeled after the Cremona school. My grandmother bought it for me when I turned professional, and it cost a fortune. Even now I can't bear to be parted from it. Anyway, evidently Jay had decided that all I needed was a push, to get playing again. So he legged it to my room, and returned with the violin. Then he went through the business of tuning it, and I sat there like an idiot, scarcely able to believe that he could make me go through with this farce. It was absolutely ghastly. Almost worse than the accident."

Even now, sitting in the truck beside Hori, she could remember her anguish, and tears were once more pricking behind her eyes.

"When he gave me the instrument I refused to take it. I tucked my hands into my armpits, and let the bow fall to the floor."

Hori grunted sympathetically. "So what did he do then?"

"Picked it up, and gave it back to me, as though I were three, and refusing to eat my spinach. He was patient in a fatherly way and so incredibly patronizing that I wanted to scream."

"Why didn't you?"

Emily tried to muster her reasons, in order to explain them. Possibly for herself, as well as for Hori. "Old habits die hard. I thought Jay could do no wrong. So, although I was still finding it hard to comb my hair with my dud hand, a part of me reasoned that perhaps he was right. I could do it, if I put my mind to it. He used the old clichés, like when we were children. You know the stuff. 'Of course you can do it. You're a Merivale,' and 'Nothing happens if you don't throw your heart over.' All equally awful."

"And what about his wife? Your sister-in-law?"

"Oh, Chelsea had nothing to do with this. She's absolutely super, but she's no match for Jay. But it was Chelsea who gave me the strength to tell him where he could shove his 'mind-over-matter' garbage. When I looked at her she was actually crying on my behalf. When I saw that tears were rolling down her cheeks, I could see him for the petty tyrant he was. He might have thought that he was helping me, but in retrospect I think all he was doing was hauling me back into line. His line."

"And so?"

"So I tried. I did all the right things, adjusted the chin rest, picked up the bow. And tried. The noise was absolutely hideous. Like a tomcat screeching. And I absolutely knew it didn't matter what I attempted, it was never going to be any less hideous. So I threw down the violin, and screamed at him that he was a monster, and didn't understand anything. That it was my hand that was crushed, not my head. Then I ran out of the room."

As she came to a halt in her narrative, Hori patted her shoulder sympathetically. "Insult added to injury, to find that your hero has feet of clay."

Emily sniffed hard, because even recalling her furious response was to place one hesitant toe on a slippery emotional slope. "But it had its plus side I suppose, because I was so furious with him, and anger's far more helpful than self-pity. And I was able to focus on him all that frustration and rage which was eating me up inside."

"But that doesn't explain how you happened to arrive here, among us."

Emily fished out a tissue and wiped her nose. "That was accidental, in a way. You see, the doctors had told me to keep away from the sun while my grafts were healing. Scar tissue can burn very easily. So that really ruled out the more obvious places, like the Bahamas, and the Mediterranean. And Chelsea had met this New Zealand woman, who ran a real estate business in Auckland. It was Marge who found me Bateman's bach."

"Marge Palmer. I remember her. The family used to holiday in Whangapouri."

Emily tucked away her tissue. "And that's the end of the story."

Hori turned the truck onto the approach road. "No it's not. That's the end of chapter one. Chapter two is waiting to be written."

Emily glanced at him.

"Maybe you're right." And she hoped her tone was sufficiently discouraging, without sounding rude. She turned her head to concentrate on the passing landscape, although out of the corner of her eye she noticed Hori look across at her, and smile.

The click-clicking of typewriter keys added a new dimension to life at the bach. Somehow it seemed more purposeful. Emily wanted to know what Bill was writing, but she was afraid that to ask might be misinterpreted as invading his personal space. In her mind there was an invisible barrier between the living room and the sunporch, not of exclusion, but of comprehension.

She showed her support with a constant supply of coffee, using that as an excuse to enter the little room. He always thanked her politely but automatically, on occasion not even pausing in his work. Sometimes the contents of the mugs were drunk, sometimes they remained untouched. Then she would quietly substitute one hot, brimful cup for the forgotten one.

She was very much in awe of his single-mindedness. It was reminiscent of Jay, and the ferocious concentration with which he applied himself when studying a new piece of music. Separated from her brother by both ocean and sufficient time to allow her anger at him to cool, she was impressed and a little envious.

But when Bill closed down the battered lid of the machine, and left the sunporch, he abandoned his writing persona and was once more her comfortable, easy companion.

"Do you think it's based on fact?" She glanced up from her attempt at letter writing as he emerged. Behind him the sunporch was filled with the dull purple of early evening shadow.

Bill rubbed the stiffness out of his neck muscles and stretched. "What?"

"The legend, about the bay. Or is it one of those tales that has grown in the telling? You know, conveniently trimmed to fit the geography."

Still caught up in the act of stretching, he yawned and shook himself. "Fact. I'm pretty sure. This isn't stuff embellished over the centuries. For one thing, it's too recent."

"Really?"

"Why do you ask?" He crossed to the hearth and warmed his hands.

She gathered together her letter-kit and began to lay the table, preparatory to the evening meal.

"I keep thinking about what happened to the lovers."

"Then there must be some sort of thought transference going on. I'm trying to write about them."

"You are?" She nearly dropped the cutlery in surprise. All afternoon her thoughts had returned, ping-pong style, to Te Manawanui and Waikura. "Do you mean just as a legend?"

He turned around so the glowing logs could warm his back. "Not just as the legend. I'm using it as an allegory."

"How? What's it supposed to illustrate?"

"Inevitability."

"I see." But actually she had no idea. She gathered up two water glasses and the salt and pepper, while she worked on that angle of the Maori legend. Inevitability. "Do you mean that they had no choice? Once they'd fallen in love?"

"In a way."

He sat down in his armchair. Mendelssohn, the opportunist, immediately took advantage of the available lap, then stood on his hind legs and butted his nose against Bill's chin.

"But do you believe that? All the business about our futures being laid out before us? 'The fault, dear Brutus, lies not in ourselves, but in our stars . . .' and so on?"

"Not entirely."

Emily tickled the cat behind his ears. "I think it's a convenient excuse for not taking responsibility for your actions."

"I'm not sure that's what Shakespeare had in mind. It's not what I intend, anyway."

"Then tell me what you're writing about."

"I have this idea to write a parallel story. One strand of it will deal with the legend. Alongside that I've got a hero who's fought with his own, personal demons and is climbing back to the surface. hope that the reader will see the connecting threads."

Emily wasn't sure that she would see them, but to suggest such a notion might indicate that she was too thick, or that the idea was too erudite for the average reader. Clearly it was easier not to pursue this line of thought.

"Tell me about your hero."

Bill ran a gentle hand the length of Mendelssohn's long, white belly. "I'm basing him on Garth."

"Isn't the AIDS side of things rather overdone? I mean, there have been so many books about it. And films and television programs." When Bill remained silent she hurried on. "I do appreciate that he was very important to you, of course."

Perhaps it was part of the process of mourning. Maybe he thought that writing it all down would help.

"That's why I want to include the legend. The inevitability doesn't arise from his death. Or their deaths. It deals with how, once a certain decision is taken, or a certain event occurs, subsequent actions are unavoidable."

This she did understand. It was tied up with looking before you leaped, thinking out the consequences of your decisions. Having absorbed his meaning, she returned to the legend.

"So you think that they died, Te Manawanui and Waikura? You don't believe they escaped?"

"I have absolutely no idea."

She looked at him doubtfully. "But won't that affect how your story finishes? Or will you just make up the end?"

"Possibly. Without evidence, what else can one do? Everything has to be conjecture."

A sudden thought hit Emily. "We could investigate."

"What?"

"Investigate. Put on our Sherlock Holmes hats and try to find out what happened. Maybe solve the mystery. Do you know if anybody has done that, in the past? Had a go at delving?"

Bill's response reflected his habitual caution. "Probably not. Why would they?"

Emily thought why not, but she held her tongue. Caught up with her idea, she swept aside his reluctance. "Don't you see, we can gather together what's actually known to be true, and start from there. Maybe retrace the path they took."

Bill leaned back and closed his eyes, as if by doing so he could divorce himself from her enthusiasm. "What role in this whodunit am I expected to play? Hercule Poirot?"

"Of course not. You're the wrong shape. You're more like . . . like Inspector Alleyn. And that's appropriate, because he was created by Ngaio Marsh, and she came from New Zealand."

"Great."

She eyed him. "You're not going to be a wet blanket, are you?"

"That depends upon what you want me to do. Remember, I might write fiction, but I'm not into mysteries."

Really, when she thought about it, all she wanted was for him to share some of her pleasure.

"Just a bit of support. Don't you think it would be fun?"

He opened his eyes and squinted at her. "It might be. It would certainly give some purpose to the daily walk."

"And help you come up with a rational conclusion to your story. Even if we finish totally empty-handed, at least we'll have eliminated certain possibilities." She paused expectantly. "Bill?"

His eyes were closed again. "What?"

"You don't feel like a walk to the store, do you?" She used her pleading tone. "Perhaps we could ask Hori to go over it all again, while we write down the basic ingredients. Then we'd have the core, for our investigation."

"Absolutely nothing short of nuclear war will persuade me to interrupt Hori's evening meal."

Bill spoke so abruptly that Mendelssohn took offense and jumped hurriedly off his knee. The cat sat down by the fire and washed himself with short, angry licks while the black tip of his tail informed the humans of his annoyance.

"Sorry." Emily felt an unexpected frisson of satisfaction at the thought of their sharing a common purpose. "I suppose tomorrow morning will be soon enough. Would you like me to waken you?"

⚘

But, as it happened, it was Kaffi, and not Hori who provided the Whangapouri sleuths with their first clue.

Bill had taken the aluminum dinghy out to inspect his set lines when Kaffi appeared with a bag of large, fat mussels. They would become the basis for Emily's and Bill's evening meal, and in exchange Emily offered her an assortment of vegetables and some sausages. Then the girl settled down at the table to read.

Emily made her a plate of hot, buttered toast, spread with Vegemite. "Kaffi?" The child looked up. "You remember when I met you the first time?"

"Yeah."

"You were washing your clothes, in the brook."

"Yeah."

"Well, I was simply wondering, why? Why there? The brook that runs down to the cove is much closer to your home than where I found you."

"Yeah." Kaffi tucked into another slice of toast. Emily waited expectantly until she had swallowed her mouthful. "That stream comes dirty, when it rains."

"What do you mean, 'comes dirty?'"

Clearly Kaffi was anxious to return to the tale of *Robert and the Fly-Away Island.* "It's okay while it's sunny. But after we have rain the water turns all red. From the dirt."

Something in Emily's brain went click, as if a light had been switched on. The lovers met where the stream changed color. Heneti had mentioned that her grandson had found the place.

"Later, when you've finished reading, will you take me there?"

"You mean climb right up the hill?" Kaffi employed her special look which she reserved exclusively for Emily. It was that "there-she-goes-again, busy-being-stupid" look.

"Yes. To the place where the brooks meet."

Kaffi shrugged. "Okay."

And she buried her nose again in the adventures of Robert.

The ascent was far steeper than Emily had anticipated. She began to appreciate the mild scorn Kaffi had evinced. They climbed to the headland, from which she could see Bill in the dinghy, almost having reached the shore. Then they turned north, skirting the thicket of dense bush that filled the gully, pushing their way through scattered flax and *manuka* shrubs, avoiding gorse bushes with their ferocious thorns. Then there was a rocky outcrop to be tackled, and the primitive path dropped again toward the cove that housed the Morrison's shack. The cove toward which, if she'd understood correctly, Te Manawanui and his beloved had been heading on that particular night.

Kaffi led the way through another thicket of bushland. This copse had thick-trunked growth of many centuries. Clearly it must have escaped the torches of the early settlers, when they cleared the land for grazing. It was like entering another world, a still, green world of *pungas*, moisture underfoot, countless mosses and ferns, and tiny, darting brown birds.

Kaffi flopped down on some ancient, knotted roots at a convergence of two small streams. Emily, trying hard to control her breathing, squatted beside her.

"It looks clear today," Kaffi explained, "But one time me and John Wayne come up here, when we'd had a storm, and this side was all red. Like that river in the Moses story, turned to blood? I read it in school, and I told John Wayne about it."

Actually, the small tributary that she indicated wasn't entirely clear today. Closer inspection showed that there was quite a deposit of rich, terra cotta sediment. It was easy to see that any precipitation would stir up that sediment, along with more clay from higher in the hills. In rainy times the contrast between the crystal clarity of these waters and the mud flow must be startling.

"You know the story of Te Manawanui?" Emily asked.

"Some."

"Well, I'm pretty sure that this is where he and Waikura met. The legend says 'where the stream changes color.' How frightened the poor girl must have been, having to evade all those prying eyes, to sneak away to meet her lover. It would have been easier for the Te Manawanui, of course, because at first he could come and go when he chose. When Kui told me the story she said that, once they'd been forbidden to see each other, they tried to meet twice before they finally succeeded. Just think, Kaffi, of having to climb up the path we've just climbed, in the darkness . . ."

"Really spooky."

"And sitting here, waiting and hoping. Because the chief had set a spy to watch his son."

Kaffi considered. "I'd be frightened, ay."

"Me too. I'm not sure that I'm made of the right stuff to be a heroine. In the legend she left him a sign, to show that she'd been there. Leaves, laid out in a pattern."

Kaffi got to her feet and started to gather a handful of large, silver-backed leaves.

"She'd use *rangiora*, because that way he could see them in the dark, ay." She arranged them on a patch of damp grass, laying them carefully in a circle with the blotting-paper underside of each leaf uppermost. "Like that."

"Perfect." Emily smiled. "I can see you'd make a wonderful heroine. One day, when you're grown up, you'll have to bring your lover here, and leave a message for him."

Kaffi's look was one of total scorn. "I'm never going to have a boyfriend. Boys are dumb. I'm going to live with me dad, when I grow up."

Emily laughed as she stood and brushed some leaf-mold from her knees.

"I'd not bet on it. Attitudes have a habit of changing, and you're going to be a knock out, one of these days." She took the girl's hand in her own. "Let's go and see your mum."

SIXTEEN

Bill leaned back in his chair, not too far, because it was somewhat decrepit and the legs protested warningly if he put too much stress on them. Most of the furniture in the place was suitable only for firewood. His gaze follow the flight of black-backed gulls, as they wheeled and turned against the silver-gray sky. He could hear their raucous screams as they circled.

Emily had come closer to the truth than she knew when she suggested that, in writing about Garth's death, Bill was facing old skeletons. And not just Garth's death. There was Jaime's to consider, too.

He was conscious of Emily's delicacy in not presuming upon their relationship. Even when absorbed in his writing, in the business of finding the very word that fitted, he could pause and reflect upon her determination not to rock his particular, creative boat. And he appreciated it. He was also pretty sure that such behavior did not come automatically, but took effort on her part. It reminded him of a song they'd sung at church school, in the days when his mother had slicked down his hair with water and sent him off to join the congregation of kids looking awkward in their unfamiliar Sunday best. Something about Jesus bidding him to shine, which he'd done anyway, after all that face-polishing. He couldn't remember the rest, apart from the final lines.

You in your small corner
And I in mine.

At the time he'd wondered why Jesus would expect you to be in the corner, which was generally connected with bad behavior in Mrs. Jessop's kindergarten class, but perhaps Jesus assumed you were always in trouble.

Now he could associate the words with space, personal space, which was exactly what Emily was affording him. He thought that in doing so she must have grown, to some extent. He'd noticed the small warning signs when she'd been about to flare up, and had quickly put a lid on her temper. That time in the tea shop, for one. It had been touch and go, that afternoon. He found her consideration endearing, which was why he was prepared to be generous over this detective business. It seemed only fair that he should compromise in certain matters as well.

He had no real objection to their amateur sleuthing, apart from the time it might take him away from his typewriter. Once in full flow, he found any interruption annoying. But it did make sense, and any facts that added to their understanding of the legend might well prove worthwhile. For himself, he thought they'd get nowhere and the whole exercise would probably waste precious writing hours. He could add to that his fear that Emily might be disappointed. After all, the whole thing was separated from them by a couple of hundred years. Distance allowed fiction to color things, age made the edges blurry and unclear.

Unlike the Kaffi Morrison family, Emily's other cause, which was only too immediate.

He had to admit that Kaffi was a nice kid, well mannered and not given to intruding upon him, but he still thought that Emily was intrinsically wrong. Without her spelling it out, he was pretty sure that things over the headland were desperate. It was only a matter of time before she started dragging him into this crusade, as well. After all, her lease on Bateman's bach had only seven weeks to run. If the mythical father hadn't materialized out of the blue, what then? No doubt she'd expect him to pick up the baton. He knew that this reluctance to become involved was his problem, and that in refusing to consider himself in the role of champion he was surrendering to yesterday's baggage. However acknowledging this fact, and acting upon it, were poles apart.

As he sat at his typewriter, he could hear the pair of them behind him. Their voices penetrated the door, not loudly, but enough to remind him that they were there. They were seated at the living room table, and he thought Emily was explaining fractions. Words like "portions of a pie," and "quarters" filtered through. He could remember learning about fractions from Mr. Gough Every time Mr. Gough barked he, Billy, had jumped as though stuck with a pin. That was one advantage in leaving Alexandria. He'd been spared another year of Mr. Gough's math.

And thinking of Cape Cod brought him neatly around, full circle, to Garth and his writing.

He dragged his thoughts back to the present, which meant Emily and this damned detective work. After lunch he guessed he should abandon the written word, walk to the store and talk with Kui and the Webbers. Fulfill his part of the bargain.

❧

"Bill, sit still."

"I can't. I'm nervous."

Emily flashed what he assumed she thought to be a reassuring smile. "Oh ye of little faith. I've cut loads of people's hair."

"But never beards."

She stood back and considered him. "No, not many of us had beards at the Meinhardt. They were rather frowned upon, because they got in the way of your bow."

Bill wondered how on earth he had allowed himself to be talked into this. Here he was, sitting on a kitchen chair like some half-wit, with a towel of sorts draped over his shoulders and Emily dancing about with a pair of scissors that looked positively lethal.

"Can I go back on this? If I promise to drive into town tomorrow, and have a trim?"

"Coward. Of course you can't. I'd take it as a personal affront. Now sit still, or I'll carve a chunk out of your ear by accident."

He had to admit that he was in need of a hair cut and his beard, which he'd allowed to grow during his time at Whangapouri, was decidedly shaggy. Nonetheless . . .

"Bill."

She seemed quite professional, in the way she approached the job in hand. A clump of hair fell to the ground. He had grown quite attached to that particular lock.

"Tell me how you got on with the Webbers." She stopped to cast him an inquiring look. "You did go, didn't you?"

He was about to nod, then froze. Moving could be perilous.

"Uh huh, but they hadn't a great deal more to add. The problem is that, apart from Kui, none of the Maori who live here these days belongs to the Ngati Tarapunga tribe, and Te Manawanui's people, the Ngati Kura, have been absorbed into other tribes. And tales can get embellished over the years, in the telling."

"Don't talk for a minute, while I trim around your ear." She concentrated on that as Bill stayed obediently still.

When she returned to cutting excess growth from around his collar line he felt safe to say, "It may not be relevant at all, but Heneti did mention something about the headland."

"You mean the one to the north?"

"Yes."

"Up high or at sea level, to do with the actual rocks?"

"High, in this case."

"Oh." She paused, clearly a bit disappointed by his reply. "Don't you think the area where they disappeared is integral to the mystery?"

"Obviously. But are you prepared to wade and swim in that water, at this time of year?"

"Have you tried climbing over the rocks? Ever?"

She'd countered with another question, a habit he'd always found infuriating in JoBeth. In Emily, surprisingly enough, it was rather charming.

"No." He made sure that his meaning could not be misinterpreted. "And I don't intend to now. I've seen how the waves slap against that rock face."

"Dangerous?"

"Suicidal."

She stood back to admire her handiwork. Bill wished that there were a mirror, so that he could monitor progress.

"And what about the headland? Are you going to share what Heneti told you?"

"No. I'm going to show you. We'll walk up there tomorrow."

"Tomorrow I thought I'd ..." She bit back what she was about to say. "Would it be all right if we went another time?"

He shrugged, and then regretted it as cold steel came into intimate contact with his chin. "Hey! You'll draw blood."

"Then keep still." She used the sort of voice generally employed by adults addressing young children. "And if you're very good, Emily will buy you a lolly next time she's at the store."

Not for the first time he wondered whether he'd actually lost his sanity. Perhaps this was the final proof that he was, indeed, a madman. Then he watched Emily's concentration as she stood back again to check that her work wasn't lopsided, a slight smile hovering about her mouth, and decided that madness, in certain circumstances, might not be such a terrible fate.

❦

One of the loveliest things about Kaffi was her enthusiasm. The excitement she had displayed when the fruits of the library visit were revealed must have warmed the iciest heart. Emily would have liked to burst into the sunroom and say, "Look at this, Bill. This is why I haven't rung the Welfare department. Just watch her face." But Bill was writing, and that was sacrosanct. So she just hugged to herself the delight of watching Kaffi unpack the books, handling each volume with the care that might have been accorded a piece of Dresden china. Emily had also bought exercise books, and a supply of pencils and erasers. Kaffi might have entered paradise.

And, surprisingly, Emily discovered that the teaching part was easier than she had dared hope. Kaffi was like a sponge. She soaked up all that there was to learn and demanded more. It was a far cry from summer school at the Meinhardt. At that time an excess of energy was concentrated in her obsession with Marco, and whether he found the other stipendiary teacher attractive. Jealousy, even in minute quantities, diffused the teaching effort quite successfully. Sex negated the rest.

But with just the two of them seated at the table, and Kaffi falling over herself in her desire to learn, the process became one of unalloyed pleasure. They finished the morning with mutual regret.

"I'd better get home, ay."

"You can take the book, if you like."

Kaffi looked with longing at *Elementary Arithmetic*. She had already covered two pages in the exercise book with carefully set out columns of figures. "Better not. Might get ripped. I'll come tomorrow, ay."

Because their relationship was grounded on a strong foundation of mutual respect, there was no longer a need for Emily to prevaricate. "While I was in town I bought some special shampoo. I thought it might be sensible to wash everybody's hair."

Kaffi, as was her habit, put her head to one side, resembling a small, wise bird. She didn't ask what sort of special shampoo. "Okay. I'll help, too. But you can do John Wayne's."

Emily awoke in the middle of the night and sat bolt upright in her bed. Outside it sounded as though the Mongolian hordes had descended upon Whangapouri in their thousands. It took her less than a second to register that it was wind gusts shaking the bach, and not an invading army. The gale penetrated every crack in the weatherboarding, rattled the window frames and howled down the chimney.

Was Bill awake? It must have disturbed his slumber, as well. Probably he, too, was sitting up in bed. It might well sound even louder in the sunroom, with all that glass. Mendelssohn appeared to take the storm in his stride. He'd been sleeping; now he rolled over and stretched, as if showing scorn that this stupid human should find the elements cause for alarm.

"You're right, chum. No reason to panic."

And anyway, she reflected, lying down again and drawing the quilt up to her chin, what on earth could she do, what could Bill do come to that, if the very cottage saw fit to fall down about them? That was clearly Mendelssohn's view. He turned around twice in the time-honored manner and resettled himself. The wind was making too much of a racket for her to hear him, but she knew that he was purring, because the vibrations traveled to her through the fabric. It was a very reassuring feeling.

As she was ascending the track that led to the Morrisons' the next morning she thought to question how last night's squall had affected that frail dwelling. At least Bateman's bach was of sturdy construction. The efforts of the weather gods had wrought very little damage that the naked eye could discern. Not so the rest of the bay, however. Daylight had revealed the fruits of the storm littered about the beach and hillside, branches torn away and flung at random, logs cast ashore and deposited high on the sand. Great ribbons of kelp lay rubbery and dark above the old high-tide line.

"We got a hole in the roof. The wind blew a branch down. We got water all over the bed."

Kaffi's first words of greeting answered her fears. The girl met her several hundred yards along the track.

"How horrible. What did you do?"

Kaffi walked several steps upside down, on her hands. Her skirt flopped down, revealing a pair of the new panties Emily had bought her. "We shoved the bed across, me and Mum. Then we got some buckets for under the holes. I put the sheets out to dry, ay."

"Very sensible."

Kaffi brushed soil from her hands. "You got the shampoo?"

"Yes."

"They used it at school, once. All the kids, all the teachers. Everybody. For nits, ay."

"Yes." What else could she say? It was scarcely appropriate to enter into a treatise about how head lice could appear on the cleanest heads, belonging to the most high-born in the land. Kaffi would see straight through such a statement.

But Kaffi took things as she found them. "I'm glad you got it. Nits make you itch, ay."

Upon inspection the damage to the roof proved to be worse than Emily had feared. The whole sheet of corrugated iron was corroded and flimsy. Light filtered through in many more places than just those penetrated by the offending branch.

"Me dad was going to mend it. He got the sheet and that. It's out the back."

She tossed up which took priority, leaky roof or hair. Clearly hair could wait.

"Show me, Kaffi."

But one look at that slab of metal and Emily knew that reconstruction on this scale was truly beyond her efforts. The Morrisons would require more professional, or at least stronger, hands. Reluctantly she returned to her original purpose for the day.

To begin with, the stuff she'd bought at the chemist shop smelled foul. She arrived at the Morrisons' to discover that Kaffi had done her part, the family was assembled, there were towels and an assortment of gap-toothed combs available for inspection. The solitary hairbrush lying alongside had also lost a goodly percentage of its tufts. She set the girl to work with newly acquired disinfectant, sterilizing this motley collection.

Ani and Tama were seated docilely on the edge of the bed looking a little confused, while John Wayne had clearly been instructed to prevent their escape. Inevitably Winnie was nursing the baby, but she looked up with quite a degree of animation, and there was more warmth in her greeting than at any time hitherto. Gary Cooper did not pause in his breakfast, but he rolled an interested eye at Emily's approach.

The instructions on the box said that the shampoo must be left on each head for a full fifteen minutes. They worked together, starting with Winnie, once the baby had been placed safely on the bed. Emily wet the hair, Kaffi squeezed the tube of paste. Together they created a lather, and Winnie did precisely as she was told. When, at last, she was upright Emily drew the mass of her soap-filled hair into a cock's-comb high on her head.

She handed the young mother a mirror, so that she could enjoy the sight of herself. "There you are. You look just like a Kewpi doll. Do you think you could help by taking off the children's pullovers, when we ask?"

Tama was next, and then Ani. They had watched with wide-eyed wonder as their mother was treated, and in turn offered very little resistance. But John Wayne was another matter. He sat on the edge of the bed, his legs swinging, looking through the open door into the bathroom. He observed his siblings being transformed into white-headed oddities, and even giggled a couple of times. He saw how Gary Cooper, held carefully under Emily's arm so that the shampoo would not sting his eyes, allowed his hair to be washed. That, evidently, was a different matter.

"Okay, John Wayne. Your turn." Emily straightened up to ease her back. "Can you turn down your collar, so that we don't get it wet?"

John Wayne sat very still and shook his head.

"Come on! You're the eldest. You have to show the others how grown up you are."

He lowered his eyes but did not budge.

"He doesn't like having his hair washed." Kaffi was certainly stating the obvious. "Our dad has to do it. Or threaten to lick him."

If one head remained untreated it might very well re-infest the household. All Emily's efforts would be in vain.

"I'm certainly not going to lick . . . beat you, John Wayne. But we do need to shampoo you, too. Please."

Again the boy shook his head. His lower lip protruded sullenly and he knotted his fingers together in tight, nervous patterns.

Emily wondered what on earth she could do. He wasn't large, but she could scarcely gather him up under her arm in the way that she'd held the baby. She compromised, for the moment.

"Kaffi, let's do your hair next, and mine. Perhaps John Wayne will see that there's nothing to be worried about."

The glance Kaffi cast her brother was one of pure scorn. She slipped out of her sweater and thrust her slender neck over the basin. The action reminded Emily, briefly, of Anne Boleyn's head, extended across the chopping block. And, like that ill-fated woman, she maintained her dignity with true nobility as Emily rubbed the bad-smelling lotion into her scalp. Her look, when she was again upright, was triumphant. Completely spoiling the image of nobility, she stuck out her tongue at her brother and crossed her eyes. Emily pretended not to see, but she did think that this was not the behavior likely to improve her chances of getting the eldest Morrison to the hand basin.

She had not planned to wash her own hair today. She'd thought to wait until Bill was safely out of the bach, and then have a very private session in the bathroom. However, for the greater good she refilled the bowl, removed her own pullover and allowed Kaffi to pour a stream of water over her head, then to rub in the shampoo. Kaffi was nothing if not thorough. Emily felt as though her eyes had been glued shut far longer than the actual few minutes that the operation required. Perhaps John Wayne had a point.

When she, too, resembled a Kewpi doll, she turned back to the final member of the party. "Okay. Your turn, John Wayne."

The boy twisted his head away and scrunched his eyes tightly shut, as if by avoiding eye contact he was safe from persecution.

Emily turned for help to his mother, aware that she was probably wasting her breath. "Winnie, could you ask him to come, please?"

Winnie was rocking the baby back and forth, crooning quietly to him. She looked up, and then at her firstborn. "Doesn't listen to me."

Now was clearly the moment of last resort, when desperation played its part. A technique perfected at the Meinhardt when some difficult brat had refused to come into line. As ever. You employed bribery.

Emily spoke very quietly, so that her voice would not carry. "Kaffi, dear. What is John Wayne's specially favorite food, or a particular thing that he likes to do? Can you tell me?"

Quick as ever to follow her drift, Kaffi replied, "He loves to go out in the boat with our dad. Set the lines and that. Our dad promises to let him go fishing."

Ouch. Not exactly within her orbit, but . . . dare she?

Desperation produced the answer. The thought of the last hour and a half being wasted, of that horrible smell which invaded her nostrils and the physical effort involved, provided ample motivation.

She raised her voice. "John Wayne, my friend . . . the person who shares my house is a fisherman. If you let us wash your hair, perhaps he would take you out with him. Would you like that?"

John Wayne opened his eyes again and stared at her. "Promise?"

She took a deep breath and resolved to cross this bridge when she came to it. "Promise." And, as a vow more to herself than to the boy, "Cross my heart and hope to die."

John Wayne didn't speak, but he slid off the bed and tugged his sweater over his head.

The walk to and from the Morrisons' home always afforded Emily the opportunity for contemplation. For a good deal of this time, on most days, she thought about Bill, because the more she came to know him, the more she liked him. The liking was tinged with an increasingly large dollop of regret. It seemed such a waste to the female half of the population that so engaging a man should be the exclusive property of other guys. He looked fantastic with his hair and beard neatly trimmed. It had been a stroke of genius to buy that pair of barbers' scissors. And there wasn't a hint of a weak chin lurking under those whiskers. In fact, he'd mentioned that the beard was only as old as his time in Whangapouri.

But today on the homeward journey, his physical features and sexual proclivity were a long way down on her list of priorities. Somehow, in a really annoying way, she'd been maneuvered by circumstances into making a promise that was going to take some fulfilling. Impossible, if left to her own devices. She'd never ventured out in a fishing dinghy in her life. And even more pressing was the matter of the Morrisons' roof.

She knew that Bill was going to resist her request for help. He would tell her to call the Welfare people, and he was right. Common sense dictated that she should, but stubbornness would not allow her to do so. Maybe, with hindsight, she should have contacted them originally, but not now. They'd come a long way together, she and the Morrisons. Kaffi was having lessons, and she had plans for the other children, because one of her borrowed books spelled out the importance of stimulating mental growth in small children. As if common sense didn't tell you that. And there was John Wayne to consider. He needed help too, and she'd made him a promise, a commitment that was very nearly as binding as her one to Kaffi.

Which brought her thoughts neatly back to Bill again. Her hopes, and the fulfillment of that promise, rested fair and square with him. She practiced various opening gambits, saying them aloud for the benefit of her ears, so they could play their part as arbiters.

Clearly it would be sensible to start with a disclaimer. "Bill, I know that you're not interested in the Morrisons, but . . ." No, that sounded apologetic at the start.

She might appeal to his better nature. "Bill, you're such a kind person, and the Morrisons have this gigantic hole . . ."

And, if that were not enough, while he was reeling from all this, she might add, "Oh, and by the way, I promised John Wayne that you'd take him out in the boat with you. When you tend your set lines." That, undoubtedly, would be the clincher.

It didn't sound at all convincing. In fact, it sounded extremely lame, but she was running out of possibilities, and the bach was in sight. She could see the roof and the slender column of smoke rising from the chimney. She'd be home within ten minutes. And she was as far from a solution as when she'd left the Morrisons. She cursed her particular good fairy, that she hadn't been blessed with the gift of tongues.

SEVENTEEN

ill used his remote voice which really got to Emily. The debate had started badly. "You've read Pope. Have you forgotten about angels fearing to tread?"

"Are you saying I'm one of the fools who rush in?" She was a great deal crosser than she'd intended, but she'd tried all her carefully rehearsed phrases and got nowhere. Bill had simply retreated behind his book and looked inaccessible. Even though there was no reason for her to expect otherwise, she found his refusal hurtful, and it was becoming personal. He had never really departed from his original stance but, because she tried so hard to seek his approval and support, it was like frequent slaps in her face. She was even further away from mentioning John Wayne and the fishing trip. Things had progressed only as far as the Morrisons' roof. It was that reference to Pope that ignited her temper. And after all, she'd held it in check a long time, which probably provided additional fuel.

"That is what you mean, isn't it. That I'm a fool, because I care about them."

"You figure it out." He carefully turned the page of his book.

"Then you're bloody well wrong." She spoke through gritted teeth, trying to keep the bubbling anger under control. "And if you would only look at this family you'd realize how much they need help."

"I've never doubted that they need help. My point is that you're not necessarily the right person to provide it." His eyes scanned the page. "And if it's all so catastrophic you're being even more irresponsible, not informing the Welfare people. As I said, they're trained for these situations. They can handle everything with the subtlety you lack. And provide long-term assistance."

"Subtlety?" Emily latched onto that word, preferring to ignore the rest of his response. In other places, at other times, she would have let rip at this moment. Even now she was sorely tempted to take his wretched book and hurl it across the room. She thought of that little pot of strawberry jam, back in the tea shop. How close he had been to having preserves all over his face. How close he was, right now, to something similar. Sanctimonious prig. Goodness only knew what she'd found to like about him, only yesterday, only this morning.

"Listen . . ."

He did look up but, although he wasn't the sighing sort, his body language spoke more eloquently than words.

Emily was not to be deterred. "Could we go through this again? Slowly? I want you to understand why I feel so strongly."

The volume was half-closed, his long, slender fingers lay across the cover. One, she noticed with irritation, kept his place. She leaned over and practically snatched the book, then placed it on the table out of reach.

"Your full attention?"

She thought she had it. She sat down with her elbows on the table and fiddled with his bookmark to give her temper time to simmer down, and to formulate her justifications. It seemed at this moment that only the inadequate power of her oratory lay between that leaking roof and Bill's willingness to help the Morrisons. If only she could come up with the perfect combination of nicely balanced arguments.

"Firstly, the roof is awful. We dragged the bed well clear of the worst holes, but now there's no space for anything else. If I can borrow your word, the way they were living was close to catastrophic. I did think about finding somebody in the town who would do the repairs, but you know jolly well they're terrified of the Welfare people. And they'd be bound to think I was about to hand them over to the authorities. I gather, from what Kaffi has said, that when Matu spirited them out of the tribe originally, it was to avoid having the little ones taken into care."

"Doesn't that tell you something?"

Bill glanced with some longing across at his book. *The Golden Bough* by Frazer, she noticed irrelevantly. Trust him to be buried in ancient lore, when she was fighting the battles of today.

"And what about when you're not here?" he continued. "Have you considered that? In the long run they'd probably be better off in care. At least eat decent meals. And get the older kids into some sort of school."

"Perhaps." Emily sighed, trying to be fair. "Probably. I have thought about that side of things, too. Or that they might return to the tribe. I've explained to you how Winnie is, but you should see how much effort she's been putting into things lately. She really worked hard today, when we . . ." She stopped. The hair washing saga was better left unmentioned. He might regard it as additional proof of his argument. "And John Wayne. He's trying, too. And you know enough of Kaffi to appreciate what a bright little button she is. For her sake alone I'd hate the family to be broken up. According to her, when their father was home Winnie could cope quite well. It seems quite likely, because recently her housekeeping has improved enormously."

"Only because you're making yourself into their slave. When you're not playing at being Lady Bountiful."

"Playing at . . . ?"

He shrugged, no more than a very slight raising of the shoulders. "Sure. Dispensing largesse."

Largesse. The word hung in the air, brimful of offensive connotations. She thought of all the cleaning, the scrubbing and scouring, that foul-smelling nit shampoo, and she could have strangled him. But though an all-out battle topped off by a session of screaming might be more satisfying to her, it would certainly not conclude with a patched-up roof for the Morrisons.

Motivated by her strength of purpose, Emily swallowed hard and started again. "Just listen to the facts. There are five children in that shack, Bill. We know their father disappeared at least three months ago. They were without electricity for several weeks, and ate *pipis* and sea urchins and anything else they could scavenge. And yet they survived, almost entirely because one small girl worked her tail off, caring for them as best she could. Surely that tells you something. And yet your only response is that I should inform the authorities, so the family can be institutionalized."

She put a lot into that speech, partly because it meant a great deal to her, but there was also just a hint of the actress, the performer doing her utmost to sway the audience. Surely he would be moved. Surely he would share her admiration of Kaffi, acknowledge the improvements Emily had wrought, and have pity on the family. Even if cool judgment were on his side, he must be able to see it all through her eyes. She sought for some response in his face, but even the neatly trimmed beard hid too much. The only access to his thoughts was through his eyes, and it seemed that he deliberately avoided looking her way.

She paused for the epilogue, feeling the drama almost as much as she felt compassion for the Morrisons. She temporarily abandoned the less pressing business of John Wayne's bribe, in favor of prioritization.

"Bill, all I'm asking you to do is come and look. Not get involved you understand, just look. The sheet of corrugated iron is already there because Matu, their father, was going to mend the roof. And the correct nails, and a ladder. But I know I can't manhandle a whole sheet. That's why I need you . . ." mentally crossing her fingers, " . . . and there are no other strings attached."

⚛

Somewhere, deep inside, Bill felt a wrenching of his soul. He refused to accept that fear was the sole motivating force behind his reasoning, but he had to acknowledge that it existed. He glanced briefly at Emily's imploring face, all eyes and eagerness. It would be easy enough to agree. Half a day's work probably, replacing an eroded section of roofing. And yet, the same old fear held him back. Getting involved with this family would mean opening too much of himself, allowing his vulnerable side to be exposed. It was far easier to retreat behind the old barriers.

His reluctance to get involved was a habit developed over so many years that it was now finely honed. Even agreeing to share the bach with Emily had chipped away at the edges of his shield. "Run," said his bolt mechanism. "You're getting too close. And close can be spelled as pain."

"No." He was careful not to meet her eyes. He knew that, if he did, his resolution might fail him. "I won't meddle. It would be better all around for them to be taken into care, and if you really feel anything for the kids, you'd be the one to make the call. Now, may I have my book?"

At that moment the taut elastic of Emily's tightly reined emotions snapped.

"Oh, you're so bloody remote! So sure of yourself and holier than thou! I hate you, you screaming pouf."

She seized his book from the table and hurled it out the open door in a long, arcing spin. It landed with a resounding splash in a large puddle.

That did it. "Dammit, Emily! That was my father's copy."

"Oh, dear. Forgive me." The sarcasm in her voice was as heavy as rain-laden cloud. "So much more important, burying yourself in the past, isn't it? So much safer. Instead of allowing the present to intrude, or perhaps considering somebody other than yourself."

Then she burst into tears.

※

When they met again, some hours later, Emily's fiery temper had abated. It was like that, a quick conflagration which evaporated as speedily as it had flared. A solitary walk down the beach to gather driftwood had done wonders. She was even prepared to accept that he might be right. For all the wrong reasons of course, but perhaps he did have a point.

He had identified the Achilles heel of the situation, her fear that what she had achieved was no more than an exercise in shoring up. Perhaps the family would be better off elsewhere. After all, she would be leaving in a few weeks and who could foretell what was in the future. The whole process of reclamation might well be turned about. But when she thought of Kaffi's eager face, and tried to imagine Ani and Tama, that inseparable duo, maybe parted and taken into care, she knew that she'd returned full circle. She couldn't do it.

Nonetheless, she owed Bill an apology. There was no real excuse for allowing her anger to get the better of her. She opened the door rather gingerly, as if expecting him to leap out from behind it, cleaver in hand.

But he was sitting in the armchair, his armchair, still reading. Her display of temper might never have happened. It was as though today was like every other day. Mendelssohn was curled in blissful slumber on his knee. She cast a quick, careful glance at the book. The dye from the cover appeared to have developed an interesting pattern, a bit like watered silk.

She didn't beat about the bush. "I'm sorry I called you that."

He looked up. "What?"

"A screaming pouf. I really am sorry. It was only my temper; because you refused to help the Morrisons. I've absolutely nothing against gays."

Bill surveyed her dispassionately. "I'm not gay."

"You're not?"

"No. What made you think I was?"

Emily was stunned into silence. She could have quoted a catalogue of reasons, upon which many of her recent decisions had been based, most of all the decision to suggest he share the bach. Newly found tact, however, kept her from voicing this litany.

He repeated the question, as though unaware of her tongue-tied amazement.

She eyed him cautiously while she did some pretty nimble mental footwork. "I suppose . . . I suppose it was your telling me about Garth. I put two and two together."

"And they totaled five?"

"Obviously they did."

She hoped she hadn't offended him. He seemed serene enough, although so often there appeared to be a vestige of homophobia in the breast of the average, heterosexual male. Perhaps, having watched his friend die, Bill didn't share that phobia. Once more confused silence threatened to engulf her.

Finally she said, "Well. Good. That's nice." And wondered where they went from here.

All her reckoning had been based on his being gay. There was something ultra-safe about living with a bloke, knowing that he wasn't by so much as half an inch attracted to you. It allowed friendship to develop unencumbered by other issues. Friendship and trust. And now he was knocking down that set of skittles, which left . . . what?

Depressingly, it left one bald, indisputable fact. He didn't find her attractive. The thought was so immediate that temporarily it shoved the problem of the leaky roof well off center stage. Clearly, in these last weeks of their living together, casually going through the day-to-day minutiae of life, all he had sought of her was companionship. Which in one way was comforting, but still something of a put-down.

She selected her words with care. "Bill, what did you imagine I had in mind, when I invited you to share this place?"

He looked up from his book again. "I'm not sure that I thought a great deal about it. Not at the time, anyway. You caught me off guard."

"But later?"

"I thought you needed companionship. Support."

"And what did you have in mind?" She didn't dare as much as to glance at him.

"A period of consolidation. And maybe a chance to help you."

"And that was all?"

"I guess so. What did you expect?"

She shrugged slightly. "Just that. Nothing more."

She dumped the driftwood she'd collected onto the hearth and squatted to stack it tidily against the chimney. It needed several days, occasionally weeks, of drying out before it was ready to burn.

It was useful, having an excuse to kneel. She felt quite wobbly as though the earth, her solid underpinning, had given way beneath her. Perhaps it really was her scars that made her unattractive. That jagged line which crossed her left temple, still looking like an ugly zipper. Maybe he found it repulsive. Some people did, she knew. Some people sought perfection in themselves, and their partners. It had not occurred to her in the past, but perhaps Bill Thackeray was among that number.

Not that they were exactly partners. And then she became still, looking into the glowing core of the fire, a concentration of scarlet and orange. The heat made her wind-chilled cheeks feel burning hot. She was wrong. That was precisely the word to describe them. Equal in everything, which when you analyzed it, was why his refusal to come to her aid hurt so deeply. Partners stuck together, presented a united front.

A piece of black pine flared in the grate and a shower of sparks winged its way up the chimney. She knelt back on her heels, poignantly aware of Bill's presence behind her. He had returned to *The Golden Bough*, apparently oblivious to the turmoil this conversation was causing within her. "I'm not gay." Three easily uttered words, which, like the trumpets of the Israelites, brought down the walls of Jericho.

Whatever their status now, it meant an end to the easy camaraderie which had characterized things until today. In the future she would certainly be more careful that the bathroom door was fully shut, that she dressed with greater circumspection. Had he thought, all this time, that she was tossing out sexual lures? Which in a way was even more of a slight, because he had never, by one tiny move, indicated any interest.

Evidently that was what he wanted. Nothing remotely amorous. No hint of romantic entanglement. So it was up to her to maintain the status quo; keep everything on an even footing. She stood abruptly and discarded her jacket.

"I'll put on the kettle. Do you want tea or coffee?"

But, of course, it wasn't as easy as that. Emily found that she approached each small activity as if seeing it with eyes unblinkered for the first time. The small things became significant, like an occasional brush of hands as they washed the dishes, the accidental meeting of shoulder or knee. On such occasions she would glance at his face and look away quickly, before eye contact was made.

She did not reopen the matter of the Morrisons' roof, and mercifully the rainy spell appeared to have worked itself out which made repairs less urgent. Arguing their case before the row had been easy. Bill, after all, was her live-in partner. More than a mere lodger, because of all those hours of conversation, experiences shared and discussed. To solicit his help had seemed a natural step. But now things were different. He had subtly changed. Now he was ... what?

He was someone who she'd have fallen for in a big way, given any encouragement,. She, Emily Merivale, who had taken a vow of celibacy after the sad affair of Marco. Until this time she had packaged away any feeling for Bill which might have surfaced, behind a four-foot thick wall labeled "inappropriate behavior." Suddenly that barrier was as useless as the Iron Curtain.

She took note of things about him which, hitherto, she had almost subconsciously avoided registering. The clarity of his intelligent, gray eyes, the almost indecent thickness of his lashes. The set of his head and shoulders. The sort of lazy sexuality that she'd assumed to be the property of another chap. And particularly his hands, because musicians always looked at hands.

Most disturbingly, it gave rise to some very confused and confusing thoughts. She vividly recalled Kui telling her about the thermal area, around Rotorua. The old lady had instructed her to think of apple pie, and to imagine a crust on top of the pie. There, underneath, was all the boiling-hot apple. That was what it was like, the volcanic area.

Emily knew all about that apple pie comparison though because it described, very precisely, what was happening inside her. The thermal activity was bubbling and boiling away, accumulating pressure. And every small, involuntary gesture added to the intensity of the emotional built-up. She would picture his mouth, and the next small step was to contemplate his kissing her. She could recall the texture of his hair as she trimmed it, at the time when it was simply a companionable thing to do. Now, when she thought along those lines, it was to imagine running her fingers through his hair, pulling him down towards her, to her height . . . vows of celibacy were all very well, when there was nobody about for whom you felt the least attraction.

The only thing she didn't know, dared not even contemplate, was whether Bill knew for a micro-second how she felt. She was longing to share her feelings with him one minute, dreading his reaction, possibly his appalled amazement, the next. Or his scorn. Please God, she would pray silently then. Not his scorn, or a retreat into that awful remoteness.

The time it took her to walk across to the Morrisons' gave her ample opportunity to contemplate certain scenarios, small snatches of possible conversation. Perhaps she could say, "I really like you, Bill. How do you feel about me?" Appallingly naff. Try again. "Bill, what about a bit of a roll in the hay? Just for the fun of it?" Gross. Unworthy of him, or of her. Another attempt. "Bill, we're two adult, unencumbered people. Why not, er . . . give it a go?" Worse and worse, and maybe untrue, because she had no way of knowing whether or not he was married, or at least attached. But every essay in conjecture seemed to deteriorate into something farcical which made her wince. And always there was that fear that he might look at her, and say no. Or, horrors, go to bed with her only because he felt sorry for her. Pity, as the prime, motivating force. That would be worst of all.

When it came to sexuality animals had it made, she decided. They smelled right. They put out signals that indicated receptivity. Perhaps she should start wearing scent; whatever line of perfumes Hori's Store had in stock. Bill might read that as a hint.

EIGHTEEN

John Wayne took matters in hand. He arrived at daybreak two mornings later, before yesterday's ashes were cleared from the hearth, before, even, the first person had grabbed the bathroom. He appeared on the verandah of the bach in an overlarge but serviceable jacket, clutching a plastic pail. Subsequent investigation revealed that this held a tangled array of lines and lures, hooks and sinkers. It was the first time he had demonstrated anything approaching such enterprise, which indicated how important the right motivation could be. When subsequently she reflected upon the whole occasion, it gave Emily cause to hope.

Emily could never quite pinpoint John Wayne. Observing him impartially you saw a nice enough looking kid, with straight, fair hair, pale blue eyes, and skin so anemic that it was hard to imagine any Maori blood coursing in his veins. And yet Emily knew that the genetic pool of any one individual was a peculiar lucky-dip. She'd once holidayed in Tahiti, and noticed there enchanting children, Polynesian featured but blond and blue-eyed; this mix being the legacy of accommodating local maidens and lonely French sailors.

And by way of exemplification you could take Kaffi, who was as sharp as a barrelful of monkeys, but whose mother was, to employ the most charitable of terms, slow. John Wayne displayed the same slowness of wit. He was a good natured boy who, like Winnie, was happy enough to perform a simple task if asked. He responded to Kaffi's exasperation at his ineptitude with his customary, slack grin. He neither retorted, nor returned her needle-tongued criticism. Occasionally he was known to exhibit a simple, pig-headed stubbornness, witness the lead-up to this present scenario. Until now he had never displayed the least hint of self-motivation.

Emily might have preferred to orchestrate the timing a little better, because she was still wrestling with other matters considerably closer to the heart, but she had to admire the boy's initiative. The fact that he had located the correct bach was not lost on her, either. She opened the back door in response to his pounding, grabbing a jacket to cover her night attire. She knew, with a sinking heart, exactly why he was there.

"Come in, John Wayne. Have you had breakfast?"

He smiled his vacant smile and shook his head.

"Then take off your anorak and we'll get things started. We haven't eaten, either."

John Wayne showed every intention of bringing the pail, to which he was clearly devoted, indoors. It stank of fish-related gear.

"Perhaps you could leave your bucket out on the verandah?" He looked at her, his darting eyes a fair indication of what he was thinking, then at the pail. "I'm sure it will be quite safe there."

The sounds emanating from the bathroom informed her that Bill was showering. She wondered how he would react, emerging to discover that they were now three for breakfast. And, fast on the heels of that thought came the next. Somehow she needed to introduce the intelligence that this particular visitor fully expected to accompany him out in the aluminum dinghy. Looking rather ruefully at John Wayne, it occurred to her that, denied the promised reward for good behavior, he might decide to remain their guest into the foreseeable future.

"Here's a magazine, John Wayne. You sit at the table and look at the pictures, while I get dressed. And this is Mendelssohn. You must stroke him very gently. Okay?"

"Okay."

Who cared about showers, anyway. The Western world was known to be obsessive in its predilection for soap and water. She hauled on jeans and a sweater, forsaking even shoes in her haste.

Working on the well-known maxim that bad news is received better on a full stomach, she hurried into the kitchen and began to prepare the best repast available. Grapefruit, speedily halved and dissected, topped with brown sugar and ready to be popped under the grill, eggs set to scramble on the lowest possible heat, so that they remained creamy and moist, toast prepared from Hori's nicest granary loaf. The kettle on for coffee.

"Do you think that you could set the table, John Wayne? For three."

"Okay."

Nonetheless Emily had to put three of everything onto the table, and even then one setting had two forks and no knife, and the arrangement was, to say the least, original. It would have taken her half the time to do it herself. But once he had found a home for everything, John Wayne's smile was triumphant. He might have just discovered the logic behind calculus. He was placing the final napkin on the final side-plate, having examined it with the care generally accorded something wondrously exotic when Bill, clean and clothed, emerged from the bathroom.

"Well, hello."

Emily couldn't see the pair from her position at the stove, but she could imagine how John Wayne was looking. Perhaps she should leap out and introduce them. Pretend that the boy's presence was coincidental. Fib like mad, and pray.

Of course, John Wayne did not understand equivocation. "I'm going out with you. In the boat. Em'ly said."

Emily, stirring eggs very gently as they coagulated, held her breath. There were certain things in this world that you could orchestrate, she realized, and certain things which were outside your control.

"You are?"

Dared she take a peek? It was important to see how Bill was responding to this flat statement. It would be ghastly if he simply looked remote, denied all knowledge and sent the boy packing.

"Yeah." There was the scrape of a chair being drawn back. "'Cos I didn't yell 'n kick when she washed m' hair."

"Ah."

Only a coward would stay, craven, in the kitchen. She grabbed two of the grapefruit halves from under the grill, carameled surface sizzling, and entered the living room with all the assurance she could muster.

"Bill, this is John Wayne." She kept her voice matter-of-fact. "Kaffi's brother," she added unnecessarily, in the face of his silence.

"I guessed."

"And he's right. I did say that if he allowed us to wash his hair he could go out with you." She spoke as confidently as possible, defying him to question the fact, willing him to accept this new crew-mate as inevitable. Praying that this wasn't the end of their relationship forever, that it didn't abort then and there before having a chance to develop.

John Wayne scooted his behind onto a chair, joining Bill at the table. He tackled the grapefruit before him with more enthusiasm than skill and a jet of juice squirted in Bill's direction. John Wayne appeared not to notice.

"I go out with me dad. He goes fishin' sometimes."

"I see." Bill wiped the offending liquid from his cheek.

"Catch *kahawai* and that. *Terakihi,* too."

"You do."

Emily removed the scrambled eggs from the heat and carried her own grapefruit half to the table. She looked across at Bill, challenging him to meet her eyes, speaking briskly. "So that's settled then."

The pause before he replied was so long she could have used the time to read half of *War and Peace*.

Goodness knew what was going through his mind. Any number of reasons, excuses why he couldn't, shouldn't take the boy with him. Safety to be cited, or his ignorance of children and children's ways. Above all, without doubt, his overwhelming dislike of being manipulated in this way. He did have a point. Except, of course, that this had not been her intention, and the timing was not of her doing. John Wayne, eating with enthusiasm, appeared indifferent to the tautness of the atmosphere; Emily could scarcely bring herself to swallow. And the grapefruit, which should have been delicious, tasted as sour to her tongue as neat vinegar.

Finally Bill broke the silence. "I guess it is." He still didn't look at Emily, but glanced across the table at John Wayne. "We'd better see whether we have a life-jacket to fit you."

The relief that she felt was so overwhelming that her legs turned rubbery. Her voice, when she spoke, emerged huskily.

"Thank you." She cleared her throat. "I did intend to ask you."

He put down his spoon. "I'm sure it just slipped your mind."

"No, I . . ."

But she had no time to continue, because Bill stood up and turned to the boy. "Come on, young fella. We'll have to get a move on, if we want to catch the tide."

"Bill! There's scrambled eggs to follow, and toast and coffee."

He hadn't once looked at her and even now kept his head averted as he spoke. "I'm sure there is, but we haven't time. You can enjoy them by yourself."

John Wayne, also denied the rest of the meal, offered no resistance. Fishing would probably take precedence over everything anyway. He slid off his chair and clambered into his jacket. There was a closing of doors, the clanking of a bucket, and within two minutes Emily was on her own. Unless you counted the cat, and the gigantic lump lodged in her throat.

Mendelssohn enjoyed the eggs for his morning repast. Then he went outside and disgorged them under a bush.

Bill had bought the dinghy very soon after arriving at Whangapouri. He chose with care, a craft large enough not to be swamped by a moderate swell, but light enough to be hauled up the beach without help. He kept the outboard motor in the wood-shed off the verandah because strangers were known to drop in on the bay occasionally.

He had spent many comfortable, untaxing hours in that small boat, learning from Hori how and where to set his lines, which of the local fish were prized eating, which were better thrown back. In a way the boat offered a personal sanctuary, a place that was his alone, during those long weeks and months when he was starting to make sense of the world again.

And now he had been manipulated into having somebody invade his private space. A kid with strange, darting eyes, a loose, pink mouth and a ludicrous name. But a boy not so different from that gangly thirteen year old whom Garth had befriended.

John Wayne helped him push the dinghy down the beach toward the receding water, placing his life-jacketed shoulder against the bow and digging his heels into the wet sand. He appeared oblivious to the sharpness of pebbles and broken shell. Once the small craft was bobbing gently on shallow waves, he scrambled in with surprising agility. Bill gave the dinghy a further shove toward deeper waters before he, too, swung his legs over the gunnel. At the same time he swiveled the stern about so that the outboard motor, secure on its mounting, could be lowered without damage. The engine fired, spluttered a couple of times and then settled into a steady drone. Bill took the tiller and pointed the bow toward the east.

They fished for an hour and a half, chugging gently out to the first cluster of bobbing corks, hauling in the line to inspect the night's catch or lack of catch, re-baiting the hooks and letting the sinker fall once more to the seabed. One line, with bait virtually untouched, they re-sited. John Wayne, Bill discovered, was an easy, unexacting companion. Having, it appeared, used up his conversational quotient around the grapefruit, he didn't attempt irritating small-talk. Somebody had taught him well. He knew what to do, even when it came to dispatching fish with a sharp blow of the short, heavy bar used exclusively for that purpose. Nor was he a menace in the boat. He didn't act in a foolish manner, or make sudden, jerky movements. He knew about keeping his weight to the center of the craft.

Bill kept a plank aboard, on which he cleaned and scaled his catch. John Wayne was quite adept at that too, holding the tail of the silver-sided fish, inserting the tip of a knife into the lower belly, carefully slitting the flesh. As soon as they began this operation the air was filled with the usual circle of shrieking gulls, demanding their spoils.

And by the time they had finished, and the nose of the dinghy was once again pointing towards the shore, Bill had come to a few conclusions. His initial annoyance at Emily's manipulation had been replaced by several, somewhat more charitable, reflections.

She could not have known that the kid would appear at first light. That had been apparent from the start. She would have gotten around to asking Bill, if John Wayne hadn't forced her hand. And would he, in all honesty, have given her the time of day? He knew the answer to that, and it did not sit comfortably on his shoulders. He was suddenly, blindingly, aware of the difference between them. He might consider Emily to be misguided in her dealings with the Morrisons, but she had, from the start, shown a generosity of spirit that was in stark contrast with his own self-absorption.

All very well to retreat behind time-honored armor. That was no more than a knee-jerk reaction, influenced by the past. Surely he had grown beyond such a response. If his time at Whangapouri had done nothing else, it had given him the opportunity to do that.

The tide had retreated to the extent that they faced a difficult task hauling the dinghy above the high-water line. Had he been consulted, Bill would have planned this trip to coincide with high tide. As it was he could view the extra effort as a form of penance.

They parted company on the track behind the bach. Two silvery, torpedo-shaped fish lay in the precious bucket, contributions to the Morrisons' table.

"You fishing tomorrow? Can I come again?"

There weren't too many days that Kaffi didn't show up. It appeared that he now was to gain a similar shadow. Where would all this end?

"Yes, you can come again. But not until afternoon, when the tide's in."

John Wayne's grin was just as loose as before, his eyes scarcely less vacant. And yet he had shown himself to be a capable fisherman. Bill had known all along that sooner or later Emily was going to drag him aboard. It was probably easier to accept the inevitable with whatever dignity he could muster. Perhaps try to emulate her abundance of humanity.

NINETEEN

ntent upon pursuing his resolve, Bill thought about what gift he might find to cement the newfound *esprit de corps* within Bateman's bach. He wanted to give Emily something special and memorable. Easy to say, far harder to achieve. So it took a day or two before it occurred to him that the very thing he looked for was already at hand.

It had to be something he cherished and kept to himself, to be shared only reluctantly with others. In Bill's case, his private treasure was the colony of little blue penguins, those he had described for his mother in that first, tentative reentry into the world of words. Sure, they couldn't be considered exclusively his because they were wild creatures, and accessible to anybody who might take an interest. But in the past six months nobody had displayed any curiosity about this particular community.

It was three days after John Wayne's initiative. Twilight, or what there was of it, promised to be still and warm enough. He closed his typewriter and went into the living room. Emily was sitting at the table, her dark head bent over a notebook, the line of her neck elegant and very appealing.

"Emily, put on your jacket. I've something to show you."

She looked up, the last rays of the sun making her hair glow copper. She sounded a little impatient. "Is it important? I'm preparing Kaffi's lesson."

"No. But I'd like you to come." Bill, determined to appease, wasn't about to be daunted. "Please."

Emily abandoned the intricacies of multiplication without further protest. It was that marvelous time when the day is on the cusp. A near-full moon hung, white and ghostly, in the late afternoon sky. Together they walked past the McDuffs' then, abandoning the track, into the dunes with their sparse, coarse grass and dottings of fluffy-headed *toetoe*. Some distance beyond the last house Bill hunkered down on the dry sand.

"This is it. Now we wait."

"For what?" Emily looked baffled. There was very little to see at this minute, beyond marram grass, and straggly lupines, and the fast-darkening sea.

"The penguins. They should be coming ashore any time now."

"Really?" Suddenly she was all alert eagerness. "Are they fairy penguins, like those in Victoria?"

"Uh huh. Except here they're called 'little blues,' or *korora*."

"Oh Bill, how fantastic. They're a real tourist attraction on Phillip Island, you know; and I kept on hoping to get down there but I could never fit it in."

Perhaps taking her cue from him, she kept her voice low, although at this minute there was no evidence of the objects of their interest.

"I think there are viewing areas for tourists somewhere in the South Island. Here, they're left to themselves, apart from the predations of domestic and feral animals."

"Crumbs, yes. What an awful thought. I hope Mendelssohn hasn't discovered them."

But, Bill pointed out, it seemed unlikely. They had crossed the greater part of northern Whangapouri to reach these sand dunes.

He spoke under his breath. "Look."

As dusk gathered, the first intrepid little bird left the whispering sea and traversed perhaps a dozen yards, before losing heart and scuttling back to his companions. Looking closely, it was possible to make out half a hundred small, dark heads bobbing about just beyond the shore.

To his considerable pleasure, Emily sat transfixed. A second foray was mounted. Perhaps a dozen birds this time, making the most of a ripple of wave to scoot ashore on their bellies, then struggle upright and waddle like clockwork toys up the smooth strand. And quickly the dozen became twenty, or thirty, and then a procession. They came quite close to where their human observers were seated, scarcely pausing to assess the potential danger inherent in this alien presence, before trudging determinedly on toward the line of bush and the safety of their nests. In the soft moonlight it was possible to see their bright, boot-button eyes and silvery chests. For maybe twenty minutes the cavalcade continued, until the last small creature scuttled by on hasty feet, obviously anxious not to be late.

It was only then that Emily turned to Bill, and her voice was warm with gratitude. "Thank you. That was absolutely wonderful. A private viewing; I feel really privileged."

Emily's praise was all that Bill could have hoped for. He took her outstretched hand and helped her to her feet. "I'm pleased you enjoyed it. And them. Now, let's get home, before we get chilled to the bone."

They walked along the dunes and reached the track in silence, but it was a companionable silence, rich with their shared experience. Being generous, Bill reflected, wasn't too hard when your munificence was appreciated; more so because, during the trek homeward, Emily's hand remained tucked warmly in his own.

❦

It was amazing the difference the first hint of winter's end had on one's psyche. The tiniest new, tightly-curled leaves appeared, there was the promise of fresh growth on the trees by the store;

pohutukawas, New Zealand Christmas trees. And, coupled with that, Bill had actually said he was sorry. Emily had expected him to arrive home after the episode with John Wayne and start packing his bags or, failing that, evince some other token of his extreme displeasure. Instead he'd laid two fish on the countertop and apologized. Prepared as she was to launch into a litany of justification, it had quite knocked the wind out of her sails. However, she was careful not to allow her expectations to take flight. An expression of contrition did not mean that he accepted her position about the Morrisons. It simply meant that he realized John Wayne's crack-of-dawn arrival was not entirely her fault. But added to his apology, he had actually taken her to see the penguins.

So Emily walked home from the store with a spring in her step, swinging the carrier bag in time to her humming.

> Morning has broken, like the first morning;
> Blackbird has spoken, like the first bird . . .

Except that it wasn't a European blackbird filling the air with its joy, but the liquid song of bellbirds somewhere in the gully. How aptly named, she thought. A few yards away a small fantail flitted from the nearby bush and dived across the track, pulling itself up just short of a puddle and swooping away into the foliage. She skirted the puddle, and wondered what Bill might be doing.

> . . . Like the first dew fall, on the first grass.

That had been one of her favorite hymns, as a child. Even humming it brought hauntingly to mind early school assemblies, at the small academy to which she, Sarah and Jay had gone. Run by two old biddies call Miss Phipps and Mrs. Rogers, Ma Rogers to the daring. At the time she'd considered them as venerable as Methuselah; in retrospect they were probably in their forties or early fifties. Sisters, she recalled, with identical hair-dos which looked to her childish mind as if spun from wire-wool. And brother, were they strict about table manners those two, and spelling lists to be learnt by rote each evening. And multiplication tables. She knew them all, up to the twelve times, by the term she progressed from Miss Phipps in the baby classroom to Ma Rogers.

Jay had departed when he was eight for the Cathedral Prep, but she and Sarah stayed with the old biddies until they were eleven. Then Sarah went off to Malvern, and she'd won her scholarship to the Meinhardt.

It must have been hard for Sarah, being the oldest, and the least gifted musically of the trio. Perhaps she still harbored resentment in her breast, that the talents had not being shared out equally. If she really was a seething cesspit of bitterness, it might explain her general prickliness when they were growing up. But nobody had a God-given right to any particular ability. Surely she could see that. Had such been the case, Emily might have shared Jay's aptitude.

... God's recreation of the new day.

Perhaps her accident had taught her something else. Not to be so judgmental. She'd make a special effort, when next they were together, to meet Sarah half way. Or maybe she'd learnt that from Bill. He didn't judge people, and he had accepted John Wayne as fishing companion with far more patience than she'd ever imagined.

There was the *kowhai* tree, the landmark which indicated the edge of the drive. Fat buds promised spring fulfillment any time now, if this warm weather continued. There were newly uncurling fern fronds along the edge of the path. She elbowed open the fly screen and dumped the string bag on the table.

The kitchen was cleared of breakfast things but Bill was nowhere in sight. Perhaps, on such a gorgeous morning, he'd decided to go fishing. But when she scanned the expanse of the bay there was no sign of the aluminum dinghy and anyway, he'd talked about the tide being at its ebb. She shrugged. He'd probably taken his paint box and set off to ramble.

She sorted out the groceries and gathered together the items she'd bought for the Morrisons. They were nearly out of washing-up liquid, so there was a new bottle, also stewing steak and some lamb which she'd show Winnie how to prepare with carrots and *kumera*. Lastly, she'd bought a little bar of chocolate for each of the older kids.

Of course, having started to hum, "Morning Has Broken," it now clung to her brain like a barnacle, determined not to be abandoned. And it forced her to walk in time with it, like a soldier having to keep step with the platoon.

> Praise for the morning, praise for the singing,
> Praise for the dawning of a new day.

She stopped at the top of the rise to scan the bay, wondering if she could spot Bill, but her quest was fruitless. The bushes over-hanging the path which led to the Morrison's shack were heavy with dew. They spilled into her way, making her shoulders quite wet as she pushed past them. But there was wild garlic in flower, and buds on the native clematis, and a verdancy about everything which gave the walk a charm she would not have altered in a single, tiny aspect. Not by so much as one bedewed leaf.

As she emerged from the bush she heard rhythmic banging, muffled by the foliage. Someone was mending the roof, and sounding quite professional. It seemed unlikely that it was John Wayne, but perhaps there was more to the kid than she'd realized. But that was ridiculous. If she couldn't maneuver that sheet of roofing, what hope had a slender, eleven year old boy.

Winnie was out at the back, hanging a row of newly laun-dered nappies along the line. Gary Cooper's dark head peeped from the shawl hung, Maori style, across her back. Ani and Tama were together, squatting in the easy manner of small children, beside another shallow puddle. They were creating their usual mud pies, having merely changed venue. Perhaps the slush in that puddle was superior. However, this time Ani acknowledged Emily's presence with a shy smile. Emily noticed that today she was wearing panties, which was another improvement. Tama watched her with great near-black eyes and his habitual, impassive face. The hammering was louder, now. *Thwack. Thwack. Thwack.* Whoever it was must be working on the far side of the hut.

"Hello, Winnie. How are you? Isn't it a gorgeous day? I've brought some groceries. And lamb. I thought we'd make a stew."

" 'ullo." Winnie's face broke into a smile that animated her features. "Ta. That's nice." She clipped the last peg and hitched her infant load a little higher. "Baby was sick in the night."

Emily came across and looked at the small, brown face. She put a hand on his brow; it felt quite normal. No fever, at any rate.

"Important, Winnie? Really sick, or just baby throwing up?"

"Baby throwing up. Don't like *kumera*."

"He shouldn't be eating *kumera* yet. You have plenty of milk, let him have that. And I'll see what the store has in the way of baby foods, if you think it's time to wean him."

Thwack. Thwack. Thwack.

Emily cocked an ear in the direction of the noise. "Is that John Wayne, mending the roof? How did you manage to get the sheet onto the roof? And is he using the galvanized nails?"

The younger woman shook her head. "Not John Wayne."

"Then who, Winnie? Who's doing the repairs?"

By way of reply Winnie plodded towards the south of the shack. And even before she followed Emily knew who it was, hammering the replacement sheet across the rusted area. And something inside her warmed, and curled at the same time, tightening in her chest. Her heart felt as if it were reforming itself. She wanted to hang back for a few seconds and think about the enormity of his being there, to relish the feeling that it gave her and to capture it for future cherishing, but Winnie took her arm and pulled Emily around the corner.

Bill was working at the top of the most hazardous, accident-waiting-to-happen ladder she had ever seen. He had on an old cotton hat with a floppy brim. Kaffi was squatting on the edge of the roof, holding the new sheet steady. John Wayne had been entrusted with a bag containing the galvanized headed nails. Bill would say, "Next," and John Wayne would delve importantly into the bag, select that very nail, and hand it up.

Bill, unaware of her presence and intent upon the task in hand, said, "Next," but Kaffi looked up and squealed, "Em'ly!" and he stopped in mid action. And turned.

In Emily's perception he turned like somebody in an action replay, so slowly did he move. She knew that she had to say something, but it had to be the right something. It would be terrible if she spoiled it all now. But all that came to mind were clichés that could not, should not be said. Instead she just smiled. Grinned like a hyena, if truth be told, like the Cheshire cat. As if her mouth could not help itself.

Bill smiled back at her, his light gray eyes squinting against the brightness of the sunshine. "Hello, Emms. Everything okay with Hori? And the store?"

Emms. The name Jay and her father used. He'd never called her that before. His use of it must have been serendipity. She cleared her throat.

"Fine. Everything was fine." She paused. "I bought some neck of lamb chops. Winnie and I are going to make a stew." Then she met his eyes and knew that there was no need to say anything at all. Or certainly not about the roof. "Will you be staying for lunch?"

TWENTY

s if by mutual agreement, Bill's change of attitude was not discussed. That he was now prepared to help the Morrisons was tacitly acknowledged and acted upon. It went without saying that John Wayne had discovered an idol to worship. Bill might find the boy's presence occasionally chafing, but John Wayne accepted without rancor the stricture that the sunporch was out of bounds, and that he was welcome only when invited. This meant on fishing excursions, or when Bill was doing something about the disgraceful condition of the Morrison's home. At these times he became a willing, totally inept henchman. The simple skills that he displayed when hauling in lines and replacing bait were not carried through to other areas. A little of his presence, Bill admitted to Emily, went a long way.

Emily was only too aware of the boy's shortcomings. She was doing her best to introduce him to the written word. It reinforced her avowal that she was no natural teacher. Kaffi, supplied with the correct textbooks, could probably have learned Sanskrit, John Wayne struggled over the adventures of Spot the Dog.

But there was something infinitely touching in his attempts to please, the abundance of effort that went into tracing letters with his finger, mouthing them silently, seeking a clue to possible content from the illustration. And the way his face lit up when praised was almost reward in itself.

The acquisition of patience did not come easily, and not just in the business of teaching. Even more, now that the one bone of contention had been dismissed, did the thermal activity of her emotions threaten to erupt. If only she could persuade Bill to lower the wall of his reserve.

"Bill," she could start, "Now that I know you're not gay, I've been thinking . . ." Awful. Schoolgirlish. Perhaps she should appeal to the animal in him. "I suppose you're a hothouse of lust, after all these celibate months, Bill." Worse. Gross. And what if he turned around and replied that he was impotent, or celibate by choice? Or, simply, that she lit no responding fire within him.

But she knew that he liked her. Not only had he said so, but there was also that list of the parts he liked. And occasionally she caught him looking at her, and there was something very warm in his look. Practically intimate.

How about "Let's make love?" Definitely a cliché, but the least awful, to date. The problem was that she habitually skirted around the word "love." It had been debased by extreme over-use. Men, or at least certain men, saw it as a virtual *open sesame*. Mouth the magic words and you would fall, swooning, into their arms. Or they would leap, lustful, into your bed. Marco had certainly availed himself of it. "*Cara mia,* I love you," professed in his delightfully accented English, was his overture to an enthusiastic session of sex. Something like grace, said before a meal. Of course, it was also followed by whispered promises of permanent devotion. "Ah, sweet one, I shall love you into eternity," and "We have been united by fate, forever," had certainly sounded marvelous to her ear. These days, remembering her gullibility, the same phrases brought a sour taste to her mouth. No, she could not say to Bill, "I love you." Not yet, maybe not ever.

And time was ticking by.

There was a small, awkward moment, when she'd decided that it might be sensible to have some sort of protection at hand, just in case, and following the dictum of "traveling hopefully." Unable to hitch a suitable ride into the township, this had led to half a minute's extreme embarrassment at Hori's Store. On Emily's part, at least. Heneti had merely added several small boxes to the groceries on the counter and totted up the bill.

Emily could have hugged her for her tact, even though the little boxes were still there, unopened, some days later. She wondered, a little wryly, whether knowledge of her purchase would be shared with Hori and thus give rise to a gross misinterpretation of facts, as pertaining to the occupants of Bateman's bach. More so because it began to seem that she would have to wait forever until the opportunity presented itself.

Why couldn't Bill read the depths of her feeling for him, not to mention her frustration, and set the ball rolling? Ruefully, she acknowledged that if she had to wait for him to initiate things she might be a very old lady indeed, or her departure from Whangapouri would leave the issue unresolved for eternity. One of those soul-wrenching "might have beens" about which elderly, unloved women dreamed.

༺༻

The spell of glorious, spring-like weather, lasted three days, just long enough to lull Emily into assuming it might be permanent. It was the line of pink and purple clouds above the horizon one morning that indicated less clement weather was on the way.

"Do you know that saying, Kaffi? 'Red sky at night, shepherd's delight. Red sky in the morning, shepherd's warning.'"

Kaffi looked up from her sums long enough to nod.

"Our nan says that." John Wayne was also sitting at the table, practicing his letters. When he worked he clutched the pencil as though fearing it might escape, and wrote with his nose no more than inches from the paper. It took all his concentration. It was just as well, Emily thought, that he did not resent his sister, and he might well have done so because she was extremely short on the very tact that was so admirable in Heneti. And yet he came daily, and labored good-naturedly at the three R's, and smiled his loose smile when Emily praised him. The clatter of typewriter keys seeping through the door was a constant background to the schoolroom activity.

She gave them lunch most days, before sending them home. Shepherd's pie, today. Bill abandoned his writing to join them.

"Have you noticed? It's building up to be quite a storm."

She glanced out of the window. The bay was overshadowed by heavy, rain-laden cloud.

"Eat up, you two. Then we'll be off. Your mum will be needing you both."

By the time she returned from accompanying the children to the crest of the headland, the rain had become a reality. She wondered if Bill, too, had been caught. He'd said, at lunch-time, that he would like to move his set lines, but he'd not allowed John Wayne to accompany him. Not with that ominous weather threatening. She pushed open the door and stepped inside, discarding her outer gear, the boots by the door, the jacket left to drip from a big hook under the verandah roof.

From his favorite seat by the fire Mendelssohn yawned widely and came across to insinuate himself about her ankles.

"Go away, you misbegotten beast." She nudged him gently with a woolen-clad toe. "You're on a hiding to nothing."

Mendelssohn added a vocal plea to his fawning, before giving up and returning to the chair. Emily glanced into the sunroom. There was no sign of Bill.

Then the bathroom door opened and he emerged, drying his neck and ears as he did so. He was completely bare, and drops of water from the shower glistened across his shoulders and clung to the hairs of his chest. He was as long and lean as she'd imagined, still tanned from the summer apart from the white patch where some brief garment had maintained standards of decency. He looked up.

Emily's feet had suddenly grown roots, while her insides started to melt. "Should I say, 'Oops! Sorry?'"

"That's okay."

At this time, in Emily's opinion, he should be retreating, fast, behind the bathroom door. Instead he slowly wrapped the towel around his lower half. The way he stood there, not moving, did seem almost like an invitation.

Was this that gently reached, special moment about which she'd speculated at such length? Then what about all those carefully rehearsed phrases. And who cared, anyway.

"Let's fuck."

"What?"

"What's wrong with that?"

Was it all a ghastly mistake? Perhaps she'd misread the message. Or did he think she was merely horny, that any guy would do at this minute? Horrors.

"Well, it's certainly blunt."

There was that awful, familiar fear of rebuff creeping in, but his body appeared interested in the suggestion. Desperate with her longing for him, she spoke defiantly. "It's an old, Anglo-Saxon word of impeccable origin."

"One I'll bet you weren't encouraged to use at the Meinhardt."

Shocked by her own crudeness but committed now, she started to take off her clothing. Rain had seeped through the jacket and her shirt clung to her back.

"There were lots of things we weren't encouraged to do at the Meinhardt. Fornicate with the guest lecturer, for one. That doesn't mean you take a pledge for life."

Her pants stuck to her thighs. Bill didn't move as the legs turned inside-out when she peeled them down, revealing the legacy of scars from her plastic surgery.

She was poignantly aware of his silence. "A gentleman might help me, you know."

"Who said I was a gentleman?"

But he came across to the chair, and kissed her lightly upon the top of her wet hair. Then he hunkered down before her, and looked deeply into her eyes as though needing to ascertain that this was, truly, right. Finally he ran one gentle fingertip across the new, baby-pink skin inside her thigh. The result of this simple action was staggering. It was as though somebody had tossed a bucketful of petroleum onto the conflagration within her, creating a bonfire of sensations. Then he began to undo the buttons of her shirt.

And, even if not a gentleman, he was certainly a very well-endowed peasant.

Presently she said, "Wow! Bill . . . Aaah. . . ." and finally, "Where did you learn to do that so well?"

They lay on the saggy old bed under the faded patchwork quilt, skin touching skin the whole length of their bodies, as close as two people can be.

"You make love amazingly, for somebody I thought was gay."

Bill's arm was around her shoulders. Feeling more relaxed and contented than he'd thought possible, he was able to appreciate the humor of her earlier mistake.

"The credit's all yours. It was a good idea."

"Good?" Emily echoed. "I thought the English were the ones given to understatement."

"What would you prefer?"

"Staggering? Earth-moving? Planet realigning?"

"Hyperbole, the lot. I'll settle for good. Or very good, if you prefer. I was just a bit surprised by the timing."

Emily nestled against him. "I've wanted to for ages, but couldn't find the right way to suggest it. Then you solved the problem."

"I did?"

"Of course. Standing there, all bare, looking so ... so fantastic. And not running for cover."

He realized the truth in what she said. Although, for the life of him, he couldn't have said why he'd not returned immediately to the bathroom. He took her left hand and gently traced the scars along the fingers with his lips.

"I guess the moment was right. For both of us."

"Yes."

"Shall we try it again?"

Emily pulled herself back so that she could look at him without squinting. "Making up for lost time, huh?"

"Perhaps." He smiled. "Perhaps I'm afraid it was a one night stand. I want to consolidate the experience."

She wriggled her hand down in the bed, between them. "I don't think you need fear that. Consolidation, I mean. You're very well consolidated indeed."

After that they were silent, concentrating on matters that required no words, although Bill did wonder, with a disengaged part of his mind, when she'd bought that package of condoms.

He lay in the darkness, looking toward the lighter gray around the curtain that heralded daybreak. Emily was curled up asleep against his shoulder, her breathing light and regular. He knew it had stopped raining, because of the absence of noise. Whatever happened in the future, he would only have to hear rain drumming on an iron roof to be transported back to this time in his life. The thought was accompanied by a sensation of great warmth that wrapped about him, like a blanket.

He was still caught up in what had happened, and the speed of it all. He needed to sort out precisely what it meant, both now and for the future. The analytical approach was probably best, he reasoned. He should stand back and try to get everything into perspective.

Yesterday he had woken, like every other morning for the last weeks. There was no perceptible difference in the start of the day. The day had proceeded like every other day, with Kaffi and John Wayne arriving for their lesson and the trio sitting at the table, heads close together, concentrating on the weighty matters of multiplication and the printed word.

Emily had decided to accompany the children homewards, at least part-way. But at some time, between when she left and when she returned, the status quo had altered. He was not aware of it, clearly she was. And it had crept up on him unawares.

But as he lay in the darkness that preceded dawn and thought about it, he realized that, very gradually, a great deal had happened. In him and to him. To begin with, the obvious. He was writing again, and the catalyst had without doubt been Emily. It was her presence, her influence, that had lit the creative spark. The words were bouncing about in his mind like squash balls off the walls of the court, each angle creating a new, exciting approach, triggering fresh responses. And when he wrote confidence in his ability, and himself, flooded back.

Add to that the feelings now stirring within him, of the sort he'd thought dead forever. Feelings that included great tenderness and understanding, as well as desire. And the remarkable thing was that, apart from his impulsive agreement to move into Bateman's bach, he could not remember having made any conscious decision. Sure, he could say that he thought Emily appealing. He valued her friendship. But that was where it stopped. He had never thought that there was something in this for him. He had not looked at Emily in that way at all. And, to be honest, he had thought his sexuality well buried. Which made what had happened all the more surprising, discovering that his body had resolved matters entirely by itself.

But there was one thing he could say with certainty. He'd never again think of Emily without remembering the joyous intensity of her love-making, and exulting in that memory. He thought of her abrupt invitation and its startling effect, and in the darkness he grinned to himself. That, from a person who had rebuked him for the occasional less-than-delicate phrase. She'd probably shocked herself as well. It wasn't a word he'd have chosen. And yet it had had the desired effect.

Now all that needed facing was tomorrow, and all the other tomorrows. As things stood, Emily would soon be packing her bags, leaving Whangapouri and returning to some semblance of her old life. That time was less than five weeks away. By then he knew she would be healed, and whole. Bill didn't want to contemplate life without her. He would be the person left behind, when she moved on. The thought should have been horrendous, auguring of one of his darker moods. Instead he drew her sleeping form a little closer to him, and smelled in her hair the salt blown up from sea-spray, and knew that he had regained the strength to face all the tomorrows that life could throw at him, and that included the probability of their parting.

❧

He rose at six and walked down to the edge of the water. Yesterday's squall might not have happened. The sea was once more in a benign mood, gray and scarcely ruffled. Small wavelets teased the toes of his sneakers, and a flock of tiny shore birds scuttled along the washed sand like self-important people on their way to a meeting. He felt very contented.

He wondered whether last night could have happened with another woman, or whether there was something unique about Emily, herself. After his divorce he'd made a few, feeble attempts to date other women, and various among his friends had gone to great lengths to fix him up for cozy twosomes. Sometimes those dates had culminated in sex. Stupid, dumb, occasions. They'd left a bad taste in his mouth, which was no reflection on the women, but a major condemnation of himself.

Emily was different; and he didn't know why. Nor did he care. There were some things that didn't need analyzing down to the last period. What was important was that fusion of two souls, which felt intrinsically so right.

Emily was clearly enjoying the sleep of the dead, still in bed when he returned half an hour later. Mendelssohn, ensconced in the armchair, stretched, climbed down, and came to demand breakfast. Bill scooped out remains of yesterday's can into his enamel bowl. Mendelssohn crossed the floor as though bestowing a favor and sniffed at the offering. Then he evinced his disdain by shaking all four paws, one at a time, and very deliberately.

Bill grinned down at him. "Too bad, fella. That's it. You starve, until the landlady decides to take pity on you."

He went into the sunporch and sat, looking at the keys of his typewriter. For the first time in days the words did not flow. At this moment, in earlier times, he would have seen that as terrible failure. He would be holding off black despair, the demon that lurked just at the edge of his perception.

Today the fact that he wasn't a wellspring of ideas didn't matter. He knew that his ability was still there, simply relegated to secondary status by something altogether more important and immediate. It was a wonderfully comforting thought.

Mendelssohn woke Emily. Refusing to accept yesterday's leftovers as his due portion, he nosed open the door to the bedroom and jumped up, landing heavily on the somnolent mistress of the house. And, in case that wasn't sufficiently indicative of his distressed state, he added a plaintive mew, the sort calculated to melt the most flinty of human hearts.

"Aah!"

Emily had been lying in that marvelous twilight zone between dream and reality. She knew that something momentous had happened. She wasn't able, at this moment, to pinpoint exactly what. Then it all came flooding back. Yesterday, and Bill, and how they had spent the late afternoon. And evening. She felt like purring to rival Mendelssohn who was, at this moment, pressing his nose insistently against her cheek.

"Okay, I get the message."

She pushed the cat away and stretched her hand across the bed to confirm that Bill wasn't there. There was only a dent in the pillow to testify where he had slept. Then she squinted at the clock. Eight-fifteen. He'd have been up for eons and, as if her senses were just coming alive, she detected wafts of smell drifting in from the kitchen. Bacon. He was cooking breakfast. She lay awake and thought about the next few minutes. The next hour. She wondered what she might say to him, how should she behave after the events of last night, the staggering change in their relationship.

Mendelssohn abandoned her as a lost cause and departed, drawn towards that delicious aroma. Emily wrapped the quilt about her and followed him. The fire was in the early stages of ignition, small flamelets toying with the wood.

"That smells fantastic."

She felt inordinately shy. But something was required, some acknowledgment of moments shared. Perhaps she should say, "My word, you're a terrific lover," or a throw-away line, like "I enjoyed it, yesterday. Thanks a lot."

"Hi, there." Bill smiled at her and turned back to his cooking.

She sat down at the table, tucking her toes into a fold of the quilt which was draped around her like a muumuu. She tried to detect whether there was anything different in today's smile from yesterday's.

"Coffee?"

"Yes, please."

He put a plate before her. Bacon, grilled tomatoes and mushrooms. He was becoming quite English in his culinary tastes. Then fresh toast, coffee. It smelled wonderful, and she realized with a shock that they'd not actually eaten, last night. That the afternoon and the evening had become one, and not included food. Or not food of the tangible variety. No wonder she was so ravenous. She set about her portion with the enthusiasm of a long-deprived person as Bill came to sit down.

"Did you sleep okay?" he asked. Loaded words, she thought.

"Wonderfully well. Like a log." And then she realized that he'd given her the very opening she needed. "I think we should renegotiate the sleeping arrangements."

Bill spread a slice of toast with marmalade. "I was hoping you'd say that. It's a great idea. I'll have the bedroom, and you can try the divan in the sunporch. I should warn you it's hideously hard, but your back becomes conditioned after a few nights."

She glanced at him sideways. "That wasn't exactly what I had in mind."

"Really?"

"Bill."

He put down his fork and covered her hand with his. "You look like a butterfly in that quilt, you know, about to emerge from its cocoon." His smile conveyed a lot of tenderness. "What do you really want to say?"

"You know what."

"Consider the sleeping arrangements altered. But we agreed that by implication last night, didn't we. And you know by now that I don't snore." He paused, then repeated, "What did you really want to say?"

It wasn't to do with what she might say, it was more about what she wanted to hear. Something from him, like, "At last I've found my soulmate. We'll be bonded together for all time." No, that wasn't it. Shades of Marco. She tried again. Maybe, "Moments like this don't happen too often. Isn't it marvelous that we've found each other." Couldn't he say that? Perhaps she should give it a try. But she was tangled in an awkwardness of her own making. It would have been easier if she'd just gone over and kissed him, before they began to eat. Around breakfast it all became a bit tricky and there were too many crumbs. Most of all . . . most of all she needed him to initiate some dialogue about commitment. And yet, while the idea was there, hanging in a state of limbo between them, she was terrified that she was rushing things and that Bill would feel threatened.

"I know that this means nothing permanent, Bill. Not the for-ever-and-ever-ride-off-into-the sunset." It sounded dreadfully bald, stated like that. And all wrong. Worse still, he didn't appear the least bit reassured. "No, no. I didn't mean that. I meant . . . I meant that last night was wonderful . . . but . . ."

Bill was silent for a long minute. "I must have changed, without noticing." He spoke in a manner she recognized to be deliberately casual. "Do I look like a ball and chain?"

She shifted uncomfortably. "No. You know I didn't mean that. I was saying it for you. Not for me."

But he disregarded her denial. He leaned back in his chair, temporarily abandoning the food. "I know all about relationships that weigh you down. Do you think I'd saddle you like that?"

"No. And not you. Me, saddling you. I just thought we ought to spell it out." This was getting worse and worse, the morass into which she was sliding deeper and darker.

"You were taught that honesty is always the best policy?"

His voice was so comical, and the pseudo-English accent so awful, that Emily was forced to laugh. The sound, in her own ears, resembled one of the harpies. "Something like that. But I was only thinking of you. Not me."

He rose to replenish their coffee. "Sometime I'll tell you all about my marriage. When you have an extra hour or two."

"You were married?" Emily stared at him.

"It happens."

"No ... but ... "

"Yeah, yeah. I forgot. As well as being gay you'd decided I had something against marriage. Is that what you thought?"

The quilt was beginning to slip down. To hide her confusion, Emily rose and wrapped it more firmly under her arms. The action gave her time to think. "You're just one big box of surprises, aren't you," she remarked.

"All the better to keep you amused."

"And you do understand?" Understand that she was digging her own grave. Sealing her own fate.

"I do."

But he didn't say whether he cared, or not. He didn't tell her that she was mistaken. Nor did he say, "I can't bear the thought of your leaving."

The absence of any such words was like a knife, twisting against her heart.

TWENTY-ONE

I t was a gorgeous afternoon, mild and serene. Emily was delighted when Bill suggested that he abandon his typewriter and that they go for a walk. She was awash with that glow of discovered mutual attraction, feeling sated with sex, at peace with the world about her. She chose not to dwell on their breakfast conversation of three days ago, when her mouth had spouted all the wrong words. Although goodness only knew what she had expected, anyway. No, she reflected, she was asking too much of him, too soon. It was better to keep her hopes firmly rationed, and accept the pleasure that each day brought. Four and a half weeks to go. All sorts of things could happen in that time. With luck he'd realize how essential she was to his happiness.

She had completely forgotten, with all that had materialized in the intervening days, about Heneti's mention of the headland, and its relevance to their detection work. In fact, for the same reason she'd given the tale of the lost lovers very little airing recently. So she started out with no clear-laid plan as to where they'd walk. When Bill headed north she simply followed, and it seemed appropriate because the area to the north was certainly the more interesting.

There was a track of sorts that climbed steeply from the shore. She would never have tackled it previously, but two months of living here had strengthened her muscles and reawakened some of her old confidence. Even so, half an hour of scrambling up that steep, narrow trail was enough to recall her limitations. She sank with gratitude onto the sparse ground cover at the top. Her calf muscles felt like jelly. Bill stretched out beside her. Apart from the vigorous spikes of native flax, everything growing on the headland bore evidence of a daily struggle against the wind. Low gorse bushes and stunted trees bent in grotesque shapes.

"Bill . . .?"

"Yes?"

She wound a blade of long, tough fescue around her fingers. "You said you'd tell me about your marriage, sometime."

"Uh huh."

So characteristic of him. She would introduce a topic and he would be in no hurry to help her. It was a form of gentle teasing, as if he enjoyed watching the mental scrambling she employed to find the correct words.

"Now is sometime."

He leaned back on the grass. "Now is also a fantastic day, with a spring sky overhead and three Arctic terns practicing para-sailing. Why spoil it all with a squalid little tale?"

Emily could have told him why. She could have said that she lay awake at night, when he was dead to the world, trying to imagine what his ex-wife looked like, how he was as a husband. She might have added that, totally irrationally, she felt very jealous of this unknown woman. Because Bill was so special, and clearly the woman had not appreciated it. Otherwise they'd still be married. She voiced none of these thoughts.

Bill, obviously reading her silence, turned to look at her. "You really want to know?"

"Yes. If you don't mind telling me."

"It's old history. Painful at the time, less so now."

"What's her name?"

"JoBeth."

"And what does she look like?"

Bill made a pillow of his hands and closed his eyes. "Very beautiful. Lean, not an ounce of extra flesh, and all the poise of a fashion model."

Emily wondered if she could bear this. Perhaps it would have been better not to know. At this moment every fiber of her body hated JoBeth Thackeray. Asking for more of the same punishment was almost masochistic. But necessary. Imagination was far more insidious than knowledge.

"And how did you meet?"

"JoBeth, among other things, is an intellectual snob. She fancied herself as a writer. I think she'd submitted several manuscripts, and had as many rejections. But she loved the literary world, so when she realized she wasn't going to make it, she altered course. Decided to woo writers, instead. First guy she got her claws into was Garth. But she's an intelligent woman. Pretty quickly, she realized she was barking up the wrong tree. So I was number two. Garth actually introduced us."

"Was he match-making, or trouble-making?"

"Probably neither. I don't think he meant to be malicious. He couldn't have known how disastrous it would all be."

"And that you'd fall in love."

Bill was silent a minute. "Did I fall in love? I guess I did. I was flattered. I've never been too hot at the self-image stuff. And JoBeth, having scented the prey, didn't let me out of sight. I was swept up in all her great plans for me, for our future."

As he lapsed into silence Emily prompted quietly, "And . . . ?"

"And not much. Four years of marriage. Three-and-a-half years of those four, a farce. An empty vessel."

Emily carefully selected two other blades of tough grass and began to plait them. Four years was a long time in a person's life. "Go back. Fill in a few details."

She was aware of the glance Bill threw her way, but she concentrated on her braiding.

"You really want to know?"

"Yes. Please."

"My second book was just out. *Burning Bright.* The reviews were fantastic, and I was on cloud nine. I'd proved that I wasn't a 'one book' author. That's every writer's dread. My agent threw a bash and JoBeth was there, of course. JoBeth was at every literary affair in New York."

She tried to detect from his voice what he was feeling, and failed. He sounded as detached as if he were explaining to her the plot of someone else's book. Deliberately void of emotion. She wondered if that was a screen, to hide painful yesterdays.

"I saw her, talking to Garth," he continued. "She was wearing a black sheath, I remember. Slinky. She came across the room like a sinuous cat. I was knocked sideways. I guess I remained stunned for the next few weeks."

"And you came to your senses a married man?"

"Engaged, anyway. Amid a flurry of Long Island social whirl. No decent way to turn back."

"You mean, you wanted to turn back? Even then."

Bill was silent. Finally he said, "No. I wanted to marry her. She didn't drag me to the altar. I was caught up in the magic, and I really believed I was committing myself, willingly, for life."

Emily managed to weave her grasses to within an inch of the bottom. She discarded them and lay back beside him.

"Was she an utter bitch?"

"No. That's too harsh. It wasn't all JoBeth's fault. And dealing with a depressive personality isn't easy. I couldn't cope, at that time. I hadn't found the right medication, so I wasn't stabilized."

Emily wondered if she could be so generous, so honest in a similar situation. It was far easier to dump all the blame on the other person. She had very few charitable thoughts left for Marco.

"And she never came to terms with my way of writing." Bill spoke quietly. "I think she fondly imagined herself as a fantastic source of inspiration for me. Like the pillar of fire before the children of Israel. But you know me. That's not my way. Every word I write is hauled painfully out from inner depths. What I need is quiet support, not a barrage of someone else's brilliant ideas."

Emily thought of those cups of coffee quietly cooling untouched, and hoped.

He squeezed her hand, as it lay on the grass. "Like you."

She briefly closed her eyes and offered up a small, silent prayer of thanks.

"That's why Whangapouri is perfect," he continued. "We're perfect. I'm writing again, and it's going well."

He'd said, "We're perfect." Two words more precious than all the jewels of the Orient. Perhaps he was, after all, seeing her as an essential ingredient in his life. She weighed up putting it to the test.

"I'm glad you said that. I think we're perfect, too."

Bill bent over and kissed her. His lips tasted deliciously of sea-salt and man. His beard tickled. Fleetingly she wondered if she should seize this moment, and try to build something tangible upon it, here and now. Sort of test the waters. But equally swiftly she discarded the notion. If there was one thing within her power to give Bill, it was freedom from emotional shackles. And anyway, the timing was anything but appropriate. She could scarcely say, in the midst of a discussion about a failed marriage, " . . . by the way, I was wondering if you'd be prepared to give it another go. Same options. Different woman."

As it was, some time elapsed before she could talk again, let alone pick up the threads of the conversation.

"How long ago were you divorced?" She assumed that they were divorced, that she wasn't sleeping with a married man.

"You really want to talk?" He sounded reluctant, but from Emily's point of view there was important ground to cover.

"Please."

Reluctantly Bill pulled himself upright. "Two years ago. July the twenty-third. A Wednesday."

As significant as that. "No children?" Was it only her imagination, or had there been an almost imperceptible pause?

"No."

"And where is she now?"

"Who knows? Probably dragging some poor bastard through the hell of New York's high society." He stood. "And time's up. You've had your twenty questions."

Emily scrambled to her feet. So the topic was closed. Anyway, she knew enough to sleep more easily in her bed. Their shared bed. Clearly Bill was harboring no deep-seated regrets about the demise of that relationship.

He turned eastwards, along the bluff. Emily had never explored this headland. Even on this still, spring-like day the updraught made itself felt, comfortably cool against her face.

"Do you know the name of this area?"

"No."

"According to Heneti, it's Ruatangi. That translates as 'Hole in the earth that echoes with mourning.'"

"What sort of hole?"

"I'm going to show you."

They followed a narrow, worn sheep-track. There were no recent signs of animals, domestic or otherwise, only a scattering of sheep droppings, pellets weathered to dusty gray with age. Some distance along the track Emily noticed the remains of a fence ahead of them. The posts looked as if they had given up the unequal struggle against the elements. No more than a few still stood, the others sagged as though the wire threaded between was the only impediment to merciful defeat. Bill took Emily's hand as they approached, and it made her feel safe and cherished. Like a continuation of their kiss.

"Go easy. There's no guarantee that the ground is solid."

"What is it? What's there?"

"Listen."

Emily did. At first all she could hear were the screams of sea birds, playing aerial tag against the blue of the sky. Then she heard something else. A sigh. A long, deep sigh, like a very tired person. It seemed to carry on forever.

"What is it?"

"A vent. Possibly an ancient fumerole. Or that's my guess."

What on earth did she know about fumeroles? Something to do with volcanoes. She retreated two cautious steps. "This area isn't active, is it?"

"Not to my knowledge. Although there's a geothermal belt that runs across the North Island. From Mt. Egmont in the west to White Island off the East Coast. But this area was probably active in the recent past, geologically speaking. "

Emily didn't feel particularly secure. The thought that the ground had once been sufficiently volcanic to create a vent was quite disturbing. But then, it was with reason that New Zealand was nicknamed The Shaky Isles.

"Heneti was telling me about it. It acts as a blowhole, now," Bill continued, "That noise must mean there's some access to the sea."

She knew a lot more about blowholes. Not all that many years ago there'd been an awful accident in Australia, when people viewing the one at Kiama were killed. She'd been in Australia at the time, and she'd visited that particular place, on a sunny day quite like today. She could picture it well. The gaping hole in the rock, the swooshing of waves as they were forced through a narrow submarine channel, then the fierce explosion of spume and spray. It rose twenty or so feet into the air. She'd stood, feeling totally safe behind the sturdy barrier, watching with fascination the surge and ebb of water. Then, less than a month later, half a dozen people were dead.

They carefully approached the fence around the hole. This sorry collection of rotted posts and saggy wire wouldn't have held back diddly. Emily stood still and listened again, as the sound of another low sigh hung in the air. This blowhole didn't give the impression of being life-threatening. But the Maori name suggested otherwise. She tried to imagine how it would sound when the weather was less clement. What happened at the base of this headland, hundreds of feet below? Perhaps the waves forced their way through a similar, narrow channel in the rock, sending a rush of compressed air surging up the vent. If weather as serene as today's could cause a whisper, it stood to reason that, with a bit more air pressure, it would become quite dramatic.

She laced her fingers through Bill's, seeking reassurance.

"Shall we go on to the point?" He indicated with a nod.

"Yes."

She was quite pleased to leave the area behind. As they climbed the steep ascent, Bill's grasp on her fingers tightened slightly.

"Don't charge ahead. Cliffs can become undermined, there's no guaranteeing that these are safe."

Still holding fast to him, Emily cautiously approached the edge. Far below she could see the jutting rocks that extended into the Pacific, gleaming with wet, dark seaweed.

"Remember Te Manawanui, and Waikura? From this height you can see why Kapiti thought they were mad. Imagine those rocks on a stormy night."

"You're forgetting the freak conditions," Bill reminded her. "The rocks were high and dry at the time. The tide was far out to sea."

Emily agreed reluctantly. "But not for long. Not in Kui's account. By the time Kapiti was searching for the lovers, water was right up to the cliff face."

"Probably. I don't know a lot about weather patterns. But common sense suggests that as soon as the offshore wind dropped the sea would surge back, on an incoming tide."

She cast one final glance down onto the coastline far below and drew back from the edge. "Bill?"

"Hmm?"

"Do you think there might be a connection?"

"I don't follow you."

"Between that vent, and their disappearance. You said that the noise we heard indicates some association with the sea." She hoped that he would appreciate the drift of her thoughts. "I was thinking, could the connecting passage not be just a narrow channel, but be some sort of cave, instead? Would that allow for air to howl up the vent?"

There was no need for him to hold her hand any longer, they were safely back on terra firma. But he didn't seem eager to release his grasp.

"It's an idea. A cave, where they sought shelter." He paused, weighing up this possibility. "Perhaps only approachable when the sea retreats."

Emily was pleased with this idea. "It's like *Brigadoon*."

"Kilts and bagpipes?"

She didn't bother analyzing whether that was deliberate obtuseness, or his customary teasing. "No, stupid. Get-at-able once every hundred years or so. Whenever there's that freak ebb-tide."

They were retracing their path. They passed the decrepit fence that offered such scant protection for straying feet. Emily stopped walking long enough to hear a sad, low exhalation. It sounded incredibly mournful.

"Possibly more frequent than that. Any phenomenon which has its own name, like El Niño, generally occurs at least once in a generation. Otherwise the name's discarded, or forgotten. That indicates *he tai rereke* occurs about four times a century."

As usual, at mention of the tragic tale of the lost lovers, Emily felt a frisson of excitement. The cave might not exist outside their imaginations. They might never actually know, but the possibility that there could be a reasonable solution to the disappearance was spine-tingling.

She followed quickly with her next train of thought. "And Bill, what if they actually escaped through the vent. Could it be wide enough for people?"

"It must be wide enough for somebody, at some time, to bother putting up a fence."

"And then they'd creep away, maybe to Waikura's tribe. Kapiti would be combing the rocks down below, and they'd be climbing to freedom, a hundred feet above him."

"Three hundred, more likely."

Emily dismissed such minor details. "And, of course, the Ngati Tarapunga tribe would never let on. They'd be safe, there."

"No. They'd do the opposite." Bill stopped walking long enough to retie a shoelace. "They'd crow. Imagine the humiliation of the chief. A publicity coup of monumental proportion."

But Emily was reluctant to abandon her argument. "No they wouldn't. They'd already suffered a humiliating defeat, not all that long ago. Probably the tribe wasn't strong enough to risk another battle. They'd just have hidden the lovers, maybe disguised them. And gloated."

Bill smiled. "Whatever. I like your theory, and I'll bear it in mind."

She'd temporarily forgotten that too, that the tale of Te Manawanui and Waikura was one of the strands in his most recent writing. She liked the notion that she'd helped contribute to his work, even if only marginally. Fresh ideas and new approaches were certainly more relevant than merely providing an endless supply of coffee. And perhaps there'd be a follow-through. Further proof that they made a perfect couple.

TWENTY-TWO

Putting her latest reading back on the bookshelf, Kaffi turned to the fiddle case. "Can I see your violin?"

"May I," Emily automatically corrected, hearing echoes of her mother as she did so.

"Oh, may I?" Kaffi was a pretty shrewd mimic, and Emily was forced to laugh.

"All right. But we'll have to be careful."

She had not opened the case in weeks, partly because so much more occupied her days, partly because sand was invasive. Now she put it gently on the table, flipped back the clip and lifted the lid.

"Oooh . . ."

The wood was richly patterned, so opulently varnished, the shape so satisfyingly perfect. There was something incongruous about the beauty of the instrument, and the disparity of the cheap Formica surface of the table. There was nothing incongruous about Kaffi's awe.

"Will you play it for me? Please?"

This time around there was none of the agony associated with Jay's insistence that she make that painfully futile attempt.

"Look, sugar." She extended her fingers. "In order to play the violin you need to have very sensitive fingertips. The nerves in my hand were all crushed, in the accident. I'd hate you to hear me try. It might put you off the violin forever, and that would be a pity, because when it's played well it's the most wonderful sound in all the world."

Kaffi inspected the hand before her. Then she looked again at the *Vuillaume.* "That's really sad, isn't it. That you can't play it any more. And it's so lovely, and that."

Emily carefully closed the case again. "Nobody ever said that life was meant to be easy. You could say I was lucky, that I could do so, for such a long time."

"You don't care so much?"

"I've found other things to do." She returned the case to the shelf and gave Kaffi a quick hug. "Be friends with you, for instance."

It was not sleeping with a man that was different. It was waking up beside him. Of course, it was something about which she had certainly thought in the past, especially where Marco was concerned. But their relationship had blossomed during two summer schools at the Meinhardt, and the best they could manage was a shared smile over the communally prepared break-fast. It wasn't too easy to be intimate when four other people, to all intents and purposes strangers, shared your table.

Added to that was the knowledge that what they were doing would not win Moshe's unconditional approval. Actually, that feeling of slight excitement added an attractive edge to the risqué nature of two summers. In retrospect, a spur to the infatuation.

But Bill was different. Sleeping with Bill had a flavor all its own, as did wakening beside him each morning. She would be aware of the warmth of his body and his smell, faintly musky and infinitely masculine. The iron bedstead would groan as he turned over, and squeal as he sat up and swung his legs over the side. The mattress would tilt slightly to one side, then return to horizontal as he stood. She'd frequently told herself that, were Bateman's bach hers, she'd invest in new bedroom furniture. Something with inner springs, at least. Now she was less positive. They had experienced some wonderful times on that paint-chipped frame.

Best of all about the bed, she thought, was that it enabled a continuation of the evenings' conversations. They would lie together in the dark when other appetites had been satisfied, sharing tales from former lives, and recalling pivotal events. Talk, Emily reflected, was a marvelous connector.

Again, it was far easier for her. Her life held very little that caused a shudder, or even a wince. There was no particular and vulnerable underbelly to be revealed. She could even consider her disastrous liaison with Marco in a more detached fashion, now that her impetuous vow of eternal solitude had bitten the dust. So it was that Bill knew all about Marco, about his dark Italian charisma, his ability as a musician, his talent in the bed.

"I know it was motivated in part by lust," Emily confided. "But that was only half of it. He wasn't my first boyfriend, or anything like that, but he was the first person I honestly thought I'd end my life alongside."

"How did you manage to coordinate all that carnality? In the lecture halls, behind the podium?"

Visions of steamy sessions atop the teacher's desk were almost too much for Emily's sense of humor. "You forget, I was at school there for seven years. There wasn't a hayloft in the vicinity we didn't know about. And all the fire escape doors from the dormitory blocks."

"Which did you find more appealing? Grass rash, or operating in total silence while students slept on the other side?"

There wasn't enough light for her to see his expression, but the rueful note in his voice did more than hint at experiences in common. "You sound as though you know all about it."

"Sure. Along with the rest of the fraternity, and every other student body in the world. I'm assuming you didn't have a vehicle."

"Not until years later."

"Then you were spared. A car is the pits. Undignified and uncomfortable. No place to put your legs. And there's the horn, which has a habit of intruding at critical moments."

She laughed. "So I discovered, subsequently. You have to be pretty desperate to resort to a car."

Bill returned to their original topic. "So what went wrong?"

"Nothing, at first. It all seemed made in heaven. Not just the musical part. I had an Italian Grandmother, whom I adored. We even shared that his father was a surgeon, too."

"That's not necessary, though. Having things in common."

"It makes life easier." Of course, it was all old history, but there was still that vestige of hurt. Mostly to her pride.

"We left at the end of the summer, Marco to go back to Rome, me to do my second season with the Royal Northern; and I was actually one of the first violins. We spent that final night together in an hotel. We pooled our resources and decided we could afford a bedroom, as long as we did without dinner. It was wonderful. And we talked about the future. We promised to write as we had the previous year, when hearing from him had kept me going. I'd just live from week to week for those envelopes with his curly writing. The rest of the year was bleak."

"And?"

"And he sent me the usual stunning letters, especially when you consider that English was about his third language, or fourth. Pages and pages, saying how much he missed me, couldn't wait for us to be together. And I replied, trying to put half of what I felt into words." Again she found herself drying up.

Again Bill prompted her with a gentle, "And?"

"Moshe was delighted that I'd decided to come back, the following summer. It was all agreed. Marco would be returning, and I really thought, this time, that we'd get engaged. We'd had our time apart as we agreed, proving ourselves in the big, wide world. I thought we'd marry, I'd find a job in Italy, perhaps with the orchestra he was contracted to. I'd even started learning Italian, in secret. I was going to surprise him. Then, about the end of June, he writes to say that he's bringing somebody very special with him this year. Somebody he's longing for me to meet."

"Ouch."

"I didn't see it as an ouch. I didn't get any vibes at all. I thought, stupidly, it might be his kid brother or a grandparent. I just looked forward to seeing him."

"And the rekindling of the lust?"

She laughed a little shakily. "Of course."

"And was it his girlfriend?" Bill hazarded.

"Oh no. Not his girlfriend. His wife. His wife of two years. Sofia. And you mustn't forget the *bambino*. Bruno, about to celebrate his first birthday."

"Ouch, again. A double whammy."

"Yes. And worse. Imagine me standing in the staff common room on the upper floor, waiting for Marco to arrive. That way I can watch the drive. And this taxi pulls up, so down I sprint, my legs all shaky with the thrill of seeing him. He climbs out of the car, and sees me, and smiles. He doesn't rush across like last year to hug me. He just smiles, and turns to the driver to pay him . . . and there I am with my heart thumping at the sight of him, and out of the car climbs this angel. The most perfect woman, dressed in something so clearly designer that you automatically look for the label. And while I'm wondering who this piece of flawlessness might be, she leans over and picks up a truly enchanting baby. And honestly, Bill, he was just a tiny Marco."

Bill's arm about her shoulder tightened slightly. Emily wriggled closer to him and drew the quilt up under her chin. Her voice was very small, remembering her mortification.

"Then he says, 'Emily!' in a bright, interested way, as if he were addressing a puppy, or a servant, and turns to the gorgeous woman. In Italian he says, very quickly, 'So, *cara mia*, the unsophisticated little English girl I told you about. The violinist. You see, there was nothing whatever to fear.' And, of course, he didn't know that I could understand most of what he said, and guess the rest."

Bill kissed her brow. "The guy's the archetype of all jerks."

"Of course."

"And you're better rid of him."

"I know. It's history. Five years old, to be exact. *Bambino* Bruno will now be six. It's more the hurt to my pride."

"What happened next?"

She shrugged slightly. "You know how these things go. Subsequently I thought of half a dozen smart, cutting things I might have said. At the time I just stood there, looking like an idiot, and feeling as though I'd had my vital organs removed before my eyes. It was such a shock. He'd monopolized two full years of my life. And all the time he's married to Mrs. Perfection. I wondered at first whether they read my purple prose together and fell about laughing, but later, when I was in Rome, I discovered that the address he'd given me was his parents' place. Sofia would never have known."

"What did you do?"

"Nothing. I crept away to lick my wounds, as the saying goes, and thanked my lucky stars that we'd had the sense to be discreet. I'd told only my family. But nobody knew about us at the Meinhardt, which is what counted, then."

He brushed the hair back from her brow with gentle fingers. "Nobody deserves to be treated in that way. I feel I should apologize on behalf of all men."

"That's kind of you, but unnecessary. Maybe it's just a part of growing up. Creating a tough outer skin."

"But I'll bet that summer seemed long."

"It was the longest seven weeks of my life. And I think I was savage with the students. As I told you before, I realized at that moment how hopeless I was as a teacher."

"You're wrong there," he said. "You're a great teacher with the Morrison kids. I know. I've seen you and heard you."

She lay very still in his arms, wondering whether this was the truth, or whether he was simply being nice to make her feel better.

"Anybody could teach Kaffi. But do you think I'm making headway with John Wayne?"

"I think you show infinite patience, which is what he needs. And encouragement."

She sighed. "I hope so. And you, too. You're just as important to him." She turned her face to nuzzle up against his cheek, gently nipping the lobe of his ear with her teeth. "And thank you for that, Bill. Actually, thank you for everything."

Bill held her closer. "If we're talking about gratitude, I think I'm heavily in your debt. Thanks to you I started writing again."

"Me? It was really thanks to me?"

"Uh huh."

"But you were finished with the depression, weren't you? Before I arrived in Whangapouri?"

"Oh, yes. But it was like a plateau. I didn't miss the black despair, but in the process I seemed to have lost the ability to feel happiness. True happiness, as opposed to mere contentment."

"No troughs, but no peaks, either?"

"And a ghastly void of creativity."

She ran her fingertip down his nose. "You know, Bill, it makes me feel really chuffed, to think that I've helped you."

"I guess by 'really chuffed' you mean pleased?"

"You guess right. You don't say that in America?"

"Not in my vocabulary."

They lay in each other's arms, silent and very close to sleep. Then Emily said, "Bill?"

He was in a twilight area, about to slip into oblivion. "What?"

"Was JoBeth the cause of your breakdown?"

"Only partly."

"Was there any one thing, one event that caused it?"

He didn't want to talk now, least of all about that bleakest period in his life. "I guess." His voice was no more than a murmur. "Yes, definitely."

"Bill . . . could you tell me about it?"

"Now?"

"Yes, now. Please."

He rolled onto his back, as sleep receded. It was probably only fair to tell her. After all, she'd set the record straight about the Italian Lothario. Jerk that he was.

"It doesn't make for happy listening."

There was a pause. Emily drew spiral patterns on his chest with one fingertip. "You don't have to tell me. Not if it's really painful."

But, because he wanted her to stay with him, kept hoping that she'd present him with the opportunity to ask, he knew this was one hurdle that must be overcome. And he was horribly wide awake again. It was a tale that reflected no credit on him, he thought bitterly.

"Our marriage was finished. Had been finished for years. We still shared the apartment, JoBeth put in appearances at literary functions, but apart from that we might have been strangers. She was certainly seeing other guys. Made no secret of it. Then she became pregnant."

"It can't have been your child, not if you weren't even . . ."

"Life isn't as straightforward as that. There was one time. . ."

He winced, remembering that night, when he'd tried unsuccessfully to stave off his desperate mood with Scotch. And JoBeth had met him halfway. It had been a miserable experience, arising from anything but love. In the morning, JoBeth had turned the screw by informing him of how useless he was, in that as in every other way. She thought she'd married a famous author. He wasn't even writing. And he was the worst lay she'd ever had. But eight weeks later she was definitely with child.

"I do understand." Emily was quick to reassure him. "Things are never black and white. Go on."

"The baby was a girl. JoBeth called her Jaime. I remember looking at her, and trying to find something of me in her, or some feature of anybody connected to me. But all I could see was this tiny, fragile creature, dependent on me for the next twenty years of her life. It was a terrible thought."

"But not these days. Family courts are far more accepting."

"I couldn't sever myself from those bonds. Even when we did divorce, which was inevitable. The child would still need a father."

He could recall it all so vividly, standing beside the crib, looking down at the doll-like creature, feeling totally hopeless.

"JoBeth and the she-vampire made sure I had nothing to do with her. JoBeth went straight to her parents' place, although that was never going to last. They might have been comrades-in-arms against me, but they couldn't live together for more than two days without World War III erupting. She returned to our apartment, happy to have me pay the bills, and applied herself to maternity. You know, Emms, I never held that little girl. Not once."

Actually, he'd have refused to do so if asked, he reflected silently, willing the anguish to abate. There was that fear of bonds being forged, ties that would be infinitely painful to sever. From the start he knew that he must not become fond of Jaime.

"I watched her grow, wanting to love her, not daring to. She was a pretty little thing, blond and blue eyed. She didn't look like me, and she didn't look like her mother."

"And you didn't divorce?"

"Not then. I simply retreated."

"And then what happened?"

He held Emily as if her closeness could offer a shield against the horror of what happened. "Jaime was killed, in a car crash."

"Oh, Bill." Her response was filled with her agony.

"JoBeth was driving, there had been heavy rain and she skidded. The rear of the car smashed into a power pole. Not even the best car-seat in the world would have saved Jaime. And I'll live with the knowledge I was to blame for the rest of my life."

"But it wasn't your fault. What could you have done?"

"It was my fault. Indirectly perhaps, but that's no real excuse."

"Why?"

He heard his voice, sounding dry and almost clinical, as he explained. "JoBeth had once again taken herself off to her parents' place. Then she appeared at the door demanding more maintenance for them both. She tried her whole arsenal of tricks, including having Jaime there, and I saw that little girl's face pucker up as her mother screeched at me. I told her to let the lawyers sort it out. Then I closed the door on her. I could hear her out on the landing pounding on the door, and the baby crying. JoBeth skidded the car because she was so mad at me she was practically blinded by her rage. And an innocent life was lost."

"Oh, Bill. I'm so sorry." He heard the distress in her voice.

"I told you it didn't make happy listening."

"But I don't see why you should blame yourself. JoBeth wasn't some immature girl. She can take her share of the responsibility."

"That's easy to say. I say it often. It doesn't really alter things."

"Didn't your therapist help?"

"Eventually. Six terrible months later. And I've come to terms with it, since then."

Emily sat up in bed. "We'll never get to sleep. Not now. I'm going to make us something to drink. Why don't you see about bringing the embers to life?"

He was still reliving those agonizing weeks. He reached for his toweling robe, acknowledging that there was still a great deal of talking to be done, and turned to watch Emily wrap herself in the quilt.

"You remember the Serenity Prayer? About needing courage to change what you can, and the ability to accept that which you can't change?"

"And asking for the wisdom to know the difference. Yes, I remember it."

"Well, of the whole sorry mess the hardest part for me was discovering that wisdom."

❧

Healing, Emily realized, was not something that followed any particular formula. Nor was it external, to be applied like a Band-Aid over the wound. Healing came from the core and spread, like a pebble dropped into still water, in increasing and concentric circles. She was immensely moved by Bill's story and, more than that, impressed he had weathered so severe a storm to emerge the person he was today. His was a form of pain far beyond anything physical, beyond anything of which she could conceive. Perhaps there was some truth in the old saw that nobody is burdened with more than he or she can bear. And maybe confronting despair was perversely enriching, in the long run. Like the pain of exercise, as a necessary precursor to ultimate fitness. And out of the pain came the wisdom to accept.

And it helped her, too. Having been raised in England, there was a residue of doubt when it came to all that navel contemplation stuff. Maybe even a touch of scorn. Therapy was part of the American way of life, a luxury of the rich, to boot. Stiff upper lip, and all that, was the British alternative. Avoid any unpleasant thought, dissociate yourself from it, pretend it hasn't happened. Now Bill's story put her own, smaller crisis into perspective, forcing her to look to her inner resources. And from there, she knew, she could move on.

TWENTY-THREE

E mily's thoughts, as she trudged her way across the headland towards the Morrison's place, concentrated on connections. Obviously, their shared telling of failed relationships was the kick-off point. She could blame the sorry tale of Marco on her own naiveté, and find reassurance in the relatively light scarring it had left, but the awfulness of what had happened between Bill and JoBeth took a lot more understanding.

She tried to put herself in JoBeth's shoes but found it almost impossible, because such apparent viciousness was not in her nature, any more than the idea of using a child as a weapon would occur to her. Unable to comprehend she was forced to abandon the effort, and allow her thinking to move onto more rewarding couples. The older generation, for starters. Clearly, from what Bill had told her, he was the fruit of a very happy union, if of relatively short duration. Polly Thackeray, Emily decided, must embody some of the qualities of sainthood, in the way she'd abandoned a fortune in favor of family harmony; and there were her own parents, approaching their ruby wedding, demonstrating the power of deep and abiding love.

And then there was Heneti, with a foot in both generations. It might be worth asking her, at some time, how she'd come to terms with the life Hori's profession had demanded of her.

To her catalogue of relationships, she could add another. The Vernons. She'd managed quite a long talk with Ruth, during one of the Saturday evening gatherings.

She had initiated the conversation while they were awaiting for the summons to the dining table. Bill, at the time, was helping Hori to rearrange the seating, the arrival of two newcomers having made this necessary.

"Where did you live, Ruth, before you came here?"

"All over. We never really intended to put down roots. Our longest stay in any one place was South Africa. The people were delightful, but we hated apartheid. So we moved on."

"And what brought you here?"

Ruth shrugged, which wasn't very wise because her shawl abandoned one shoulder. Emily held her glass of wine while she rearranged it to her satisfaction. "Karma."

"Fate, you mean?"

"Or serendipity." The older woman's smile was serene. "There comes a time when you don't want to move on any more. In my case, I came to see that what I was running away from was myself. Somehow, wherever we found ourselves, I was still there."

This seemed so self-evident that Emily was hard pressed not to come out with a smart, but quickly regretted, remark.

"You see, my dear, I couldn't have children. That was a great heartache to me, and by transference, to Vernon. He didn't mind being childless, but he did sense my grief. And for a great many years I tried to outpace this loss. It doesn't work, of course, as I discovered. Eventually you run out of steam."

Emily would have liked, at this moment, to find something erudite and compassionate to say. As ever, her mind let her down.

"I'm so very sorry," she mumbled.

"No, there's no need to be sorry. There are compensations, as I found out. Once I'd come to terms with being childless, I turned to Vernon and to our marriage. We chose to settle here, because we found New Zealand to be all we required, and the people are so very, very accepting and friendly."

"And you've never regretted it?"

Emily noticed the look with which Ruth sought her husband, and when she replied her voice was quiet. "No, my dear. When you put all your energy into a marriage, it can only be for your mutual benefit. I've never regretted it. Or our settling here."

She wished that Bill could hear Ruth. Then, perhaps, he might see her, Emily, in a different light.

≈≈

The Morrisons' house was starting to look quite presentable. Certainly, Emily no longer thought of a cup of tea as a health hazard. It wasn't all her doing. Once the necessary motivation was supplied, as well as a constant source of electricity and clean water, Winnie proved herself to be quite a capable housewife. She did most things by rote, but somebody had taught her well in the past.

It was interesting to watch as the relationship between the mother and her eldest children altered subtly. When Emily had first appeared on the scene there was no doubting who was in control. Winnie had, to all intents and purposes, abdicated the role of parent in favor of her daughter. Now there was a bit of resentment creeping in, as Winnie sought to regain the authority that was rightfully hers. The resentment was more on Winnie's part than Kaffi's, but it was asking too much of any nine year old to understand the nuances of so delicate an issue.

John Wayne, of course, presented no such threat. It would never have occurred to him to step into the vacated shoes of his father. Whether Winnie gave the orders, or Kaffi, was all as one to him.

Emily, doing her best to keep the harmony of the family intact, concentrated on showing Winnie ways to encourage her younger children. She explained the importance of talking to all three, reciting nursery rhymes to them, playing simple number games. Winnie listened gravely, and did her best. In the case of Ani it certainly looked encouraging. The little girl started to blossom, became generous with her smiles and more independent in her ways. With Tama Emily was less hopeful. It would seem, at least at present, that he was the slowest of the Morrison offspring.

What might happen to the family when she, Emily, was not about to monitor progress, still caused some worry. It gave her a few sleepless nights. Optimism, however, came to her aid. This particular quality had been relegated to the back burner during the long convalescent months of body and soul, but re-emerged, as though appreciating that the time was auspicious. Refusing to cross this particular bridge until she came to it, Emily told herself that something would turn up. Their father would reappear. She had only to pray hard and wait.

On this particular afternoon Emily encountered Kaffi appearing from the general direction of the main road. She clutched several items of mail in her hand, which she waved cheerfully in Emily's direction.

"Been to get the post. Lots, ay."

Letters. Of course. Emily could have kicked herself for her stupidity. Here she was, assuming there was little more progress to be made, when fate intervened. And that such an obvious clue had been there, right under her nose. She wondered what on earth Winnie did, with whatever correspondence came their way.

"What happens to the post, Kaffi? Do you read everything for your mum?"

Kaffi shook her head. "Nah. They're all bills and that. Not proper letters, or cards like Christmas."

"You mean, you just throw them away?"

Kaffi turned a cartwheel, which wasn't so easy when clutching several brown envelopes in one hand. She didn't reply until she was again on her feet. "Nah. I put 'em on the shelf. For when me dad gets home."

"Do you think it might be sensible for me to go through them, with you?"

Kaffi stayed still long enough to consider this suggestion. "Okay."

The pile that appeared from a dark recess of the cupboard was formidable. All but the most recent additions were covered with the grime of some time. It was easy to spot bills among the circulars and junk mail items, and it stood to reason that quite a few of those at the bottom of the heap would bear the logo of East Coast Electricity. What did not stand to reason, and actually caused Emily to catch her breath in surprise, was the name displayed: Matu Cook. Not Morrison; Cook.

Kaffi was sitting beside her at the table, sorting out envelopes from fliers and advertising pulp. Emily turned to her. "What's your father's name, Kaffi?"

"You know that. Matu. That's Maori for Matthew."

"Yes, but Matu what?"

"Cook. Like Captain Cook. We learnt about him in school, ay. But he's not my ancestor, because he's *pakeha*, and the Cooks are Maori."

She said it in the matter-of-fact voice that she might have employed to identify anybody. It was a prime example, Emily realized, of the way you could be led astray by not asking the right question. It had never occurred to her that Winnie and Matu might not be married. And, come to that, there had been the efficient young woman at the electricity office who'd mentioned Cook. It was simply that Emily, incapable of seeing its importance, had been unable to complete the jigsaw.

The back door opened at that moment and Winnie appeared, her arms filled with newly dried laundry. The baby was asleep in the shawl on her back, glossy black head outlined in sharp contrast against his mother's fairness. Winnie had her hair neatly tied with a ribbon. She deposited the load on the bed and smiled at Emily. "Baby got two teeth. This morning. I felt 'em. Time to wean him."

Emily wasn't willing to give the child's progress a lot of attention at the moment, although she appreciated the significance of this milestone to Winnie. After all it was she who, following the advice in *Practical Steps in Baby Care,* had indicated to Winnie that *kumera*, even mashed, was not the preferred infant formula. And certainly not prior to the eruption of teeth.

"That's fantastic, Winnie. He's doing very well."

She returned to the importance of the correspondence before her. Obviously, even knowing that Matu was actually Matu Cook wasn't going to spirit him back to the bosom of his family, any more than Winnie, who had never been in any doubt of his name, would now be able to say where he might be. Winnie began to sort out the freshly laundered clothing. Her eyes strayed across to the pile of bills and she looked a little uncomfortable.

"I got no money."

Following her drift, Emily hastened to reassure her. "Of course not. Kaffi and I were just making sure there wasn't anything important which might have been overlooked."

Winnie neatly folded a nappy, corner to corner, flattened it with the palm of her hand, and folded again. Then she dropped her bombshell.

"I got a letter. From Matu."

Emily's knew her eyes were goggling with surprise. "You have?"

"Yeah."

"No you haven't, Mum. You know you haven't." Kaffi sounded exasperated, employing the same tone generally reserved for John Wayne.

Winnie looked at her daughter, her chin raised slightly. "You don't know. I have got a letter, too."

"Mum, we've been through all this lot. We'd have seen if there was a letter from Dad."

"It isn't there. I got it."

A note of doubt crept into Kaffi's voice. "Where is it, Mum?"

"Here. I keep it here." She delved into the bodice of her dress and from within her bra drew out a much-folded sheet of paper. She volunteered it to Emily with pride. "Keep it under my pillow, too. I like to sleep on it. Reminds me of Matu."

Emily, still somewhat in shock at this unexpected turn of events, managed to find her tongue. "How do you know that Matu wrote it, Winnie?"

" 'Cause I know his writing. Knew it was from Matu, soon as John Wayne collected it. That's how."

Kaffi practically snatched the epistle. "Give it to me!"

"Kaffi. That's not the way you speak to your mother."

Such finesse was lost on the girl at this minute. "Yeah, but she can't read."

"That's no excuse," Emily pointed out, hearing herself validate all mothers, everywhere. "You can still ask her politely."

With some dignity Winnie withdrew the precious sheet from her daughter's fingers and handed it to Emily. "Please. You read it for me."

Emily's hands were practically trembling as she unfolded the letter and flattened the creases with care. It must have been stowed away against Winnie's heart for some time, because the surface of the paper was rubbed from continual friction, and the writing itself had become faint.

"Dear Winnie,
I am verry sorry to be writing this letter, and I am verry ashamed of myself. You will see from the adress at the top that I have been verry stupid. I met up with the Turakina brothers in town, and we went for a few beers. There was this fella down from Auckland who drove the lorry, a Tongan, and he started the fight. He said some verry nasty things, but I now I shouldn't of lost my temper. I hope you will forgive me, becose I now I promised not to drink again, and I reely ment to keep my promise, Winnie dear. The judge gave me six months, because of my other time

in jail. He sed I was a repeet offender and must lern to control my temper. I now that.

Winnie, heer is what you must do. Go to Mr Bryant and ask him to take you and the kids back to the tribe. He is a kind man and I'm shure will do this for you. Tell him I will pay eny expenses when I get out of here. Thank him for letting us have the whare. He is a kind man.

Tell the kids I'll bring them there treat when I get out of here. Tell John Wayne and Kaffi to be good and help you all thay can. Thay are good kids.

I am quite well.

Your loving husband,

Matu.

P.S. XXXXX for the kids and XXXX for you.

There was a lump in her throat by the time Emily finished reading. So Matu was in prison. She glanced at the top of the letter, looking for the date. May. She had come to Whangapouri in July. It was now September. It looked as if Matu might be released in October, early November at the latest.

She carefully refolded the precious paper and handed it back to Winnie. "Here you are. And thank you for letting me read it."

"Our dad's in jail?" Kaffi turned for confirmation to her mother.

Winnie replaced her letter in its original home. "It's the beer." She appeared somewhat bewildered, herself. "But he promised me. After last time."

"He's been in jail before?"

Winnie nodded, looking infinitely wise and infinitely accepting. "After Kaffi was born. We lived with the tribe, then. I didn't like it. They never liked me."

Emily cleared her throat. Here was the solution she had been seeking. The solution to everything. The family should return to their people, as Matu had said. That was where he would look for them, when he was released from prison.

"Shall we arrange to get you back to the tribe? We could talk to Mr. Bryant, or perhaps Bill would take you."

Winnie's mood changed. The tenderness with which she'd listened to Matu's confession and instructions was replaced by a look of unparalleled stubbornness. Emily had encountered that look before. It explained where John Wayne got his streak of obstinacy.

"I don't want to go back. They don't like me. Say I'm stupid."

Emily spoke gently. "But that's what Matu wants for you."

"Matu's in jail." Her tone was heavy and sullen.

"Yes, but . . ."

The other woman sat down heavily on an available chair. "He can't say. He's in jail."

Kaffi voiced her thoughts. "Mum, that's what Dad told us to do."

But Winnie remained obdurate. "I like it here. I got no friends in the tribe. The welfare lady will come and take the babies away."

"Our nan's there, Mum. And Kui. She won't let them take the babies away." She turned to Emily. "And I could go back to school."

It was all too much for Winnie. Her temper snapped. "You'll do what I say, Kaffryn Mary. I'm the mother. I say what we do. And we stay here. You hear me? We stay here, I say, and you'll do what you're told."

Kaffi looked at her mother with round eyes. Emily wondered if she had ever before seen her so forceful.

She spoke with awe. "Okay, Mum. We'll stay here. And I can have my lessons with Em'ly, ay."

Thank heavens for Miss Phipps and Ma Rogers, and their insistence on Educational Basics. Emily was constantly amazed by how much she remembered of those early schooldays. She could even hear herself parroting Ma Rogers, explaining the difference between an adjective and an adverb, which preposition followed "different," which followed "similar."

Kaffi had a tremendous gift for story telling, and was happy to get all her ideas down on paper. Now letter writing was added to the English lessons.

It did not appear to bother her that Matu was in prison. Emily had done some nimble skipping, and mentally rehearsed phrases like "sometimes we can't be judgmental," and "your father was very sorry about the fight. And it's always important to forgive." The phrases remained unspoken. Kaffi accepted where he was and had already decided when they might expect to see him. She wrote him long and newsy letters, almost one a day, updating him on their doings and the baby's progress. At Emily's suggestion she didn't mention that his family had practically reached their nadir before rescue, or that during the coldest part of winter they'd lived without electricity. After all, Emily explained to her, as he couldn't undo those bad times, why give him the worry of knowing?

"But I'll say that you lent us the money, ay?"

She glanced up from helping John Wayne with some simple addition. They were using assorted shells as counters, a large scallop representing ten, smaller ones the units. "If you wish."

"How d'you spell Em'ly?"

"E-m-i-l-y."

Kaffi looked at the word. "Funny name, isn't it."

The owner of that name thought not half as funny as calling your family after 1940s film stars, but held her tongue. "Say there's no rush to pay me back. I don't want him to feel anxious."

Kaffi sucked the end of the pencil. "You very rich?"

"No. Why?"

She shrugged slightly. "I just wondered. You could be a princess, in disguise. Like in stories. And you talk posh."

"I'm nothing in disguise. Just me."

Kaffi returned to her writing, no more bothered by this dashing of her hopes than anything else. "That's okay." She smiled kindly. "I like you and I mightn't like you if you was a princess."

"Were," Emily corrected. "If you were a princess."

"No, I'm not," said Kaffi saucily, and laughed so hard at her own joke that she nearly fell off the chair.

❦

New York was sweltering. The humidity out in the street was such that every morning Janice O'Dell offered up thanks to the guy who'd invented air conditioning. If she hit the traffic right she could reduce the period between her apartment and the office to thirty-three minutes. It might have helped if she rationalized on her clothing, perhaps discarded a layer or two, but Janice wasn't into compromise.

The problem was that, if the truth be told, she was bored. Nothing on the immediate horizon got the adrenaline flowing.

Then, at the very moment when tedium seemed likely to countermand all else, she received a letter from Bill. She recognized his handwriting immediately. What she hadn't calculated upon was the effect it would have on her. Her fingers shook so much she had to will them to behave properly and open the fucking envelope, without reducing the enclosed letter to ribbons. It was a very short note, no more than the back of a postcard, actually. But each word carried such weight that their worth, to Janice, could not be measured.

He had turned the corner; was on the mend. Her patience had been rewarded, and that gorgeous hunk of man was writing again. Now all she needed to be certain that heaven really did exist, would be to hear that he was on his way back to the real world. Back to New York, and to her.

But then another thought formed itself. Why the hell wait? There was nothing to hold her in the city, and all he might be needing was a tiny nudge in the right direction. A touch of the proverbial carrot, as it were.

TWENTY-FOUR

t was about a week later that Kaffi appeared one morning with wings on her heels. John Wayne, who was usually the faster of the two, was having a tough time keeping up with her. She didn't even wait to say hello.

"We got a letter from Dad."

"Have you read it to your mother?"

"Yeah. Of course."

Emily took the envelope that was thrust under her nose. It felt a little intrusive, reading something not addressed to her. Kaffi noticed her hesitation.

"Mum said I could bring it for you to see. Dad mentions you."

She opened the sheets with reluctance. Matu had begun:

Dear Winnie, and dear kids,
I was verry pleased to get Kaffi's letters. I was verry worried about you, becos Kui said you were not with them. It is good to now that you are all OK, and that Gary Cooper has four new teeth. Is he sitting up yet? Emily must be a good person to help you. I will pay her back when I am working again.

Deer Winnie, the reverend has visited me here in jail and we have talked a lot. He is a very good man. I have becum a member of the church and red the books he has lent me. I will be baptized soon, here in the jail. I promise you there will be no more booze, becos I now it is rong.

Then I wont lose my temper. And the reverend says no more babys. Five is a very fine famly, he says. He has talked to me about it.

Becos I have behaved well I will be home in just four weeks.

I love you all. Your loving husband,
Matu Cook.

Emily folded the paper and slotted in back into the envelope. She liked the sound of the reverend gentleman.

"That's a lovely letter. Thank you for letting me read it.

Kaffi tucked her skirt into her pantie legs and stood on her hands. That way up she took half a dozen confident steps before righting herself. "He's going to be home, in a month. Then you can meet him.

"Four weeks," John Wayne corrected her. "Dad said four weeks."

Kaffi stuck out her tongue at him. "That is a month, dummy."

Emily parted them. "You're both right. Now, what about lessons?"

Janice drove the Range Rover as she did everything in her life, with verve and flair. She swept down the final half mile descent to Whangapouri, although her mood was considerably more benign than the driving might have indicated. In fact, she was positively buoyant.

Having made the decision, she was on her way to reclaim Bill. He'd wallowed long enough in his emotional mire. Six months was sufficient time for anyone to convalesce.

The sleuthing ability she'd discovered in herself had been gratifying, once the idea of coming to New Zealand had surfaced. The flight to Auckland had been long and tedious, even though she'd splurged on a first class ticket. Those shabby, narrow seats in cattle class were never designed to accommodate generous proportions such as hers, anyway. Then, when she was signing for the Range Rover, she'd had the sense to ask the guy exactly where this Whangapouri was. Driving on the wrong side of the road was hideous after all these years, and she'd left more than one idiot gaping open-mouthed in her wake, but that was their problem. If you were dumb enough to disregard the driving habits of most of the civilized world, you got what was coming to you.

As she swept around the corner by Hori's Store she wondered, not for the first time, why in the hell he had chosen such a hellishly remote corner of the globe for his convalescence. He could have gone anywhere, and he'd picked Whangapouri. Casting a jaundiced eye over the bay made her shudder. She saw nothing attractive in sand dunes and ocean. All that nature made New York seem appealing, even in high summer.

"Bateman's bach," the envelope had said. What the hell did "bach" mean? A plank, the name roughly painted on it, identified the place. It was secured with two rusting nails to a nearby tree. But she was a bit surprised by the shabbiness of the cottage. It was difficult to imagine the sophisticated, immensely attractive man that she knew, shacking up in a dump like this, illness or no illness. Talk about slumming it. She pulled the Range Rover into the driveway, climbed down with a swirl of her full skirt, and walked purposefully around to the front. Her knock on the door was followed by silence.

"Anybody about?"

Further silence; but the door was not locked, so she went in and cast a searching glance about the room. Hmm.

A cat chose this minute to make itself known. An unforgivably plain cat, which stretched and yawned, and showed signs of impending approach. Janice was wearing her favorite emerald green, and she had no intention of allowing brindle and white hairs to spoil it. The cat protested quite vigorously, but judicious prodding with the toe of her natty leather boot encouraged a hasty exit out the door.

She closed the door briskly and continued to inspect the house, although house was far too dignified a name. Inside it was everything she had expected, a clone of all the leased cottages they'd rented in the Australian holidays of her childhood. Her parents had favored The Entrance, a couple of hours north of Sydney, for happy family gatherings. Even thinking of them made her shudder. This place, like those, was furnished with Auntie Susan's cast-offs, the discarded articles from Uncle Ted's refurbishment. Other people's tat.

Ten minutes later she thought she knew what she needed to know, and not all of it was pleasant. There was definitely a female person in residence, and if the two pairs of panties and the wisp of a bra hanging out on the clothes line were any indication, the female was trim and young. Janice hated her for these facts alone.

However, on the credit side she had discovered, in different rooms, two beds neatly made up with sheets and pillows, and no actual evidence of Bill in the large bedroom. No pajamas under the pillow, no masculine attire hanging in the totty wardrobe. She had no compunction about opening drawers and snooping. After all, this man provided a large part of her bread and butter so, if nothing else, self preservation played a sizable role in her calculations.

But that wasn't all of it. She had known and lusted after Bill for eight years. Of course, while he'd been married to JoBeth one glance at that woman dispelled any notions of a bit of nookie on the side. Janice recognized an equal in JoBeth. But the marriage had crumbled without any intervention on her part, and Bill was legally free. It was just too bad that in the process he should have become so damned depressed.

She still felt smug the way she'd guided him through that, too, finding the best of shrinks, shielding him from stressful situations, nursing his interests. Blessed Saint Janice O'Dell, so help her. Dash it all, the guy owed her; big, as they said in America. And, by her reckoning, it was pay-up time.

From outside the door the cat mewed plaintively, begging entry. It had started to rain again, a fine drizzle. In Janice's memory it always rained in places like Whangapouri. Countless holidays cooped up in too small a space were remembered as damp and uncomfortable. The washing out on the clothes line would be getting wet. Too bloody bad. She tossed another log onto the fire, sat down on the second, cat-hair-free chair, and prepared to wait.

⟫⟪

Emily and Kaffi returned from the store by way of the beach. The rain was no more than a mist, not the sort to penetrate outer wear, so they simply discarded gumboots on the verandah and opened the door to let Mendelssohn precede them inside. You didn't need Mensa intelligence to read his annoyance. It was evident in every sharp twitch of his tail.

"Well. Hello there." The voice that greeted their arrival was rich and confident.

It was impossible to say who was more surprised, but the honors probably went to Emily. To her as well went the award for first regaining her wits. Kaffi, by her side, just stood and gawked.

"Who are you?"

This was not quite the gracious welcome of a stranger that might win a mother's approval, but the discovery of a woman built on Junoesque lines making herself at home by your fire isn't an everyday occurrence. Emily was out of practice.

The woman didn't exactly answer. Instead she said, "I'm looking for Bill Thackeray. I assume this is his address."

"That's right. He should be back soon." Emily tried to make amends for her earlier lack of manners. "By the way, I'm Emily Merivale and this is my friend, Kaffi Morrison."

Kaffi had continued to gawk, as if the stranger might be an alien from a far-off planet. Now she extended her hand politely. "Pleased to meet you."

The woman replied coolly, but did not respond in kind.

Emily held her hostility in check because, to be fair, the owner of that self-same hand had not five minutes earlier been demonstrating her skill at turning cartwheels on the sand. Her palm showed ample evidence of this feat.

"Can I get you anything to drink? Tea, perhaps, or coffee?"

"No, thank you. I believe I'll go and find some sort of accommodation. I'm told that the town has a bearable hotel. Tell Bill that I'll catch up with him later."

She stood as she spoke, delicately removing two or three silvery cat hairs from her skirt, and suddenly Emily had the feeling that the room was too small. Seated, the newcomer's presence was large, standing it was overwhelming. She had too much hair, and too much bosom. Resting on the latter was a concoction of copper and brass that brought to mind the dowry of an eastern princess. Her jacket fell from the shoulders in a series of pleats, and her skirt swept to the tops of smart leather boots. Emily owned a pair of boots like that, in her other life. Funnily enough, she'd not given them a thought in eons.

"May I tell him who called?" She spoke coolly, as if the appearance of strangers in your house were such an everyday occurrence in Whangapouri that the odd one might slip from memory. Although she knew who this woman was. It had all fallen into place. And who else, apart from his mother, might know that he was living at Bateman's bach. This overwhelming person had to be Bill's agent.

It was curious that he'd never mentioned her being female.

❧

"You got a visitor!" Kaffi almost fell over herself in her eagerness to break the news. "A lady."

"I have?" Bill, with John Wayne in attendance, appeared in the kitchen not half an hour after the Range Rover had departed amid squealing wheels and kicked up sand. His eyes swept the empty living room. "And you've hidden her. Or eaten her."

Kaffi loved the fun inherent in this idea. "Yeah. She was num. Juicy, ay."

"Your agent, Bill. Although she didn't actually leave her visiting card." Emily kept her voice casual, but looked carefully to ascertain Bill's response. However, he could conceal emotion so well that it was like trying to read a slab of stone.

"Janice? Here, in Whangapouri?"

"Not quite. She disappeared to find somewhere to stay. I didn't offer her the sunroom."

"You didn't?"

"You said yourself that the divan was jolly uncomfortable. But she'll be back."

Bill shrugged himself out of his jacket and found a towel. He rubbed the excess moisture from his hair. "Good. I've a load to discuss with her."

Jealousy seeped through Emily like the pain of toothache. It wasn't just that the O'Dell woman was large and dominant, and rudely intrusive. It was that echo of his other life. Life before Emily. Temporarily it robbed her of her new-found confidence.

"I'll put on the kettle," she said gruffly. "John Wayne, wash your hands before you sit down. It's like having a fish stall invade the house every time you two arrive home."

⚘

Bill had always known that Janice, given half a chance, would try to seduce him. He also knew that, although admiring her as a person and happy with her as an agent, not even that half chance would be presented to her.

But he owed her a considerable debt, and he did have quite a lot to tell her. He was fired with his new writing, and it was flowing well. He thought Janice would approve and he respected her judgment. She was, indeed, a four-star agent.

She appeared shortly after the Morrison kids had departed. The same old Janice, larger than life, sweeping in as though blown by a gale, reassuring in her confidence.

"Bill!"

She cast not as much as a glance Emily's way, but bestowed upon him a hug of grizzly proportions. He extricated himself with care. Becoming entangled in all that cloth might be life-threatening. She always seemed to drape too much fabric about her.

"I think you met Emily before, Jan? This is Emily Merivale."

Emily looked at Janice. Bill had not mistaken those earlier indications. For heaven's sake, Emily was actually jealous. Jan, he could understand, she'd always considered him her property, but he was surprised by Emily's response.

"We met before." Icicles formed, six inches from Janice's mouth.

Emily matched the chill, crystal for crystal. "I'll make some coffee. You two will have a lot to discuss."

He smiled at her, wondering whether by such an action he could warm the frost. He managed to catch her eye and wink, and was rewarded by seeing her shoulders relax a little. She smiled rather tautly back.

"Jan, sit in the sunroom. I've quite a lot to tell you."

Emily went into the kitchen. "You can stay in here. I'll walk along to see Hori, if I'm in the way."

They replied simultaneously. Bill said, "Don't be silly. You're never in the way," and Janice said firmly, "Yes, do that. Bill and I will want to talk in private."

Emily looked from one to the other, and stayed. Janice deliberately ignored her. She seated herself at the table, taking some care to spread her skirt out about her. She flicked away two or three crumbs, vestiges of the Morrison children's most recent repast. Emily pretended not to notice.

Janice fixed her gaze on Bill, peacock-shadowed eyelids heavy with intimacy. "You're writing again." A statement that required no reply. "And I have news, too." Her voice was loaded with significance. From out of her large, black portmanteau she withdrew a file. "Hollywood is interested in *The Forests of the Night*."

"It is?"

She set a pair of half-moon spectacles on her nose and looked at him over the top. "It's early days yet, but they're talking big bickies. There's a hint that De Niro has asked to see the part of Jake."

Bill tilted the chair back and twirled one of Kaffi's pencils in his fingers while he thought about this. If there was one man he saw filling the role of Jake to perfection it was De Niro. The part might have been tailor-made for him.

"Who're they thinking of, to do the screenplay?"

Janice shuffled her papers. "You. That's what I'm holding out for."

Too good to be true. "Honest?"

"They're playing hard to get. But I've stipulated that at the very least you have final rights, or we offer the whole shooting match to another studio. That made them sit up."

Through Bill's mind raced all the horror of *One Witch*, transformed into something suitable for the family channel. Bereft of its bite, bereft of its message. A process he'd vowed never to repeat. But if he could be involved in the screenplay for *Forests* ...?

Emily plonked down a tray on the table. Coffee, two mugs, sugar bowl, a plate of chocolate cookies.

"Did you hear, Emms? Hollywood, interested in *Forests*."

"That's very nice. Congratulations."

But, despite the formality of her words, he knew that she was feeling less threatened. She waited until they had finished their coffee before standing. "I think I'll walk along to see the Webbers, anyway. I'll be about an hour. Enjoy yourselves."

Janice paused only until the door was shut before she started.

"Bill, who is that woman?" She placed a lot of emphasis on the "is."

"My landlady."

"When I arrived there was the most appalling, ragamuffin child here that you ever saw."

"That was Kaffi."

"And who is Kaffi?" She didn't wait for his reply. "She looked unkempt and filthy, and her clothes were a disgrace. Not to mention the nasty, raw patch on her cheek."

Bill had also noticed that injury. Kaffi had explained that she'd been a bit too enthusiastic when climbing rocks in search of *pauas*. The scrape was the result of a carelessly placed foot.

"She's neither filthy, nor is the wound on her face anything you might catch. She's one of a family that Emily has befriended."

Janice leaned across the table, placing a heavily beringed hand on his arm. "Bill, you shouldn't be bothered by a child like that. You should be nurturing your talent."

Not all that long ago he might have agreed with her. Now he saw the remark as extremely irritating. He found himself justifying Emily and, incidentally, himself. He launched into a brief summary of how Emily had met Kaffi, how she had helped the family get back on its feet. He omitted certain parts, such as the fact that Matu was being detained at the New Zealand Government's pleasure, but he did include Winnie's slowness as validation, and emphasized Emily's growing skill as a teacher.

When he again mentioned Emily, Janice pounced on the reference with the enthusiasm of a trout leaping at a fly.

"You sound far too deeply embroiled in all this, Bill. It must be terribly time-consuming. And difficult for someone of your disposition. How did she manage to trap you into playing handyman?"

"My disposition?"

"A sensitive, creative artist."

"That's hogwash and you know it, Jan. And I wasn't trapped. It was my decision to help."

"So this young woman is your landlady."

"And friend."

"Is that all?"

He withdrew his arm, on which her hand was still intimately resting, and looked at her. The look was deliberately remote. Now, he thought, was the time to quash once and for all her personal interest in him.

"I don't see that as any business of yours."

"You know it is. Your happiness is vital to me. And your mental health. After all, you've only recently weathered an extreme crisis in your life."

"You think I'm unbalanced?"

She was quick with her reassurances. "You always did have inner strengths. I knew you'd emerge, stronger than ever. And you have so much talent, Bill."

"Which translates to mean I'm a good meal ticket."

Janice appeared to have missed the thrust of his words. Or had chosen to ignore it. She softened her tone and leaned across the table again, looking into his eyes. "More than that, darling. Much, much more."

She could have laid her message on with a trowel. He tried once more to put clear blue water between them.

"Jan, you've been a good friend when I needed you, and a fantastic agent. I'm more than grateful for both, and as a friend I'll always be in your debt. But my private life is my own, and that will never change. Now, let me tell you about my current project."

He wasn't too certain that she'd taken in his words but, without being deliberately cruel, he could think of no other way to spell out the boundaries of their relationship.

TWENTY-FIVE

ary Kelly, senior officer of the Social Welfare Department, drew her car onto the side of the road and re-scanned her notes. It was as well to reacquaint oneself with the known facts, before taking action. A family with several small children, she read, clearly living in very bad circumstances. Reduced to begging for food. A mother who was intellectually challenged, no mention of a father. Squalor. Health hazard. All potent stuff, although depressingly familiar, these days. Even the name of the child, which seemed to be dogging her at present. Kaffi Morrison, run to earth at last. Funny how, on occasions, fate took a hand while you were waiting for things to happen. Certainly, the idle Jim McGuire's half-hearted probing wouldn't have come to anything, without this recent spot of good fortune.

It had taken Mary Kelly a bit of delving to pinpoint where, exactly, the family was living. By a process of elimination she concluded that they must be on the Bryant Estate, so her first visit would be to the homestead. She knew of the Bryants, without having met them. Two elderly brothers, one widowed, the other never having married, who farmed the land which had been in the family for some generations. They weren't known for their up-to-date farming methods, but were generally agreed to be perfectly approachable.

One look at the homestead and she could appreciate that remark about old-fashioned. The whole place could do with a general taking in hand. No woman of her acquaintance would tolerate so run-down a house. The door was opened, in answer to her knock, by an elderly man sporting several days of stubble on his chin.

"Mr. Bryant?"

"That's me. Unless you want my brother, Godfrey." His voice was pleasant enough, without being overwhelmingly friendly.

Mary smiled. "I'm sure you will do. I'm actually making inquiries about a family called Morrison."

Mr. Bryant looked as if about to close the door. "Sorry. No Morrisons here."

From somewhere behind him a voice called, "John. She might be talking about Matu's family. Isn't his woman a Morrison?"

The man turned his head in response to his brother, then looked back to Mary. "Perhaps you'd better come in."

The room wasn't dirty but it, like the rest of the property, badly needed a woman's touch. Dishes were heaped to dry on the draining board, there were newspapers and farming periodicals in waist-high piles. Two cats wove, fawningly, in figures of eight about her ankles. From in front of the old-fashioned range a semi-comatose collie did no more than thump its tail a couple of times by way of greeting. A second elderly man, clearly the brother, rose to his feet from the table where it appeared he was doing the farm's accounts. The surface was covered with bills and papers. Mary sat on the edge of the proffered kitchen chair.

John was putting the kettle onto the stove. "You'll have a cup of tea, Miss . . . er, Mrs. . . . ?"

"Kelly. Mary Kelly. I'm from the Welfare Office. And I'd love a cup of tea."

"And you say that you're looking for Matu's family?" The brother she knew to be Godfrey spoke.

"If he is Matu Morrison."

"Well, he's actually Matu Cook. The woman is Morrison. What's her name, John?" He scratched his head. "Winnie, I think. Or is that one of the children?"

"No, you're wrong there," John replied. "The little girl's name is Kaffi. Don't you remember Matu telling us, and roaring with laughter? Her mother called her Kaffi after Katharine Hepburn, in *The African Queen.* Evidently can't get her tongue around 'th.'"

Godfrey smiled at the memory. "You're right. How could I have forgotten?" He turned back to Mary. "What's up? Kids playing truant from school?"

"Possibly."

"Well, I'm afraid you're too late. We can't help you. The family was here, for about a year, and we let them have the shepherds' *whare*, over in the ewe country. Matu did a bit of work for us around the place, in exchange for rent. And he was getting the *whare* into shape, too. Good chap, wasn't he, John?" His brother nodded in agreement, and Godfrey continued, "But he got drunk in the town one day, and ended up in a fight. I think it was his third offense, and Matu's a big chap. Strong, like. The other fellow was a bit knocked about, so the magistrate gave him six months. The family left, to return to his people."

"Are you sure?"

"Sure I'm sure. Matu wrote to us, from the prison. Very apologetic, thanking us for our kindness, etc. etc. Explained that his woman would be leaving. And the kids."

Mary accepted the cup that John offered her. There was one thing you could always guarantee about farmers. They knew how to make a good, strong pot of tea.

"No, I meant are you sure that the family left?"

Godfrey turned to John with an eyebrow raised inquiringly. His brother shook his head. "I thought that someone from the tribe would come'n pick them up, but I can't be certain. We don't go up there too much, in the winter. The ewes are brought into the holding paddocks, for lambing. Only a few run cattle up there, and they care for themselves mostly, or come down to the mangers for fodder. No need to go out into the ewe country."

"Mr. Bryant, would you mind if I take a look? We've had this report that I should follow up."

Clearly the same idea dawned simultaneously in two very attuned minds. John voiced their thoughts. "You mean, you think those kids and their mother have been living up there alone, all these weeks?"

"We do."

"But that's terrible. I mean, how will they be getting on? What will they be eating?"

Godfrey put down his cup with a clatter. "They could be going down to Whangapouri, you know. There's Hori's store, there. Our local celebrity, like. Used to sing with the New Zealand Opera. Keeps a store, these days. Maybe they're getting what they need from him."

Although the name did ring a distant bell, Mary had very little interest in opera in general, and none at all at this moment. She finished her tea and stood up. "The report we've got suggests that things aren't too good. I must find out whether they're coping."

"And what will you do then?"

"That depends. As the final resort we may be forced to take the children into care, although obviously I'd rather not. I gather that there are at least three infants."

She noticed the brothers exchanging looks, and read their thought all too clearly. Typical. People always reacted badly, when you mentioned taking kids into care. But they had never seen the conditions she'd witnessed. Even though the current thinking was heavily weighted in favor of keeping families together, there were some cases where that solution simply was not practical. Least of all when you were dealing with a very disadvantaged parent. The dice were too loaded against it.

Godfrey voiced the brothers' concern. "We'd be happy to help, Mrs. er . . . Kelly. Maybe Matu has a bit of a temper when he hits the bottle, but he's a good chap. Works well."

She kept her voice coolly professional. "That's very kind of you, Mr. Bryant." She turned to John. "Perhaps you'd be good enough to show me which way I get to the *whare?*"

〜〜

She mulled over the alternatives within the system and available for this family, as her four-wheel drive vehicle bounced over the ruts of the track. She seemed to be driving to the end of the universe, although the meter told her it was not much more than a kilometer. Then she rounded a hill, and the small dwelling was there before her. Wisps of smoke from the chimney immediately indicated that the place was inhabited, so at least one part of the report was true. The rest remained to be ascertained, but it was best to anticipate the worst. Her heart sank at the prospect.

But the initial indications were surprisingly favorable. She switched off the engine, climbed out and walked around the dwelling. A dozen white nappies flapped cheerfully from the line, alongside several articles of children's clothing. Elderly garments but, her professional eyes noted, clean and mended. Two small, dusky-skinned children sat on the verandah. They had a set of plastic pots and pans which they were carefully filling with mud. They looked up at her approach, and the older of the two, a girl, smiled shyly. Mary knew what to look for; seventeen years of social work gave one experience aplenty. These children were clean-headed, it would appear, although their lips were chapped, and the smaller one appeared to have a bit of a cold. But they were clad in warm pullovers and sensible lower garments. Their feet were cased in little red gumboots.

"Hello. Is your mummy in?"

The child said nothing, but her eyes swiveled toward the door.

Mary knocked. "Hello. Is there anybody at home?" She was marginally surprised when the door was opened by a white woman. "Are you Winnie Morrison?"

There was no doubting the fear on the young mother's face. The initial reaction, when she'd first appeared, had been one of pleasure, as if she expected to see someone welcomed. A friend perhaps. This response was quickly succeeded by a look of deep distrust. It was as if an ember had been damped inside.

Her voice reflected her resentment. "Who are you?"

Situations such as this were everyday events. The first thing necessary was to set the person at ease. "My name is Mary Kelly. I'm from the Welfare office."

The young woman made as if to close the door. "Go away."

Mary quickly inserted her foot between door and jamb. "I'd just like to talk to you, for a minute or two."

"Go away," the young woman repeated sullenly.

Mary kept her foot firmly in place and tried another tack. "I saw your little boy and girl. They're lovely children."

"Yeah."

"What are their names?"

"Ani and Tama."

That was better. A response. She was getting somewhere. "They seem to enjoy making mud pies."

"Yeah."

"And don't you have a daughter called Kaffi?"

"Yeah."

"That's an unusual name. Is she here, right now? Or is she at school?" Mary knew that not to be the case. For heaven's sake, she'd ploughed through school records several weeks ago.

"She's not here. Nor John Wayne, neither. Back soon."

Mary eased her body forward, so that she had a knee in the half-opened door. She gently pushed it a little wider. Winnie, if Winnie it be, did not resist.

"John Wayne? You do choose unusual names. Perhaps I could wait here to meet him and his sister?"

Suddenly the young mother appeared to give up the struggle. She let the door open abruptly, so that Mary was very nearly catapulted into the room. Her voice sounded defeated.

"Okay. But then you go away."

In fact the children did not appear for another half hour. During this time Mary made quite a few interesting discoveries. The *whare* might not be everybody's dream home, but it was clean and functional. It smelled of no worse than cooked fish and a certain mustiness that comes with old timber. The bathroom was at least serviceable, in her time she'd seen many worse. Clearly the family congregated in this one room, because a child's crib and the two ancient settees in the second room, almost certainly intended as a bedroom, were not made up. The large bed in the living room had clean sheets, and if the family elected to sleep all together, that was not entirely desirable, but also not sufficient evidence to suggest abuse. And Maori families often chose the closeness of communal slumber.

The mother was clearly very slow, but she was managing all right. Once her initial mistrust had subsided, she showed Mary the daisy clasp which held back her long, fair hair, and its matching necklace. She allowed her to inspect the cottage and admire the baby, sleeping in the shawl on her back. He was an attractive infant, clearly well nourished. His abundant black hair was glossy, his skin had the bloom of infancy and looked healthy.

There were other touches about the place, too, which Mary found surprising. The fresh, yellow and white gingham curtains at the window, the matching tablecloth, the small vase of ferns and grasses in the center of the table.

"You like a cup of tea?"

The brew she had drunk far too quickly with the Bryant brothers was still swilling about in her, and had probably scarred her throat forever, but Mary didn't want to undo the progress she had made by appearing ungrateful.

"A cup of tea would be lovely, thank you."

She watched with studied indifference the attention with which Winnie performed the small chore, the careful way she filled the shiny electric kettle, plugged it in, heated the teapot. Then, with equal care, how she added three tea bags to the pot and poured in the boiling water.

"One for each person and one for the pot," Winnie recited.

While she watched Mary was mulling over that report. Had the informant been malicious? It was not unknown for a spiteful neighbor to rat on a family. But not in this case, Mary reflected. She had been there at the time and had talked to the woman. A large person, with an abundance of hair, dressed in garb more appropriate to the set of a costume drama. There'd been a ring of authority in what she had to say. She seemed to know a lot about the family, come to that. Apart from where they actually lived.

Mary was taking her first sip when she heard noises that heralded the approach of the older children. Laughter, and cheerful voices, and the sound of running feet.

"I won!" The door burst open and a small girl bounced into the room, then stopped short as she saw the visitor. She was followed immediately by a fair-haired boy, his face flushed with exertion. And, hard on their heels, a third person appeared, a young woman with chestnut-brown hair, in whose hand was a laden carrier bag. All three were shocked into a silence that Winnie broke.

"This is my boy, John Wayne," Winnie said. "And this is Kaffi." She stood and walked over to the children, proudly putting an arm about each. Then she turned to the brown-haired young woman, and her voice was warm. "And this is my friend, Em'ly."

TWENTY-SIX

By the time Emily arrived home her temper was finely honed. There had been ample interlude to rehearse what she would say, and how she would say it. So it was unfortunate that such rhetoric didn't have a chance to spill from her lips. She saw the Range Rover at once, and realized that Janice O'Dell was yet again in residence. The fourth time in so many days. There was something about the Range Rover which fueled her annoyance. Perhaps it was the height compared with lesser wagons, perhaps it was that inherent assumption of the life-style for which it stood. Her father had one, back home in England, but his wasn't a spankingly new vehicle like this. His was mud-spattered and serviceable. And yet, she'd frequently told herself that she would invest in a very similar vehicle, should she ever consider living here for good.

She had no intention of confronting Bill in the presence of his agent, furious though she might be. There were limits to everything. It didn't take too much in the way of simple arithmetic to appreciate it had to be Bill who'd reported the Morrisons, for the simple reason that nobody else knew about them. Whenever they walked to the store, she and Kaffi, the girl never approached the building but melted into the bush to await Emily's return. There was just a chance that a second figure had been spotted in the dinghy by some far sighted person, but that possibility seemed remote.

She'd had quite an informative conversation with the Social Welfare woman who appeared, at least, to be fair-minded. And from that exchange she learned that somebody had, indeed, contacted the office to file a description of a family in need, small children, a mentally retarded mother. You couldn't see any of those details from spotting a boy in a boat, albeit using binoculars.

She did her best to explain Bill's motivation, although none of it rang true to her ears. She worked her way through the only scenario which held any water at all. He'd tolerated John Wayne and his single-minded adulation long enough. Being the object of hero worship became tedious. The moment had come to have this distraction removed. Perhaps it was the knowledge of Matu's being in jail that had been the final straw.

A large part of Emily refused to accept that any of these arguments could be true. She'd have laid down her life to vouch for Bill's integrity, and it was equally out of character for him to be underhanded. Surely he'd at least have told her of his intent. But, outweighing what she wished to believe, were the indisputable facts.

It would have been fine, had she been able to fling the door open and burst into her fine phrases. They'd have fought it out, cleared the air, and progressed from there. Or gone their own ways, if that were the only solution, although her heart twisted painfully at the very thought.

As it was, she entered the kitchen from the back verandah and silently began to prepare the evening meal. Ham and potato broth. Sustenance, she thought as she worked, for the ensuing altercation. She could hear their talk through the half-closed door. Janice had been on the phone, and was back to report the latest offer from Hollywood. Emily removed the meat from the cooked hock and peeled a large potato as she listened to the finer details of the impending deal. Then she selected one of Hori's more substantial onions.

She assumed Bill would have to go to California to write his screenplay. She knew so little about how these affairs were set up. But surely being on the spot would be vital. She did know that Jay had added the musical score to *One Witch* after its completion, but obviously that could not apply in this case. She tried to imagine Bill surrounded by the paparazzi and plastic inhabitants of Hollywood, and failed. He'd stick out among them like a sore thumb, too genuine, too three dimensional.

She removed the papery skin of the onion and started to chop. The fumes stung her eyes and she began to weep, the tears rolling down her cheeks. She mopped at them ineffectually with the sleeve of her sweater. Bill, two empty glasses in hand, pushed the door ajar three minutes later.

"Emms? What's up?"

"I'm . . ." She intended to continue, " . . . peeling onions," but somehow the hurt she felt about the Morrisons spilled over, and instead she sobbed, "How could you, Bill? How could you do it?"

He looked mystified. "Do what?"

"Be . . . betray them."

"Betray who?"

"The . . . the . . . Morrisons. To the Wel . . . Welfare Department."

He dumped the glasses in the sink and put his arms around her. She found herself clinging to his chest, sobbing into the rough texture of his sweater, and somehow the tears were not just onion-inspired, but were a genuine expression of her response to his possible deceit. She wept for some minutes.

"Bill? Are you coming?" The voice intruding from the living room was decidedly peremptory in its tone.

Bill held Emily back from him, so he could see her face. He ignored the obvious command. "What's this, Emms? Are you saying someone from the Welfare office has visited the Morrison family?"

Emily nodded and scrabbled in her pocket for a tissue. She scrubbed at her eyes.

"And you thought that I was the informant?"

Again she nodded, but then decided she'd better justify her reasoning. "Nobody else knows about them. And I talked to the woman. She said a report was filed, in some detail. Approximate ages of the children, all about Winnie's being slow, although she called it 'challenged.' Even that they were having to beg for food. And you know that's not true. Kaffi has never begged in her life. We always barter."

Again the voice from the living room interrupted them. "Bill. What's keeping you?"

The woman was laying claim to him, Emily appreciated. Of course she would have heard Emily crying, and known that she was home.

Bill gave her a quick hug and spoke into her hair. "Hold it, Emms. Stay here, will you?"

He pulled the door behind him, but his voice, although very quiet, carried plainly enough.

"Janice, I think you've taken information I shared with you in confidence, and made use of it."

There was the sound of fingernails clicking testily on the Formica table and the rather irritable tapping of a foot. But Emily, mopping her eyes, awarded Janice marks for not prevaricating.

"Darling, the authorities are always best at dealing with these situations. It was clear to me at once that somebody had to take matters in hand. And I knew that you wouldn't want to offend your landlady." She said the final word archly. Emily could imagine the look which accompanied it. Eyebrows raised, crimson-shadowed lids half lowered, mouth pursed a little. "I decided that I must act for you. It was for everyone's benefit, you'll agree."

Emily had never seen Bill angry. Not truly furious. There had been the occasion when she'd thrown his book into the puddle, but that was as nothing to this. Of course, she couldn't actually see him because he'd told her to stay put, but the vibes from his rage permeated the intervening space.

His voice was even softer but it carried just as clearly. "You overstepped the mark, Janice. And betrayed the trust I placed in you. You intruded where you'd no right, and badly damaged a young woman you've not even met. That damage might be irreparable."

"But darling, I only did what I thought was right for you. In the circumstance."

"Let's get this straight, Janice, once and for all. I'm not your property. Sure, I'm grateful to you, and I always will be. That doesn't mean you own me. And I don't need you deciding what's right for me."

"Bill . . ." Emily could imagine her. Coquettish. Gross.

"I guess I'd better spell this out; we have a professional relationship. I thought it a good relationship, and I'd like it to continue, but that's all. There'll never be anything else between us. And if writing the screenplay for *Forest* is dependent on any other sort of connection, then the deal's off. I'm not interested."

There was a gasp. "Not interested in the best thing I've ever negotiated?"

"Not if it means dancing to your tune, in and out of the bedroom. Not if it includes you nosing into my private affairs. Not if the price is this sort of manipulative, emotional blackmail."

Emily was starting to feel sorry for the woman. The exchange had gone far enough. She wiped away the last vestige of her tears and emerged into the living room.

"Bill, you've told me so many times that Janice is a brilliant agent. That she always remembers to read the fine print." She stopped when she saw their faces.

There was a startled silence. He looked at her, surprised that she was pinning her colors to the wrong flagstaff. Janice cast a thunderstruck glance her way, too. She was a far cry from the confident, overbearing woman who swept into the bach as though owning it and its inhabitants.

Bill broke the silence. "So?"

"Then that's it, isn't it? You don't want to say things you might regret, and find that you can't ever work together again. And there wasn't really too much damage done to the Morrisons."

"What?"

"The Welfare woman was quite impressed. She told me so. She's going to say that they're managing well, and I told her about Matu coming home in a few weeks. She was surprised to hear about him. Perhaps you'd forgotten to mention that." She turned to Janice. "Matu is their father. He's in prison, right now."

A sort of groan escaped from Janice, although whether it was because of Matu, or because of what Bill had said to her, was hard to ascertain. Emily chose to assume the former.

"He's not a bad person. In fact, she said that the Bryant brothers, who own the *whare*, think quite highly of him. But he got drunk, and there was a fight. Now he's become religious. He wrote to say he was being baptized. Oh, and he's giving up alcohol, so it's probable he'll never get into trouble like that again."

She could hear herself babbling, but it seemed to be working. The atmosphere improved almost discernibly, as both antagonists used the space she had created to simmer down. She glanced up at Bill and saw him grinning wryly, obviously aware of her motive. That was more like the chap she knew and loved.

He turned his attention back to the seated woman. "Well, Jan?"

Janice O'Dell made quite a display of placing all her papers together in a tidy stack. Then they were returned to her black portmanteau with equal precision. She kept her eyes averted for some time before speaking.

"Well, Bill," she replied coolly, echoing him. "I'll relay all that we've agreed over the phone, and get back to you in the morning. I certainly hope that they agree to those final terms, because I can't hang about in Whangapouri much longer. Staying in that nasty little hotel is driving me distracted. I'm afraid I find it hard to leave civilization, these days. And all this nature is so very wearing, compared with city life."

She stood and gathered up the shawl that lay draped across one armchair. The gesture with which she threw it about her shoulders could not have been bettered by Sarah Bernhardt, at her most gothic.

"And if you have plans to remain here much longer I'm afraid I'll have to insist that you install a phone. I guess it'd be too much to ask for e-mail? That is, if New Zealand has managed to emerge from the Dark Ages into the era of technology. The use of carrier pigeons just isn't the same."

꿍

To Emily's relief, Janice left Whangapouri two days later. Even now that the ground rules had been established, a little bit of her went a long way. By the time of her departure the contract with the Hollywood studio looked all but settled. It was, to quote Janice, merely a matter of crossing the t's and dotting the i's, and perhaps Bill wouldn't mind borrowing some sort of wheels when it came to signing the contract. She didn't think she could face another trip to this barbarous outpost.

She was very gracious. You did not require x-ray vision to see how desperately she lusted after Bill. Having to climb down and admit defeat was always painful, probably even more if you were of Janice's personality. She must have had several pretty tough hours of contemplation, while she came to terms with the fact that her lust was to remain unreciprocated. Emily had only to think of Marco to be fully appreciative.

So it was that she found herself held by the shoulders and kissed in an affected, half-peck manner, as Jan's lips just brushed her right ear.

Janice spoke in that woman-to-woman voice which always managed to put Emily's teeth on edge. "Look after him, dear, won't you. He's a special guy. I'm entrusting him to your care."

It was on the tip of Emily's tongue to reply that she wouldn't be here all that much longer herself, but then she extinguished the thought at half-birth. Bill had known Janice for eons. Perhaps it suited him to establish a purely working relationship, once and for all. To tell Janice that she might not be about, that there wasn't, actually, any commitment agreed between them, would be to allow a rekindling of hope. And Bill could, once more, be forced into a corner. It was for the better that she stay silent. So she smiled in wordless agreement, and left it at that.

Janice turned to Bill and hugged him. Having never made a concession to the informality of Whangapouri life, she was, as ever, draped in yards of jersey wool.

"Oh, you wicked wicked man. Electing to stay in this backwater, when I could have you under my thumb in the Big Apple."

"Maybe that's why I prefer it here, Jan. Away from that thumb." Although his tone robbed the words of any sting, and was accompanied by a smile, Emily noticed that it was his remote smile, not the one which wrapped tenderly about you.

Janice wagged a roguish finger in his direction. "Naughty boy. Teasing your number one fan." She sighed deeply. "Anyway, I'll have the contract faxed through to that address you've given me, and you can toddle along there to inspect it. And if they're on schedule at the studio, I'll see you in sunny California in January."

The way she said "you" was all-embracing, including Emily with Bill and his writing.

Emily sincerely doubted it.

❧

That was part of her trouble. Time was slipping by. She had less than three weeks left of her lease, and things seemed to have ground to a halt. Under that general term "things" she lumped such matters as the solving of the Whangapouri mystery, and some determination of their current relationship, hers and Bill's. Only the Morrison/Cook family seemed destined for a happy ending.

She knew such a lot about Bill. She thought she knew what made him tick. Unfortunately, with that understanding came the knowledge that any permanence in their relationship might well be seen as threatening. Shackles, similar to those associated with JoBeth. Or Janice. And she knew that she'd offered him any number of opportunities to dispel this assumption. When she gave it some thought, it all stemmed from what had been said on that wretched morning, the time when her mouth took on a life of its own and betrayed her.

And, of course, that was fine with her because she had no desire for a long-term commitment, either. Far be it from her to foist herself, willy-nilly, onto a man who did not need her. Really, the only undertaking she could see for herself was to civilization, and shops and city life. In that she shared a mild sympathy with Janice, who was bolting back to the neon lights of Times Square.

Emily had casually mentioned the proposed time in Hollywood, just to sound out the water. Bill had replied, briefly, that the shorter it was the happier he'd be, although he knew himself to be a novice in the business of screenplay.

On the second occasion the subject arose he explained, equally fleetingly, that he'd have the first draft with the director soon, via Janice. The studio could take it from there.

It was just too bad that whenever she thought of the future without him there was that awful sensation of hollowness. Complete emptiness, actually. But, looking on the brighter side, she had come to Whangapouri in far worse state. She would be leaving knowing that she had, indeed, healed, that she was strong enough to face the future. Alone.

In time Bill would probably find himself back in New York, picking up the pieces of his old life. Or perhaps not New York, but Cape Cod. It seemed likely that he'd find somewhere on those windswept beaches where he could write.

She thought very seriously about suggesting a compromise, along the lines of their spending part of the year together, in some center of civilization, the rest of the time in a place of solitude. Maybe even here. But she could never quite voice the words,,which was stupid when you considered how frequently they shared far more intimate exchanges. Somehow she thought she knew his response without going through the motions. It was as though she feared the worst, and was too cowardly to put it to the test.

Instead she could be grateful that they had experienced so much together, that he had helped her to mend, inside and out. And, she repeatedly told herself, she would soon forget him of course, in the excitement of her new career.

Whatever that might be.

TWENTY-SEVEN

I t was Bill who suggested that they invite the Webbers to dine with them. Reciprocation in part for those Saturday get-togethers. It was Heneti who thanked them, then turned the tables by pointing out that they couldn't leave Kui alone, so why didn't Bill and Emily join them for an informal, family meal. "Tea," Heneti called it. Just the five of them, to be eaten at about six p.m.

It was a comfortable, low-key affair, the conversation general. Occasionally it needed to be repeated because Kui dreaded being left out, and voiced that dread in high, peevish tones. Emily was once again impressed by the boundless patience Heneti exhibited where Kui was concerned, especially when you remembered that the old lady was her grandmother, not her immediate parent. She wasn't too certain whether this trait was shared by all the Maori, or whether Heneti, to quote Bill, was a very special person.

Once they were satisfactorily replete, and a decent interval had elapsed in which to appreciate the quality of their fare and to assist digestion, Emily rose to assist their hostess clear away. Kui, having eaten a sparrow's share of the repast, nodded off, and the men were left to entertain themselves. Men might help clear away following the Saturday soirees by virtue of sheer volume, at other times the kitchen was exclusively Heneti's domain, and fiercely guarded accordingly.

She was even reluctant to accept Emily's help with the washing up, agreeing, it occurred to her guest, because good manners would allow for no other. So Emily was granted the favor of swiping a cloth across those articles for which space could not be found in the dish washer. Most of this was done wordlessly. Originally Emily had found this daunting, reinforcing her own loneliness, these days she was sufficiently comfortable with Hori's wife to accept the silence as part of the fabric.

"Has Bill ever told you the story of Hinemoa and Tutanekai?"

Emily shook her head, fully aware that when Heneti chose to talk it was to some purpose.

"I'll tell you, then, while the coffee's brewing. It's not a legend, it's a true story, like the lost lovers. Hinemoa and Tutanekai lived on the shores of Lake Rotorua. Well, Hinemoa lived on the shore, and Tutanekai lived on an island in the lake, called Mokoia. Hinemoa was a young woman of great beauty, and her fame was such that everyone in the surrounding tribes had heard about her. Many of the young men wanted to marry her, but she would have none of them."

Heneti paused long enough to take down five mugs from their hooks. Then she found a tray. Emily, watching, wondered where this tale was leading them.

"Tutanekai was a fine musician. While his brothers were boasting that soon this one or that one would win Hinemoa, he would play his flute and think about her beauty and her gentle ways. And in her village on the shore Hinemoa would hear the notes, which carried clearly over the water. It was inevitable that at some time these two should come together and fall in love, and that is exactly what happened. One day the people from the island paddled across in their canoes to the mainland, and the young couple had only to meet to know that each had found a soulmate. But the elders of Hinemoa's tribe were not about to let their most beautiful daughter marry Tutanekai. They had far more important plans for her.

In a stolen tryst the pair agreed that Hinemoa would wait until nightfall and paddle across to Mokoia, to join her lover. But the elders had seen how she looked at Tutanekai, and they'd ordered all the canoes to be pulled high out of the water. Hinemoa didn't have the strength to launch even the smallest. And, across the water, she could hear the sweet music of Tutanekai's flute conveying his message of love.

Night after night she crept down to the shore, night after night she found the canoes high and dry. She began to despair, wondering whether Tutanekai had started to doubt the strength of her love. And out of her desperation came a solution. If she could not paddle, she would swim across to the island. That was a very brave thing to do, because it was quite a long way, and the night dark. She slipped off her cloak and slid into the cold water, taking with her some gourds tied together to help her stay afloat. Then she began to swim towards the sound of her lover's music. She swam until her strength was all but exhausted."

As she listened to the tale unfold, the thought occurred to Emily that perhaps here was a parable of Heneti's life, as she followed Hori about the world. Was that why Heneti had chosen to relate it?

"Over on Mokoia Tutanekai sadly put away his flute and returned to the *whare*. Clearly Hinemoa would not be coming tonight. So now the girl had no direction to follow, and no music from which to draw strength. It was only the resolve within her that gave her the ability to carry on. And so it was that, some time later, she heard the sound of waves lapping, and knew that she had reached the island. When she dragged herself ashore she felt the chill of the night wind, and wondered whether, exhausted as she was, she would die before she could find shelter. Fortunately, with the last of her strength, she fell into a thermal pool close to the shore. The swirling warm waters revitalized her.

But now she had the problem of locating her lover. She had shed her clothes in order to swim, and her nakedness made her feel shy. Then she heard someone coming, and she sank down in the pool. The person approaching stooped to fill a calabash, and Hinemoa, speaking in a gruff, deep voice, challenged him, asking who he was, and why he was stealing the water. Startled, the man replied, 'I have been ordered by Tutanekai.'

'Give me the calabash,' Hinemoa ordered in the same deep voice, and taking the gourd she broke it against the rocks. Of course this frightened the slave, who would have to return to his master empty handed, and who thought he had met an evil spirit. He ran back to report these strange events, and Tutanekai, assuming the man was trying to explain his own carelessness, ordered that he take a fresh vessel. Well, of course, the same thing happened again. Once more Hinemoa seized the slave's gourd and smashed it against the rocks, and then again, a third time. Now, at last, Tutanekai began to believe that this was not just negligence. 'Let this evil spirit show itself to me,' he said, taking up another pot. And he approached the hot pool and cried, 'Come out of the water, cowardly one, and face me, Tutanekai.'

Well, those were the words Hinemoa had been waiting for. Using her own voice she spoke softly. 'Don't be angry, Tutanekai. It's me, Hinemoa. I broke your pots.' And she rose out of the water, naked and beautiful.

Then they were married, and the residents of Mokoia accepted her as one of theirs, and her own people realized that the power of her love had overcome all the obstacles they had put in her way, and they agreed that Tutanekai was a worthy husband.

So that is the story of Hinemoa and Tutanekai. One day, if you go to Whakarewarewa, you can see them, carved above the gateposts of the *pa*."

The end of the tale was followed by silence. Emily was still trying to connect its message with Heneti and Hori, and their marriage. The idea of following the music was easy enough to accept, but she could not fathom where the rest of the saga lead them. Unless to Whangapouri.

The coffee machine registered that it had completed its task with a series of rich gurgles. Heneti placed the sugar bowl on the tray.

"Do you understand what the story tells you?"

"Sort of . . ." Emily gave up the fruitless effort. "No, not really. It's a lovely tale, but I'm not too sure about its message."

To her surprise Heneti took Emily's hand between her own warm, brown pair. "Think about it, *e hine*. You can follow the music only so far. You can find yourself in the warm water of the pool. But sooner or later you have to be brave enough to climb out of the pool."

"Me?" The surprise she felt echoed her voice. She'd been a long way from equating the tale of the lovers with her own life.

"Yes, you. What are the walls of your pool? And the depths? Are they tied up with your music? Or with your other life?"

Emily, mildly confounded at this abrupt change of direction, remained silent.

"And what about Bill? It takes courage, you know, to make that final commitment. That's what I mean, about climbing out of the pool."

"But . . ." She was about to launch into a litany of how it wasn't she who could not commit to anything but Bill, whose unhappy marriage had made him trigger-shy. But then she remembered her own unconsidered, ill-advised words, and she closed her mouth. Perhaps it had been her inner self talking, advising her to flee. Or, to share Heneti's analogy, to stay in the water, hiding her nakedness. Not the nakedness of the body in her case, but the rawness of the soul.

And suddenly, immediately, the unthinkable happened. She found herself floundering in panic mode. Cowardice of the worst, most craven sort seized her from within; and with the cowardice came a huge rush of adrenaline. How had she found herself here, in this remote place, among these alien people? She, who needed the succor of the city, and the feel of solid pavement under her feet. Surely they were trying to trap her, by insisting that Bill could not exist without her. It assumed the guise of some awful plot, designed to ensnare.

It took all her will-power not to abandon her cup of coffee right now, this very instant, and summon Bill to set off along the track with her. As it was her hand shook slightly with the effort, spilling a brown puddle across the table-top. Heneti appeared not to notice.

The men, left behind in the living room with the somnolent Kui, had also lapsed into companionable silence.

After a decent period had been observed Hori asked, "Got any further with our mystery? Our lost pair of lovers?"

Bill was thinking how nice a port would be at this minute. He'd enjoyed alcohol in the past, and regretted that it was no longer available to him. A small matter when compared with the troughs of his despair, but in retrospect something which added incalculably to the sense of well-being that follows partaking of delicious food. Like saying 'Amen' at the end of a prayer.

"I can't pretend the sleuthing business is flourishing. But Emily's an optimist. She lives in hope."

"You went to the headland? Found the vent?"

"Yup. Magnificent views."

"But not a lot for Sherlock Holmes."

"No, although Emily's pretty sure she's located the place where they met. Where the stream changes color."

Hori's look, Bill thought, was a mixture of mildly smug and avuncular-benign. The sort of expression which might well be seen on the face of a benevolent grandparent, dropping clues for a kids' treasure hunt. He could understand that look, because on certain occasions he had a tough time living up to Emily's expectation.

"And what about the author stuff? That flourishing more happily?"

His writing was progressing, although he was honest enough to admit that creating a screenplay was fresh territory. He rarely considered it good, and was inclined to re-work a scene or a conversation until unable to separate the leaves from the trees, but that was the only way he knew to write. However, the outline was in shape. Infill would follow.

"I've been thinking about passion. Juggling about with it. Nothing to do with this script for Hollywood, but with my novel. I'm not talking about the sexual sort, but the extremes of emotional depth."

"Passion." Hori rolled the word about his tongue, savoring it as he savored Heneti's delicious food. He was partaking of the very port for which Bill longed. He held the glass up to the light so that it glowed a rich, soft ruby. "Passion," he repeated. "The stuff that makes life worthwhile. And it changes, doesn't it. Maybe with age. Certainly with maturity."

Bill agreed. "When you're in your teens, you can feel intensely about things that would leave me cold, today. Whether the school team wins or loses. How well your country does at the Olympics. Unimportant things."

"But important at the time."

"Sure. To quote Pope, passion's a good servant, but a bad master. Like fire, and water. Both destructive, when they get out of control." He paused to reflect. "Have you ever stopped to think how many of our great writers died from alcoholism, or suffered from mental illness?"

Hori gave this thought the consideration it deserved. "Can't say I have."

"It's as though the flip side to being creative is the problem of dependency."

He was aware of Hori's anxious look. "But not you. You don't need alcohol."

"That's not my particular cross to bear. But when the doctors wanted to prescribe drugs after my breakdown, I refused them initially. I was frightened that they'd numb my senses too much, so that I'd be unable to feel in sufficient depth. And if I couldn't feel, how could I write?"

Hori grunted. "Same with singing. Getting into a part. You have to experience it deep, deep inside, if you're going to convince your audience. Can't just pretend to feel, because any audience'd see through that." He was silent long enough to enjoy another sip of port. "So what did you do in the end? Compromise?"

Bill flexed his shoulders. "In the end I accepted treatment with ill grace. As the least awful alternative."

"And you lost the passion?"

"At first. It was as though I'd been enveloped in a vast, senses-numbing shroud. I had to re-discover it. By degrees."

Again Hori grunted, but his glance was shrewd.

Bill did a bit of mental editing. The re-discovery of the passion was still recent history, and as such something of a surprise to him. He'd been sitting in the sunporch, temporarily bereft of words, and tossing about the concept of emotion, as pertaining to his hero. How, he pondered, did the guy respond. It seemed reasonable that it was tied to his feelings for the girl, the beautiful young slave woman. And in part his pride would be in his people, his position within the tribe. The Maori were a fiercely proud people. How would he, Bill, respond in a similar situation? He'd abandoned the typewriter and instead doodled on a scrap of paper alongside. His thought pattern encompassed euphoria, and yearning, and elation, and despair. The extremes of passion, he mused. It was when he allowed his eyes to focus on his doodling that he'd realized that he had written and rewritten one word. *Emily. Emily. Emily. Emily. Emily. Emily. Emily. Emily.*

It came as a shock, to discover how much of him focused on her, how intense were his feelings where she was concerned. It made the possibility of her departure even more painful, more poignant.

As the silence lengthened he became aware of Hori's quizzical expression and hauled himself back to the present. "I'm going to miss Emily. When she leaves."

His friend didn't appear to find the abrupt turn-about in the conversation at all unusual. His smile merely broadened. "Aren't we all? But my Heni most of all. Since her accident she thinks of her as a special friend."

〰️

"The Welfare woman explained it all to me. Suggested that I might follow it up. It's called Correspondence School, although these days, of course, they also use modern aids."

Emily was folding the household laundry. She crossed to where Bill was sitting at the table, a copy of *The Auckland Herald* spread before him, and silently held out the corners of a sheet. She had mended the cuff of that shirt last night having decided that, like Janice, she should cross the t's and dot the i's before she left. Bill could, at least, look kempt.

"How does it work?"

"I'm not altogether sure. Evidently a packet of lessons arrives by post. An adult has to supervise the children, as they work. Then it's all sent back to the teacher for marking."

Together they folded the fabric and tugged to get it into line.

"What's the alternative?"

She shrugged as she gathered up the sheet and completed the folding process. "The school in the town, I think. It's called a District High School, and it caters for all ages."

"Mightn't that be better? Especially when you've gone."

Every time he mentioned her departure Emily's heart wept a little. Not once had he said, "Don't go. Stay here with me." But it was so important that this conversation be initiated by him, not her. Then there would be no hint of shackles. And yet he seemed to accept that there was no alternative to their parting. He spoke of her going with regret, but he'd not once gone beyond that, given her so much as a fingerhold on which to cling.

She brought her thoughts back to the education of the Morrison children.

"It's the distance they'd have to travel, and the time. Over an hour and a half, morning and evening. That's three hours out of the day, spent in a bus."

Bill accepted the second sheet and aligned the corners. All this had an easy solution, he thought, if she were to stay. Move the family into Whangapouri; supervise them herself. But he wasn't going to beg her to change her mind. He'd kept hoping that, given time, she'd hint at the possibility that she saw them as more than ships passing in the night. That she might, even, see something permanent in the relationship. But recently her talk had been all about when she returned to her other life. There were repeated allusions to the pleasures of restaurants, the picking up of old threads. What did she want? That he play devil's advocate, perhaps. Or that he beg.

Well, he would, if he thought there was any point. He'd get down on his knees and plead. But he'd come to a decision, too. He wasn't going back to New York. Nor would he live in any place where getting from A to B was a daily battle. Even now he was not wildly excited about the thought of California. A time to be endured, although worth the price for keeping the screenplay of

Forests his own. It wasn't as though you met your ordinary, decent American amid the artificiality of Tinseltown. He'd made up his mind to settle in Whangapouri. And, to be honest, the faster he could return to this place of blessed solitude the happier he would be. In Whangapouri, he felt, he'd rediscovered Cape Cod as it used to be. As it was during his adolescent years, before the tourists took over.

In his perfect world Emily would be there, beside him. But not Emily as she now appeared, busy keying herself up for imminent departure. It was important that his Emms return of her own free will, to accept all that Whangapouri and its way of life had to offer.

And, even more vital, was that she left unencumbered by guilt, the guilt motivated by her perceived abandonment of him. He could only hope that, if he allowed her to return to that other existence, she might discover it wasn't all she'd anticipated. And if that proved not to be the case . . . then they were probably better apart. Although the idea hurt like hell.

He handed the neatly creased cloth back, watched as she doubled it over, then again, smoothed out the material with one hand and added that article to the pile. He looked at the curve of her back, and the set of neck and shoulders, trying to absorb even the smallest details about her for the future. He'd never seen her decked out for city living. Hose and heels, skirts and smart jackets. His Emms wore jeans and sweaters, and no make-up. He wondered whether he would find the other version as appealing.

〰️

Emily was still wrestling with the tale of Hinemoa and Tutanekai, and Heneti's allusion to its parallels with her own situation. She could understand the reference to the swimming and to her, maybe, being at this moment in some sort of pool. If you translated 'pool' to mean hiatus. After that she confessed herself to be totally in the dark. So she was pleased when a message arrived, via Bill, asking her to stop at the store in time for 'smoke-o.' That, she knew from earlier invitations, was about ten-thirty, and meant tea.

Heneti led the way to the big living room, leaving Hori to tend the store. There was a trickle of early visitors, appearing with the warmer weather. On the way along Emily had noticed several of the holiday baches with open doors and evidence of spring cleaning under way. Kui was asleep in her chair, tiny white head drooped onto her chest. It always looked hideously uncomfortable, but Emily knew that this was her habitual position. Heneti put the kettle onto the range and measured three spoonfuls of leaves into the old-fashioned, brown-glazed pot.

"So you're still leaving."

"Yes."

"Only a fortnight to go."

Emily perched herself on a high stool alongside the breakfast counter in order to give herself more time. She knew that Heneti was thinking about the story she'd related. She knew, just as clearly, that Heneti really wanted an update on her progress, pool-wise. "Yes."

"I'm sorry. I thought you might stay here."

"Heneti, I know what you're referring to. But that was never on the cards. As I told you, I'm not a rural type."

Heneti found where the milk jug was hidden in the refrigerator. "Bill's going to miss you."

Emily bit her lip. This was not exactly a conversation she welcomed, because it put her on the spot. But Whangapouri was so small a place that everything happening within its confines was of interest to the other inhabitants. After all, she herself had been one of the first to rejoice with Talitha, when she found herself pregnant. And in telling her the legend Heneti had staked a claim to friendship. Without meaning to offend Emily was rejecting that claim, refusing, even if unintentionally, to take aboard the analogy of the pool. But there was no way that she could explain that flash of hideous panic, that moment when she had felt threatened by the very act of their caring.

She spoke defensively. "Maybe. But he's a very independent person, and he's perfectly happy for me to go. And he'll have Mendelssohn for company."

"A cat's not the same. No conversation."

She watched as Heneti poured boiling water into the pot.

"He doesn't need conversation." She played her trump card. "Actually, it was inevitable that we'd not stay together."

"Inevitable?"

"That's the theme of his new book. The one which he's weaving about the story of the lost lovers."

"It's a strong word. You'll need to explain what you mean."

Emily, having given this a fair bit of thought, felt that she was on firmer ground. "I think he realized it, long before I did. Perhaps not when he started to write, but since. The similarity between the story and us is quite obvious, once you're aware of it. He knew it was unavoidable that we'd go our different ways. Our lifestyles are too dissimilar."

Heneti poured a stream of amber liquid into each mug. "How're they so dissimilar, then? These lifestyles. You tell me."

Before their friendship developed Emily would have considered such a demand grossly intrusive. Now, knowing that her host's directness was not intentionally rude, she drew a deep breath and did her best to elucidate. She drew parallels with the time that Hori and Heneti had lived overseas, the cities they'd visited, the museums and art galleries, the concerts and the shops.

"It was the excitement that went with it that I miss. I managed a sort of juggling act. Northern Hemisphere for our season, Southern Hemisphere for theirs. I've made the right connections so I have friends all over the place, and I knew I'd always have a job. Maybe not the leader of course, or what the Americans call the concert-master, but a decent chair to park my behind, in a decent orchestra."

Heneti listened in silence. Then she shrugged dismissively. "I couldn't wait to get home. Hated living abroad. Needed to put down roots."

"But you had children. I don't."

Picking up the tray, the older woman led the way into the living room. She spoke over her shoulder. "Hated it before I had children. Hated it more, after."

The Webbers' was one of those relationships about which Emily had thought at some length. Perhaps this was the opportunity to explore it further, and at the same time remove the topic of herself from center-stage. "Then why did you go, if you disliked it all so much?"

Heneti's look was serene. "Hori needed me, right there beside him. And I needed him. That's why."

"But what about your girls?"

"You don't marry your children. You marry your husband. The girls were secure and happy, living with my mother, their grandmother. And without me Hori would have been nothing. Nothing at all. He depended on my physical presence, just as I couldn't have managed without him. That's why I arrange our musical evenings, in the winter. Each time I cook, I'm saying thank-you to him. The food and the music are my gifts."

That was an amazing speech for Heneti. Emily regarded her with awe. Clearly, her external composure hid a great depth of ardor. Emily felt a little uncomfortable in the face of such conviction. She decided to redirect the discourse.

"Kui's looking well."

Heneti glanced at her sleeping mother, as though she might have shed a dozen years in the last few minutes. But evidently she recognized Emily's remark for what it was. This conversation was getting bogged down in intractable arguments.

"We have the final dinner of the season next Saturday. I'll put a side of hogget on the spit. That's lamb, to you English pommies."

"You mean, you don't hold them all year?"

"Only during the winter. For the residents."

"Oh. I see." She'd been considered a resident, then. Quite an honor. Or maybe she'd been allowed in on Bill's shirttails, as it were. The people of Whangapouri certainly considered him to be one of them.

Heneti returned her empty mug to the tray. "We thought we'd make it your evening. Like a farewell."

"Mine?" Even more of an honor, in the circumstances.

"Yes. You can select the music. Your favorite records."

Emily felt herself going pink with pleasure. And by accepting that she really was leaving, it appeared that Heneti had no intention of pursuing the uncomfortable parable of Hinemoa and Tutanekai. "Really?"

Heneti nodded. "It was Hori's idea. One musician's gift to another, he said. But you'll have to choose what we have in our collection, unless you've got your own discs with you."

Three months ago the idea would have appalled Emily. It would have been like rubbing salt into the wounds. Agony. She thought with amazement how far she'd traveled. Now she could accept the music for what it was. An integral part of her past. Something wonderful that would be with her always, although in future in a more passive capacity. She juggled with the idea of including Mendelssohn's *Violin Concerto* in her selection, and concluded that it would be okay. The healing was inside as well as out.

"And could we have a sing-song, afterwards?" It was still novel and exciting, the way the Maori contingent could pick up their guitars and break into harmony.

"Of course."

Emily crossed to where Heneti sat, large and seemingly impassive. She wrapped her arms about the older woman in a warm hug. Of course, you couldn't really tell how she felt, because her flawless, milk-chocolate skin hid any color, but Emily had the feeling that, inside, she was blushing.

"Heneti, you couldn't have come up with a lovelier farewell. Thank you so much. And for telling me the story. Although I have to say you're wrong, about me being still in the pond. If anything, I haven't even started to swim."

TWENTY-EIGHT

mily had never considered herself to be a child psychologist, but you couldn't go through the process of growing up yourself without gaining a few clues into the working of the young female mind. Even so, Kaffi's reaction to her impending departure caught her unawares.

After all, she'd always acknowledged that Emily's time in Whangapouri was finite, and already there was the happy event of her father's return to create a rosy glow in the very near future.

And such a small remark ignited the fire of her anger. They were tackling the business of essay writing, courtesy Ma Rogers. Emily had even complimented Kaffi on her most recent work.

"The correspondence school teacher is really going to enjoy your stories," she'd concluded.

"Stupid correspondence school." Kaffi, seated at the table, shoved the exercise book abruptly across the Formica surface, crossed her arms and laid her head on them.

Emily couldn't believe her ears. "What did you say?"

The head was raised six inches. Angry eyes set in a mutinous face scowled at her.

"It's your fault. You shouldn't be going away. You oughta stay here."

"You'll like your new teachers. They talk to you on the radio."

Kaffi slipped off her chair and stamped her foot. "Dumb new teachers. I hate them. You oughta stay here and teach me 'n John Wayne."

Her brother was in the middle of a labored exercise in forming his letters. He looked up admiringly. "Kaffi's cross."

There were occasions when he really got under Emily's skin. This was one such moment, but she ignored it to concentrate on the greater issue. She put an arm about Kaffi's waist and attempted to draw her close. Kaffi stood her ground, her body rigid, her face still dark with anger.

Emily tried reason. "Darling, you knew I wasn't going to be in New Zealand forever. You say yourself, 'While you're here.' This was my time of getting over my accident. I never intended to settle down."

Kaffi fixed her eyes on some spot on the floor. "You never knew us, then."

"But your dad'll be home soon. You won't need me to help you, when he's about."

"Will, too."

Reason, clearly, wasn't going to work.

"Kaffi, I can't change the way I am. I really like you, and John Wayne, and all your family . . . no, that's wrong. I really love you all. But I can't change me, in order to accommodate you." She thought of that panic attack which had hit her at the store. If ever the subconscious had a message to tell, surely that was it. And the residue of that attack had not entirely departed. It lurked on the fringe of her consciousness, as though waiting to re-ignite.

Kaffi looked up. "What's accommodate?" For the first time in this little spat her body lost some of its rigidity.

Emily took advantage of that softening to draw her closer. "It means, I can't alter me, to make myself what you want me to be. And even if it were possible, with the help of some magic dust, you mightn't even like that other Emily." She paused to see if her words were having any effect. Kaffi kept her head lowered but peeked through her lashes. "And I absolutely promise that I'll write to you, and let you know where I am, and what I'm doing. You can look the places up in an atlas. And I'll almost certainly come back to visit."

"It won't be the same."

But Emily was sensing that they had passed through the turbulent waters, and were sailing on calmer seas. "Of course it won't be the same. Correspondence school's bound to be better. I'm not even trained, you know. I can't introduce you to all the things your new teachers will be able to. And you're so good at your lessons, that quite soon you'd be having to teach me."

Kaffi look up. "Honest? Me teach you?"

Emily smiled, her warmest smile. "Honey, I'm only a hop skip and jump ahead of you now. In a year or two you'll be wondering what subjects to choose for your career. To be a doctor, or a lawyer, or perhaps a teacher. You'd make a marvelous teacher. Believe me."

"Me, too," said John Wayne.

Emily hoped that her lie would be forgiven. She squeezed his fingers. "Of course," she agreed. "Absolutely. You, too."

It blew in the night. The gale was not like a Southerly Bluster, which came directly from the Antarctic without the impediment of land, and took three days to blow itself out. This wind came from the west, dry and insistent. It swirled down the valleys and the hillside and found fresh gaps between the weatherboarding of Bateman's bach that no Southerly had penetrated. It wailed like a banshee and roared like an animal in pain. It made Emily shiver and draw closer to Bill, in the iron bedstead. It encouraged Bill to put his arms about her, and then to wonder unhappily what the future would be like when she wasn't there, in his arms.

He woke first in the morning, and was immediately aware of a relentless, nasal whine. So the wind was still with them. He couldn't recall anything similar to this gale, during his time in New Zealand. He left the bed carefully in order not to disturb Emily, and drew back the curtains in the living room.

Something was different. Very different. The sea, even at ebb tide no more than a few hundred yards from the low dunes, was only a thin line on the horizon.

"Emms, wake up!" He shook her shoulder. She was a notoriously deep sleeper.

"What?" A muffled voice from somewhere in the pillow.

"I think it's the tide. *He tai rereke.*" She screwed up her face and stretched slowly, then settled herself again. "Remember the wind that drives the sea from the shore? Like in the legend."

Suddenly he had all her attention. She swung her legs over the side of the bed, winced slightly as her feet met the floor, and sped to the window. No doubting her alertness, now.

"Oh, Bill. This is what I prayed for. The very thing we needed."

He wasn't entirely certain of her drift, but it became clearer by the minute as she ran into the bedroom and began to scramble into her clothes.

"Quickly. We have to hurry. There's no knowing how long the wind will last."

He began to dress more slowly. "What do you have in mind?"

"To explore, you dimwit. Try to find the entrance."

"To the vent?"

"I don't know. I thought I'd never know. But now we've been given an opportunity to find out. Don't you think that's fate?" She was thrusting her feet into her rubber boots. "Bill, hurry. Please."

They must have made a bizarre sight, he thought, had anybody focused binoculars on them at this minute. A couple sprinting along the beach in the early light of morning, complete with jackets, backpack and flashlights as if about to head for an

Eagle Scout jamboree. And for what? Without wanting to put her down, he had very little faith in this idea of Emily's, that they might find some sort of sanctuary in which the lost lovers had sheltered. It was too close to fantasy. And, to give weight to his misgiving, surely some other questing soul must in the past have considered such a possibility. But no record existed, as far as he could ascertain. In his opinion they had drowned, their bodies lost somewhere along the coast. Tides could do strange things and behave in unexpected ways.

The wind whipped up the dry sand and flung it at them, so their cheeks stung and their eyes felt gritty. It took the words from their mouths as they spoke, making conversation hazardous. They found it easier to bend forward, shielding their faces from the worst of the onslaught, and refraining from speech. At one point Bill paused to pick up a length of driftwood, smoothed by the action of water into an acceptable staff. You never knew when it might come in handy, should this hare-brained notion of Emily's bear fruit.

It was a merciful reprieve to arrive in the lee of the headland, and to be spared that constant battering. The two tall pillars, Nga Ipongaro, generally surrounded by swirling eddies, stood high and dry like a pair of beached obelisks. Similarly, the outcrop of rocks which buttressed the point lay abandoned by the sea, skirted by mussels and limp fronds of drying seaweed.

"Come on," Emily urged, picking her way around the boulders.

It was important to progress carefully across the difficult terrain, because the weed was slippery, although here and there they encountered patches of smooth, virgin sand. Bill looked up. He'd never see the headland from this angle. The cliff towered above them, rough and uninviting, with only the occasional, small shelf to relieve the steepness. The further they progressed, the more he felt that this whole excursion was an exercise in futility.

They were almost around the point, and within hailing distance of the neighboring cove, when they spotted it. And only somebody deliberately searching would have noticed, even then. A low, dark opening, not much more than a meter in height, and even now guarded by a pool of water.

"Oh, Bill."

Further words were unnecessary. So, maybe, Emily's faith had been rewarded. She turned to him, her face radiant. One of her most appealing attributes, he thought, was the way her features mirrored her pleasure. There was none of JoBeth's careful and guarded arrangement of expression.

He reached across and took her hand. "You really want to go on?"

She nodded mutely.

"And you don't suffer from claustrophobia, or black-o-phobia, or any other phobia?"

"I don't think so. I've never been inside a cave to find out."

"There's no certainty that this is a cave."

But Emily swept aside such doubts. Obviously, she was as sure at this minute as she'd been when the possibility of a secret escape route first struck her. Bill resigned himself to the inevitable. He realized at this moment how fortuitous it was that he'd chanced upon that torn off and wave-tossed bough.

"I'll lead. Water has a way of playing tricks with sand."

The pool at the entrance might seem innocuous, but there was no guaranteeing it would continue so shallow. It wasn't the easiest of approaches, being forced to bend almost double, stretching ahead with the exploratory stick. He wished that, like Emily, he possessed a pair of rubber boots. Chilly water squelched through his sneakers.

The beams of the flashlight showed only a diminishing passage, which might peter out at any minute. But then, just as he was about to retrace his steps, his questing probe encountered . . . nothing. He dug the tip hard into the sand and almost lost his footing as the stick failed to find solid rock beneath the sand. He fell to his knees in the shallow water.

"What is it, Bill? What's there?"

"Wait a minute, I'll tell you."

He slung the strap of the flashlight about his neck and pushed up his sleeves as high as possible before proceeding. Then on hands and knees he crawled forward, edging his way with care until he was able to duck his head under the last ridge of overhead rock. The stick, unable to find anything substantial, informed him that, should he progress any further, he would probably be swimming at any minute. Clearly the narrowness of the entrance had created a sand bar. Already wet from the thigh down, he straightened slightly and fumbled for the flashlight.

Emily's voice followed him eerily as he swung the beam about. "Bill?"

He replied over his shoulder. "It's okay, Emms. You'll have to creep, but the water's shallow. I'll wait here for you."

She was beside him almost immediately, as if excitement had added an urgency to her movements, although the pack on her back proved awkward through the last few feet. He let the light play on the rough walls before him.

"Oh. It really is a cave."

"So it would seem." Their voices sounded hollow, echoing about the space.

It wasn't very large, the cavern illuminated before them, perhaps no larger than the living room in an average house. Before them lay a still pool of water, deep enough to hinder their progress, if its darkness were any guide. The rest of the ground was littered with rock, where the roof had obviously collapsed at some long-distant time. The fall rose like a landslide to one side, and it was apparent, from the deep stain on the walls, that the cave was usually half-filled with water.

Bill stood with care. "Come on."

They had to skirt the deeper water, Bill feeling the way ahead with the precious stick, but within minutes they were on the rock-fall. Emily shrugged the backpack from her shoulders and found her flashlight. She always called it a torch, a word to which Bill constantly objected. A torch, he argued, required a naked flame atop some sort of receptacle. Like the Olympic flame. Emily, having pointed out that the English invented the language, refused to budge. Now she let light from the disputed utensil probe the space.

"Do you think they found this place, too? When the sea retreated?"

No need to ask who. "Probably."

Emily looked about her. "Then what?"

He was still examining the area with the exploring beam, a few feet at a time.

"I don't know. The air seems fresh, which is one of the clues you look for. But I'm not sure whether constant tidal coming and going would act as a purifier."

"There must be another exit. Otherwise, wouldn't stale air just gather up by the ceiling? And it would be musty. This just smells of salt. And don't forget the noise that we heard on the headland."

Bill started to climb the heaped rocks with care. The lower ones, clearly habitually submerged, were treacherous with black slime.

He bent down toward Emily. "Here. Take my hand."

"Where are we going?"

"Following a hunch. Remember the old boy-scout trick, with a wet finger? I think there's a draft, and it's from somewhere behind this lot."

They climbed in silence, concentrating on the task. Droplets of icy water dripped from the roof onto their heads. One found the precise spot where Emily's collar ceased to afford protection and she gave an involuntary yelp. But Bill's hunch was quite quickly proven correct. Beyond the rock-fall there was another chamber. And this was a very different affair.

"Wow."

The beams of their flashlights failed to reach the extremes of the expanse before them.

"Bill, it's enormous." Her voice in the vastness sounded tiny and filled with awe.

The cave was long and narrow in shape, high enough that no more than a small pool of water had collected at its lowest point. The floor rose steeply before them. Bill stooped to touch the surface of the pond with one finger, and then tested it with his tongue.

"No salt. So the sea doesn't penetrate as far as here."

Emily leaned against a ledge of rock. "I'd not thought of anything like this."

She looked about her, the rays alighting on a series of stalactites which descended from the roof like tapered organ pipes.

"Yes, but it's still beyond anything I'd imagined. And so big."

"Shall we carry on?"

The rocky floor here was rough, but easy enough to traverse. After several minutes climbing the chamber waisted, then opened again.

"Are my eyes getting used to the dark?" Emily asked, "Or is this part lighter?"

"Definitely lighter." Bill continued along the cavern, the floor now rising more steeply. "Aha."

"What?"

"Look, up there. I'm betting that's the start of our vent."

Emily followed the movement of his head. Together they strained their eyes toward the upper reaches of the cavern. The area high above was definitely less dark. Was daylight percolating through the coarse grasses that grew on the headland? But, if so, it was doing so at least forty feet above their heads.

Emily voiced the thought that must have struck them at the same time. "Nobody could escape through there, Bill. Not without sophisticated climbing gear."

"No."

"And they'd have been stumbling about in the dark, as well."

"Yes."

"Oh, Bill." Her voice sounded so forlorn that he reached across with one arm and hugged her comfortingly. The movement caused his flashlight beam to bounce from rock to rock.

"Do you think they could have returned, out the entrance?"

"Emms, I doubt it. Not if the legend is correct. It can't have taken Kapiti all that long to descend from the headland, and by the time he reached the point the tide had returned."

She sat down on the nearest flat surface. "So they'd have been trapped."

"I'm afraid so."

"That's so sad."

"Maybe it was to be expected."

Emily had turned off her flashlight. Now she clicked it on again and let the glow linger on the surrounding walls. "No it wasn't. There could have been a happy ending."

Bill's thoughts immediately switched from Te Manawanui and Waikura to himself and Emily. They could have a happy ending, if she allowed for the possibility. Unable to voice this, he remained silent.

"Bill?"

He cleared his throat, suddenly tight. "What?"

"If they couldn't escape through the vent, and they couldn't return the way they came, they'd have had to stay here, wouldn't they?"

He snapped back to the present. "I guess."

"Then shall we look for them?"

"Emms . . ." He hesitated. "You know what you're saying?"

She stood, pulling her jacket about her. "I'm getting chilled. And my feet are freezing. We shouldn't have worn jeans, because cotton stays cold when it's wet." He could see her shiver, in the reflected light. "Yes."

"Yes, what?"

"Yes, I appreciate what I'm saying. Do we have time to search?"

Bill calculated what he knew of the tide. By his reckoning there should be several hours before it should turn.

"But we'd better not hang about. Let's get going."

It was easier said than done. In the end they returned to the first cave and tried to retrace the steps that the lovers must have taken, switching off the flashlights now and then and feeling their way, in the manner that they imagined Te Manawanui and Waikura might have progressed. Unless they had drowned in the pool, or been buried under the rock-fall, there was nowhere that might conceal two bodies in that confined space. But it wasn't so hard to find your way to the large chamber because, once they were aware of it, the fine draft they had previously noticed touched their faces as though leading them on.

Exploration of the large chamber was considerably more complicated and hazardous. There were small recesses and antechambers to investigate, and stalagmites and stalactites to circumnavigate. On one occasion Emily mistook her footing and fell awkwardly onto her newly mended arm. The fall elicited the tinkling of glass, followed by a grunt of pain from her.

"Emms? Are you all right?"

Bill covered the distance between them with fright giving wings to his heels. She sat up and rubbed her elbow.

"I'm okay, I think. But I've lost my torch."

Bill swung his beam carefully over the surrounding area. The glass of her flashlight had shattered against an outcropping of limestone deposit. But the bulb, at least, had survived. Its light was no longer diffused by the protective glass, but it was better than nothing.

After that they proceeded with more care.

It was perhaps half an hour later, when they appeared to have traversed the ground of the cave as thoroughly as possible, that Emily glanced up.

"Bill ..."

"What?"

"Up there. Are the shadows playing tricks, or is there something on that ledge?"

He followed the direction of the skinny gleam. The ledge appeared to be quite broad, and shielded from immediate view by a series of icicle-like stalactites. He let his own flashlight ascertain a potential mode of ascent, and it wasn't impossible, if you edged your way along the crack which ran diagonally along that section of the wall. And the shadows did suggest that something might be lying up there. An involuntary shiver crept along his spine, like a ripple of discordant notes.

"Do you want me to investigate?"

Emily's voice was not much more than a whisper. "No. We'll look together."

"Then be careful."

They had no choice. The narrowness of the crack which allowed them access saw to that. But there were adequate handholds, and the rock beneath their feet appeared solid enough. For fully ten minutes they edged their way upwards, toward the shadowed ledge.

TWENTY-NINE

e had encountered death before, but had Emily known it would be like this? There was no flesh left, after nearly two hundred years. Just bones lying as if arranged, side by side, the skulls grinning hideously in the light cast upon them. The first light, he thought, to touch them since they had sought refuge here. Rats would have scavenged the bodies and their clothing in the early months, although there were the remains of a cloak-like woven garment. But it was impossible not to be deeply moved by the discovery.

Emily didn't say anything for several minutes. He wondered if finding the lovers would be too much for her, if she'd cry. He wasn't too far from tears, himself. But when she did speak it was with quiet respect.

"Do you see, Bill, they died in each other's arms. You can see that his arm is shielding her. And they would have had water, wouldn't they?"

"Yes." He knew to what she was alluding. To die of starvation was bad enough, but to die of thirst was a terrible thought. Although goodness knew what the quality of the water in that pool was like.

There were other artifacts, should they have wanted proof that the taller figure lying before them was the remains of a high-born man. A greenstone *tiki*, which would have been about his neck, a small calabash, a serviceable *mere*, the Maori club, by his side.

"You were right. It was the only possible solution. I see that now."

He would have liked to put his arm about her, to copy the loving gesture of the pair before them, but the narrowness of their perch made such a move impossible.

"Emms, we know as many answers as we'll ever know. I think we should be getting back. We've no idea how long the tide will remain out."

She nodded in agreement and they began the precarious business of retracing their steps. In silence they descended to the floor, then made their way back toward the entry cave, through the narrow waist, along the rough, rock-strewn ground, over the rock-fall.

"What is that noise?"

He'd heard it too, and premonition filled him with foreboding. It was as they breached the apex of the fallen roof that his worst fears were realized. He'd gotten his calculations wrong. The noise they were hearing was water rapidly filling the smaller cave. It came in surges, driven not so much by the incoming tide, as by the sudden abatement of the wind, allowing the sea to regain its rightful bounds. The flashlight confirmed what he already knew. They sat down on the highest of the rocks. Emily's hand sought his. He wondered if she appreciated the danger they were in.

"We've been very stupid, haven't we? Not anticipating this."

"We allowed ourselves to get too involved exploring. I had given it some thought, and I reckoned that the sea would return quickly, but not this fast. Like a tidal wave coming in."

He felt her shiver through their joined fingers. "Are we going to be like Te Manawanui and Waikura?"

"Not if I can help it."

"What can you do? Climb forty feet through the air, like the Indian rope trick?"

Now was the moment for practicality. "Let's start by conserving our resources. Switch off your flashlight."

"Torch."

He smiled in the darkness. She'd be arguing with Saint Peter at the Pearly Gates.

He was thinking rapidly, trying to assess what possibilities there were. They had left the bach before seven. He glanced at his watch. Almost eleven o'clock, and high tide was due at three-twenty. This he knew, and the freakish wind would not alter that. How long was the passage? Fifteen yards? Twenty? Why hadn't he paid more attention at the time. He'd managed that sort of distance underwater often, as a kid, although always in the controlled warmth of a swimming pool. Very different. Then the width of the passage; probably less of a problem. And there was the possibility that the temperature of the water might affect his breathing, perhaps cause cramp.

They sat very still. The only sound was the whooshing as water flooded in through the narrow channel, then abated briefly as though pausing to gain strength for a further invasion.

Then Emily voiced her thoughts. "Wouldn't it be ironic, if I survived the crash in France, only to die here."

"You must be getting used to the idea.

"Of facing death?"

"Yup. This is the second such occasion, after all."

Emily took her time to reply. "Not really. I had no concept of death, last time around. My parents probably faced the possibility that they might lose me, but once I'd regained consciousness, I'd already survived the worst."

He acknowledged the truth in what she was saying.

"And what about you, Bill? Having put all those terrible things behind you, with everything looking wonderful. To die in a cave on a remote coast of New Zealand. Is this further proof of your inevitability theory?"

"I never suggested things had to be accepted passively. Nothing robs you of the ability to fight. And we're not going to die."

"You say that as if you had a plan."

"Maybe."

"What? What can we do?"

"You forget that I'm quite a strong swimmer. I think that I can manage to get out via the entrance."

Her grasp on his fingers tightened. "You can't. You'll be smashed against the rocks."

"If I went now you're probably right. But not if I wait until the tide is on the turn. It's a risk I'm prepared to take. Then I'll go for help."

"When do you estimate that to be?"

"In about another three hours."

This time her shiver seemed to shake her whole body. Shock, and reaction, he knew.

"Bill, I'm cold."

He drew her closer and she snuggled herself against him. Silence descended again.

When she spoke at last her voice was pensive. "Do you think Te Manawanui was a strong swimmer?"

"Almost certainly. Maori kids can swim like fish, from an early age."

"Then why didn't he go for help?"

He laid his cheek against her hair. It felt damp, as though the moisture of the cave were permeating their very beings.

"I think Waikura was injured. I noticed that one of her arms was lying oddly. At first I thought it might have been moved subsequently, but the bone looked as if it was broken."

"You mean, he might have chosen not to leave her?"

"It would fit Maori philosophy. And he couldn't go back, could he? Facing the knowledge that he'd defied the tribe, and certain humiliation. I think he'd have opted for death with Waikura."

"Inevitability, again, but without the fight?"

He smiled slightly into her hair. "Perhaps. I prefer to think of it as death with dignity."

※※

"Bill . . .?"

"What?"

"I was thinking . . . You remember Heneti told me about Hinemoa and Tutanekai?"

"Uh huh."

"Well, do you think it's coincidence that we should be here, trapped by the water, so soon after her telling me about them? Except in that legend it's the woman who swims to be with her lover."

They were both feeling chilled. Emily snuggled closer. Bill wondered why Heneti had chosen to relate that, particular, tale. He said, "Uh huh," again, and waited for her to go on.

"Heneti said that I was like Hinemoa. She suggested that I wasn't brave enough to get out of the pool. Do you remember how it went? Hinemoa had discarded her clothing for the swim, so she was naked, and shy."

"And can you see a connection?"

Emily's voice was subdued. "I don't think so. Not really. I think she got me wrong. She sees me as being another sort of person." She was quiet for a few minutes. "Bill?"

"Yes?"

"Do you think I'm letting you down, by not staying here in Whangapouri.? I mean, if we do get out of here."

"Yes. . . Yes . . . Yes!" the inner Bill screamed and was instantly silenced. He spoke slowly and carefully. "Sweetheart, I could never hold you anywhere against your will. So there's no question of your letting me down. You are a free spirit, and I've been lucky enough to fly briefly alongside. That's all there is to it."

He prayed that was the correct response. Emily's face was turned against his jacket, muffling her response, but the involuntary movements of her shoulders indicated that she was weeping silently.

⟫≈⟪

For the plunge he removed his sneakers and jacket, giving the latter to Emily to serve as another layer of insulation. He'd have preferred to remove his jeans too, because any extra weight was going to be a liability, but they might provide a bit of protection against rough ledges of rock.

He wasn't looking forward to the next few minutes, but he recognized that this was their only chance. How incredibly stupid they had been, not leaving any message of their intentions with Hori, or the Vernons. Probably because he'd never, really, accepted that this cave existed. He'd gone along to keep Emily company. He should have had more faith in her intuition, he thought regretfully.

"Okay, this is it. Remember what we agreed?"

Emily nodded silently.

"Return to the vent, and wait there."

"All right."

They'd said all this before, several times. God only knew why he was going through it all again. "It'll probably take several hours, assembling rescue gear and the like. Don't think I've abandoned you."

"I won't." But her voice, very small, said something else.

"Keep the faith, baby!"

He thought she smiled, as he had hoped. He drew her to him in an awkward hug, then kissed her, a long, desperate kiss as though he could draw strength from her for what he was about to undertake.

"Bill, I love you."

"And I love you, too."

"Be careful."

As if he had any choice. The flashlight informed him that the sea within the smaller cave had risen to the high water mark. It had been at that level a full half hour, there was no reason to delay further. He slipped into its deeper blackness with care, resisting the temptation to groan at the abrupt encounter with the chill. And it was worse than he had imagined. It robbed him of breath for several seconds, so that he wondered if he'd succumb to suffocation before he could die from drowning. It was like fire and like ice, painful as hell, all in one. He fought to control the action of his lungs, gaining mastery of them only with supreme effort.

His first dive was no more than an exploratory venture to locate the entrance. He knew that he had precisely one chance to negotiate it. And once through that narrow passage . . . what then? He could only hope that the wind had not veered to the east, causing roiling surf and lethal breakers. In which case he'd probably be pounded against the cliff-face like a rag-doll, before he could draw breath. And then what would be Emily's fate? He refused to contemplate that other scenario.

Good. There was clearly a patch of lighter definition, which must signify daylight outside. He surfaced again within the cave and took several long deep breaths, accustoming his lungs, to the best of his ability, for the ordeal to come. Emily might still be perched on the top of the rockfall. He didn't chance the extra effort needed to seek her out.

Then he plunged for the second time, making for that hopeful exit, kicking powerfully, seeking the edges of the passage with exploratory fingers. His body started to protest before his shoulders were into the passage, but he knew there was no going back. Remembering boyhood exercises, when to achieve the entire length of the pool submerged was to be declared the champion, he exhaled carefully, concentrating on releasing air in a fine, controlled stream as he propelled himself forward. But even so there were long, terrible seconds when he felt that his chest was about to burst.

The area before him brightened, the passage widened and, gasping, he sought the surface like a cork. He drew a deep raw breath into lungs close to collapsing. The pain was almost as bad as had been the absence of air. It hurt all the way down and made his head spin as though he was drunk. He struggled to regain control, almost anticipating the action of a breaker seizing him, hurling him against the cliff. Now, he prayed, let there be no surf. And Someone must have heard his silent prayer, because the sea, as he looked around, was smoothly unguent, its grayness meeting and merging with the grayness of the horizon. The wind must have dropped as suddenly as it had risen last night. Only last night? All this had happened in less than twenty hours.

Even so, regaining solid ground wasn't a picnic because there was no easy transition from one rocky outcrop to the next. Five times he was forced to plunge into the wintry swell of the sea. He was increasingly grateful for the protection against limpets and mussels afforded by the fabric of his jeans, ripped and battered though it was. And there wasn't one part of him that the cold had not infiltrated. Obviously, the next hazard in this bizarre obstacle race would be death from hypothermia. Or pneumonia. He was close to exhaustion when, finally, he scrambled onto the beach of Whangapouri and set off with the last of his strength toward the nearest point of habitation.

⌗

Emily tried to control the shaking of her body. It wasn't that she was afraid, she told herself. It was more a reaction to all that had happened. She did have complete faith in Bill. She watched him dive, using her own torch and reserving his for later, then saw his head re-emerge, pause, dive again. Please God, she prayed, look after him. Let him get through the passage safely. She closed her mind to the possibility of his drowning in that narrow, confining space, because it brought forth latent panic tinged with a sizable dose of claustrophobia, and she was determined that she, too, would be nothing but resolute. The British bulldog and all that, she reminded herself, did not give way to an attack of wobbles, simply because she was marooned in a cave without obvious means of rescue. Might, in fact, never be rescued.

She waited for what seemed like an eon before she stood and made her way into the larger chamber, respectfully lowering her eyes as she passed the final resting place of the lovers.

They had talked about them, during the long, slow hours while they waited for the tide to turn.

"Bill," she had said, "Te Manawanui and Waikura. They've been together so long. I'd prefer that we don't actually mention to anybody that we found them. I'd like to think that they'll be there, like that, forever. Not disturbed."

"You don't think they deserve burial?"

"You could look upon this cave as their burial tomb. Private and exclusive. Nobody need ever know, apart from us."

Bill had been silent for a few minutes. Then he'd said, "All right. We might have to lie, say that we found nothing, if we're asked. That okay with you?"

"Yes. It's worth a lie. They're worth a lie."

They had not, for one moment, considered out loud the possibility that one or both of them might not leave this cave. That Bill might fail, and Emily might stay here until she starved to death, because nobody would ever, ever think to look for her at the bottom of a remote vent. Instead they had talked about this and that, so much and so little. Bill had returned, again and again, to his youthful years on Cape Cod, describing for her the beauty, and the wildness of the winter storms, and the gentleness of the summers. Also his regret at how the place had gone up-market, becoming a fashionable watering hole for people he so often found himself despising. Had she needed confirmation of his determination to settle in Whangapouri, she could not have asked for clearer evidence. But he'd also talked about his writing, and about the proposed visit to Hollywood, and about her future as well.

They had discussed healing, and facing the future, and how nobody need accept predestination in a defeatist way.

She wished she wasn't so cold, and that her arm hurt less. The early fall had jolted it more than she'd realized at the time. It ached all the way through. Even with the extra warmth that Bill's jacket afforded, she felt chilled to the bone. Underneath the place where they estimated the vent to be she found the flattest slab of rock and huddled down on that, Bill's well-padded jacket around her lower half. But perhaps that was wrong, she thought. Perhaps she should exercise to keep warm. So she paced up and down the cave floor, picking her way with care, because she knew that another accident would be disastrous. Five times she traversed the length of the cave, but it appeared to do very little good. Thirst was a problem too, more so than hunger. She returned to the small pool and dipped her hand into its cold waters. It tasted intensely bitter, but better than nothing.

She paced again, willing legs that were becoming increasingly stiff and intractable into action. What time had elapsed? Her watch, viewed in the last feeble light from her own torch, told her it was nearly six o'clock. The dimness of the space high above suggested that, outside, daylight was dwindling into darkness. She had shoved two packets of crackers into her haversack, and they had eaten some while waiting for the tide to turn. Or rather, Emily had nibbled and Bill had toyed with those she offered him. She wasn't too certain whether altruism was the motivating force, or a fear that even a small quantity of food might cause stomach cramps when he swam. She'd preferred not to ask. Why on earth had they not stopped for breakfast before they set out this morning, or paused long enough to seize more in the way of sustenance from the kitchen. One packet of water biscuits, even if she chose to consume the lot, would do no more than dent her hunger. And, perhaps, she should ration them even so.

Sleep seemed a reasonable alternative, but she knew that if she settled down she might never get up again. She thought about Te Manawanui and Waikura. She wondered whether they'd taken food with them, when they eloped. It was possible, because they'd have had no idea when next they might eat. But, perhaps, having supplies would simply prolong the agony. Maybe death from starvation was easier if you didn't attempt to stave it off. And Waikura's arm, like hers, was also injured, maybe broken as they scaled the rocks. Her lover would have had to help her, on their final climb up that narrow crevasse. She could imagine their slow, laborious progress. Were they, even then, weak with hunger? And they'd probably chosen the ledge as a suitable, final resting place, high enough to be safe from flash-flooding within the cave; safe, perhaps, from rats.

Rats. She'd given no thought to the possibility that she might not be alone in the cave. They might very well be attracted to the smell of crumbs. The notion induced another onrush of shivers that engulfed her body and made her teeth chatter. She perched herself timidly on an available outcrop and strained to hear the scrabbling of small, rodent feet. But there was only the incessant dripping of water, and the muted sound of the tide ebbing through the passage several hundred feet away, and the pulsing of her own blood, loud in her ears.

※

"Emms? Can you hear me?"

The words, echoing through the darkness that surrounded her, finally penetrated Emily's consciousness. She had drifted into a state that was half sleep, half atrophying numbness. She could understand how, in certain circumstances, death would come to seem a very reasonable alternative.

"Bill?" Her voice refused to obey her, as though her larynx had already given up the struggle to survive.

"Emily?" She could hear the note of anxiety in his voice.

She cleared her throat and shook off the enveloping lethargy. "I'm here, Bill."

"Are you okay?"

"Yes."

"Is the flashlight still working?"

Her broken torch had petered out some time ago, but the beam of Bill's was still quite powerful.

"Yes."

"The Reynards are here with rescue equipment. They're experienced mountaineers, and they're getting everything set up, now. I'm going to lower a vacuum flask for you, with food. Look up."

There was a series of clanks as the metal container encountered rock, then the flask swung into the arc of light and continued its careful, uninterrupted descent. Emily stood to receive it, the thought of food so overwhelming that she was temporarily bereft of strength. But, shades of Tantalus, the ache in her arm had spread throughout her shoulder, and she could not find the force necessary to unscrew the steel top. The flask and its contents represented a terrible, agonizing torture.

"I can't, Bill. I can't open it."

Their voices seemed to take an age to traverse the space separating them.

"Hold on. I'll pull it up and loosen the cap."

The flask spun into space and receded, banging once more against the sides of the vent as it ascended. No more than minutes elapsed before it reappeared, but they might have been hours.

And this time the lid was one easy turn from release. She had no idea of the contents. Something hot and milky, but her taste buds had gone on strike so beyond that it might have been anything. But nothing had ever been so welcome, or so good. As she drank she could almost feel the strength flooding back through her body, a sweet infusion of power-enhancing warmth.

"You got out all right?"

That, she thought as the words left her mouth, really was the stupidest question anyone could have uttered. Of course he had got out all right. He was there, high above her, talking to her in the flesh. He was safe. He was rescuing her. He was wonderful.

"Sure. The sea was surprisingly calm. But I'd not choose to try that little caper again."

She smiled to herself. There would be no need to try that little caper again. They had solved the mystery of the lovers. They were at rest with each other, together for all time. And she, Emily Merivale, had been cured of any desire ever again to enter a cave, in any way, shape or form. In the future she would seek only sunlight and fresh air. Perhaps leaving this place was like her stepping out of Hinemoa's pool, although not in the way that Heneti could possibly have forecast. It would be sensible to think about any similarity when she had more strength, more time to concentrate.

"Emms, the Reynards say that they're all ready. Listen while we tell you what to do."

She prepared for her rescue with a combination of dread and anticipation. The clanging of the flask against the narrow confines of the vent had suggested it would not be a comfortable ascent.

Vernon Reynard took control. His voice, descending from the heavens above her, was calm and reassuring, and he issued instructions as though she were the most amateur of all amateurs in this business. Which, she reflected, was the exact truth.

They lowered a harness on the end of a rope, and at first sight it was no more than a confusing, unintelligible assortment of straps. Vernon had to talk her through it. The webbing belt that went around her waist was easy enough, but the straps from it, which created a loop for each leg, refused to be manipulated to slip over the half-moon piece of metal which would secure them in front of her. Frustration, and the thought of imminent exodus from the cave, made her fingers clumsy, and the webbing seemed to have a mind of its own. Finally, on the third, fumbling attempt, she managed to get the D shaped clasp to close and twisted the securing thread.

"All right?"

"I think so."

"Right. We're going to haul you up, now. Don't try to bring anything, apart from yourself. The vent is quite narrow, so I want you to call out when you can put your hand up to touch it."

"Okay."

She was reassured by the quiet confidence in her fellow countryman's voice. He sounded as though rescuing maidens from caves was as everyday as changing your clothes. As she felt herself lifted like some grotesque Peter Pan, Emily had a sudden vision of somebody, in the distant future, maybe stumbling upon this cave. What would that unknown person make of an abandoned haversack, complete with water-biscuit wrappers, and Bill's cast off sneakers and jacket. Manmade fiber, environmentalists told you, took hundreds of years to disintegrate.

"Now. Stop now." She could reach out a hand to feel the rough edges of the vent.

"Good."

High above to her left, maybe thirty feet, the dazzle of a powerful beam caught her eyes, before veering away to light her surroundings. She could see for the first time the diagonal perimeters of the passageway between herself and freedom.

"Vernon . . . Bill . . . I can't get through there. The vent is too narrow."

"Yes, you can," Bill replied steadily. "It's not going to be easy, but you can do it."

She could hear snatches of conversation from above, Ruth's voice and the men's. Then Bill spoke again.

"We're wondering about your parka. Whether it's better for you to keep it on for protection, even though it adds to bulk. The preference is for you to stay as you are."

Dangling, as she was, like a sack of spuds at the end of a pulley, Emily felt that she had very little say in the matter. "Bill, my shoulder's really weak. From my fall."

"We'll bear that in mind. Just listen to Vernon."

Looking up, she could see a man's head in silhouette against the beam.

"Listen, Emily. You have to make yourself as thin as possible, but we know it can be done. Put your good arm above your head, hold onto the rope, and breathe out. We'll go very slowly, so you can maneuver yourself as much as possible into the widest part of the gap. And take your time. There's no rush."

Even going very slowly indeed it was agony from start to finish. Like a rebirth. There was a limit to how narrow you could make yourself, even by breathing out to the best of your ability. And her capacity for breath-holding was inadequate at the best of times.

She tried not to scream, she tried not to allow the pain in her shoulder to influence her thinking. She gritted her teeth and thought of all Bill must have been through, and simply let the tears roll down her face.

So it was that, despite the most careful of handlers, after half an hour of pain-racked scraping her shoulders at last emerged from the vent, sufficiently for Bill to tuck his hands under her arms and lift her the final few feet. And it was, indeed, very much as she'd imagined being born again might feel.

Without his support she would have collapsed onto the ground, because she felt as weak as a kitten. She looked at the smiling faces of Ruth and Vernon, illuminated in the darkness as they were by an efficient hurricane lamp, and by the lights of a four-wheel drive vehicle. The rope attached to her harness, she noticed, was knotted to the front fender of the truck.

Bill still kept his arm sustainingly around her. He leaned over to kiss the top of her head. "Welcome back to the world, Miss Merivale."

She made a valiant attempt to pull herself together. "Thank you, all of you. Thank you so much. I . . ."

But then it was all too much for her, and she burst into tears against his comforting shoulder.

It was only when they were safely within the confines of the truck that Bill allowed himself the luxury of relaxation. Not physically, because he was supporting Emily and the lack of space made everything very difficult. But mentally. He felt a profound rush of love, and a small, but equally important, sense of pride. No, that was too strong. Of contentment. He'd spent so many bleak, unhappy hours knowing that he'd failed Jaime. Swimming from the cave, rescuing Emily, did nothing to bring her back, but it did count for something.

Maybe that was in Te Manawanui's mind, when he lay down beside Waikura and waited for his own death. He could very likely have abandoned her, swum away and survived. And perhaps you could follow the comparison with another legend, similarly analogous. Because surely Emily, in being drawn up through the narrowness of that vent, had stepped out of her own, personal pool.

THIRTY

It was almost as close in the cab of the Reynards' vehicle as it had been squeezing through that confined space. Four adults were jammed onto a seat designed for two, or at a pinch three, while allowing sufficient room for Vernon to employ the stick shift. Emily, as the smallest, sat on Bill's knee, which was all right with her. Anything would have been all right with her just then, but to have his warmth supporting her back, and his arm circling her waist, was especially comforting. She felt so tired that she would have nodded off at any given moment, but for the jolting of the truck. There was not even the vestige of a track to follow, and the moon had yet to show itself. The headlights bounced drunkenly, springing from stunted tree to coarse grass and back again, occasionally catching the amber eyes of some small, nocturnal creature. All Vernon's attention was concentrated on the business of returning them home in one piece.

Ruth, however, was clearly anxious to converse. She had been marvelously supportive during the rescue and, were she feeling more gregarious, Emily would have responded happily. As it was, she would have preferred to be left with her own, silent thoughts. The idea of a long, hot bath was paramount at this minute.

"We went down, once," Ruth began.

Emily dragged herself back into communicative mood. "You did? Through the vent?"

"Yes. It was a long time ago, now. We've lived in Whanga-pouri coming up for fourteen years. We'd heard the story of Te Manawanui and Waikura of course, and the relevant facts about the retreating sea. We discussed it together and agreed that perhaps they'd managed to find shelter in the cave, if there was one."

Emily lived again her rebirth through the narrowness of that rocky confine. She was feeling bruised and scraped from fingertip to toes. "How did you manage to get through the vent?"

Ruth smiled in the darkness, her features illuminated in silhouette by the dim lights of the dash. She put out a hand to steady herself as the four-wheel-drive plunged into a shallow rabbit warren and out the other side.

"It was hard, particularly for Vernon. But we were descending by abseil, and we were a lot younger than now." She paused to reflect. "And thinner. Bill was telling us about how you entered this morning, from the sea face. I feel quite cheated, not having witnessed for myself *he tai rereke*. Maybe today was the only chance in our lifetime."

Emily ignored the other aspect of the older woman's conversation, not possessing enough energy to discuss the phenomenal tide.

"But you still had to get out of there."

"Yes we did, and it wasn't easy. But we thought it was worth it."

Emily could feel Bill's arm about her, comforting, reassuring. She leaned her head against his shoulder and said nothing.

"I was just wondering . . ." Ruth continued, clearly choosing her words with care. "Did you find anything down there? Anything significant?"

Bill's arm tightened just a little.

"No," Emily replied slowly. "We were exploring with the legend in mind, as well. But we found nothing. Nothing at all."

Ruth's body was jammed between her husband's and Bill's, preventing much movement.

"Good." She turned her head to smile, and her eyes met Emily's in the dimness of the cab. "That's as it should be, isn't it."

※

The evening was tremendous. Something Emily would cherish forever. It was nobody's fault that on the other side of the scale, balancing her pleasure, was the regret that would accompany her departure. Her body had recovered from the battering it had received as she was hauled through the vent, the occasional twinge of pain in her shoulder was the sole reminder. The story of all that had happened should remain private, they and the Reynards had agreed, to be shared only among themselves and with the Webbers.

Ruth had voiced the thought. Emily had agreed readily enough. She had not been too happy about not telling Heneti and Hori, when they had been so good to her.

"Shall we tell them everything?"

Nobody had actually spelled out what "everything" meant. The agreement was tacit, but intrinsic.

"Not necessary." Vernon was as sparing as usual with his choice of words. "Not necessary at all. It's our opinion that they know already."

And the matter was not mentioned again.

She looked around the table, at the McDuffs, almost a caricature couple, at Abraham with his bizarre, pompom hat atop a headful of dreadlocks, and Minnie, his wife. There was sweet-faced Talitha, already a friend and wearing her pregnancy like a badge of honor, and Vernon and Ruth, with whom she'd shared their adventure. In another life she could become good friends with them, too. She'd have liked to see how Ruth ran her animal rescue center, and to inspect Vernon's seascapes. Evidently there was quite a market for them, here and overseas. She never would, now. Time had run out.

And Minnie Tu'utu had arrived with a present for her, a pair of her own *pois*.

"You've got to practice," Minnie warned her. "It'll make the muscles in your arm strong, ay."

Emily thought of her clumsy attempts to get the small, flax balls circling at the ends of their strings and wondered whether a new pair of hands might not be more useful. But she was immensely touched that Minnie should have thought to bring her a gift.

The lamb was wonderful, succulently roasted, glazed with red currant. Mouth-watering.

Hori had them all raise their glasses in a toast. "To Emily."

She was seated beside him, the guest of honor. He turned towards her as he continued.

"It's not so long ago that she arrived here, and I delivered enough food to that bach to feed an army. And, I tell you, she needed that food. Thin! You could see light through the girl, when she stood sideways. She came here, this little English person, looking like a white mouse." Everybody laughed and Emily, fiery-faced, attempted to defend herself, but Hori gestured expansively and continued. "And look at her now. Color in her cheeks, filling out to look like a proper woman. Even a few curves."

More laughter greeted this.

"And now she's leaving us. Even Bill couldn't hold onto her, although I'll bet you he tried. But we're not going to let her disappear without extracting a promise." He looked around the long table, catching the eyes of the diners, seeking their endorsement. "We want a promise that, one day, you'll come back and visit us. Will you give us your word, young lady?"

Suddenly it was Emily's turn. She rose to her feet as Hori sat down, burningly aware that she should have anticipated such a speech, and prepared a reply. It was even hard to find her voice, because there was a tightening in her chest. She cleared her throat to buy time.

"I can't say how much I'm going to miss you all. As you probably know, because there aren't too many secrets in a place like Whangapouri, I came here after an accident. I had to re-think my life, and I always saw my stay here as a period of healing, with a finite time. You've all been wonderful, but I'm a nomad. I wander. And I'm afraid I'd become too restless, were I to stay here forever. But I promise you that I'll be back some time, as long as Heneti promises to roast a haunch of venison that evening. Or New Zealand lamb, like tonight. And in the meanwhile, thank you, all of you. For your friendship, and for your understanding. It's meant so much to me."

She sat down abruptly, aware that tears were very close to the surface. It seemed amazing that in only twelve weeks these people should have become special to her. She had never expected leaving to be so hard.

Hori came to her rescue. He put a hand on her shoulder. "Enough of that. We'll all be crying in a minute. Now, Emily has selected this evening's entertainment, so let's get this table cleared away. What do you say, ay?"

She had chosen with care, music that represented her past life, and perhaps her future, whatever it might hold. She thought that she'd chosen well; anyway, her audience seemed to appreciate the selection. She wrapped up the evening with Gershwin's *Rhapsody in Blue*, which was her tribute to Bill.

Hori insisted upon driving them home, as though her legs might be incapable of the walk. He pulled the truck into the drive, switched off the engine and fumbled for something in his pocket.

"Didn't want to give you this, in front of everybody. It's a little something from Kui and Heneti and me. For you to remember us."

"Oh, Hori. Shall I open it now?"

He grunted. "Inside. Open it inside."

Emily leaned across and kissed his cheek. "I promise that I'll never forget any of you. And thank you so much for my gift."

To her surprise he put an arm quite roughly around her and pulled her close. The hug was something of an ordeal, crushing her as it did to his large frame, but the discomfort was nothing, when compared to the sentiment it displayed.

She undid the tiny parcel, once she was in the bach and the sound of Hori's truck had retreated into the night. And it was a small, greenstone *tiki,* beautifully carved out of the New Zealand jade. It lay in the palm of her hand, the curious, stylized features of the face staring up at her. The only other such ornament she had seen was in the cave, where it lay for eternity around the neck of Te Manawanui.

"Is it symbolic then, Bill? Do you know what it means?"

He was hanging up his jacket. A new, green oilskin had replaced the one abandoned in the cave.

"I believe it was a symbol of fertility, originally, before it became valued just for the stone itself. Tiki was the first mortal man."

"Oh."

Not entirely appropriate, then, but still to be cherished. She wondered why Hori had selected a token suggesting fertility for her, when she was not even married. To promise her abundant progeny in the future? Or was it merely because greenstone represented wealth, and he wanted her to remember the richness of her life here.

And who would have thought, on that dismal, wet evening of her arrival, that words like richness and wealth would ever go hand-in-hand with Whangapouri?

⚡

She had been given fair warning of the party to be held in her honor at the store. That the Morrisons should put on a ceremony of farewell was as unexpected as it was appreciated. After some consultation with Mary Kelly, the social worker, in the decision making part of which they included Winnie as much as possible, it had been agreed that John Wayne and Kaffi should, at least for the foreseeable future, register with the Correspondence School. This might change when Matu returned but, with some things tactfully not spelled out, it was generally accepted that Kaffi was far too important within the family to be absent nine hours each day. Winnie was managing fine right now. It would be foolish to upset the status quo. And Mary had sorted out the financial side of things too, so that there was now a viable account for the family at Hori's, where the children could shop at least twice a week.

The Friday before Emily's departure. Probably the last time that she would be making this walk across the headland. She thought back to that first occasion, when Kaffi had agreed Emily should meet Winnie. She recalled not only her horror at the state in which the family was living, but also how physically exhausted she'd felt. Strange to remember now, when her muscles were honed and she covered the distance in half the time. And today was one of those marvelously mild harbingers of summer warmth.

John Wayne met her first, bursting through the growth of bush a full twenty paces ahead of his sister, and she could tell at once that he was excited. He was absolutely useless at hiding his emotions.

"We got somethin' to show you. And we made you a party."

"Dummy!" Kaffi slipped her hand into Emily's. "It's s'posed to be a secret. A surprise."

It must be something really special, because Kaffi positively glowed.

"Yeah," John Wayne agreed, at his most animated. "A surprise."

"A party, really? For me?"

"Yeah. *Ka pai*, ay."

Before coming to New Zealand Emily would have been openly incredulous at the notion that this family, or any such family, could have wormed itself into her affections. But they had. Not just these two, with whom she was best acquainted, or their mother, but also Ani with her shy smile, Tama, who was responding so well these days, and gorgeous Gary Cooper, with his silky hair and great, dark eyes. Somehow they had become intrinsic to her journey of healing. Despite mutual promises to correspond, she was going to miss them terribly.

"I know it will be a lovely surprise."

But it proved more than that because the party of seven, it transpired, was to be a party of eight. When she entered the living room it was to find a young man seated at the table, a small, brown toddler on each knee. No need for conjecture. Here was living proof whence Kaffi and the babies inherited their fine looks.

Matu started to put Ani and Tama gently down, but Emily was quick to discourage this display of good manners.

"Please don't get up for me. You must be Matu and, of course, I'm Emily Merivale." She crossed to the table, hand extended and, somewhat awkwardly because of his double burden, Matu shook it.

"Pleased to meet you, Emily. And I gotta thank you, too."

She dismissed his attempt firmly, because a torrent of gratitude was the last thing she needed at this minute. "I'm only too delighted that we've had the opportunity to meet, before I leave."

They made an enchanting small tableau, the father and his children. Nobody seeing them could doubt the bond of love that united this family, and if ever she had sought justification for her actions it was manifest before her, right now.

Kaffi, who had disappeared into the tiny kitchen, appeared at this minute, tray balanced precariously. Winnie followed, wiping her hands on the gingham apron that had been one of Emily's gifts. And she was radiant with happiness. Clearly, all was now right with her world.

Kaffi unloaded the tray with care. "We made tea and that."

Emily vividly recalled the ghastly concoction of sugar and milkiness which found such favor with Kaffi, and offered up a serious supplication. But she was spared that, at least. On the table, along with Kaffi's seasonal bunch of leafy twigs and buds, was a jug of luridly orange fruit squash, and a plate of egg sandwiches, and a *kumera* pie. Scarcely the lavish abundance of the Webbers, but perhaps appreciated even more for what it represented. Even the *kumera* pie, which she found unusual to say the least, but on which she lavished most praise, because she saw in its creation Winnie's desire to thank her.

"I got you a present. So you'll remember us." Kaffi delved importantly into the cupboard.

Emily had to master the lump in her throat before she could reply. "I promise I'll remember you, always. I don't need a present to do that."

"But this is special, ay. I found it, and it's whole. Not chipped or anything."

The small gift had been carefully wrapped in a square of the tissue which is used to protect fruit in transit. Emily unfolded the paper to reveal the perfect, pinkish globe of a sea-urchin skeleton.

Kaffi hopped from foot to foot. "You like it, ay?"

"Sugar, you couldn't have found anything I'd like better. It's the best present I'll ever have." Kaffi nestled up very close, and Emily put an arm about her. "And you'll always be the best friend I'll ever have."

John Wayne pressed close on the other side. "And me, too."

"And you, too. And all of you. My family of best friends."

Winnie's smile would be etched for all time on her memory, and the manner in which it transformed her plain, colorless face.

She was so different from the withdrawn young woman of their first encounter, the Winnie who had lost all hope. When she smiled you could see what had attracted Matu. And even more, Emily reflected, looking about the *whare*, here was abundant proof that a happy home was not exclusively dependent on the consumer goods of the twentieth century.

～≋≋～

Matu's elderly, serviceable pick-up was parked behind the *whare*, which was why Emily had not spotted it originally. She didn't demur when he offered to run her back down to the bay because, to crib Janice's phrase, she was aware that there were i's to be dotted and t's to be crossed. It was only fair to offer Matu the opportunity to do so. She was impressed by the quiet but firm manner with which he refused to allow the older children to accompany them.

"Emily and me got grown-up things to discuss. You two stay here and help your mum clear up."

She was equally impressed by the way John Wayne and Kaffi accepted his authority. You often read about fractured families, unable to function as a unit after a parent's extended absence. This would not appear to be a problem threatening Matu and his clan.

"Isn't it a very long way, down to the bay?" She had to shout over the din.

Matu drove as though the rough terrain was one of the Queen's highways. "Nah. No need to go all the way up to the road, y'know. There's a track along the back'a the ridge. Bit rough, but cuts out four or five mile."

"Bit rough" was a staggering understatement. Once again Emily found herself all but swinging from the handle above the door. It was a blessed relief when they negotiated the "track" and were on the final descent into Whangapouri. It was only then that

Matu pulled the truck into the side of the road and switched off the engine. The ensuing silence was blissfully sweet.

"Miss Merivale . . . Em'ly. I know you don't want me to thank you again. But I got to. And I need to know what I owe you."

She'd been considering this, in disjointed spasms, while the truck bounced and wove. "Are you planning to stay on here, or go back to your own people?"

Matu scratched his ear, which she interpreted to signify embarrassment. "John Bryant, he's a true Christian. Said he was happy t'have me work for him again. Don't reckon we'll be going back to th' tribe. They never liked my Winnie."

"Was that why you came here, originally?"

She could tell by his glance that this was painful territory. Again he scratched at his ear. "Some've the *wahine* . . . that's the women . . . they kept tellin' Winnie that the Welfare people would come and take away our babies. Made her really unhappy. Problem is, you hear some't said often enough, you kinda believe it. I kinda believed it m'self. And it'd break my heart t'have them babies taken away. But the reverend in the prison, when I explained it to him, he said that was nonsense."

"I'm sure he's right. I can see at once that the children think you're a wonderful father. In fact, Kaffi would stand before any court in the land and vouch for you."

Matu's smile reflected his delight and pride in his elder daughter. "Kaffi's a good kid. Sharp, too, like me mum. Me mum's as clever as any of them teachers."

"That's rather what I'm coming to. Can we strike a bargain?" His look was inquiring, and amazingly like Kaffi's in similar mode. "I don't think it's good for any of the family to be isolated out there, in the *whare*. Children need other children as playmates, and I think Winnie would benefit from more friends, as well."

"You sayin' we should go back to the tribe?"

"No, not that. Winnie told me how much she disliked it. But why not live down here, in the bay?" She could see doubt collect behind his eyes, so hurried on. "This is what I propose; you can pay me back on a monthly basis, for the amount I've spent recently, but in exchange I'd like to put down a year's rental on the bach next to the store. It belongs to the Webbers, and I know that they'd be happy to have it occupied for the year. It would be my farewell present to you all."

"But . . ."

"Please, Matu. Your family has become so very special, and they've helped me as well, more than I can say. This would be my way of saying thank you. Like barter. And if you don't understand, ask Kaffi. She's the world's expert, when it comes to bartering."

THIRTY-ONE

ill offered to drive her to Auckland. Emily refused his offer. " I came by bus. It seems appropriate that I should go by bus."

So he borrowed Hori's truck and transported her, and the Vuillaime, and her two battered suitcases, to the junction. They drove in silence, because all that Emily wanted to say had been said, apart from the most important thing of all. But from the start of their relationship she had made the decision, very painfully, not to burden Bill against his inclination, and if nothing else she would stick to that resolve. It was the most important factor, far more relevant than the transparent ruses of the bay's residents to keep her among them. She had not been surprised by Bill's statement that he would stay here, return permanently to Whangapouri after his time in California. The local folk saw him as one of them. You could say it was almost pre-destined.

They drove past the store. Heneti was cleaning down the wrought iron chairs and tables, in preparation for the summer bunch. Hearing the familiar engine, she waved a bright yellow cloth in their direction and Emily, attempting to remain cheerful, waved back. Heneti had said, "We're getting on, Hori and me. I'd kinda hoped you might think about helping us with the store. Maybe do a bit of summer catering, for day visitors and that."

Emily had made negative noises, and scarcely thought about the casually dropped suggestion again. Now, seeing her friend, she wondered whether the proposal had been so casual. Without doubt it, too, was a well-considered part of their plot to hold her there. She saw but scarcely registered the passing scenery, the thickets of bush, the snug homesteads with their sheltering screens of trees. The drive was much too short, the time they had allowed for it far too long, so they were faced with an awkward period to fill while they awaited the appearance of the coach.

"You'll let me know about your writing? And how you get on in Hollywood."

"Sure. If you send me an address."

"You have my parents' address. They'll always re-address anything."

"Uh huh."

"And you'll remember to take Mendelssohn to the clinic in town, for his shots?"

"I'll remember."

"And you'll arrange for Kaffi to feed him, while you're gone?"

"Sure."

Time-spinning nothings. They'd said it all before.

The coach rounded the bend in the road. Panic gripped her, far more closely than had the walls of the vent.

"Bill . . ."

"What?"

"Bill . . . I don't want to go. I want to stay here. With you."

He turned her squarely to face him, holding onto her shoulders. "Yes, you do. You're speaking out of fear of the unknown."

"No . . . honestly. I should have told you before. I really don't want to go." She was nearly shouting in her determination to make him listen to what she was saying.

His hold on her shoulders was quite painful. "Emms, listen to me. Now is not the minute to look back. You must lead with your chin and face the future. Spot decisions are disastrous. The heart in charge, instead of the head. Accept that you've made up your mind. That you made it up weeks ago. This is not the moment for a Technicolor, 'ride off into the sunset,' ending."

"Please, Bill." She could hear herself pleading, begging him to understand. The bus had pulled up alongside them. "Please, don't make me leave."

"You have another life to go to. Remember? A life filled with symphonies, and sidewalks, and trendy lunches with your girl-friends. In two weeks you'll forget all about us. All about the bay. Apart from swapped cute little anecdotes about how primitive it all was."

"Bill . . ."

He was handing over her suitcases to the driver, and they were being stacked into the baggage hold, and he was helping her onto the bus, clutching her violin case. And she was walking the length of the aisle like a zombie, almost blinded by her tears, not caring what the other passengers thought, until she could sink down on the rear seat and look for him out of the panoramic sweep of glass. She'd always remember him like that, standing in silhouette at the bus stop, tall and thin, with one arm raised in farewell as the coach pulled smoothly away from the verge, and gathered speed.

〰️

Auckland was hot. She'd forgotten how busy even so far-flung an airport could be, but there was something immediately familiar about the smell of aviation fuel, the shape of the airplane seat behind her shoulders. Even the blandness of the meal served by cloned flight attendants seemed surprisingly normal.

She was doing her best to follow Bill's instructions. "Don't look back," he'd said. "Face the future." It helped to remember that wholesale panic into which Heneti's challenge had originally plunged her, when she related the tale of Hinemoa. Thus armed, she fell upon every aspect of normalcy like a beggar seizing cast-off scraps. In some way they provided justification for her departure.

She tried to imagine what Bill was doing, at this moment. Three o'clock. He'd probably be sitting in the sunroom writing, or the warmth of the day might have driven him outside. It was nice to think he had Mendelssohn for company.

Sitting in the darkness of the cave, Bill had said, "Try to imagine yourself in two or three weeks time. And then in two or three months. That way you'll set yourself small goals, more easily achieved, but still rewarding."

She closed her eyes as the plane droned its way across the Tasman Sea and thought about the future. What would she be doing in a fortnight? In a year?

Jay and Charlie were at the airport. Remembering her hasty departure, she wondered whether there might be a slight awkwardness in their meeting, but Jay had never been one to dwell upon anything he found uncomfortable. He kissed her on the cheek and hugged her, which wasn't easy with his small daughter in his arms. Together they made a confused collection of limbs and cheeks. Charlie, all bright eyes and shiny brown curls, pressed her lips pertly against her aunt's face and beamed a three year old's approval.

"Poor old Chel is in the grips of the dreaded morning sickness. Except that it lasts all day. She thought she'd escaped this time around, but it hit with a vengeance last week."

"The price to pay for parenthood?"

Jay's smile was a touch rueful. "I suppose. But it does appear to be a bit one-sided."

They retrieved her bags and Jay led the way to the car.

"You're looking tremendous, so I don't need to ask whether New Zealand was a success. You'll have to fill us in on how you whiled away your idle hours. Never out of bed before noon I'll bet, and carousing with the locals until all hours of the night."

Emily thought of all that had filled her time. The Morrison/ Cook saga, the discovery of the cave and the drama of her rescue. Her moment of rebirth. There was a sense of achievement at having solved the mystery of Whangapouri, although it might never become public knowledge. She thought about Mendelssohn, and about meeting Bill, and getting to know him. And all that happened in only three months. It felt like an entire lifetime.

She thought about the process of healing . . . and about scars and their therapeutic value, as Bill had explained them. A constant reminder that one has weathered the storm and emerged a stronger person. She looked down at the criss-cross lines on her hand. It seemed that already they were starting to fade.

Jay brought her back to the present. " . . . and any plans. How far have you got?"

At least he had not mentioned her violin. Clutching the Vuillaume, Emily watched a familiar tram rattle by, filled with tourists and locals; women toting shopping bags, uniformed schoolchildren looking bored, men in dark business suits. Comfortable. Cozy in their familiarity.

"Not really. Although I can tell you, before you say anything, that it will involve nothing to do with music. But right now I'm just feeling culture starved."

There was a moment's silence, when she could all but read his mind. Whatever else, he was thinking, avoid mention of the orchestra. Or her own playing. She flew off the handle last time, a repeat might well be untenable.

"Culture we can handle. I can promise that in a week's time you'll be begging for mercy."

She smiled a touch smugly to herself, feeling for the first time in her life that for once, and in a very minor way, she had gained the upper hand. "Sounds good to me."

※

She unpacked her city clothes, and climbed into pantyhose and high heels for the first time in months. Her feet protested that they disliked the cramped feeling, the loss of liberty. At first the clothes felt strange on her back. She leaped on and off trams, she shopped with a will, relishing the array of fashionable etceteras in the stores. She ate at as many different restaurants, sampling almost forgotten pleasures. She swam in Jay's and Chelsea's pool. A swim considerably warmer than Bill's essay into wind-driven waters, although not exactly Hinemoa's hot springs, either.

The legend had never left her. Nor could she say with certainty she knew to what Heneti had been alluding. It appeared to hinge on what was her, Emily's, metaphorical pool.

"You're looking well," Jay said. "That bit of weight you've gained really suits you." Whangapouri did that to you, restored your health.

Together the young women visited the gym.

Chelsea had a neat little bulge in the front, to presage the arrival of a Merivale son. "You're fantastically fit," she remarked admiringly. There was nothing like frequent treks over the headland to hone muscles, not to mention the daily gathering of driftwood.

She sat through several movies, and watched with pretend interest the antics of assorted people on the television. They had the appeal of an alien race going through some strange ritual. She couldn't imagine Bill's movie being as shallow, or as trite.

She attended Jay's concerts. The orchestra was attempting to woo the youth of Victoria. The concerts were as polished as everything Jay undertook, the music as lovely. Nothing new about that. But it was not her music, because she would no longer be contributing to it. And the thought had lost the ability to hurt.

She played with Charlie, taking her off her mother's hands. She read to her and walked with her, and it was delightful and a little bit disappointing at the same time. Charlie had no need for further mental stimulus, because her parents could already supply all that was required.

She basked in the new-found respect which Jay accorded her, and she thought about the future. She had no idea where she would go from here, but such a decision had lost its immediacy. She could afford a few days of vegetating.

So it was all as she'd remembered it, deeply satisfying in its familiarity.

And yet, somehow, she felt herself on the outside of Jay's and Chelsea's charmed circle. She could see that there would be room in that circle for another member of their family, a further manifestation of their love. But, that aside, it was already complete. The perfect circle didn't really extend to her, and never would. Aunts were, by their nature, fringe members.

It all came to a head ten days after her return to Australia, and might well have done so earlier, had she not been deliberately obtuse. Blinkered by her determination to look only ahead, and by that long-held determination that she should not become Bill's metaphorical shackles.

She had hopped on a tram to the downtown shopping area, enjoying the close proximity of so many bodies, the assorted nature of her fellow passengers. Melbourne, she thought appreciatively, was like a mini United Nations. Shopping was fun. And then, standing in the middle of Collins Street, weighed down with an assortment of smart carrier bags, she found herself overwhelmed, once more, with panic. It was a fear as cloying as syrup, and as jolting as a charge of electricity. Suddenly the shop windows were too bright, there were too many people, and too much traffic. The fumes and the city smell invaded her nostrils and created a disgusting film at the back of her throat. She longed with all her being for the sweetness of uncontaminated air, and the feel of the beach soft beneath her heels, and sand percolating between her toes.

And, most of all, she ached for Bill.

The yearning was so strong that it made her head dizzy and turned her legs to jelly. She was forced to seek a bench and sit down, before she made an utter fool of herself and collapsed on the sidewalk. Seated, her immediate view was of human shapes crossing and re-crossing within her field of vision, but they remained blurred and unfocused while she wrestled with the message imparted by her panic.

What was it she thought so important? Traffic lights, and gridlocked streets, and pollution? So that was how she saw her future. Emulating Ruth Vernon in a mad dash to escape from herself, until she ran out of steam. Trying ineffectually to re-create her old, nomadic life, during which the very thought of putting down roots had seemed like a life sentence.

And, equally blindingly, she understood for the first time the message of Hinemoa, and Heneti's allusion to the pool. It had nothing to do with the cave. Heneti could not have been thinking about that. Heneti meant you must come to terms with things as they were, be brave enough to take your life in your hands like Hinemoa and commit yourself. Make decisions. And, paramount, she meant you should refuse to allow notions of predestination to come between you and that which was truly important. It was easy to be diverted by false suggestions of inevitability.

And, having understood, she knew that it was time to climb out of the pool.

❧

An old bag lady shuffled by, pushing a hijacked shopping cart. In it were the scant possessions she called her own. To the top of the pile were added two pairs of shoes by Gucci, a matching bag, and an Armani skirt.

"If these aren't comfortable, I suggest you sell them," Emily told her cheerfully. "Try one of the 'almost new' shops. But I think the skirt should fit. And they won't be too much use to me, where I'm going."

※

Another plane. But this one was traveling eastward, and was far more satisfying because this time she knew she was going home.

She thought of the list Bill had made, the one she'd discovered in the sunroom. Perhaps one day she would tell him that she'd read it. She scrambled about in her bag, found a scrap of paper and began to create her own, parallel list.

Things about him that are important to me. She stopped to chew on the end of her pen. It seemed vital that she get this exactly right. Nothing frivolous or secondary.

1. He doesn't find my scars repulsive. That was certainly important, because it had helped her to accept her altered body.

2. He has learnt acceptance the hard way. And from now on there will be nothing we can't talk about.

3. He has achieved wisdom and serenity.

4. He was actually prepared to let me go, when I'd persuaded myself I couldn't climb out of the water.

5. I need him.

She paused again, looking out of the plane's window at the whispy clouds below. They were like little islands of cotton wool against the blue of the sea.

And he needs me. She wasn't so certain about that, but still . . .

She tried to conjure the image of Bill before her, but distance was usurping her imagination. Only parts appeared. His long, beautiful fingers, the hairs on the back of his hands. The parts were all there, but they refused to meld themselves into a whole. He was slipping away from her already, she thought with alarm. Like a crumbling mosaic, the pieces were disintegrating into tiny squares which meant nothing. Somehow she had to hold on, attach him to her. To quench the fear she returned to her list, thinking hard and urgently.

6. He is long, and lean, and lovely. His hair was receding at the temples and she couldn't pretend to understand all that he wrote, but it didn't seem particularly important. And he was angry with Janice, when she interfered with the Cooks. He'd been prepared to chuck her and find another agent, which was an act of true valor.

7. I love him. Achingly. And why shouldn't they have a go at creating their own perfect circle? Bill would make a wonderful father.

She read and reread her list. There seemed no more to say, after that. It appeared to cover everything quite neatly which, for somebody who didn't pretend to be smart with words, was a little rewarding. And by writing it she felt she had formed a connection between them.

She had two commissions to undertake in Auckland. The first was to visit Marge.

The door to the estate agent's office had not changed by one lick of paint from her first visit. Neither had Marge, although she looked mildly surprised when Emily was ushered in.

"Hello. I thought you'd be well and truly back in England."

"I got as far as Australia. Then I changed my mind."

Marge looked complacent. "The country got to you, then?"

Emily allowed her that bit of smugness. "I suppose you could say so. As you told me before, they're friendly people, New Zealanders. And a certain person got to me, as well."

Marge laced together the fingers of her pretty, plump little hands. "And? What can I do for you."

"I've come about Bateman's bach. You remember telling me that it was for sale? I was wondering whether it was still on the market."

Marge spoke with regret. "I'm sorry, Ms. Merivale. The bach was sold . . . oh, quite a few weeks ago."

Emily looked at her blankly. "Quite a few weeks ago? While I was still there."

"I'm afraid so."

She remembered those earlier words, about red-blooded New Zealanders snapping up holiday places as soon as the air smelled of spring. And spring had well and truly sprung.

"But how could you sell it, without telling me?"

"The buyer knew it was leased at the time of purchase. He did not appear to mind. I simply transferred the rental you were paying to him, instead of to Mrs. Robertson's account."

The disappointment was like a drenching of cold water. She'd had this wonderful notion, that she'd return to the bach, papers of ownership in hand, and present it to Bill as a *fait accompli*. Now they would have to start looking for a new property.

She stood and turned to leave. At the door she paused, hand on knob. "By the way, who is the new owner?" Not that the name would mean anything. It was a vague desire to tie up loose ends.

Marge looked up from her work again. "That's easy. His name is Thackeray, and he comes from the States. But, sadly, he doesn't think that there's any connection with the original bloke."

Her second mission was to buy a wagon, a four-wheel drive vehicle which the salesman assured her would take the unsealed road down to Whangapouri in its stride. And after all, if you were prepared to make a commitment it was sensible to equip yourself adequately. She also bought up a supply of coffee beans, a grinder, a sensible coffee maker. There seemed no point in prevaricating. And sheets, and towels which weren't tissue-paper thin, and as many other supplies as she considered essential until her next foray into the city. By that time, anyway, there was bound to be another list of requirements. And she'd be able to gather bits and pieces in California, if Janice had done her crossing of t's in her usual, efficient manner. Which reminded her about the bag-lady, in Melbourne. She wondered who was wearing those Gucci shoes now.

She remembered the first time she'd been driven along this route, the bus trundling out of Auckland on such a miserable evening. But mostly miserable because she didn't know what to expect at the other end of her journey. And then there'd been Jack Muller, who had not said a word during that depressing drive to Whangapouri, but who had stayed to see she was safely inside the bach before departing. And the rain. How it had rained.

She approached the store-cum-service-station at the junction of the road to the coast. Fourteen weeks ago it seemed to her the outpost of the known world. She turned down the Whangapouri road. It had appeared utterly desolate then, far from civilization.

But then she had not met Bill. There had been nobody at the other end, waiting for her. She'd decided not to telephone from Auckland, to leave a message with Hori. It seemed likely, anyway, that she'd arrive before the message was delivered. And that brought to mind something else she would have to do. Get them connected to the phone. And paint the place. And start a garden, a garden brimful with native plants. And lupines. Loads of yellow lupines. And she would put up a feeder for the birds, well out of reach of Mendelssohn and his wicked ways.

So Bill had bought Bateman's bach several weeks ago. She thought about the timing. It must have been on the occasion when he'd driven to Auckland to collect the McDuffs. Or later, when he'd gone up to meet with Janice and sign his contract. It could have been either, but she knew, instinctively, that it was on his second trip. And he'd not mentioned it to her, because then the boot would be on the other foot, and she might well think he was attempting to tie her down. It all made sense, when you worked it out. And from that time he had been paying board and lodging to her, and she had been leasing the property from him. Which was all very funny, in retrospect.

Why had she considered this road so long, in the early days? With ideas of home-making crowding through her mind, jostling each other for space, it seemed no longer than a stroll into the Gloucestershire village.

The sea looked incredibly vivid in the afternoon sunshine. Shadows cast by scattered clouds created an irregular pattern across the stretch of blue. The wagon bounced along the track, past Hori's, past the holiday baches. Quite a few of them appeared to be occupied. Summer visitors of course, anticipating the holiday season. There were open windows, and tables and benches outside, with sun umbrellas up. The bach beside the store showed no signs of habitation to date. But not for long, surely. She wondered how Winnie would feel about her pretty, new little home, only a stone's throw from the neighbors. How would Heneti react, when Emily took up her suggestion, that she needed younger legs about the store, and help catering for visitors to the bay? And there was something else she had a mind to do; have Kui retell some of her tales into a tape recorder. Narrative like that should not be allowed to disappear. Perhaps Janice might be able to direct her footsteps towards the right outlet. She thought that Kui might get quite a kick out of seeing her name in print.

She pulled the wagon into the drive and found that her palms were damp, that panic was again hovering on the edge of her perception.

She needed him, she thought. And he was almost disintegrating. Breaking up in her mind. She needed him to be whole, and solid. In the flesh. But what if he'd discovered, in the last week, that he didn't need her, that independence suited him just fine?

The bach looked just as shabby as she'd remembered, each rusty nail weeping its trail of reddish tears down the corrugated iron, each sill crying out for fresh paint. But the *kowhai* was in full bloom, a cascade of startling yellow, and there were black-eyed susies spilling over the rocks. From inside she could hear the soft tattoo of clicking typewriter keys. Perhaps she should suggest that he, too, took a step into the future. They could easily buy a computer, next time they went to Auckland.

⚜

The door was ajar, only the fly screen stood sentry between him and the outside world. Mendelssohn was nowhere in sight, probably off foraging in the scrub. Bill was working, with his back towards her, concentrating on the words rattling out across the page. Shabby checked shirt with its frayed collar, the one she'd mended, hair once more needing a trim down his neck. He was long and lean and lovely, just as she'd remembered.

"Bill, I'm back. I've come back."

And suddenly she was terribly, fearfully afraid. Afraid that this was not right, that he'd reject her, or accept her only reluctantly. It had not occurred to her that perhaps he'd been relieved by her departure. Bossy old Emily, who had forced him into a haircut, whose temper flared so abruptly on occasions. It occurred to her now, inducing a rush of shyness.

The clatter of keys ceased. Bill turned, as if in slow motion. And there was a moment, an awful moment, when everything appeared to be suspended in time. Then he held out his arms, wide and welcoming. And smiled.

And that was what she had forgotten, the one thing she'd have sworn would stay with her for all of her life. Just how very sweet was his smile.

"Yes, love," he said simply, taking her into his arms. "So you've decided to climb out of the water, after all. We were waiting for you, Mendelssohn and I."

⚜

GLOSSARY

of Maori and New Zealand Words and Phrases

Ani *n.* Anne

ariki *n.* first-born male or female: leader, chief, priest

Aotea Roa *n.* Land of the Long White Cloud; Maori name for New Zealand

a, tino whaka-rerea te akaurerea te akau ah, leaving the shore absolutely abandoned

bach *n.* New Zealand name for a holiday cottage

e hine *n.* form of address to young girl or woman; also means daughter

e hoa *n.* my friend

Heneti *n.* woman's name

Hinemoa *n.* woman's name; the most famous woman in Maori history and legend

Hori *n.* George

he tai rereke *n.* tide that goes out unusually far

kahawai *n.* a fish (delicious) *Arripis trutt*

ka pai *adv. or adj.* Good! Fine!

Kapiti *n.* man's name

katipo *n.* small poisonous spider, found under driftwood or vegetation (*Latrodecus katipo*)

kororoa *n.* little blue penguin

kowhai *n.* small tree with golden flowers in spring. (*Sophora tetraptera*)

kui *n.* literally *kuia,* a grandmother, a term of respect

kumera *n.* a sweet potato (*Ipomoea batatas*)

manuka *n.* shrubs or trees, so-called tea tree.(*Leptospermum scopatium & L. ericoides*)

matutu *adj.* convalescent; in the act of healing

Maui *n.* the most important hero of Maori legends. A demi-god, known throughout Polynesia.

mere *n.* club; short, flat weapon

Mokoia *n.* an island in Lake Rotorua

morepork *n.* New Zealand owl (Maori = *ruru*) *Ninox novaseelandiae*

Nga Ipongaro *n.* the lost lovers

Ngati Kura *n.* people of the precious red ochre

Ngati Tarapunga *n.* people of the red-billed gull

pa *n.* fortified or stockaded village

Pakeha *n.* commonly used for a person of predominantly European descent; fair skinned

paua *n.* New Zealand abalone *Haliotis* of several species

pipi *n.* New Zealand bivalve shellfish, cockle in general

piu-piu *n.* ceremonial skirt made out of flax leaves, scraped and dried so they curled into tubes, and fastened onto a waistband

piwakawaka *n.* fantail; a small bird. *Rhipidura flabellifera & R. fuliginosa*

poi *n.* light, flax-covered ball on a string, generally swung and twirled rhythmically in pairs and accompanied by song.

pohutukawa *n.* large native tree (*Metrosideros excelsa*) common on the sea coast; known, because of its brilliant, red flowering in December/January, as the New Zealand Christmas tree.

pukeko *n.* New Zealand swamp hen. (*Porphyrio melanotus*)

ponga *n.* tree fern. (*Cyathea dealbata*)

rangiora *n.* native shrub with silver-backed leaves. (*Brachyglottis repanda*)

rangatira *n.* chief (male or female); master, mistress, well-born or noble person

rimu *n.* native timber tree; (*Dacridium cupressinum*)

Rotorua *n.* the name of a lake and town in the geothermal area of the North Island

ruatangi *n.* place that roars, resounds or moans; descriptive name of a coastal blow-hole.

Tama *n.* boy's name, also son.

tamahine *n.* daughter, girl

tauhou *n.* a small bird, the silver-eye or wax-eye. (*Zosterops lateralis*)

Taupo *n.* lake in the center of the North Island: at 250 square miles the largest in New Zealand; also a town of the same name.

Te Manawanui *n.* man's name: the stout-hearted one

terakihi *n.* prized eating fish.(*Dactylopagrus mactopterus*)

tiki *n.* neck pendant carved in wood, or *hei-tiki* fashioned from polished greenstone, in rectangular shape after the human form. *Tiki* was the first mortal man.

toetoe *n.* grass or sedge with feathery, pampas-like seed stalks. (*Arundo kakao* and various species)

tohunga *n.* skilled person or priest

totara *n.* timber tree. (*Podocarpus totara*)

tui *n.* the parson bird with distinctive white throat feathers. (*Prosthemadera novaseelandiae*)

Tutanekai *n.* lover and husband of Hinemoa

Waikura *n.* woman's name

wahine *n.* woman, female, wife

Whaka *n.* abbreviated form of Whakarewarewa; a village within the geothermal area near Rotorua

Whangapouri *n.* Bay of Sorrows

whare *n.* house

About the Author

Sally Ash was born in New Zealand, and has also lived in Miami, Florida; Kirkland, Washington; and Australia. At present she lives with her husband in Derbyshire, England. She taught English for many years, and has raised a family of five children, countless dogs, cats and small furry animals.

In *Matutu* she combines her love for her native country with her understanding of people, and what makes them tick.

When not writing she cherishes her husband, Bruce, creates gardens, and plays killing bridge.

At present she is developing a story that investigates the damage one dominant person can do within a family and community.

GOODFELLOW PRESS

Novels from Goodfellow Press are smooth and seamless, with characters who live beyond the confines of the book covers.

Hedge of Thorns by Sally Ash. A gentle story unfolding like a modern fairy tale, of painful yesterday's and trust reborn.
ISBN 0-9639882-0-4 $7.99/$8.99 Canada.

This Time by Mary Sharon Plowman. A man and a woman with differing expectations and lifestyles, take a chance on love.
ISBN 0-9639882-1-2 $7.99/$8.99 Canada.

Glass Ceiling by C.J. Wyckoff. Facing career and emotional upheaval, Jane Walker boldly chooses to explore East Africa with an unorthodox man.
ISBN 0-9639882-2-0 $9.99/$10.99 Canada.

Bear Dance by Kay Zimmer. A man betrayed and a woman escaping memories struggle to overcome the barriers keeping them apart.
ISBN 0-9639882-4-7 $9.99/$10.99 Canada.

Homework: Bridging the Gap by Kay Morrison, Ph.D/Susanne Brady. Empowers parents, teachers and students to solve the homework dilemma.
ISBN 0-9639882-5-5 $12.99/$15.99 Canada.

White Powder by Mary Sharon Plowman. It's hard to fall in love when bullets are flying.
ISBN 0-9639882-6-3 $9.99/$10.99 Canada.

The Inscription by Pam Binder. An immortal warrior has conquered death, now he must conquer living.
ISBN 0-9639882-7-1 $12.99/$13.99 Canada.

Ivory Tower by May Taylor. Does the scent of lilacs herald a soft haunting?
ISBN 0-9639882-3-9 $12.99/$13.99 Canada.

Cookbook from Hell by Matthew L. Buchman. One part creation. Two parts software. Season lightly with a pair of love stories and roast until done.
ISBN 0-9639882-8-X $12.99/$13.99 Canada.

A Slight Change of Plans by John H. Zobel. Mike Archer has a chance to solve a mystery and meet the girl of his dreams, if only he can get out of the moose suit. (Released 1998)

Riding Ahead: a Voyage by Bicycle by Matthew L. Buchman. To relearn what is important, a corporate refugee sets off on a solo journey around the world. (Released 1998)

Ⓖ

Goodfellow Press/*Matutu*
PO Box #2915 Redmond, WA 98073-2915
(425) 881-7699

1. How would you rate the following features? Please circle:

	readable				excellent
Overall opinion of book	1	2	3	4	5
Character development	1	2	3	4	5
Conclusion/Ending	1	2	3	4	5
Plot/Story Line	1	2	3	4	5
Writing Style	1	2	3	4	5
Setting/Location	1	2	3	4	5
Appeal of Front Cover	1	2	3	4	5
Appeal of Back Cover	1	2	3	4	5
Print Size/Design	1	2	3	4	5

2. Approximately how many novels do you buy each month? _____
   How many do you read each month? _____

3. What is your education?
   ❏ High School or less   ❏ College Graduate
   ❏ Some College   ❏ Post Graduate

4. What is your age group?
   ❏ Under 25   ❏ 36-45   ❏ Over 55
   ❏ 26-35   ❏ 46-55

5. What types of fiction do you usually buy? (check all that apply)
   ❏ Historical   ❏ Western
   ❏ Science Fiction   ❏ Action/Adventure
   ❏ Romantic Suspense   ❏ General Fiction
   ❏ Mystery   ❏ Time Travel/Paranormal

6. Why did you buy this book? (check all that apply)
   ❏ Front Cover   ❏ Know the author
   ❏ Liked the characters   ❏ Back Cover
   ❏ Like the ending   ❏ Heard of publisher
   ❏ Like the setting   ❏ Purchased at an autographing event

For current Goodfellow Press updates:
Name: _____
Street: _____
City/State/Zip: _____

We would like to hear from you. Please write us with your comments.